I0775920

Book I of the Vellichor Epic

GUARDIAN

Kate Korsak

For those who believe fantasy stories to be a horrible waste of time.
It's a shame you'll never read this dedication.

PORT PRIME
KORIA SEA
GRIT
DORIA OCEAN
BAKA
WAL
EKOBY
DAR
ZOX
HON
CIRWELL
LANK
SALTIER BAY
PORI
NEVE
SEA OF SANNIR
QUIVALE
THE LONELY ISLES
BOSA
LEIDA
AGIOS
SANNIR
GILAS
EYMERY
AM
KERY
EDOMORE
SARMOT
ATHESIAN SEA
OPENHAND SEA
GELOUS
THE MIDDLE ISLANDS
POTRI
DISKAL
PO
ABR
FOTIA
ISLE OF LANSTER
WALLIS
GRIMROCK
TRAPASTON
ROOKSHIRE COVE
FORGOTTEN SEA
SEA OF HERMON
SOKKOTA
ANDAR SEA
SAGE
REALM OF VELLICHOR
WAPOR
100 TD.
GRHAM
PLINE
0 miles   200 miles   400 miles   800 miles   1000 miles
ABERNYN
SASO
CRODON
CRESSER
PORT TURRY
FURG

CASTRO
VENI
MANCHAR
GARD
THAIN
KEIGH
OD
FARGAIN
IDOLRIDGE
XYNACK
LANTON
SHARS
CRANDOLPH
DOR
ALDER
ONESALL
TON
WOOLNET
HUBIS
NOSTER
FLOWTE
DAR
CANNONITE
LEW
MOYRA'S PASS
AXLEY COVE
MANTHORNE
Isle of
RAPHIAM
SEAINK
A
VRACH
SALBUGH
BLURRY
DORISVALE
ANTON
YARNS
TREKA SEA
JESA
RBA
STONEHOLD
FLOLN
ANDON
DENVARNI
STONEHOLD
GULF
HEIGH
JELIS
JATHE
VAKES
ORIA
GULF OF
OAKVINE
MARSKTON
LEET
MARGERINE
CELDON
GADON
REIGNA
LAKE
GLADIS
NALE
MANDEL
INFEILD
JUNIC
WRAITH
ZIRTA
GLADIS
ELMWOOD
SLOW
GULF
VLOCK
NDER
FLEY
PORT RYE
CANDON
ANTABURN
DRY SEA
MIDITH
COVE
PRELES
HALE
YORA
BLIMSTONE
MIDITH
EA OF
RILL
BUTOL
N
IPRIME
ESTRIDGE
BALDWIN
HETOL
MONT
ZEIM

TABLE OF CONTENTS

PRONUNCIATION GUIDE

Aeron Priamos: AIR-on / PREE-uh-mos
Adoni: a-DOH-nee
Afi: AF-ee
Aiyanna Ascian: aye-YA-nuh / ASS-ee-uhn
Ancelin: AN-suh-lin
Apola: uh-POH-luh
Bricru Borealis: BREE-kroo / boh-REE-al-is
Cadmus Vangelis: KAD-muhs / VAN-geh-liss
Corbin Revwell: KOR-bin / REV-well
Draven Caelum: DRA-ven / KY-lum
Eliab: EE-lee-ab
Elizus Allerick: EL-eye-zuhs / AL-air-ik
Gallot: GAL-uht
Gelio: GEL-ee-oh
Kilder: KIL-duhr
Kyler Weylyn: KY-ler / WAY-lin
Matoma: muh-TOH-muh
Moundi: MOWN-dee

Novah Elison: NOH-vuh / EL-i-son
Onys: OH-nis
Ophir: OH-fer
Orisis: or-UH-sis
Ouxileous Ascian: ocks-IL-ee-uhs / ASS-ee-uhn
Pevoth: PEV-oth
Ponos: POH-nos
Potri: POH-tree
Salcon Delmar: SAL-kun / DEL-mar
Sannir: SAN-er
Tach: TOK
Tophet: TAW-fet
Uriah Caligari: yoo-RY-uh / kal-i-GAH-ree
Vellichor: VEL-i-kor
Vera Caelum: VEE-ruh / KY-lum
Vothia: VOH-thee-uh
Xynack: ZAN-ak
Zale Acamar: ZAYL / AK-uh-mar
Zalis: ZAL-is

PROLOGUE

BEFORE ELVES WALKED THE SOIL OR DRAGONS FILLED THE SKY, before giants or satyrs or celestials breathed the air and studied the stars, there were two.

They were beings of incredible magic. But more than that, they were brothers—not by blood, but by heart—and in one another, they trusted. They were tethered at the hip by a bond stronger than love, and together, they created. They created worlds no man had walked, worlds of light and magic without borders or boundaries.

And all was well between them.

The Realm of Vellichor began as a thought, nothing more than a vapor, and yet the ever-creative mind of Adoni refused to still. So, he sought his brother-at-heart to share his idea.

"Listen to me," Adoni said. "There are things we have not yet explored, and my mind will not rest until I am certain I have brought these things to completion. Create with me and share in my glory."

Orisis listened, and when his brother was finished, he met the idea with skepticism, for he was jealous of Adoni's creative mind. "You will grow power-hungry," he reasoned. "I am your brother.

Do you not trust me? Create all you want, but let me destroy what I wish, for the one who creates must not decide what should be destroyed. Do this, and we will have balance."

Adoni agreed to his brother's request, and Vellichor was born.

Adoni and Orisis—the creator and the destroyer—worked together as one. The creator formed stone and salt, and the destroyer chipped it away until it fit like fragments of a puzzle. And so, there was Vellichor, and there was balance.

Then Adoni said to Orisis, "Why do we stop now? Let's create life so we will not be alone."

Adoni created life, and Orisis, always the sculptor, was given the power of death. What Adoni created, Orisis destroyed, and there was balance.

Life filled Vellichor, from the giants of the islands to the dragons of the sky, and to his creations, Adoni gave the ability to create. His magic was a gift to all he loved. What Adoni gave, his creations multiplied. He gave the elves herbs, and with them, they made potions. To the wizards he gave words, and with them, they made spells. Wood became ships, parchment became maps, numbers became mathematics, and Vellichor thrived. Every being alive possessed a magic they felt suited to, and every corner of the realm brimmed with new ideas and inventions.

All of this pleased Adoni, but Orisis grew weary. Everything he destroyed was remade tenfold, each time returning stronger and more vibrant than before. No amount of death or hurt could smother the burning flame that was Vellichor. The more he thought about it, the more Orisis realized his own mistake. These new lives would soon overpower him, for they could create all they wished and he could not. Adoni had outsmarted him after all.

Orisis devised a plan. He went to the creatures of the realm—

the alchemists and scholars, the wizards and beasts—and proposed an alliance.

"Share your magic with me," he persuaded, "and I will give you power over death. My hand of destruction will pass over you and your children, and you will become masters over darkness."

His promise was tempting. Many creatures found they craved the security it offered, so they traded with Orisis. To him, they gave every kind of magic they'd learned; to them, he gave the touch of death.

These were the creations of Orisis, the ones who traded their magic for service to the destroyer. They had no spells to whisper, no potions to brew, but with a single hand on the neck of their victim, they could steal a soul. They were called the afi, and with their touch, they cast creatures to Tophet—the home Orisis made for himself with his newfound magic. It was a place of tears and bruises, built for those whose magic threatened Orisis when they refused his offer.

When Adoni found out what Orisis had done, he broke through the gateway of Tophet and tore down all who stepped before him until he reached the throne where Orisis was seated.

"You defile my creations," Adoni said, the tip of his blade aimed at the one he called "brother". "You were permitted to destroy, but what you have done goes far beyond destruction. You will release my creatures and give back the magic you have stolen."

But Orisis laughed, the sound cruel and twisted. "I will do no such thing. For the first time, I have made something important, and you will not touch what I have built."

Adoni was filled with rage—the kind that burns when something one loves is taken from them—and with that rage, he created something he'd never created before: an army. He found those who refused Orisis, the elves of the mountains with arrows of steel and dragons with scales the color of snow, and from among them, he selected a leader.

Eliab was an elf with a heart that bled for Adoni, and so he was appointed as general of Adoni's army. Eliab led his soldiers into a battle like none that had been recorded.

Thus, Adoni destroyed what Orisis created, and the fabric of the realm twisted in a way it was never designed to. All who had been imprisoned were released, and when the ash settled beneath the gateway of Tophet, Orisis—the god defeated—was left to sit alone in its ruins.

But the battle had been costly. Lives were lost, and Adoni was deeply saddened by it.

Adoni sent Eliab and the survivors from his army to an island called Sannir. There he instructed his general to build his Temple, and from the Temple, Adoni created the Dragon Pass. From cloud and rain, he formed a gateway of his own above the mountains of Sannir. He built a dwelling beyond the gateway, a place where the dragons could rest away from the evils of the realm, and through the Pass, he gave his magic. From now on, he would not give it freely.

The elves of Sannir had access to Adoni's magic and were untouched by the destruction of Orisis. However, the rest of Vellichor was forgotten.

There were a few ancients who found ways of keeping magic outside of Sannir, making gods of themselves from scraps of sorcery and remnants of war. They built empires, and the empires fell. They crafted weapons, and their weapons failed. The giver of magic no longer gave, and the destroyer would not let them succeed.

Because the one who creates should never destroy, and the one who destroys should never create. This is balance.

PART ONE
THE COMMANDER

CHAPTER ONE

THE DRAGON SCALE WAS GREEN, LIKE THE PINES OF A FOREST, and Kyler had earned it. The scale stared up at him from the dirt, spinning slightly as his mind reeled from the blow. Blood dripped on his armor from the tip of his ear where the dragon scale had been fastened just moments before.

"Saints," he muttered, kneeling to pick up the piece from the ground. Dust clung to the shine of its surface, the ornament no larger than Kyler's thumbnail.

Beside him, Corbin gave a crooked grin as he shook out his wrist. "If it makes you feel better, I was aiming for your jaw." His broad smile showed just how proud he was of winning against his commander yet again.

Kyler scowled as he polished the scale against his shirt sleeve to rid it of blood and dirt. Few soldiers could best the young commander in a spar, and Corbin was one of them. The two of them had grown up together, climbing the ranks side-by-side until Kyler was promoted to Commander of the Land Brigade. It was Corbin who took it upon himself to keep Kyler's pride in check—something the lieutenant did gladly. A bit *too* gladly.

Corbin was square-shouldered and stood as tall as Kyler, and he was unreasonably good at hand-to-hand combat. The armor he wore clanged lightly as he shifted, passing Kyler a clean rag.

He accepted it with a sigh and pressed the rough fabric to the bubble of blood that stung the tip of his pointed ear. He brushed his hand down the rest of his scales, which hung like trails of emerald armor beneath the auburn braids at his temples.

The scales of Adoni's dragons were the mark of the soldiers of Sannir, identifying them as guardians of the Dragon Pass. The moment a scale was granted by the general, an elf became a soldier.

Kyler studied his newest scale, ensuring it was pristine before he tucked it into his trouser pocket. He'd received this one only a month prior, just before the former general, Uriah Caligari, disappeared. The rumors surrounding his sudden departure were widespread, but Kyler found himself more interested in what was to come.

The position of general would be granted to a standing commander, of which there were only three—commanders of land, sea, and sky. They were leaders tasked with guarding not only Sannir and its people but also the Dragon Pass, their source of magic.

There were three military branches in Sannir: the Sea Force, made up of ships and sailors to defend the waters; the Sky Regiment, who rode the backs of dragons and kept their arrows aimed at the skies; and the Land Brigade, which Kyler had committed his life to serving.

He tossed the bloodied rag back to Corbin, who scrunched his nose as he caught it. Kyler gave a playful chuckle as Corbin quickly dropped the cloth and used his shirtsleeve instead to wipe the sweat that clung to his forehead. Strands of unruly blond hair fell from his braids and into his eyes, causing him to blink against the salt. He was still grinning at Kyler, and his smile grew wider as Kyler knelt to the belt of potions he'd left on the sidelines of their fight.

"That bad?" Corbin asked. "I wasn't even trying."

"Hush," Kyler snapped. His mind was still spinning, and it was quickly becoming a headache.

Vials of potions sat tucked within the leather belt, each holding only a sip of an elixir and sealed with a cork stopper. They lay tilted in the grass, colors of orange, indigo, and silver catching the light of the afternoon sun. Kyler's fingers danced over each vial until he found the one that would calm his spinning vision. He'd brewed these himself, perfecting the mixtures until he was satisfied with each one. The cork gave a slight pop as he tugged it free from the thin vial, and Kyler tipped his head back as the silver liquid touched his tongue. Zalis was a simple concoction made for curing dizziness, and by the time Kyler opened his eyes, his blurring mind had steadied.

He corked the empty vial with a whistle. "Zalis works fast."

"You know what else works fast?" Corbin crouched beside him, dipping his voice. "Apola. Or are you going to ditch us for your princess again tonight?"

"Watch your mouth, Lieutenant," Kyler scolded, shoving the bottle back into its designated pocket. He took a moment to brush the dirt from his belt before strapping it to his waist, securing the buckles with a tug. The leather practically molded to him, sitting comfortably against his silver armor.

Kyler glanced around them, ensuring curious ears hadn't caught Corbin's comment, but he found the grounds of the barracks mostly unoccupied. Open fields ran from where he and Corbin stood to the walls of the living quarters, long buildings made of paneled wood and brick chimneys. In the distance, the sound of commanding shouts echoed from the docks where troops were in the middle of water combat training, learning the way a foot soldier must fight when the tides pulled at their boots and salt stung their nose. From here, Kyler could see the shine of the water. Gentle waves rolled against the shore of Sannir, sparkling with every movement as if made of starlight.

To the left of the docks, a simple path ran past the training fields and toward the castle of Sannir. The castle rose far above the scattered trees in layers of gray stone and stained-glass windows that shimmered just as much as the water.

"All I'm saying is you've disappeared on us one too many times." Corbin paused, laughing at himself as he realized his own joke. "Maybe you *will* make a good general."

Kyler jabbed a calloused finger at his friend's chest plate. "I will be nothing like Uriah. You know that."

Corbin shrugged and reached for the pine-colored scales that dangled from his ears, untangling them from his sweat-soaked curls. His set was sparse compared to Kyler's, with only four trails per ear as opposed to the commander's six—now seven on his right. The blood still stung where his latest addition had been knocked free moments ago. He'd have to find time to put it back on later.

The urge to turn Corbin's teases into a lecture rose, mostly because Kyler's ear still throbbed and it was bothering him, but the moment was interrupted by quickly approaching footsteps.

"Commander!"

Kyler turned, ignoring Corbin's lingering smirk as Lieutenant Salcon reached them. Like his fellow soldiers, scales of green mixed with the occasional brown adorned his ears, dangling just below his jaw. Black braids hung at Salcon's temples, matching those of Kyler's and Corbin's, though his were much thicker and fell past his shoulders, elongating his already thin face and high cheekbones.

Like Corbin, Kyler had known Salcon since they were young. Though they'd risen the ranks together, it was Kyler's brother whom Salcon had grown closer to, for reasons Kyler still didn't understand.

"Shouldn't you be in the fields with the buggers?" Kyler asked, facing Salcon with a frown.

"I was. You picked a difficult batch of trainees. The kilders are with them now."

Kyler gave a curt nod. Without a lieutenant present, kilders took over as the voice of authority, followed by soldiers, and finally 'buggers' or new recruits.

"A castle messenger found me," Salcon continued. "I was told to give you this." He passed over a cream-colored envelope addressed with Kyler's name.

Commander Kyler Weylyn.

The commander's brow furrowed as he turned it over, finding an intricate seal stamped in wax on the back. He carefully tore the seal, revealing the handwritten invitation within.

A meeting at the castle. As soon as he could make it. He felt a sudden jolt of excitement. Had the dragons finally chosen the new general?

"Has the decision been made?" Corbin voiced Kyler's question, leaning closer to catch a glimpse of the letter.

Kyler shouldered him and stuffed the letter back into the envelope. "I'll find out when I get there."

"Go ahead." Salcon slapped Kyler's back, hard enough to make him grunt. "Corbin and I can keep everyone in line."

Kyler's stomach fluttered as he stole another glance at the envelope. It'd been nearly a month since he'd been summoned to the castle. "I'll find you after." He returned Salcon's gesture before grabbing his cloak from the grass and began his walk toward the castle grounds.

"I look forward to it, *General*," Corbin shouted after him.

The silver clasps latched at Kyler's shoulders as the wind tugged at his cape, tangling it around his ankles as he started for the castle.

Troops continued training as Kyler passed, and pride swelled in his chest as he admired each one. Soldiers rehearsed battle sequences while lieutenants shouted orders, kilders corrected trainees to perfection, and the clashing of swords could be heard coming from the training arena just past the barracks. His men; his army. Any doubts about receiving the honor of general faded from his mind. The Land Brigade truly was the best in Sannir.

Kyler snapped his shirt at his wrists, ensuring he looked presentable, while ignoring glances from those he passed. Word would travel quickly that he was meeting with King Ouxileous, followed by questions when he returned. Most soldiers had never spoken with royalty, and most never would. It was an honor few received. He, however, had been amongst royalty on several occasions. The king hosted the commanders every so often for dinners and holidays, including Eliab's Day, which was quickly approaching.

Kyler waited until he was away from the curious glances to relax his shoulders. Sweat had begun to form on his palms despite the cool air, and he flexed his fingers at the sensation. It was just his training with Corbin, that was all.

The simple trail slowly turned to cobblestone, twisting and turning past trimmed shrubbery and wide-leaved trees. The back and sides of the castle were nothing grand, but coming around the front, every detail the architects had crafted was showcased. A bridge, large enough for carriages to travel both ways stretched across a creek that ran to the Openhand Sea. Pillars of marble lined the bridge and continued into the courtyard where the stone path created a maze between marble statues of dragons and perfectly rounded bushes.

Men of Kyler's own training patrolled the area, stopping to salute as their commander passed. Their uniforms were slightly different from the soldiers at the barracks, with added chainmail and heavier armor draped over tunics of light silver and navy—the colors of Sannir.

Scales that matched Kyler's hung from each of their ears, and the gentle clank of their armor filled the otherwise silent courtyard.

A set of tall wooden doors marked the main entrance of the castle. As Kyler neared, soldiers hauled them open without a sound, the hinges as unblemished and smooth as the rest of the castle.

Kyler's steps echoed across the ornate hall as he entered the foyer. It smelled like cotton and lilac, and light danced across the marble floors in shades of amber and sage, filtering through the stained glass of the castle windows. A massive chandelier made of crystal, mined from the mountains of Sannir, hung overhead like a curtain of gemstone.

Soldiers had been stationed along the sides of the foyer, blocking the wings and windows that stretched the length of the walls. The wings branched toward more rooms and staircases, but Kyler had never gotten the opportunity to explore them. The castle was massive, with several spare rooms, studies, ballrooms, and libraries on every floor. In fact, if Kyler's knowledge was correct, he'd seen less than a third of it.

That would change when he became general.

Ahead, the opening to the great hall sat atop a length of wide stairs, and the vaulted ceilings allowed the murmur of voices to carry as Kyler ascended the steps. Light spilled from the open doors, catching the shine of Kyler's armor as he neared the top.

He swept his hands over the shoulders of his cape and tugged his armor, ensuring everything was in place before he straightened himself and crossed the threshold.

The hall was one of the most beautiful rooms in the castle, wide and bright, with pillars made of the same white marble that lay across the floor. Massive windows made up the majority of the hall's far wall, showcasing the inner gardens which bloomed with seasonal flowers. Latches secured the windows shut, allowing them to be pulled open for special occasions or for the rare case in which the dragons needed entry into the castle. In front of the window was a rectangular table covered in a spread of bread, cheese, fruit, and sliced meat for the king's guests to enjoy.

Kyler wasn't alone in the great hall. To his left stood his fellow commanders, and with them was King Ouxileous Ascian.

"Commander Weylyn!" The king halted their conversation as he spotted the final commander.

"Your Majesty." Kyler paused as he joined them and placed a hand on his chest. The scales at his ears clinked against one another as he dipped his head into a bow. When he lifted his gaze, he found the eyes of the other two commanders fixated on him.

Zale Acamar, commander of the Sea Force, studied Kyler, one eye as dark as his brown skin, and the other paled by scarring. He was several years older than the other commanders, though his strength and agility would never betray his age. Years at sea were etched across his weathered face, and his once-black beard was now speckled with gray like the twisted locks that hung to his shoulders. Scales of blue and silver ran up and down his elongated ears, their number surpassing even Kyler's.

The late afternoon light reflected off Zale's armor as he turned and offered Kyler a curt nod. Kyler returned it. He'd never considered the older commander to be pleasant company, but at least Zale was respectable.

Beside him was Commander Novah Elison of the Sky Regiment. Like Kyler, she was young, with honey-brown hair braided back to reveal earfuls of orange and red scales. Though she donned an impressive amount, she possessed only two-thirds of what Kyler did, which was something he took pride in. Her uniform, which complemented her scales, was comprised of maroon fabric topped with crisp silver. Scattered freckles marked her jaw, and her cheeks appeared wind-whipped, likely a result of her hike from the Sky Regiment's post at the base of Sannir's mountains.

There wasn't much Kyler found admirable about Novah. They'd worked together for almost two years, and she'd hardly spoken a word to him.

Novah barely glanced at Kyler as he approached, her eyes flicking back to the king as he spoke.

"I'm glad you could make it, Commander. It's been too long since we've all spoken."

Kyler turned his attention to King Ouxileous, finding a warm smile on his face. "It has, Your Majesty."

The king looked so much like his daughter—dark hair, round eyes, and high cheekbones. A silver crown dotted with sapphires rested on his brow, and his hair had been tucked behind his ears, revealing long points that showed his age better than the wrinkles at his eyes.

He clasped his palms together with a smile. "Well then, shall we get started?"

He turned without waiting for an answer, passing between two pillars as he headed for the room Kyler knew well: the meeting room.

Kyler's mind flashed to the last time they'd entered this room, just days before General Uriah's disappearance. It was odd to be there without him. The former general had been a commanding presence, quick to speak and impossible to ignore.

Kyler selected a seat beside Zale. He mindlessly tugged at his scales as he sat, feeling their smooth surface and round edges. Novah took the seat across from him, eyeing his nervous fidgeting.

Kyler dropped his hands, avoiding her gaze.

The king waited until they all were seated to take his place at the head of the table. "Thank you for meeting with me on such short notice." His rings tolled against one another as he folded his hands. "As you know, it's been one month since General Uriah's disappearance, and there's been no sign of his return. The dragons are ready to appoint the new general."

Kyler's chest tightened.

"But they wanted to give you all one last chance to plead your case. This is unorthodox, after all, and I know all three of you could fit the role of general very well. Sannir has been free from war and turmoil for nearly a thousand years now, and I'd like to keep it that way."

Kyler shifted in his seat, earning another glance from Novah. Saints, she was critical. Her glare seemed to cut through him, making his nerves buzz faster.

The king continued. "Let's begin with you, Commander Elison. Why should you stand at my side as general?"

Novah remained unphased, as though he'd asked for her name or for the time of day. When she spoke, her tone conveyed confidence and knowledge. "Your Majesty, as commander of the

Sky Regiment, I spend my days alongside the wisest beings in our kingdom and have not only earned their trust but their friendship. I have traveled the Dragon Pass and know its every strength and weakness. Sannir's greatest assets are the Pass and the dragons that dwell beyond it, and I can utilize that expertise in cohesion with land and sea to lead Sannir into another thousand years of peace."

"Very well said, Elison. Commander Weylyn?"

This time, all eyes turned to Kyler. He cleared his throat.

"Your Majesty, as commander of the Land Brigade, I oversee more soldiers than my fellow commanders. I've set records for scale count, scales that I've been awarded in this very castle, and have turned even the weakest men into capable soldiers. The Land Brigade has been the strongest branch for years, and I have kept it at the top."

"Thank you. And Commander Acamar?"

Kyler struggled to hear Zale's words. His pulse had begun to pound so loudly that he could hardly remember what he'd said.

"—as an island, having a general who knows the sea would be a wise decision," Zale finished, and the king nodded.

"Very well." A sharp silence filled the room, so still that Kyler wondered if the king would ever speak again. "Thank you all for your time. The announcement ceremony is set for the day after tomorrow, and an invitation will be sent to every lieutenant and kilder. I expect each of you to have a speech prepared, should your name be called, and a lieutenant selected to take your place." He stood from his chair. "Meeting adjourned."

CHAPTER TWO

A HUM RAN THROUGH KYLER'S BLOOD AS HE FOLLOWED NOVAH and Zale from the meeting room and into the great hall. He *was* going to be general; he had to be. It was what he'd wanted since he was a bugger. But the way the other commanders had spoken, with such confidence, made Kyler uneasy.

King Ouxileous didn't linger. He disappeared quickly down a hallway, heading off to his next meeting or task, and left the three commanders alone.

Kyler turned to the table, allowing the smell of freshly baked bread and salted meat to distract his mind. Cheese, the color of white wine, lay in folded patterns, and he helped himself to a piece.

Footsteps echoed across the marble as Novah started for the doors, her haste nearly matching the king's. She strode out into the courtyard without so much as a nod in Kyler's direction, her cape dangling from her shoulders and scales catching the light of the stained glass as she exited the castle.

Kyler's lips twisted into a frown. He'd been a commander for as long as Novah, and yet he knew nearly nothing about her—except for her cold demeanor. This was why. She seemed to have little time for pleasantries, acting as though her small number of soldiers demanded her full attention.

"Good luck, Commander." Zale's deep voice filled the open room as he came to Kyler's side. "You'd make a good general."

Kyler snuck one last glance at the doors before giving Zale an absentminded nod. "You as well." He grabbed a handful of fresh bread and broke it, offering a piece to his fellow commander.

"I think the most difficult part of this is having to prepare a speech," Zale drawled, accepting the bread. "I'm not sure what I would say."

Kyler shrugged. "I'll write mine tonight." He had no intention of writing a speech that evening. Corbin and Salcon were headed to Leida, and he planned to join them for an evening filled with potions crafted to make their veins buzz.

Zale smiled, his good eye locked on Kyler. "Planning on a bit of potion to get the words flowing?"

Kyler coughed as he swallowed his bite, taken aback by Zale's forwardness. "I'm sorry?"

"I'm not ignorant. I know how soldiers like you spend your free time." He blew lightly on his food, eying Kyler through the steam.

Kyler sighed. He was beginning to wish he'd left as quickly as Novah had. "Just a night away, that's all. Though I don't believe I owe you an explanation."

Zale nodded slowly. "This 'night away' doesn't happen to include large amounts of enjoyment potion, does it?" When Kyler didn't answer, he continued, "Surely a skilled alchemist such as yourself would understand the effects of having too much Apola so late into the evening."

"I didn't realize it was your place to lecture me about how I spend my time outside of the barracks."

"Hm." Zale shifted. "Need I remind you that as a commander,

you are never truly off duty?"

Kyler chuckled, the sound low and humorless. "And you wonder why I like Apola."

"Kyler."

Kyler stilled, meeting the older man's eye with a look of warning.

"Commander," he corrected himself, "we represent the same kingdom, same throne, and same magic. I have every right to question you."

"That's the thing"—Kyler tapped a finger on the table—"you forget that we're equal. If you want to question a man's ethics, question your own soldiers."

The room fell uncomfortably silent, filled only with the slight crackle of oil lamps. Kyler kept his gaze locked with Zale's, refusing to be the first to look away. A sharp breath lifted Zale's chest, and he set the remainder of his food down.

Kyler's lips quirked. "I'll see you in two days, Commander." His cloak snapped at his heels as he turned, following Novah's path toward the entryway.

As he neared the wooden doors, a figure emerged from the west wing. Diamonds hung over the pale fabric that hugged the princess' waist and fell like liquid silver down to her heels. Dark curls framed her round face, and Kyler's stride slowed as he met Princess Aiyanna's eye.

He pressed a fist to his chest, dipping into a formal bow. "Good evening, Princess."

She smiled kindly, the freckles on her nose stretching as she did. "Hello, Commander."

Kyler stood, forcing himself to continue for the doors. He swore to make time for her tonight as well; the urge to drop formalities grew stronger every time he saw her. Soon enough, they wouldn't have to pretend.

…

Kyler sat at his desk, the scent of bitter herbs and smoke filling his room. Despite the open window, tonight's brew of rosemary and merlot was overwhelmingly potent, and Kyler blamed the assault on his senses on his lingering headache.

He stole a glance at the clock above his head. Corbin and the others were checking inventory tonight, so there was still time to perfect his brew.

The sprinkle of rosemary caught a hint of sweetness, and Kyler quickly grabbed a knob, shrinking the flames below his pot. He'd had this desk specially made, designed to shift from a place to write letters to a stove on which an alchemist could brew his potions. The small dials jutting out from the side were used to adjust the size of the open flame—crafted for the most accurate of brews.

The mixture in the pot before him began to bubble, and Kyler rested his chin in his palm, watching it closely. He left the other hand hovering above the dial. It was a foul-looking mixture, dark brown and not the least bit appetizing, but a moment later the liquid flashed pink, and Kyler twisted the knob to smother the flames.

Smooth, inky liquid revealed itself beneath the bubbles, sparkling deep purple. Kyler held his breath so as not to disturb the potion as he tipped the pot, pouring it into an empty vial. Steam rose to his face as it drizzled, and the last drop filled the glass to the brim. He set the pot aside to cool, admiring his now-full vial of Vothia.

Growing up, Kyler had been obsessed—not with the military, but with alchemy. The potions he brewed were mostly for different forms of healing, but he also enjoyed the study of mixtures, and there were many he found to be much more exciting than healing.

Kyler's potion belt lay across the tangled sheets of his unmade bed, several of its vials more than half empty. There were a few, however, that Kyler ensured were always full. This one, Vothia, was helpful for mornings after too much Apola and of course his soldiers needed Zalis when someone like Corbin sent their head spinning. Strong pain relief known as Ponos was another he kept close as well as brews like Trof for an upset stomach or Saris to momentarily calm the mind of its drinker.

Glancing at the clock again, Kyler decided to leave the fresh Vothia behind. He wouldn't need it until the morning, and he couldn't cap it until it'd finished steaming anyway.

Kyler removed his shirt, tugging it over his head and wincing as he forgot the wound still healing on his ear. He'd find a way to repay Corbin for that one. The skin throbbed as his scale snagged on the cotton, turning his ear pink and swollen.

He cursed lightly and carefully untangled the scale, sighing with relief when it finally came loose from his clothes. He reached for a clean rag, smothering it beneath the cool faucet water before pressing it to his ear. The water dripped down his scales and onto the freckles that dotted his shoulders, relieving the sting and inflammation.

With the rag occupying one hand, he moved to his clothes chest and pulled out a wrinkled tunic that nearly matched the murky green of his eyes.

He held the rag on his ear until the water turned warm, then tossed it to the floor. Kyler was careful not to snag the scale again while slipping the new shirt over his head and paused at the mirror as he passed it.

His ear burned bright red, the throbbing growing stronger with each second. He released an aggravated sigh—directed at Corbin—and took a moment to fix the two thick braids that framed his face. They hung even, beginning at his temples and landing at his jawline.

Kyler reached for his potion belt, tightening it around his waist, and replaced the empty pocket where Vothia usually sat with a miniature vial of Gelio, Aiyanna's favorite. It was a pale purple color that tasted like berries and could make even the saddest person slip a giggle. She always said it was fun to have around when ladies of the court came to visit, but Kyler could see right through her. The laughing potion was one of the few ways to lighten her mood after a full day of politics and lessons.

But for Kyler, it was Apola that lifted his spirits, and that was at the forefront of his mind as he left his quarters and stepped into the hallway.

The barracks were mostly quiet this evening, with soldiers getting as much sleep as possible before another early morning. Kyler smiled to himself, recalling his days as a low-ranking soldier. Calfner had been his commander at the time, a sour man with no mercy. He stood a head shorter than Kyler, even when Kyler was a bugger, but his voice traveled like thunder and rattled the young soldiers to the core. He taught them how to be protectors and leaders, and when he finally decided to retire, Kyler had been honored to take his place.

Just like he'd be honored to take the place of general.

Kyler quickly reached the back door of the barracks, where the night air met him with a welcomed sense of freedom. The silver moon of Vellichor was already visible in the dark sky, illuminating the fields and casting a gentle light on the pillar of Adoni positioned just beyond the barrack lines.

Unlike the Temple, which acted as the anchor to the Dragon Pass, the pillar held no connection to Sannir's magic. It was built by the early elves of Sannir and was a symbol of pride amongst the elves who lived here now. It stood taller than the barracks Kyler had come from, its tip pointing to the thick clouds above the mountains where the Pass rolled amid their peaks.

Kyler stopped at the base of the pillar and studied the marble. Tiny dragons had been embossed across the stone, circling the column as if suspended in flight. They were accompanied by simple draconic runes, markings of dragons that symbolized peace and light. The images spun and spiraled to the top, where a detailed dragon perched with tucked wings. The beast was decorated in armor-like scales, and horns resembling a ram's curled at the top of its head. It was a symbol of Adoni, a reminder of who they served.

Soldiers were not only required to give an oath to their king and the kingdom of Sannir but also to Adoni, the god of Eliab and the dragons. It was he who gave Sannir to the elves, appointing Eliab as their first general and giving the dragons a home on the other side of the Pass. Eliab was the first dragon rider, who built the Temple of Adoni and established Sannir as a kingdom.

Kyler shifted his gaze to the mountains, where the Pass spiraled like a whirlpool of cloud. Somewhere in the realm remained the entrance to Tophet, the home of Orisis destroyed by Eliab. But unlike the Pass, those who entered Tophet did not return. Beasts with scales of onyx and horns like that of a goat had once guarded Tophet, and Orisis himself was said to still dwell among the ruins.

No being alive had stepped foot into Tophet, but a few soldiers of Sannir were allowed to enter the Dragon Pass.

General Uriah had spoken of the world beyond, where dragons

roamed free amongst temples of gold and mountains taller than Sannir's.

Novah had been there. She knew of the world Uriah spoke of, which stirred something bitter in Kyler's mind. His scales were plenty, and his troops were disciplined.

He would see those temples and mountains soon enough.

CHAPTER THREE

KYLER LEFT THE GROUNDS BEHIND, FOLLOWING THE PATHS OF dirt and stone until they welcomed him into the town of Leida. There was one other town within walking distance of the barracks, but Leida had the best taverns and the best potions—particularly Apola.

It was Kyler who had banned the enjoyment potion from the grounds of the Land Brigade. Its intoxicating properties made it dangerous around weapons. Besides that, he believed healing and strengthening potions alone were suitable for soldiers to consume on base. Tonight, however, Kyler wasn't spending the evening at the barracks.

Not only did Leida have the best potions, but it also had the best sights. Countless taverns sat along the twisted streets, lined with carts full of oranges and pomegranates. Chatter filled the evening air, and street performers danced past, dressed in extravagant costumes. Leida seemed to sparkle with life the moment the sun dipped behind the mountain range, as if waiting for dark to finally wake up.

Kyler maneuvered through the busy streets and came to a stop at a tavern. Light flickered from the other side of the glass windows and live music drifted through the walls. *Lone Wolf* was plastered on the sign above the door, matched by an emblem of a howling wolf.

Music filled Kyler's ears as he opened the doors, a colorful band of stringed instruments filling the space with song. Elves talked and drank concoctions of sparkling silver and bubbling gold, and the smell of mixed potions mingled with citrus and the crisp tang of Apola. Lights were strung across the ceiling, giving the illusion of a starry sky, and birds made of enchanted parchment came to life from unseen magic, flapping around the dancers' heads.

Kyler made his way to the bar, excusing himself as he weaved through the guests, before finding a seat on a tall stool. He was greeted with a smile from a woman he'd seen working here many times and yet could never recall her name. She was lovely to look at, with bright eyes and hair that matched the black tunic she wore. Jewelry as silver as the moon dangled from her pointed ears, sparkling in the lights as she approached him.

Her brows lifted and a smirk played at her lips. "Commander, it's a pleasure to see you again."

"The pleasure is mine." He met her eye, hoping she wouldn't notice his stalling.

Her smirk deepened, and she placed her elbows on the counter in front of him. "You forgot again, didn't you?"

He attempted to hide his smile. "Perhaps. Although I'm sure I'll remember after a few glasses of Apola, don't you think?"

She hummed lightly, tugging at the sleeve of his shirt. "That's what you say every time."

Her touch sent spikes of electricity down his arm, though he did his best not to show it. "Let's find out together then…"

"Maeve." She straightened. "Raspberry, I assume?"

"You know me well, Maeve."

She scrunched her nose, turning to the tap behind her. "All by yourself tonight, Commander?"

He chuckled, lounging against the short backrest of the wooden stool. "I certainly hope not."

She faced him again, dropping a star-shaped ice cube into the glass before topping it with a single raspberry. Her fingers brushed his as she slid the drink across the counter, the ice within tapping softly against the glass.

Kyler took a sip. The tart flavor of raspberries mixed perfectly with the herbs used to create Apola. It rolled across his tongue with a sting, filling his chest with a swell of cool pricks.

He swallowed and tipped the glass in her direction. "Well done, as usual."

"Here come your friends."

Kyler turned, finding Corbin, Salcon, and Adri—another one of his lieutenants—entering the crowded building.

"I'll leave you to your boys," Maeve teased, walking down to the other end of the bar.

Kyler called after her, "Miss you already!"

She flashed a smile before addressing another customer.

"I wouldn't stand you up." Corbin slapped a hand on Kyler's shoulder, taking the stool beside him. He'd braided his hair back completely, though a few strands hung loose around his jaw. If it weren't for the scales on his ears, he'd have looked nothing like a soldier.

The other two took seats on Kyler's opposite side, and he nodded to them. "Good to see you gentlemen outside of the barracks."

"Good to be out," Adri answered. The thickness of his voice matched that of his beard, and the lights above their heads cast shadows over the dark ink tattooed on his arms.

Salcon leaned around Adri, eyeing Kyler's swollen ear. "Corbin got you good today."

Kyler chuckled as he brought his drink to his mouth again. "I'll make it up to him."

"I believe it."

The band's song came to an end just as Maeve returned to get drinks for the others. Kyler turned his attention to the lean man with a lute as he addressed the audience.

"It's a pleasure to be with you all tonight," he shouted, drawing the attention of the tavern guests. "I'd like to welcome someone very important." His eyes met Kyler's as he motioned in the soldier's direction. "Commander Weylyn, it's an honor—"

Before he could continue, applause and whistles came from the rest of the crowd. Corbin shook Kyler's shoulder, laughing as the commander tried to hide his grin.

"It's an honor and a privilege to share this evening with you," the musician finished, pressing his hands together in thanks. Another round of applause sounded through the tavern, filling Kyler with warmth. He waved a hand as the band started back up again, and eyes continued to flicker in his direction.

Maeve made her way over to him. "Mr. Popular tonight, I see."

"Don't kid yourself. I'm popular *every* night."

She rolled her eyes. "I'm going to pretend that's the Apola talking. Next one's covered, by the way."

He beamed. "You shouldn't have."

She laughed, nodding down the bar. "I didn't. Dark hair, blue shirt. You should at least say thank you."

Kyler scanned the room, spotting a woman with cherry lips and hooded eyes. When she caught his stare, he gave a subtle wink.

Corbin frowned and leaned close enough that his nose brushed Kyler's temple. "You've got a certain someone who wouldn't like that."

Kyler's head fell back with a laugh. "Take it easy, Corbin. She's not here, is she?"

He shrugged, clearly amused by the attention Kyler was receiving. "Don't say I didn't warn you."

Kyler lifted his brows and tipped his glass to finish the last of the raspberry as Maeve dropped another in its place.

"It can't be that good," Salcon scoffed as Kyler started on his second.

Kyler answered with another sip. "I'd let you try some, but it was specially ordered for me. If you could get a lady to look your way for once, perhaps you wouldn't have to pay for every drink."

"Ouch." Adri whistled.

Salcon laughed. "That's fair." Turning to Maeve he added, "I'll try the raspberry."

Corbin motioned to Salcon's half-full glass of ginger Apola. "You haven't finished your first!"

Salcon waved a hand. "Those of us who have coin can afford it."

Kyler let his laughter spill freely as Corbin stomached the insult.

Adri hid his smile behind his hand, shaking his head slowly. "You have no mercy."

"It's just the Apola talking." Kyler took another sip, enjoying the way the potion numbed his tongue.

"So," Salcon pressed, pausing to thank Maeve as a raspberry Apola was placed before him, "are you preparing a speech, Kyler? Or are you going in unprepared, like you do everything else?"

Kyler swallowed, holding up a finger. "That's not fair. I'm not unprepared for *everything*."

Salcon lifted a hand in defeat. "My apologies. *Almost*

everything." He took a drink of the raspberry, and his face twisted. "This is disgusting."

"You lack a refined palate."

He shook his head with a grimace and passed the Apola to Adri. The larger man contemplated the taste for a moment before shrugging and stealing the drink for himself.

Corbin gave Kyler a nudge to the rib. "Answer the question."

Kyler placed his elbows on the counter, shooting a glare in Corbin's direction. He hadn't yet told the others what had been discussed in his meeting with the king. It seemed his lieutenant had loosed his tongue while they were counting inventory.

"I don't have a speech, *yet*"—he aimed a finger at Salcon to exaggerate his point—"but I will." He tapped his hand on the wood and took another swig of Apola. It bubbled in his chest and clouded his mind, causing his thoughts of generals and speeches to fade.

Salcon scoffed, but their conversation was halted by Maeve once again.

"Blonde hair, black dress. Another raspberry?"

Kyler glanced at his glass, which was still half full, and shrugged. "Let's try something different."

"Oh?" She crossed her arms. "What'll it be, Commander?"

He met her eye, resting his chin in his palm and giving her his most innocent look. "Whatever you want."

She thought for a beat before nodding. "If you insist. Give me a moment."

He clicked his tongue as she started on his potion.

*Blonde hair, black dress…*Ah, there she was. She quickly looked away as Kyler spotted her, turning to her friends and whispering excitedly. He grinned, keeping his sights set on her. When she finally gained the confidence to turn his way again, he cocked his head, inviting her closer.

Her friends erupted in a series of murmurs as she made her way toward him, tucking a strand of golden curls behind her pointed ears.

"Commander," she began to address him, but he stopped her.

"Kyler, please. And you are?"

Her face heated as he leaned in to hear her speak. "Annelle."

"Annelle," he repeated back to her, letting her name roll off his tongue. "Well, Annelle, you look lovely tonight." His lips brushed her cheek as he spoke, close enough to smell her perfume.

If she wasn't blushing before, she was now. He could practically feel her heart racing. He pulled away as Maeve set his drink down, lifting the glass to Annelle with a look of amusement. "Thank you."

She finally found her words. "Of course, Kyler." She turned on her heel and returned to her group of friends, who began berating her with questions the moment she reached them.

"These poor girls." Salcon pulled Kyler's attention from Annelle. "You know it's not nice to tease."

Kyler shrugged, downing the rest of the raspberry. "She seemed to enjoy it."

"So did you," Corbin mumbled into his glass. "A little too much."

"Loosen up, will you?" Kyler started on his third potion, this one light blue. It smelled like citrus and honey, and when he tasted it, he was met with a hint of salt. "Interesting." He waved Maeve over, and she eyed him suspiciously.

"You told me to make you something. Just because you don't like it doesn't mean you get another."

He chuckled, shaking his head. "Don't get defensive. I just want to know what it is."

"It's Apola mixed with orange, mango, and blackberry, and sprinkled with salt. It's called 'The Athesian'."

Kyler admired the glass. "Well, I'm sold. This might be a new favorite."

Salcon made a face. "Good. Because the raspberry is awful."

"Don't get mad at me because you don't know what's good." He nodded his thanks to Maeve.

"You're not going to like yourself tomorrow," Corbin warned, a single empty glass before him.

Corbin was right, but that was a problem for the morning.

CHAPTER FOUR

KYLER TAPPED A HAND AGAINST HIS LEG AS HE WALKED, keeping alert for anyone else wandering about as he passed the barracks and neared the castle. None of his soldiers would dare question him to his face, but they would certainly wonder what their commander was doing at the castle so late. He didn't need rumors spreading.

Stars dotted the sky, lighting the roads that led away from Leida and toward Aiyanna. Only two people knew of Kyler's secret meetings with the princess—Corbin, obviously, and his older brother, Evander, whose dare nearly eight years prior had eventually led to Kyler's secret romance. Evander had since moved across the sea to a city in Xynack, so his knowledge didn't matter much anymore.

Kyler caught a glimpse of an open blade as a soldier rounded the hill, his back to the barracks. He was headed toward the castle, where he'd follow the back walls down to the beach and continue toward the south entrance. Being the one responsible for the soldiers' patrol routes, Kyler knew every step his soldiers took and had timed their rotations, allowing him to slip in and out of the castle without an unwanted run-in.

It was a brilliant setup and, so far, had worked like a charm.

Firelight flickered from inside the castle windows, casting warm light across the gray stone of the castle. Branches snagged at his shirt as he slipped into the hedges, muttering curses as sharp brambles raked across his skin. He pressed his hand flat against the rough wall, running it across grooves in the stone, as he turned to avoid getting more scrapes from the pointed twigs. His fingers brushed the vines as he sunk into the shadows, and stopped as he finally felt the cool, familiar touch of metal.

Evander's dare had been thrilling: climb to the roof of the castle. As a kid desperate to prove himself, Kyler had accepted the challenge. He'd spent the next several nights pacing the perimeter, avoiding the annoyed stares from castle soldiers, until he'd finally discovered his way to the top. The stones were laid evenly, making the wall nearly impossible to scale—if not for the metal ladder that stretched from the hedges to the lowest roof, hidden by vines and shadows. It was an odd find, something likely placed there should the royals need a hasty escape, and it'd become Kyler's secret.

A secret he intended to keep.

He began scaling the ladder with practiced ease, hardly touching one rim before reaching for the next. Hidden by darkness, he climbed higher and higher until he came to a stop at the second story window. Sure enough, the glass had been lifted, and the silver curtains flapped lightly in the breeze.

Kyler reached for the windowsill, his chest jumping as he caught himself on its marble hold. With a bit more effort, he hauled his body into the room, his feet landing on the silk carpet as the smell of perfume filled his lungs.

Before he could catch his balance, Aiyanna threw herself on him, nearly sending him tumbling back out of the window.

"You're here!"

He chuckled and wrapped an arm around her waist, running a hand through her dark curls. "I'm sorry to keep you waiting, starlight." He cupped her face in his hands and planted a kiss on her forehead.

The princess smiled up at him, dimples forming against her cheeks. Aiyanna was a beauty to behold, even without jewels on her ears or silk dresses. Her black hair was streaked with shades of brown that caught the light whenever she moved, starkly contrasting her porcelain skin. Eyebrows just as dark sat above her almond eyes, which sparkled like topaz, and a rounded nose fit her face perfectly. And her lips—soft and pink and Kyler's favorite thing.

She pulled his hands from her face, tangling her fingers in his.

Aiyanna tugged him away from the window and farther into the room. Like most in the castle, it was lavishly decorated, with a canopy bed and a round ottoman planted in the center of the space. Multiple mirrors hung from the walls, along with frames filled with pressed flowers that Aiyanna had taken from the gardens. An unlit fireplace sat against the wall, prepped for the fast-approaching winter.

"Tell me about the meeting," Aiyanna urged. "Oh, and your new recruits!" She paused, reaching up to brush Kyler's hair from his swollen ear. "That looks like it hurts."

"Aiyanna," he teased, unable to hide the playfulness in his voice, "one question at a time?"

She scrunched her nose. "Sorry."

"Don't be." He traced her jaw with the tips of his fingers, his rough hands skimming over her smooth skin. "I'll start with the meeting, hm?"

She nodded and took a seat at the foot of her bed, urging him to follow.

Kyler sat beside her, his mind drifting back to the meeting that morning. "The dragons are ready to pick the new general."

Her brows furrowed. "And?"

"I don't know. The ceremony is in two days."

She sighed and lounged back on the bed, her gaze traveling to the ceiling. "I wish I could ease your mind, but my father refuses to tell me anything." After another moment, she sat up. "How was your night? You smell like Apola."

Grateful for the change in subject, Kyler smiled. "I tried a new mixture—orange, blackberry, and salt. They called it 'The Athesian'. You would like it."

Her eyes floated across the room in thought. The king only served Apola on special occasions, and even then, it was lightly flavored. Kyler had managed to sneak a bit of better-tasting mixtures to the princess a few times, though not enough for her to discover a favorite.

"Who came with you?"

He laughed as he recalled Corbin's teasing and how the musician drew attention to him. He took his time describing the sights and smells, watching her face soften as she listened. Kyler hoped his words did the town justice. Aiyanna loved people, and she loved music. Kyler often debated stealing her away for an evening, but his frequent visits were risky enough.

"Salcon tried the raspberry," he finished, "and he hated it. Complained all night."

Aiyanna's laugh fell with a sigh as she glanced at the still-open window. "That sounds fun."

"I'll take you with me one day."

Her eyes met his with a playful edge, and sarcasm dripped from her words. "I had fun too. I spent all afternoon studying the history of gateways at the request of my father."

Kyler grinned. "Thrilling. Speaking of, I brought you something." He removed the vial of Gelio from his belt and waved it before her.

A tender smile rose to her lips. "You're the best."

"I know." He winked and passed her the elixir.

Aiyanna tucked the vial beneath her blanket before leaning closer and pressing a kiss to his mouth.

He could never tire of her kisses.

Her lips met his with sincerity as she wove her fingers into his hair, sending chills up his spine. She held him for a few more moments before slowly pulling away so that their noses were touching.

"You look lovely tonight, starlight," he breathed.

"So do you, Commander."

He chuckled. "You think I look lovely?"

She rolled her eyes, sitting back once more. "You know what I mean."

He didn't allow his laugh to fade as he brought his face close to hers again, studying her lovely features.

"I recently overheard my father talking about you."

"Mhm." He wasn't listening.

"Something about your skill."

"Oh?"

She sighed, shoving him gently in the chest. "Listen to me!"

Satisfied with her annoyance, Kyler leaned back on his hands, giving her his full attention. "Go ahead. I'm listening."

"He was meeting with Advisor Cadmus. He spoke highly of your scale count." As she talked, her fingers brushed his trains of scales, making them jingle softly.

He smirked. "That's something I'm glad to hear. I thought you had nothing to ease my mind?"

Her soft tone fell. "He also spoke of the other two. He's impressed with Zale's experience and Novah's knowledge and commitment."

His face turned solemn, and Aiyanna frowned. "You're the obvious choice, Kyler."

Kyler inched closer, pulling her into his chest. He fell gently on the bed, pulling her down with him, and placed his chin atop her head. The smell of lilac drifted from her hair, making him dizzy with attraction. "I need your father to trust me."

"He *does* trust you."

Her reassurance didn't help much. The king trusted him with the Brigade, but his daughter was another matter entirely. However, if the dragons appointed him as general, Kyler would be at the king's left hand. The king's life would be entrusted to Kyler from that day forward.

If *that* wasn't enough to let Kyler court the princess, then nothing would be.

CHAPTER FIVE

❖

KYLER WOKE BEFORE THE SUN, HIS BODY FILTERING THE EFFECT of the Onys he'd taken the night before. The sleeping potion had done its job, sending him into a dreamless sleep despite the tumble of his thoughts. The moment his eyes opened, however, his heart began to thunder.

Tonight.

He rolled to his side, lifting his head so his scales wouldn't poke his face. The still-dark room and soft quilt urged him to rest for a moment longer, but there was work to be done before the ceremony.

The rustle of waking men was muffled through the thin barrack walls. The soldiers' groggy chatter and shuffling blankets reminded Kyler of the years he spent sharing a bunk with Corbin.

Breakfast was served at sunrise, and if you were late, you didn't eat. A part of Kyler was tempted to make his way to the dining hall now and grab something before the kitchens opened, but he didn't quite have the energy. Instead, he tossed the quilt to the side, shivering against the cold that seeped into the room.

The bed creaked softly as he sat up, allowing the cool air to pull the sleep from his mind. He reached for his scales, gently tugging them apart and running his hands through the knots in his hair.

His thoughts wandered, picturing the ceremony where the coveted white scale would be awarded to the new general, marking his authority.

Or her. Kyler grimaced at the thought and pushed himself to his feet. He dragged his hands down his face in an attempt to shove the ceremony from his mind. He needed to order new training bows—Corbin's count from the other day showed they were running low—and he'd offered to assist Adri with training. There was also the issue of the speech, which he had yet to put together.

Layers of cotton, leather, and steel settled into place as Kyler dressed himself routinely, caring little for what he wore now. The silver chest plate rested comfortably over his shoulders as he tightened the sides, securing the armor, and topped it with a cape that matched the green of his scales. It latched in place with a satisfying snap, falling over a single shoulder.

The barracks were stirring with activity as Kyler emerged into the hallway, his boots echoing against the wooden floors as he made his way toward the dining hall. He found several of his men already there, seated at the circular tables, as the sky began to brighten. The smells of cooked sausage, eggs, and oats filled the hall, and steam rose from the kitchen. The clinking of ceramic and glass matched the chatter, and the room slowly came alive as the sun rose higher.

"Morning, Commander."

Kyler turned to find Salcon at his side. He wore a clean uniform, and his hair was still damp from a morning bath. As was customary, his even braids matched Kyler's, and black gloves could be seen poking out of his pockets.

"Cold day?" Kyler asked.

Salcon nodded. "Must've swept in overnight. Eliab's Day is coming fast." He glanced around the hall. "Any news?"

Kyler sighed, not wanting to talk openly with so many ears around. "You'll be receiving a letter today."

Salcon raised an eyebrow.

Kyler had nearly forgotten that his lieutenants were just as anxious as he was for the appointing. The first decision a newly appointed general made was to choose a new commander from among the current lieutenants. He'd already made his decision, and it would come as a surprise to no one; Corbin would do an excellent job.

"I won't ask any questions." Salcon stepped into the slow-forming line behind one of the kilders. "I'll be shocked if they don't pick you."

Kyler followed, taking a plate from the rack as they neared the buffet-style counter. "I appreciate your faith in me."

Salcon glanced back at him with a squint. "You're nervous, aren't you?"

Kyler shot him a warning look, nodding to the many soldiers that surrounded them. He should have known better than to say something like that in such a public place.

Salcon turned back to his plate in silence, dropping several sausage links onto its center. "Evander believes you'll do well," he said lowly.

Kyler sighed at the mention of his brother. Evander had the opportunity to become a soldier like the rest of them but instead, he'd chosen to take a ship across the Athesian Sea. His brother could do whatever he wanted with his life—Kyler cared nothing for it.

"What's your schedule today, Lieutenant?" Kyler asked, changing the subject.

"Another day of archery."

Kyler caught the roll of his eyes and couldn't help but chuckle.

"Did any of the buggers make the north target?"

Salcon scooped a spoonful of eggs onto his plate. "One girl did, but she was unable to make it a second time."

Kyler skipped the eggs. "Unfortunate."

The dining hall began to fill, and it took them a minute to find an empty table. Salcon set his plate down across from Kyler, and their conversation halted as he began piling food into his mouth.

Kyler's nose scrunched. "You look like an animal."

"And you look like a nobleman. Let a man eat in peace."

"He's no nobleman, but he may be a general." Corbin appeared behind Kyler and tossed an envelope onto the table. The cream parchment slid across the wood, coming to a stop at Salcon's plate.

Corbin pulled out the chair beside Kyler and turned it backward, resting his arms on the backrest, as Salcon eyed the letter.

He swallowed, glancing up at Corbin and then at Kyler. "You weren't kidding."

"Tonight." Corbin grinned. "All lieutenants and kilders are expected to be present."

Kyler attempted to return his grin, but it wouldn't quite come. The queasy feeling in his stomach returned, and he set his fork down. "The soldiers will need specific instructions for this evening. I don't want anyone getting reckless while the higher-ups are gone."

"I'll speak with the upper ranks today and find a few to lay down the law."

"Thank you, Corbin."

He bumped his shoulder into Kyler's. "Make yourself busy, Commander. You're thinking too much."

"And you're not thinking enough." Kyler stood from his seat, adjusting his cape. "I'll be in the fields today if you need me."

Corbin grinned. "I *always* need you, Commander."

Kyler sighed in annoyance as Salcon joined in with a scoff. "Quit flirting."

Corbin gave an exaggerated wink, causing Salcon to choke on his eggs.

Kyler scratched his nose to hide his smile. "I hate you both." He could hear them continuing their banter as he headed for the door, hoping to get to the fields before the soldiers did.

The frigid wind lifted the tips of his cape the moment he stepped outside. Salcon hadn't been kidding about the cold. He knew the afternoon sun would usher in warmth, but at the moment, Kyler wished for another layer or two.

The heavy cloak continued to spiral and whip as he trekked out to the field. Adri was already waiting, pulling axes from barrels and directing kilders to their designated spots. He'd trimmed his beard since Kyler had last seen him at the tavern, and like Salcon, he was dressed warmly.

"Bit chilly there, Lieutenant?" Kyler called as he neared.

Adri paused, eying him up and down. "Not as cold as you must be."

A grin brought dimples to Kyler's cheeks as he accepted Adri's firm handshake.

"I got the letter. I have full faith in you, Commander."

"Thank you, Adri."

Kyler's attention turned to the barracks as soldiers began slowly filing onto the grass, tugging coats and cloaks around their arms.

They positioned themselves shoulder to shoulder in flawless rows, a sea of sage standing as one unit as opposed to nearly five dozen individuals. As second-level soldiers, these men and women had completed basic training in every area and were ready to move on to more advanced exercises.

Kyler drew the soldier's attention, his voice rising above the wind. "A soldier knows his place—at the top." His boots sunk into the grass as he paced, hands clasped tightly at his back. "I have high expectations of all of you. Have I made myself clear?"

"Yes sir!" Their shout filled the silent field, and he nodded his approval.

"Lieutenant, please."

Adri stepped forward, a battle axe firm in his grip.

"When fighting an unfamiliar opponent, there's no telling what skills or weapons they may possess. It's important to know which pose a real threat in enemy hands and how to use their weaknesses against them.

"In this case, your lieutenant's weapon of choice is an axe, a strength weapon that can cause a lot of damage." Kyler stepped closer to Adri, who held the axe out so everyone could see it. "When facing an enemy with a weapon made purely for strength, you want to look for the weak points. Can anyone tell me where this axe is the weakest?"

The soldiers were quiet for a moment before one man shouted out, "The eye, sir!"

"Correct." He lifted a finger to where the axe head was mounted to the handle. "This point is vulnerable, and with the right technique, it's possible to sever the head from the handle." He faced Adri, who shifted his stance and gripped the axe in both hands. "You need to be faster than your opponent and stealthy with your attacks. Axes are heavy and require more effort to maneuver, so use this to your advantage."

Adri swung, and Kyler ducked under his attack. The momentum of the swing made Adri step backward, throwing him slightly off-balance.

"Now, watch as he swings again."

Adri brought his axe down, and Kyler slipped out of the line of attack. Before he could bring his weapon back up, Kyler moved in, thrusting his foot against the eye of the axe. A sharp crack echoed around them, and Adri lifted his weapon to reveal splinters sticking out from the area of impact. Though the weapon was still in one piece, it was fractured and damaged beyond use.

"Kilders."

Four kilders stepped forward, training axes in their hands. A fifth stood off to the side with a wagon full of axes waiting to be destroyed.

"I want you all to walk through this slowly. It takes a well-timed attack and just the right amount of strength. Line up."

The soldiers did as Kyler asked, talking amongst themselves as they took their places before the kilders. The satisfying snap of splitting wood filled the air as Kyler observed the training, stepping in when his correction was needed.

Even as he worked, the weight of what was to come lay heavy on his mind. He was ready to be general. He'd trained his entire life to prove himself to General Uriah. Tonight, despite whatever corner of the realm Uriah had run off to, Kyler would prove him wrong.

CHAPTER SIX

KYLER STARED AT HIS REFLECTION, HIS GAZE TRAILING OVER THE evening's attire. The emerald-stained leather at his shoulders faded into sage cotton, and he hadn't decided whether he liked it or not. He glanced at the heavy gray armor lying on his bed. It was for special occasions; the darker color revealed every scratch and dent, making it impractical for training.

Tonight, however, he wanted to look his best.

He stood there for a moment longer before stripping off the emerald leather and replacing it with the white. The new color stood out, a shade that would draw eyes to him. He cursed his fingers for shaking as he tightened the straps, rolling out his shoulders and eying himself again.

Satisfied, Kyler slipped the armor over his head, strapping it to his sides and shifting it until it sat in the grooves of the leather pads. He stepped closer to the mirror, studying his braids and checking that they were even.

"Stared at yourself long enough?"

Kyler hadn't heard the door open and startled at the sound of Corbin's voice. "Can't you knock?"

Corbin crossed his arms and leaned against the doorframe. "You're going to miss me showing up unannounced."

He was dressed in some of his best armor as well, with a forest green shirt overlaid with black leather pads. His silver breastplate was clean and polished, every engraving popping as it caught the light.

Kyler turned back to his reflection, adjusting a stray hair. "I think it's you who will miss me."

Corbin stepped in and closed the door behind him. "You're right. The only people you'll miss are the tavern girls."

"Don't worry, I'll still visit them." Kyler lifted the white cape he'd laid out on his bed. Like the one he wore that morning, it hung off a single shoulder, leaving the armor on his left exposed. Dark green dragons spiraled across the fabric in thick embroidery, eye-catching and elegant.

"Let me guess," Corbin said, cracking his knuckles as he spoke, "you don't have a speech?"

"On second thought, I *am* going to miss you." Kyler crossed his arms and faced his lieutenant. "Your daily lectures are truly touching."

A sharp knock echoed through the door, and Kyler threw a hand in its direction. "See? Knocking."

Corbin smirked as Kyler twisted the handle and found Salcon waiting in the hall. The lieutenant shifted into a salute, an excited smile pinching his lips. "Ready?"

"Lead the way, Lieutenant."

He winked playfully and spun on his heel, letting his dark cape swing behind him as he walked.

Corbin rested a hand on Kyler's shoulder and offered a reassuring squeeze before shoving him after Salcon. Kyler resisted the urge to mess with his hair, keeping his hands balled at his sides instead. Every step felt heavier and heavier, as though he would sink through the barrack floors.

Salcon led them out front, where every soldier and trainee stood in salute. They lined the path that led to the castle, filling the barrack grounds with the glint of silver armor.

From the rows of soldiers, the rest of the lieutenants and kilders stepped forward, falling into place behind Salcon and Corbin. Sixteen lieutenants and thirty-two kilders, all dressed in their best armor and donning the green shades of the Land Brigade.

As Kyler reached the end of the line, several high-ranking soldiers stepped forward from among the others, led by a young man with only a fraction of the scales his commander possessed.

He saluted, and Kyler gave him the honor of saluting back.

"Sir, I can assure you the Land Brigade will be in good hands in the absence of our commander, lieutenants, and kilders."

Kyler dropped his salute, offering a handshake instead. "I have full faith in you, soldier."

He nodded, his face like stone, though Kyler could see the pride swelling in his dark eyes. "Good luck, Commander."

"Thank you."

The soldier saluted again and stepped back into place with the others who'd been entrusted with authority for the evening.

Kyler started for the castle, followed by his men. Not a single word came from the mouths of the soldiers that trailed him, each one wanting to make a good impression. The shifting sounds of armor grew louder, and Kyler subtly turned his gaze west, toward the docks.

Commander Zale rounded the hill, followed by the lieutenants and kilders of the Sea Force. They were dressed entirely in shades of blue, their capes rolling behind them like ocean waves. Zale met Kyler's eye and gave a brief nod as he approached. Kyler returned the gesture, concealing his disdain after their previous interaction.

From behind them, the Sky Regiment emerged from the base of the mountains, their armor reflecting the sunset. There were only twenty-one lieutenants and kilders combined, and at their head, Commander Novah strode with her shoulders back and chin high. Her armor was pristine, the light metal laid across deep red leather and fabric as gray as storm clouds. Intricate braids danced through her hair and formed a knot at the base of her neck, exposing every one of her fire-colored scales.

A shadow blocked the setting sun, and Kyler's eyes shifted to the skies. Wind whistled from the mouth of the Pass, the only opening in the cloud above the mountain, and from it emerged beasts of ivory and flame. Three broke through the cloud, one to represent each branch, but the fourth was the most breathtaking.

The dragon was called Atlas, one of the few whose scales remained the pure white of Eliab's army. He was as old as Sannir itself, and it was he who would grant one of his scales to the commander he deemed worthy.

The dragons made their slow descent to the castle, disappearing behind its stone with swift elegance.

"Showoffs," Corbin mumbled.

Kyler chuckled.

The Brigade reached the gates first, pausing to greet the others as they arrived.

Zale offered a gloved hand as he approached, his good eye fixated on Kyler. "Good luck, Commander."

"You as well." Kyler got the sense the older commander was still bitter from their last conversation, but he wasn't in the mood to push. Instead, he turned to Novah, who approached with a stiff spine.

She placed a fist on her chest and dipped her head in respect.

"Good evening."

Kyler mimicked her movement as her men came to a halt behind her. Zale gave her a nod, along with the same well wishes he'd given Kyler, but Kyler kept his mouth shut.

Novah's burning gaze met his, and like him, she said nothing.

The gates to the courtyard swung open, and Zale motioned for Novah to enter first. Her troops fell in line, following her along the cobblestone path and between the lines of castle guards. Flags rose from the grounds, flapping just above their heads as they marched silently. The Brigade followed, and then the Sea Force. Tension hung heavy in the air, and Kyler's mouth grew dry.

At last, the line of guards and flags came to an end, stopping before the doors of the largest ballroom. It was a building separated from the rest of the castle, complete with a large balcony and a side wall made entirely of glass that mimicked the one in the great hall. The doors opened before the soldiers, creating an opening large enough for all three commanders to walk side by side with their armies trailing behind their respective leaders.

Sannir's nobility already filled a quarter of the ballroom, and the chatter silenced at the opening of the doors. On the balcony stood the king, whose ivory robes framed him like sheets of bone. It was nearly impossible to avoid looking at him. He watched the three commanders with intensity, his face revealing nothing of the decision made. A thick navy cape draped from his shoulders, and his polished crown rested firmly on his head.

Princess Aiyanna stood to his left, dressed in a silver gown with sleeves that flared at her elbows. A silver circlet matched the cloth, with beads of blue draped through her hair and laid across her collarbone. She was the stark opposite of the advisor who stood to the right of the king.

Advisor Cadmus Vangelis was as old as the king, with peppered hair and a trimmed beard. He stood straight, donning black and silver like a raven against the moon. His steel eyes cast across the audience and studied the approaching troops with diligence.

But as striking as the three of them were, they didn't hold the room's attention.

Beside them, with curved horns nearly brushing the domed ceiling, was Atlas. Scales colored like cloud and cotton danced along his back and chest, running in lines from the tip of his nose to the end of his tail. Eyes, slit like a cat, bored into the commanders as every breath of the beast seemed to fill the room with power.

On the floor beneath the balcony, the other three dragons sat like stone; their only movement was the gentle pulse of their nostrils with each breath. Though the three were large, their size was a mere fraction compared to that of Atlas—a sign that they were quite young. Unlike Atlas, their scales danced in fragmented colors. Green as deep as the forest, browns and golds, flashes of orange and red, and shimmering blue caught the light of the chandeliers like the scales that hung from the ears of the commanders.

Kyler reached the front, stepping out from among his men to stand beside Novah. Zale did the same, placing himself on Kyler's opposite side, and the ballroom fell still. Kyler's ears rang in the quiet, his face hot and blood racing. The heat from the dragons' chests radiated, burning Kyler's skin and flooding his pulse.

The king took his time, looking over all three groups and letting his eyes sweep the audience of nobility and soldiers.

"People of Sannir," he began, his voice booming across the ballroom, "as you all are aware, we lost a great general. General Uriah Caligari was an honorable man, who brought success and victory in all Sannir's feats. Today, we come together to celebrate the appointment of his successor."

The king paused, and Kyler feared the entire audience could hear his pounding heart.

"The honor of becoming general is a great one. When Eliab built our kingdom under the instruction of Adoni, he demonstrated what a true general should look like. We have before us three exceptionally gifted commanders, each with their own abilities and distinctions. The decision was not easy, but the time has come for an appointment.

"Now, it is my honor to share with you the new general of the armies of Sannir."

Kyler's breath hitched.

"It is with great pride and a clear conscience that we welcome to the ranks…General Novah Elison!"

CHAPTER SEVEN

APPLAUSE ERUPTED FROM THE CROWD, BUT KYLER COULDN'T hear it. His body went numb as Novah stepped up the stairs, her face glowing. The world felt as though it were moving in slow motion.

It was a mistake. It must have been.

His mind spun as he watched Novah reach the balcony and kneel before the great dragon. Atlas lowered his head to hers, pressing their foreheads together as smoke drifted from his nostrils. She lifted a hand to his nose, stroking the tiny scales at the tip until one fell into her palm, and the dragon straightened once more.

Kyler sucked a breath, snapping back to reality, and joined in with the applause. Beside him, Zale remained expressionless as always, clapping along with everyone else.

Novah secured the scale to the end of her chain of red. She rose from her knees and dipped her head to Atlas. Princess Aiyanna moved aside, allowing Novah to take the general's place at the king's left, as His Majesty lifted a palm to silence the applause.

"General Novah Elison, your skill and self-control have served you well, and Adoni's favor has come upon you. I entrust the armies of Sannir to your leadership."

Novah bowed. "Thank you, Your Majesty. I will not disappoint you."

He smiled and stepped back, allowing her to have full control of the audience for her speech.

Kyler didn't listen. He couldn't. Dread crept into his senses, filling his stomach with a poisonous mixture of anger and disappointment.

Somewhere in this forsaken realm, Uriah was laughing.

When she finished speaking, Novah descended the marble stairs while the audience rose with applause. Kyler couldn't look at her. Heat burned his eyes, and his jaw began to ache with tension, but he still managed to lift a hand in salute. Zale did the same as he waited for the Sky Regiment to fall behind Novah before leading his troops from the ballroom.

Kyler stood until the final Sea Force soldier passed, then guided his men after them. The vibrant red of the Regiment's uniforms ahead made him dizzy, but he kept a steady pace through the courtyard and out of the castle gates.

The sky had turned to dusk, and the tip of the moon was already peeking out from a sea of dark clouds. The air attempted to cool Kyler's burning skin, but it was to no avail. Every inch of his body seemed to spark and smolder.

It wasn't until every soldier was through the castle gates that Kyler dropped his formality, pressing his eyes shut. It was done. The decision had been made.

"I look forward to serving under you, General."

Kyler glanced up to find Zale offering a hand to Novah, the two lingering as their troops continued on.

Her cape fluttered behind her as she stepped closer, accepting his sign of respect. "I look forward to it as well."

She turned toward Kyler but he avoided her eye, addressing his troops instead. "You're dismissed, Corbin. Take them back."

"Yes sir." Disappointment filled his voice, only adding to the anger bubbling within Kyler's chest. He didn't want pity.

The Land Brigade began their walk back to the barracks as Novah approached him, out of earshot of the Regiment troops who were following their new commander back toward the mountains.

"Commander Kyler."

Kyler sighed, facing her.

"I look forward to getting to know you better, as we'll be working closely now."

He clicked his tongue. "Don't count on it."

Novah lifted her chin in cool hubris. "I see." She glanced at the rest of his men, their shadows still visible as they rounded the castle. "I expect you to learn your place, Commander."

He scoffed and stepped closer, lowering his voice. "I know my place. If you want my respect, you'll have to earn it."

Her russet eyes flicked between his. "I believe I already have, though, evidently, you refuse to acknowledge it."

The unpigmented scale that dangled from her right ear seemed to taunt him, and he hardened his gaze, masking his jealousy.

She took a step closer, swallowing the space between them. "You answer to me now, Commander."

"You're not Uriah."

His comment must've stung because her hard features softened, though only for a moment. "No. And I don't intend to be." She turned, and the tips of her cape smacked his shins.

Kyler dug his teeth into his tongue, biting back an insult. This evening had been terrible enough; he didn't need to lose his position due to disrespect on top of it. He forced himself to watch as she strode toward the castle and wondered if she could feel the heat from his gaze.

Novah looked to the Pass as the four dragons rose into the darkening sky. Then, she glanced back at Kyler, her gaze cold. "Goodnight, Commander. You're dismissed."

She left him alone, silver and red fading into the shadows cast by the lanterns of the courtyard. It wasn't until she disappeared entirely that he slammed his fist into a column of stone, curses rolling off his tongue. A crack shot through his hand, and he winced, having hit the column much harder than he'd intended. The throb of his knuckles momentarily drowned his anger, pulling him from his spiraling thoughts. His eyes shifted to Aiyanna's room, where the curtains flapped through the open window.

He rolled his shoulders and turned from the courtyard, pacing toward the castle's side. His hair caught in his lashes and poked at his eyes as he circled, keeping his head downcast.

Branches snagged his clothes, but he cared little. His palms scraped along the castle walls until they met the familiar metal. It was risky—the white cape wouldn't hide him well, and the castle grounds were still scattered with guests—but he allowed himself to be rash and gripped the ladder. Wind stung his face and cut through his armor. When he reached the windowsill, the warmth from within Aiyanna's room welcomed him.

Her room was dark, with only the moonlight from outside filling it. Kyler stumbled over the rug as he landed. Pain shot through his wrists as he caught himself before his face hit the ground.

"Sannir's Saints, Aiyanna!" he hissed, his kneecaps throbbing from the impact. He didn't get up right away. Instead, Kyler paused, allowing the pain to subside and frustration to ease. He had no reason to be upset with Aiyanna, and yet the thought of her brought waves of curdling anger.

She'd told him he had nothing to worry about. She'd been so *certain.*

So had he.

Kyler sat back on his heels and closed his eyes. Aiyanna's silky curtains waved, brushing his shoulders and tucking themselves into his armor. With more effort than necessary, he lifted himself from the ground, careful not to trip again as he kicked the rug flat.

He took a deep breath as he leaned his back against the wall. His eyes slowly adjusted to the darkness and the sounds of servants walking the halls reached his ears. The castle was alive with excitement tonight. He could hear it; he could feel it. But the pit in his stomach wouldn't allow him to take part. Everything he'd ever worked for seemed to slip through his fingers like drops of water.

He knew the decision was final, but his mind wouldn't accept it. He continued to search desperately for a solution in which he came out as general, but every thought led him to a dead end. Unless Novah died or stepped down, she would continue to hold the title.

Novah. *General* Novah. It was absurd. If it'd been Zale, Kyler might have been able to understand—at least he was experienced and strategic. But Novah? She had nothing to offer.

If Uriah came back—

His thoughts were interrupted by the creak of the door, and light from the hallway filled the room. Aiyanna stepped inside, apparently unaware of Kyler's presence. Her silver gown reflected the moonlight as she stepped to the lamps, lighting the nearest one.

Kyler stayed silent, watching as it sparked to life. The lamp illuminated a dinner gown that'd been laid across her bed, made of blue silk and decorated in fine embroidery. She was to prepare for a customary dinner with the king and general. The king and Novah.

She turned to light the next lamp but caught sight of Kyler's armor and jumped at the sight of him. "I didn't see you there."

He didn't answer.

Her gown wrinkled as she stepped toward him, her heels clicking until they reached the carpet. The light of the single lamp cast shadows across her face as she neared, but Kyler could easily read the disappointment etched on her features.

"Are you alright?"

Kyler's jaw shifted. "Of course, I'm not *alright*, Aiyanna."

His tone made her pause, and her dark brows furrowed. "The general serves the good of Sannir. If Novah can do that—"

"*I* can do that." He pushed off the wall, sharpness slicing his words. "I've done that for years."

"It's not about you, Kyler. We have a kingdom to serve. You are not the only soldier capable of leading Sannir's armies."

"Look at my scales, Aiyanna! I earned these!"

Her face hardened. "Do you hear how prideful you sound?"

"Prideful?" He didn't bother hiding the appall in his voice as he inched closer. "That's what you think of me?"

She lifted her chin. "Right now, yes."

"I'm starting to think you didn't want me to be general." He was almost yelling. "Did you know? Did your father tell you?" He was close to her now, his heart pounding.

Aiyanna held her posture. "You know I'm not involved in this."

"Don't play innocent with me."

Her voice was steady. "You will not shout at me."

Kyler could hardly see her through his anger. "You don't care, do you?"

"You have no respect."

"You could have convinced him! If you truly cared—" Kyler fell backward as Aiyanna shoved him.

"You're selfish and arrogant!" She shoved him again, the rings on her fingers echoing off his armor. He stumbled into the wall, his back hitting it hard enough to steal the air from his lungs.

"I am not your servant, Kyler!"

Shock replaced the anger, and his mind began to clear. His shoulder ached from where he'd collided with the wall, but that was nothing compared to the way Aiyanna's words cut him. It was then he noticed the tears welling in her eyes, which she blinked away as silence engulfed them. He'd never seen her like this.

He stared numbly as Aiyanna drew a deep breath. "I do not know why the dragons chose General Novah, but it's clear to me why they didn't choose you."

"Aiyanna—"

"No," she snapped. "I think you've said enough." Her shoulders straightened as she turned to the dress laid on her bed. "It's time for you to go. I'm having dinner with the general."

He was still for a moment, stunned by her harsh words.

"Leave."

Kyler swallowed hard and nodded as he turned and swung his boots over the windowsill. It wasn't until he was on the ladder that tremors overtook his body. His limbs shook violently as his foot hit the first rail, and he feared his hands would slip as he descended. Aiyanna's voice echoed through his mind as her anger burned his memory. Tears fogged his visibility, which was already low given the dark sky, but he refused to let them fall.

He reached the ground and staggered through the bushes, glancing back at the window as he sunk into the outer gardens. Though light fell from inside, it was filtered through the thick glass. She'd closed it.

Kyler gritted his teeth as the cold came in a wave. He flexed his palms in an attempt to stop the shaking, and he forced his legs to carry him toward the barracks.

His armor clinked with each step. He squinted against the wind, the cold catching the saltwater at his lashes in painful, burning gusts. He could still hear her voice shaking as his mind replayed their encounter over and over. He wanted to tell himself everything was fine, but he knew it wasn't. The world seemed to fracture like broken glass, sharp edges slicing his skin with every movement he made. The jealousy that'd inhabited his chest had been traded for bitter emptiness. He didn't want to think or feel or be. He wanted to close his eyes and open them to sunlight, but every time he blinked, he was met with darkness and ice.

Through the rawness of his thoughts, low murmurs caught his attention, and something about them made him stop. He was still near the castle walls, and trees from the gardens scattered the area. The wind suddenly shifted direction and the voices seemed to float from along the wall, somewhere deep within the shadows.

Kyler turned back toward the castle, inching closer to the voices. It sounded like two men, their tones cautious yet edged with excitement. He stayed low, tucking his white cape behind him and keeping close to the trees. Suspicion entered his mind, and Kyler wondered if they were a couple of his men sneaking time off duty. As he got closer, however, the shadows of their dark armor revealed a design he'd never seen before.

Engravings of legless dragons known as amphipteres twisted

along their breastplates, the dark beasts highlighted in gold. Large swords hung at their hips with no sheath to cover them, and though their faces were shadowed he could make out the edges of helmets resting over their heads.

It wasn't until their conversation halted that Kyler realized they'd spotted him. His eyes lifted to meet theirs, only to find two sets of horns, ribbed together in sheets of black metal, set atop their helmets. The horns angled back, forming sharp points at the end that resembled those of a goat.

The horns of Orisis.

Kyler stared at them, almost convinced they were a delusion of his tormented mind.

One of the men stepped forward, his height towering over Kyler. The man's dark gaze flashed to Kyler's hand as he reached for his blade, and Kyler halted with his fingers hovering above the hilt.

A screech erupted from beyond the clouds, tearing through the night. Kyler tore his eyes from the man to see a massive shadow pierce the air, setting the sky ablaze with fire.

CHAPTER EIGHT

AMPHITERES SHOT THROUGH THE NIGHT, THEIR HORNS glinting from the sparks that flew from their mouths. They were creatures of Orisis, twisted and dark and full of rage. They were supposed to be legend, demons crushed by Eliab's army a thousand years ago.

Heat pressed Kyler's skin as embers caught the trees, engulfing the area in flames. He could see clearly now. The soldiers of Orisis were advancing toward the Temple of Adoni. Shouts rang from the distant barracks as soldiers prepared for the sudden battle.

Kyler stood motionless, allowing the fire to dance dangerously close. He'd spent his life training for battle, mastering every kind of weaponry and turning men into soldiers.

But this wasn't training. This was *real.*

The afi hadn't been seen in years—centuries. The armies of Orisis were disbanded long before Ouxileous was king or Uriah was general. And yet here they were, coated in armor as dark as the night sky and marking Sannir with death.

Kyler swore as the flames caught his cape, pulling him from his trance. Through the blaze, the sounds of shifting armor faded, and he looked up to find the two men strolling through the trees, leaving him alone in the burning gardens. Kyler fumbled with the clasp at his shoulder, and the moment his cape fell, he shot through the smoke, gasping for fresh air. His eyes trailed upward to the sky full of beasts, long and snake-like, with no limbs and massive wings protruding from their backs. Each was topped with a rider, whose horned helmets matched the beasts. They circled the castle, shouting curses and raining down fire. Scales of midnight shadowed them in the now-starless sky.

The Land Brigade came pooling out of the barracks, disorganized and chaotic, unease filling their shouts.

"Soldiers!" Kyler's voice carried as his men raced toward the castle. "Guard your necks!"

At least that much of the legend he'd remembered. The greatest danger of the afi wasn't their fire or blade, but their hands. With a single touch to the neck, an afi could steal a soul, condemning it to eternal torture in Tophet—or whatever remained of it.

Kyler caught a glimpse of Corbin as he passed, tugging at the collar of his shirt. The troops appeared tiny compared to the amphipteres, and fear welled deep within Kyler's core.

A rush of white shot through the air. Atlas was the first to break free of the Pass, emerging in the sky like a beacon of light. He met the ambush with the clamp of his jaws, sending the nearest amphiptere tumbling to the ground. Snaps echoed in the night as the Pass released countless dragons, their scales ranging from pale ivory to rich pigments of green and red.

A flurry of steel arrows shot forth from the peaks of the mountains as the Sky Regiment rushed into battle alongside the Brigade. The dragons swooped to the mountains, slowing just long enough for the soldiers to leap onto their backs with practiced ease, before launching back into battle.

Cannon fire erupted from the shoreline as Zale's troops turned their vessels into weapons, adding to the smoke that now choked the air. Kyler's hand fell limply to his sword, fingers brushing the weapon gifted to him by his father—a soldier before him.

It will always protect you when I can't, his father had sworn.

That promise now felt like a lie. A blade could do nothing against the strength of Orisis. Fire ate at the castle. The metallic tang of blood filled the air.

Kyler pulled a deep breath, wrapping his hand firmly around the hilt of his blade. He drew it from its scabbard with a hiss, and the metal caught in the light of embers. Orisis or not, he was a soldier, and he was sworn to guard one thing above all else—the Dragon Pass.

Through the smog, Kyler could make out the Temple of Adoni, the arched structure of white stone marred with singes. It was a rounded building, engraved with runes and dragons like the pillar and hauntingly pale against the black smoke. If the Temple fell, so would the Pass. If the Temple fell, so would Sannir.

Kyler lifted his blade and brought it down on the nearest afi. Metal rang like bells as the soldier of Orisis blocked his attack, a grunt escaping his lips. He swore as Kyler's weapon pierced his side and stumbled to the dust with a groan of pain.

Their armor was thick, but it had weak points, and that was what Kyler focused on as he struck again, soaking his sword in blood.

The afi fell before him. The black helm tumbled from his face and revealed a man with round ears and light stubble. He stared aimlessly at the dragons above.

Kyler set his jaw as he tugged his blood-soaked sword from the dead man's abdomen. He tore his eyes from the corpse and cleared a path for himself to the Temple. Smoke clung to his lungs and armor, and soldiers of Orisis and Adoni alike crumbled as the battle grew.

"Commander!"

Kyler spun at the shout, just in time to dodge an afi whose hand was merely inches from the back of his neck. Kyler's blade whistled as it cut air and flesh, slicing through the fingers that could have stolen his soul with one touch. The large afi soldier shouted in pain as blood poured over his exposed hand, and he clutched it to his armored chest.

Kyler turned to find that the call of warning had come from none other than Novah.

General Novah.

The white scale on her ear was slicked with blood, as was her armor and blade, but she hurried to Kyler's side as he continued toward the Temple. She constantly looked up, where the soldiers she'd trained battled the beasts of Orisis in the sky.

"Not how you imagined your first night as general?" Kyler asked as they reached the outskirts of the Temple. It stood nearly two stories high, with scattered windows of stained glass and large wooden doors now barred shut by soldiers.

Novah ground her teeth and sunk her blade into another one of Orisis' men. "Not how anyone imagined it, Commander." She flexed her fingers around her hilt. "Just buy time. The dragons will drive them out soon enough."

Kyler hissed a laugh. "How much time, *General?*"

The flames reached higher, dancing along the Temple walls and sending sparks like fireflies into the night. Another fleet of dragons shot from the mountains, horns curved to their jaws and teeth sharper than knives. The tiny charms at Kyler's ears seemed minuscule compared to the thousands that caught in the light of the fire as the dragons of Adoni joined the battle. At last, their numbers matched the amphipteres.

Feeling like he could breathe once more, Kyler scanned the

grounds before him. His sword sat firm in his grasp, raised for an attack, but his sights stilled on a single man who stood a good distance from him. The man held no weapons and wore no armor besides a helmet. Robes black as ink with golden stitching dressed his form, and his hands were clasped calmly behind his back. His gaze was set on the sky.

As though he felt Kyler staring, the unarmed man turned his face toward the Temple.

The man knew who he was. Kyler could feel it.

The sensation was haunting, as if this man dipped into his soul and tore knowledge from within. It nearly stole the air from Kyler's lungs.

Another came to the man's side, dressed in black with dark purple designs spiraling across his chest. Tips of bone-white hair stuck out from beneath his helm, and he followed the gaze of the other. The first man turned to the second, and the second lifted a single hand to the sky.

In one swift movement, the amphipteres dipped to the grass, grabbing hold of the afi soldiers on the ground, and shoot back into the clouds. The soldiers of Sannir stilled as the beasts disappeared into the darkness, leaving nothing but ash and sparks in their wake. Atlas was the only one to move, his unpigmented scales trailing after the flight of the amphipteres.

The cries of war quieted. Kyler's mind stumbled to reconcile what he'd just witnessed. In the silence, the remnants of the battle seemed to scream.

Orisis had issued an attack on Sannir. Whatever his intention was, the message was clear: Sannir's time of peace was over.

…

Novah kept pace with Kyler as they neared the castle. Elves called upon their magic, some dousing fires with water pulled from the river and others passing healing potions to the wounded. Soldiers scattered the bridge and castle grounds, and Kyler's throat tightened as he beheld the castle ruins.

The main building was intact, but the west wing was nothing but crushed stone. Ash as thick as foliage rolled into the midnight sky, and Kyler caught glimpses of shattered glass and singed tapestries. His and Novah's steps disturbed the dust that had begun to settle against the stone, sending puffs of gray into the air, as they reached the cracked door of the castle.

The surviving soldiers from every branch carried the wounded to the infirmary and lay the dead beside one another in the hall. Bodies filled the castle foyer. Sannir's soldiers. *Kyler's* soldiers. Scales of emerald, ruby, and sapphire alike were smeared in blood. The putrid scent of burned flesh and fresh wounds made his eyes water. Where was Corbin? Salcon?

"General." Zale found Kyler and Novah quickly, his armor bent and hair dusted in ash. "The king."

Novah's face hardened. Before she could speak, a scream broke free, echoing off the bare castle walls. Aiyanna shoved through the men who attempted to hold her back and fell to the marble beside the body of King Ouxileous.

The king lay lifeless amongst the fallen. Burns covered his arms, and blood spilled freely from a deep wound across his torso. His ivory robes were stained in blood and ash. No one dared pull the princess from her father's side; her cries sank deep into the chests of the surrounding soldiers.

Novah didn't move. Her lips parted as if to speak, but no words came. The new general looked as though she might crumble along with the stone.

Kyler pushed past Zale and stepped into the center of what had previously been a stunning entryway. His armor clanked as he knelt beside Aiyanna, placing a gentle hand against her shaking back. Her father's blood soaked her embroidered dinner gown, and tangles of her hair fell across his stilled chest.

Kyler sat there, fixated on the king's face.

Aiyanna whispered softly to the king, her words so muddled by tears that Kyler couldn't make them out.

He turned to the nearest soldier. "Get them both out of here, but do not separate them. Let her mourn."

The soldier nodded, taking Kyler's place at the princess' side as Kyler stood and faced the new general once more. His gaze hardened like steel, and he stalked closer until Aiyanna was out of earshot.

"First night as general and you've managed to get our king killed."

"Kyler," Zale snapped, placing himself between them.

"That's *Commander* Kyler." Kyler pushed Zale's shoulder away and found red webbing through Novah's eyes as he met them. "It's been quite a night, don't you think, General?"

She set her jaw against the tears that begged to spill for the king. "You will stand down, Commander."

"I will do no such thing."

A hand fell heavy on Kyler's shoulder, and he turned to find Corbin. "Commander, you're needed."

Kyler relaxed a bit. At least Corbin was fine.

He looked once more at Novah before stepping away, trailing Corbin around the scads of mangled bodies and debris. "Where's Salcon? And Adri?"

"Alive." Corbin finally stopped, standing near enough that Kyler could hear his low voice. He looked angry. "Keep your wits, Kyler. She's still the general."

"You're joking."

A small huff escaped him. "No one could have prepared for this. Had you been in her shoes, you wouldn't have done anything differently."

"The king is dead," Kyler snapped, "under *her* protection."

"And as the commander of the Land Brigade, you have a duty to ensure that no one else dies." Corbin's brows lifted, his silent plea making Kyler sigh.

"Commander Kyler!" Zale motioned for him to come back, and Kyler moved away from Corbin to find Novah and two Sky Regiment soldiers grouped near the front door.

Kyler recognized one of them—Idar Arcus was his name. He'd been a lieutenant under Novah, but she'd named him commander of the Sky Regiment when she became general. Idar was short and broad-shouldered, draped in the scarlet of the Regiment. He scanned the scene before them, his thick brows buried in thought. His scales of auburn and mahogany brushed his shoulders beneath braids of dark gray hanging from his temples.

"I hope we have a lead." Kyler crossed his arms over his chest and met Idar's eyes.

The new commander stared back, his gaze like iron.

"We do," Novah said, nodding to the other Regiment soldier. "This is Kilder Draven Caelum."

He was taller than Kyler, with a sloped nose and high cheekbones. Dark hair covered his head and chin, cut clean and sharp, and his hooded eyes matched the brown of the rest of his features. Scales of sunset trailed along his elongated ears, and like the rest of them, the armor he wore was smeared with blood and soot.

Draven straightened, looking between the three commanders and the general. "Atlas has returned. The amphipteres of Orisis have flown south and landed in the Middle Islands."

Zale's brow sunk with the same confusion that Kyler felt. "The Islands are full of cities and keeps. There's nowhere for an army to hide unless they're camping at the peaks of mountains."

Draven shrugged. "It's not impossible. The Regiment does it."

Novah bit her tongue. "That seems highly unlikely."

"Unlikely as it is, it is what Atlas perceived. You can speak with him yourself if you wish."

Kyler's suspicious mind refused to rest. "It may be a decoy. The afi must've known Atlas was following them—perhaps they led him astray."

The kilder shook his head. "Atlas is certain they landed there, which means there must be somewhere on the Islands that hundreds of afi and amphipteres can safely rest."

"Even still, we must play the game of 'what-ifs', Kilder." Zale took Kyler's side for once. "Let's not ruin ourselves with false certainty."

Idar frowned, his eyes grazing the room of fallen men. "Then let's play the game. What if the afi *are* in fact at a hidden base in the Middle Islands?"

"Then they're close," Kyler answered. "Most likely regrouping to strike again."

Idar nodded. "Exactly. If we move our pieces right, we might be able to attack them first."

"Hit them when they're weak," Novah finished his thought. "But the Islands are massive. It would be foolish to send an army into such a broad area with no clue where to strike. We'd risk attacking the wrong group and have another enemy on our hands."

An idea sparked in Kyler's mind. "Don't send an army. A few of us can search the area in silence and send word when we've found their base. Then we'll know how and where to attack."

Novah raised a brow. "Are you suggesting we send you, Commander?"

His blood spiked at her condescending tone. "Do you have an issue with that?"

"None at all." She faced Zale dipping her chin with a nod. "I'll go too."

Kyler gave a hollow laugh. "You just don't know when to stop."

"The amount of faith I have in you is impossibly small and, unfortunately, your oversized ego doesn't make up for it," she snapped. "Commander Zale, I would like you to take over in my absence, and Commander Idar, I expect you to treat him with the same respect you show me."

"You're joking." Kyler shifted so he could face her fully. "I knew you were full of yourself, but you've exceeded my expectations."

Novah sucked a deep breath, and Kyler could feel her struggling to regain control of the conversation. "You're playing a dangerous game, Commander. You may not like me, but I am your superior, despite how you feel about it."

For a moment, the two just stared at each other. Kyler could taste the anger on his tongue, as sour as lime and sharp as an arrow, and he swallowed it. "Lieutenant Corbin Revwell will join me. He's an excellent swordsman and a skilled foot soldier. I believe he'll be a good asset."

"Kilder Draven will join as well"—Novah glanced at Kyler before turning back to Idar—"if that's alright with you, Commander."

Idar dipped his head in a nod. "You should take Aeron too."

The informality made Kyler curious, but he chose to focus

instead on Zale. The Sea Force commander straightened and ran a hand down his worn face. "And what if this is a decoy? Are we certain this is the wisest option?"

Idar began shaking his head before Zale had finished. "This may not be our safest option, but if it works, it will save us from another surprise attack. You're right to go, General. Commander Zale and I will prepare forces here. Even if your search of the city comes back empty, our armies will be ready."

CHAPTER NINE

TENSION HUNG LIKE FOG, FILLING KYLER'S LUNGS THE MOMENT he stepped into the barracks. He knew he looked exhausted, with heavy bags beneath his eyes and his dark armor now riddled with scrapes and grime, and his skin tingled as the eyes of every soldier landed on him.

He'd assumed most of his men would have gone to sleep, but it seemed everyone was still on edge. His soldiers were scattered around the common room, their elbows and blades resting on the round tables. Warm flames crackled in the fireplace, casting shadows across their faces. They looked just as tired as Kyler felt, but he could sense the unease that was keeping them awake.

"What's the consensus, Commander?" Corbin's voice pulled his attention, and Kyler found him sitting at a table near the fire with Salcon and Adri.

Kyler had sent him to check on the wounded in the infirmary nearly an hour prior. If he was back already, that meant there weren't many wounded to report on. The injured were dead.

Kyler sighed, rubbing his temples as the room of soldiers waited for his response. "This isn't the time or place. I need to speak with you alone, Corbin. Salcon and Adri, go round up the rest of the lieutenants and meet us in the dining hall." He nodded to the rest of the room. "The rest of you will be informed shortly."

Light murmurs rose amongst the soldiers as Corbin stood. Though his eyes were bloodshot, he moved with purpose as he followed Kyler down the hall and toward the kitchens.

"Is everything alright?"

Kyler glanced over his shoulder. "We've just been attacked. What do you think?"

He scoffed in response. The voices from the common room faded, and the silence of the hallway engulfed them. Ringing filled Kyler's ears, and the musty smell of the barracks flooded his nose. Sweat caused his shirt to stick to the skin beneath his armor, and his scales knocked against one another as he swung the door open and entered the empty dining hall.

Light poured from the kitchen and brightened the space, revealing chairs that'd been placed upside down on top of the clean tables. The kitchens were alive beyond the swinging doors, the cooks preparing to serve the troops in just a few hours.

Kyler lifted a chair from the nearest table, letting it clatter to the floor as he turned it upright. Corbin did the same. The uneven chair legs wobbled as the lieutenant sat, his eyes fixed on Kyler.

Kyler placed his arms on the table and buried his face in his hands.

"Spit it out," Corbin urged, leaning back in his seat.

Kyler glared at him through his fingers. "We're going to the Middle Islands. And by *'we'* I mean you, me, and that mess of a general."

Corbin raised his eyebrows. "What for?"

Kyler dropped his head back, his eyes begging him to close them. Saints, he was *exhausted*. "To gather intel on the afi. Two Sky Regiment soldiers will be joining us. We might be gone awhile."

Corbin nodded slowly. "When do we leave?"

The doors to the hall swung open, and Salcon ushered in the rest of the lieutenants. From the messy hair and wrinkled clothes, it was clear that some of them had managed to fall asleep. Kyler stood from his chair and answered in a low voice, "Tomorrow."

"Tomorrow?" Corbin hissed.

"Please, take a seat." Kyler addressed the lieutenants before Corbin could ask any more questions.

The room filled with the thumps of chairs hitting the ground as the soldiers settled.

Kyler leaned his palms on the table, waiting until the room was silent to begin talking. "Thank you all for coming. As you know, we've been issued a threat from the followers of Orisis, and Sannir will not bend to the enemy." He paused. Every lieutenant was watching him closely. "It's been decided that a team will go to the Middle Islands in search of information on the afi. Part of that team will be Lieutenant Corbin and myself. We set sail tomorrow morning, and in our absence, Lieutenant Salcon will be acting commander."

Surprise fell over Salcon's face.

"I need everyone on guard. An attack like we experienced tonight is not a joke, and our mission is not without risk. If you have any questions, please don't hesitate to ask."

The men glanced at one another and, after a beat, Kyler nodded. "Very well. Thank you for your time. Dismissed."

The soldiers stood from their chairs, many of them turning to congratulate Salcon. Their support of Salcon only confirmed Kyler's decision, and pride welled in his chest as he saw Salcon step up to the challenge.

A shoulder brushed his, and Kyler found Corbin at his side.

"You think he can handle it?"

Adri tossed an arm over Salcon's shoulder, making Salcon grunt from the impact.

Kyler gave a tight smile. "He'll be fine. So long as we do our part in ensuring this doesn't happen again."

Corbin pinched the tip of his tongue between his teeth. "Did the healers have any luck with the king?"

Kyler didn't answer, but the look he gave was enough for Corbin to understand. The lieutenant nodded slowly, clearing his throat in a way that sounded like he might shed tears for the king. "How's the princess holding up?"

"Fine." Kyler's voice was sharper than he'd intended, gaining him a side-eye from Corbin.

"Tell me later."

"I don't want to talk about it."

Corbin *hmm*ed lightly, pursing his lips. "Whatever you say, Commander."

His voice was camouflaged by the men as their light chatter turned to scattered conversations. There was an uneasiness among them, as evidenced by their stiff stances and hushed tones.

"So, the position of general—"

Kyler turned, jabbing a finger at Corbin's chest. "Don't push it. I'm only putting up with her because of this threat. It's clear the dragons made a mistake."

Corbin lifted his hands in defeat. "Alright, I get it."

Kyler tried to ignore Corbin's smirk. "The sooner we get these afi under control, the happier I'll be." He clapped a hand on Corbin's shoulder as he passed, headed for his room. "I'm going to sleep. Hopefully we can find these afi quickly, and everything can go back to normal."

...

The morning came crisp and light, a gentle welcome to the start of autumn. Potions clinked at Kyler's waist with each step, the sound mingling with the press of his boots against the dry grass. The armor he'd chosen was light and flexible, sitting comfortably at his shoulders and hugging his torso.

Across his back hung a bow—a beautifully crafted weapon he'd helped design himself. It was a horse bow, compact and slightly curved in the middle. He'd chosen the design because of how powerful it was and how smooth it pulled. Carved from redwood, the sleek finish made it not only useful but a gorgeous weapon. At his shoulder, a leather quiver was strapped into place, filled with white feather arrows, and at his side hung his sword. His bag bounced against his hip, filled with brewing supplies and spare potions that didn't fit in his belt.

Corbin walked beside him, his eyes on the ground and his gaze distracted. Like Kyler, his sword hung at his side, and a similar bag held changes of clothes and medical supplies.

They hadn't spoken much since the previous day, but that was because both of their minds seemed to be elsewhere. Neither had left Sannir before and had things been different, Kyler would have kept it that way.

The Middle Islands were messy, with few rules and many gods. Though the kingdoms seemed to thrive, the people there had no respect for Adoni or his magic and even less for the elves of Sannir. Any magic the Middle Islands possessed was nothing but a remnant—a shattered piece left over from the battle of Tophet—and all seven territories had made it clear that they cared nothing for a political alliance with Sannir.

The docks came into view, along with Novah and Draven, who

waited on the shore along with the man Kyler assumed to be Aeron. Light caught the pale white of Novah's scale like a cruel tease, standing out amongst her trails of orange and red as she turned to face the Land Brigade soldiers.

She wore silver armor and carried a single satchel. Draven was dressed similarly, with a short sword at his hip and silver armor across his chest. He stood with his face to the ship, a small frown on his lips.

Aeron, however, had his arms crossed over his narrow chest, and his gaze sliced across Kyler as he neared. He was fairly young, with a square jaw and a straight nose. Scales of red danced along his ears, partially covered by dusty blond braids. His most noticeable feature, however, was the scar that ran from beneath his left ear down his neck, dipping beneath the armor at his collarbone.

Kyler met this newcomer's gaze with one just as cold, tearing away only as Zale strode down the dock, followed by Commander Idar and Advisor Cadmus. Kyler found himself looking past them, hoping to find Aiyanna following after, but she was absent. The ship towered over them, though small in size compared to the rest of Zale's fleet.

"Good morning, Commander." Zale slowed as he reached the end of the dock, his face like stone and hands flexing in the cool air. He nodded to Corbin. "Lieutenant."

Zale was dressed like a sailor, with a coat of azure hanging from his shoulders. The fabric was worn and grayed from years at sea, and the blue embroidery was faded. From his hip hung a cutlass that shined as if it'd been cleaned recently, and atop his head sat a simple tricorne, designed to keep both sun and rain from his face.

Advisor Cadmus stilled, studying Kyler. "I hope for all of our sakes this isn't a mistake."

A smirk pulled at Aeron's thin lips.

Kyler had never been fond of the Advisor, and the distaste was mutual. Cadmus hardly bothered to hide his feelings about each of the soldiers, making it very clear that he only approved of Zale and Uriah. The fact that Cadmus enjoyed Uriah's company told Kyler all he needed to know about the man. Uriah was a great soldier, but he'd never been *pleasant.*

"Thank you for your support, Advisor," Zale snapped. "Shall we?" He motioned to the ship, whose gangway had already been laid out for boarding.

Novah's men stepped up first, nodding to Idar as they passed. Novah, however, paused as she reached the new commander, her voice dipping too low for Kyler to hear.

Kyler frowned and slipped past her, convincing himself he didn't care what they discussed. He gripped the strap of his bag as he strode up the gangway, keeping his eyes forward and face calm.

The ship's crew was already on board, working quickly to prepare to set sail. This vessel was a cargo ship, and the crew was busy loading wooden crates and livestock below decks—the perfect ruse for the soldiers to sneak onto the Islands undetected. Several barrels and additional crates had been strapped to the rails to keep them from sliding. The crew wore no uniform aside from the blue scales hanging from their ears and swords at their waists; most of them wore heavy coats to fight back the chill in the air.

"Commander."

Kyler turned to find Zale stepping onto the deck. He waved a hand to Kyler, urging him to follow.

Zale's coat flapped behind him as he started for the helm of the ship. Footsteps caught up to Kyler, and he turned to find

Novah making her way to his side.

Smells of fish and sweat coated Kyler's nose, and he could already feel the salt settling in his hair. His boots tapped against the worn wood as Zale brought them up the steps of the quarter deck to where a soldier was stationed at the wheel.

"Lieutenant Sorien," Zale introduced him.

The man faced his commander, revealing a face full of freckles. His light hair was covered by a hat similar to Zale's, and he carried an identical sword.

"This is General Novah and Commander Kyler."

The lieutenant saluted, his stance stiff and well-rehearsed. "It's an honor to captain your ship."

The lieutenant was young, and while Kyler knew age didn't determine the ability of a soldier, he felt odd knowing this was the man overseeing their journey. Zale, however, seemed to have full faith in the lieutenant. He waved Kyler and Novah away from the wheel and motioned to a set of doors nestled behind the helm. One of them was nailed with a golden plaque inscribed with the words *Commander's Quarters*.

"The general will take the first mate's cabin." Zale motioned to an adjacent door. "Lieutenant Sorien has offered to sleep with the crew, so the rest of you can decide who takes the commander's quarters. At the moment, it's set up for two."

Corbin came to Kyler's side, nodding to the commander's quarters. "I can handle the bunks. You're the only commander with us."

As he spoke, Novah quickly entered her room, closing the door behind her without a word.

Kyler frowned. "She hasn't said much today, has she?"

Zale shrugged. "Got a lot on her mind, I suppose. Good luck, Commander." He turned back to Lieutenant Sorien, offering a word of encouragement before seeing himself off the deck.

Kyler stepped into his room and found it surprisingly spacious. A single bed sat bolted to the floor in the left corner, with a window looking out to the ocean beyond. A desk, also bolted down, was placed along the opposite wall, and a hammock that appeared to have been pulled from the crew's cabins swung from the ceiling. In the center of the room lay a rounded carpet, with spiraling designs of maroon and gold stitched throughout it. Red fabric made up the bedsheets, with a matching pillow on the desk chair. The room was noticeably void of the smell of fish, but the air was still musky and damp.

Kyler tossed his bag to the ground with a heavy thump.

His moment of quiet was interrupted as the door swung open once more, and Kyler turned to find Aeron closing it behind him.

"So, it's you I'm sharing with?" Kyler asked lightly.

Aeron took a slow breath, studying the room. "You'll take the bed." His voice had a rough edge to it, and his eyes refused to meet Kyler's as he stepped to the hammock, tugging a loose thread in the fabric.

Kyler straightened. The man's tone was offsetting. "Remind me of your rank?"

He remained aloof. "Lieutenant."

"And as a *lieutenant,* I don't believe it's your place to be giving me orders."

Aeron dropped his hand from the fabric, facing Kyler with a glare. "Novah isn't one to complain but believe me when I say your disrespect hasn't gone unnoticed by those closest to her." He tilted his head slightly and the scar on his neck caught in the lamps of the cabin. "I'll show you respect when you show the same to her. Until then, you'll take the bed."

Aeron dropped his bag beside the hammock, his cool

nonchalance returning.

Kyler's jaw ticked as he snatched his bag from the floor, throwing it onto the bed without care. "You're walking a thin line, Lieutenant."

"I'm loyal, Commander," his voice drawled, "and I don't like you."

"You don't have to like me. I'm not inclined to be your friend, Lieutenant, but I'd rather not be your enemy. You seem like the type of man who has enough of those already." Kyler glanced at him, nodding to the scar on his neck.

Amusement danced across Aeron's features, but he said nothing. His shoulders straightened as he stepped toward the door, leaving Kyler alone in the room once again.

"Bastard," Kyler muttered to himself. It seemed arrogance ran like a plague through the Regiment.

The sounds of the crew penetrated the thin walls, and the ship lurched slightly, letting Kyler know they left the dock. It took him a moment to find his balance, his hands landing on the grooves of the desk chair. Its legs scraped against the wood from the movement. Kyler's eyes flicked to the window, where the docks slipped from view at the ship's slow rotation.

He could see the barracks from here, nothing but a speck beneath the towering mountains of Sannir. The Pass, made of cloud and magic, spiraled in the sky, like the gateway of the dragons was waving farewell to its soldiers.

Everything had happened so quickly. It wasn't until now that reality began to sink in. He ran a hand through his hair, lowering himself slowly into his seat. A thought had come to him before the attack, and even after all that'd happened, he still couldn't seem to let it go.

Before Novah's appointment, Kyler hadn't cared much about

what had become of former General Uriah. Some claimed he became overwhelmed by the duties of general and ran away from Sannir to escape his life. Others claimed he'd gotten lost in the Pass, searching for a more powerful magic.

Kyler's fingers danced aimlessly across the pommel of his sword. Perhaps he was working with Orisis. Maybe his disappearance was the very beginning of their plan of attack, and General Uriah was hiding with the afi somewhere in the Middle Islands.

If this were the case, then he didn't resign. He was a traitor, and the law of Adoni was unclear on the succession of a general who turned on Sannir. The only thing Kyler knew for certain was that Uriah wasn't captured or overpowered. The former general was many things—ruthless, calculated, and cruel—but never weak.

Kyler shifted, reaching for his potion bag. He'd brought a handful of supplies to brew with since he'd been given so little time to gather his things after the attack. He was low on potions for cleaning wounds, something he thought might be useful, as well as Ponos for pain relief. It took him only a moment to set up his supplies across the desk, laying out several vials and placing a round metal bowl before him. He took his time, allowing his mind to wander as he filled the bowl with kindling and struck it with a match.

Kyler hung a small iron pot above the flame and added scattered ingredients to the mixture. The potion bubbled and steamed, hissing at just the right tone. He listened closely to their frequency, waiting until the right moment to add the herbs and plants.

This is what he could lose if Novah failed as general. Magic was in his blood. He was born for it. If the Temple fell, the Pass would close, and the people of Sannir would lose their magic.

Unlike Sannir, the rest of Vellichor had no access to magic. It was scrounged and sold and bargained for—remnants of a lost world and a creator who'd once looked kindly upon them. There were rumors of shapeshifters accessing magic through the caves of Vrach and the ancestors of a powerful mage called Regona, who held the power of the ocean deep in their blood, but it was all twisted and wrong. True power came from Adoni alone.

The afi were a difficult enemy. At the time of Eliab's Army, they'd possessed the same magic that coursed through the veins of the elves of Sannir and had traded that magic to Orisis. But those afi had been destroyed. Now, the afi were beings desperate for protection and power, and so long as they swore themselves to Orisis, he gave them just that. Twisted and destructive power, but power nonetheless. While they remained in his service, Orisis kept his destructive hand away from them and their families.

They weren't supposed to be soldiers—just fools who searched for strength outside of themselves. This attack had been intentional and organized.

The hiss raised in pitch, dragging Kyler from his thoughts. He quickly lowered the flames and watched the silvery-blue liquid bubble and pop as the heat subsided. Moundi was one of the best-smelling potions, with floral hints trailing its steam. Despite its pleasing scent, Moundi was one of the few elixirs that wasn't meant to be consumed. It was poured over wounds to cleanse them.

The smell satisfied him as he pulled the mixture from its hook, using a piece of cloth to guard his hand against the metal. Unlike Vothia, Moundi wasn't bottled until it nearly finished cooling. That way, it would settle in its glass without scorching it. It had a history of melting vials when poured straight from the fire. Kyler set it aside for a moment and turned to the next potion.

"Moundi?"

The voice startled him, and Kyler snapped his head up to find Corbin leaning against the doorframe, his nose scrunched.

"Saints, Corbin." He pressed his fingers to his temple. "Just knock for once."

A smile joined his scrunched nose. "No thanks. I'm right though?"

Kyler turned back to the desk. "Yes. And if you keep doing that, I'll make sure there's none left for you when you need it."

"How kind of you."

Kyler ignored his sarcasm. "Are you ready for the Middle Islands?"

Corbin stepped away from the door, shutting it behind him. "That doesn't matter. I'm here to find out what happened with your princess since you were grouchy with me yesterday."

"Still am."

Corbin waved a hand to the closed door. "Everyone else is below deck, and Novah's trapped in her quarters. It's just us."

Kyler glanced up at him, finding his eyebrows raised in expectation. A sigh fell from Kyler's chest, and he turned back to his potion, measuring out a sprinkle of powdered limestone. "She shoved me."

A laugh of surprise fell from his lips. "You're kidding! Aiyanna *shoved* you?"

"She called me prideful, and when I got mad, she shoved me."

Corbin whistled, his eyes wide. "Did it hurt?"

"No," Kyler lied.

He brushed the powder from his hands and watched the new potion bubble. Ponos was pale yellow and bitter smelling, but acted as a powerful pain relief and was simple to brew. He was careful not to splash as he pulled the pot from the flame and tilted it, letting the mixture drizzle into the nearest vial. When every drop had been cleared from the pot, he corked it and watched the warmth fog inside of the glass.

Corbin continued to hover, his silence indicating that he wouldn't leave until he'd gotten the answers he wanted.

Kyler gave an agitated sigh. "She was upset, but so was I. It doesn't matter."

"It kind of sounds like it does."

"It doesn't." Kyler snapped. He slipped the vial into his potions bag and faced Corbin. "You got your answer. This conversation is over."

Corbin shrugged, eying Aeron's bag beneath the hammock. "If you say so."

"I do. Go make yourself useful. I'm sure Lieutenant Sorien has some pointless chore to assign you."

"Thrilling." He dropped his shoulders, moving for the door. But before he reached it, he paused with his hand resting on the knob. "I know you don't want to hear this, but Novah's in charge right now. I don't want you ruining your reputation over her."

Kyler pursed his lips. He knew Corbin was right, and he didn't like it when Corbin was right. "Point taken."

Corbin gave a sharp nod and closed the door behind him, leaving Kyler alone with his thoughts and his potions.

CHAPTER TEN

WAVES PUMMELED THE SIDE OF THE SHIP AT A STEADY PACE, AND the movement was making Kyler drowsy. He'd gotten so little sleep since the attack. His forearms rested on the rail of the ship, balancing him as the vessel rolled over the sea. He'd ditched his armor, the metal having turned into an oven under the open sun, and he found he didn't mind the cool air that rushed through the sails and rigging.

A shoulder bumped his, and Kyler didn't need to look to know who it was.

"How's the crew's cabin?"

"Awful." Corbin chuckled. "It smells like those soldiers haven't showered in weeks."

Kyler snorted. "They probably haven't."

He squeezed his eyes shut. "I don't want to think about it."

Kyler grinned, watching the water dance below them as Corbin continued.

"Draven's a quiet one. I can't get much out of him. How's sharing a room with Aeron?"

They hadn't spoken since they boarded, and Kyler intended to keep it that way. "Better than sharing with Novah, I'm sure."

Corbin looked out to the water, the wind knocking his braids against his cheeks. "Novah probably doesn't snore. Aeron on the other hand…"

"I can neither confirm nor deny." Kyler gripped the rail as they rode over a large wave, landing safely on the other side.

It had been only a day, but the ship had already begun to feel small and cramped. The cargo took up a good amount of space, but it was necessary. It would be easy to dock in the Middle Islands and slip off the ship while the crew unloaded.

"Any idea what the general's plan is?"

Kyler glanced toward the quarterdeck, where Novah's door remained shut. "No clue. She hasn't left her room." He turned back to the ocean. "She's struggling."

"Anyone would be. First night as general and the kingdom is attacked. No one was expecting that." Corbin picked mindlessly at a hangnail, causing it to bleed.

"The least she could do is give us a solid plan of action, but apparently that takes too much energy."

The sound of approaching footsteps made him quiet, and Kyler glanced toward the sound to find Aeron descending the steps.

"The general asked for us."

Kyler tossed a lazy salute in response.

Aeron frowned, and Kyler fought the urge to stare at his scar before he turned toward the hatch, where Draven remained below deck.

Corbin waited until Aeron disappeared beneath the hatch to mutter, "He's so formal."

"He's cranky."

"Hm." Corbin brought his finger to his lips to stop the bleeding, a loose grin on his face. "I'm surprised you haven't told him off yet." He paused. "You haven't, right?"

Kyler swung his hand, his knuckles colliding gently with

Corbin's chest. "Don't be ridiculous. I know not to start fights."

Corbin raised a brow, making it clear he didn't believe him.

The hatch opened again, and Aeron emerged. He held the door open for Draven, who squinted as his eyes met the sun. Aeron waved for Kyler and Corbin to follow.

Kyler pushed off the rail, specks of wood and paint sticking to his shirt. His teeth dug into his tongue as he started toward Novah's room.

Aeron let them into the first mate cabin. The room was smaller than the one Kyler shared with Aeron, with a circular window making up most of the left wall. A simple bed was bolted across from the window, and in the center of the space was a small, circular table, with its chairs secured to the ground. This is where Novah was seated, a spread of maps laid before her. She barely glanced up as the soldiers entered, her focus locked on a leather journal in her hands.

Kyler sat, and out of habit, he attempted to scoot the chair closer.

Once everyone was settled, Novah finally looked up from her page. The deep purple hue under her eyes matched Kyler's, and he wondered if she'd slept at all since the attack.

"Thank you all for agreeing to accompany me on this mission," she started, closing the leather cover and tucking the book in her lap. She folded her hands on the table before her. "For those of you who have never met, allow me to introduce you. This is Kilder Draven Caelum and Lieutenant Aeron Priamos of the Sky Regiment."

Kyler nodded to the two men across from him. Draven gave a small nod in return. Aeron did not.

"Men, this is Commander Kyler Weylyn of the Land Brigade and his lieutenant, Corbin Revwell. This is the team that has been selected to gather information on the afi of Orisis. Commander Zale is our contact in Sannir. Any information we come across will come first to me, then I will pass it on to Zale. That's non-negotiable."

Kyler tried not to be offended as her eyes paused on him. He turned his gaze to the table and picked at a splinter.

Novah brushed aside the scattered papers, revealing a large map of the Middle Islands. Sketched stars marked notable areas, while dotted lines stretched across to show roads and trade routes. The parchment took up nearly half the table, and she twisted it to give them all a better look.

"My goal is to remain as subtle as possible, avoiding too much time in one location. We'll be docking in the city of Potri, which houses the main trading port of the Islands." Novah traced the area with the tip of her finger, starting at the docks and moving toward the city's center. "We'll start on the north side near the ports and work our way inward. If we have no leads, we move west. Any questions at this point?"

Aeron worked his jaw as he studied the map. "How do you suggest we remain inconspicuous?"

The Middle Islands were full of travelers of every kind, but dragon scales were notable even in Sannir. Word would travel quickly that so many elven soldiers were staying nearby.

Kyler's skin began to burn at the thought of removing his scales. He looked to Novah once more, hoping she wasn't foolish enough to ask her soldiers to dishonor themselves in that way.

Novah brushed a hand down her trails of red, her touch lingering on Atlas' scale. "Keep your scales hidden beneath your hoods and hair whenever possible. We won't remove them unless we have no other choice. I want to avoid moving as a large group, so we'll split up during the day to cover more area. It'll be important not to cross paths. One soldier is a rare sight on the Islands, much less several of them. Each morning, we will make it clear where everyone will be, so we can ensure a thorough sweep of the area. At night, we will meet back at our inn and share what we've found. Take note of anything and everything, and do not keep any information to yourselves."

She paused for a breath and turned to Draven. "Lieutenant Sorien will remain nearby. Keep your distress signal close should we need to alert the ship."

Draven gave a sharp nod.

"Remember, we are looking for any signs of Orisis or his afi." She brought her journal to the table, flipping to a page with sketches of goat horns and spiraling designs like the ones that covered the afi armor. "Stay low and move fast. I don't want unnecessary hang-ups. We're not here to fight the afi, just find them." She closed her journal and leaned back in her chair. "That's all. You're dismissed."

Everyone else stood, but Kyler remained seated, scanning the maps before him. Corbin hesitated for a moment before heading out the door with the rest of the men, leaving Novah and Kyler to themselves.

Novah turned her back as she stood, setting her journal atop a small dresser. "You are dismissed," she repeated.

"I know." He stayed where he was, studying the map of Potri. His eyes trailed the roads and towns until Novah sighed, facing him.

"'Dismissed' means you can go." She crossed her arms and leaned back against the dresser.

He didn't look up. "I know very well what it means, General."

She nodded slowly. "Try this then—it's time for you to go, Commander. That's an order. Surely you know what that means?"

Kyler's scales brushed his neck as he turned to face her and was met with a sharp glare. "Very well." He stood slowly, pressing his tongue to his teeth as he fought the urge to argue.

He hadn't noticed before, but her eyes had a certain spark to them, like the crackle of flames or the burn of whiskey as it settles in your chest. It was almost intimidating.

"Do you have something to say, Commander?" Novah lifted her chin as she spoke. Her head tilted, and she watched Kyler from under her furrowed brow.

He had a lot he wished to say, but he decided it wise to keep those thoughts to himself. His chest rose and fell with a huff. "Am I not allowed to look at the maps you've acquired?"

A small smile tugged at her lips for a moment before vanishing. "They're right there. I'm not hiding them."

"I'd like to study them myself."

She watched him for a moment, her fingers finding a resting spot at her temple. "Very well. Take them to your quarters. But I want them back in an hour."

"Two hours." Kyler pressed, but her expression remained motionless.

"One and a half. Not a minute later."

Satisfied, Kyler stepped to the table and rolled the map of Potri so it fit in his palm. He held the parchment gently as he turned back to Novah. "One and a half."

He started for the door, feeling as though he would trip beneath her glare. It wasn't until he heard the door swing shut behind him that he took a deep breath and unraveled the map, scanning the ink.

"What was that about?" Corbin strode across the deck, squinting in the sunlight. "You flirting or something?"

Kyler ignored his comment. "Come with me. I want to study

this map and get a head start."

"A head start on what?" Corbin came to his side, looking over his shoulder. "It's not going to tell you where the afi are."

"No," Kyler squinted, lifting the map closer to his face. "But it might give us a hint as to where Uriah could be hiding."

"Uriah?" Corbin stepped closer, his voice dipping. "I don't know what you're thinking, Kyler, but drop it. General Caligari is gone."

He lowered the map. "I'm not so sure he is."

Corbin sighed, his hands catching on his braids as he combed through his hair. "I get it, I do. It's just—"

"I don't think you do, Corbin." Kyler tapped his shoulder with the map. "I knew Uriah better than I would have liked, and things aren't adding up. It's been centuries since afi were seen, much less seen in Sannir. Then, Uriah leaves without notice and on the night of his successor's appointing, Sannir is attacked. There's more going on here, and I think Uriah is involved."

Corbin pinched his tongue between his teeth, eying the map. "You're sure this isn't personal?"

Kyler shot him a look.

"Fine. But if there are no leads after the first week, you'll drop it."

"Deal." He started for his shared room, hoping Aeron wasn't there already. "Keep up, Corbin. I'm losing time."

CHAPTER ELEVEN

CORBIN'S LEG BOUNCED, THE SOUND OF HIS TAPPING BOOT ONLY adding to Kyler's growing headache. The commander had barely slept. He'd spent the early hours of the night meticulously tracing Novah's map onto a piece of spare parchment and studied it. By the time exhaustion finally took over, the wind had become fierce, battering the ship and jostling him in the process. He'd taken Onys after the third time he was nearly thrown from his bed, but even the sleeping potion couldn't help him rest.

The inside of the ship was more pleasant than Kyler had expected, though the air was stale and smelled faintly of mold. All four soldiers were below deck, but Novah had made no move to join them. She kept herself locked in her quarters, and when Kyler had returned her map—after exactly an hour and a half—she'd hardly spared him a glance.

Pressure built behind his eyes as the headache pressed to his forehead. "Stop that."

Corbin stilled, glancing at Kyler from the corner of his eye. "Someone's in a mood."

"I didn't sleep well," Kyler mumbled, leaning against the back of his chair as he massaged his brow.

"I gave you the bed." Aeron barely looked over his shoulder

before placing a card on the table between himself and Draven. "The hammock was much worse."

Draven looked at his hand of cards and played his turn, nodding to Aeron for his next move.

Kyler didn't respond. He gave a subtle roll of his eyes and shot Corbin a look that made his lieutenant crack a smile.

"At least you're not with the crew," Corbin said lightly, running his knuckles along the ship's wall. "We were swinging into each other all night."

Draven placed another card. "There is nothing that states you can't sleep on the floor."

"I can't imagine that'd be more comfortable."

Draven's lips quirked—the first emotion Kyler had seen from him yet. "No. But it is more pleasant than sleeping beside you."

Kyler lifted his head with a grin. "I wasn't sure you could talk, Kilder."

He sighed. "I only speak with those worth my time, Commander."

Corbin leaned towards Kyler, speaking loud enough for the others to hear. "Draven is a recovering mute. He speaks best with his eyes." Draven shot Corbin a glare, and Corbin grinned. "That means he's mad."

"No." Aeron snorted as he dropped his final card, ending their game. "That means you're a fool."

Kyler laughed. "In that case, I must agree with Draven."

Draven's glare turned into a chuckle as the hatch above them opened, and the face of Sea Force Lieutenant Sorien appeared in the doorway. "We're nearly there. Keep your cloaks on; there's a storm rolling in."

Aeron and Draven stood from their seats, swiftly tucking the cards away, and started for the ladder. Kyler, however, made no move to join them. He began to pick at a loose thread on his cloak, slowly unraveling it with each tug.

"You alright?" Corbin asked, tossing his cloak over his shoulders.

Kyler sighed and dropped the thread, tilting his face to the beams above. "I'm not sure I like this plan."

Corbin slowly sat back in his seat, the wood squeaking beneath him. "Go ahead. What about this plan is bad, other than the fact that Novah came up with it?"

Kyler couldn't help but smirk at the jab. "It's rigid. If she'd let me go into a tavern or two, this would be much simpler. They don't have potions on the Islands—all I'd need to do is slip a few drops of Apola and people would start talking."

"That's very illegal."

"It'd get the job done. And it might reveal something about Uriah."

Corbin leaned forward, resting his elbows on his knees. "If anyone found out, you could lose your position. And these." He swept a hand through Kyler's scales, making the commander pull back. "It's not worth it."

Kyler scrunched his nose. "Right. *Novah* will take my scales."

"She can." Corbin shrugged. "You're already picking fights with her."

Kyler contemplated this for a moment. Corbin was right. Besides, his potion supply was limited as it was.

"Alright. No potions. But I still think taverns could be our best bet."

"I don't disagree, but you're not the one leading this mission."

"I should be."

"But you're not." Corbin's tone caught Kyler's attention. "She is. I don't want to see you lose everything for a shot at finding

Uriah."

Kyler dropped his voice, anger clipping his words. "If Uriah is behind this, I will prove it."

Corbin's expression was unreadable, but for a moment, Kyler thought he saw a hint of worry cross his features.

"Alright then." Corbin pressed his hands to his knees and stood from his chair. "I'll be on deck."

Kyler joined him a moment later, finding the sky gray and angry. A drop of water hit his skin, its prick chilled like ice. The dark clouds ushered in the type of cold that sent shivers along Kyler's neck and back, even with his cloak on. He glanced to the sky as a second droplet followed closely after, landing on his cheek with a sting. He quickly brushed it from his face and tugged his hood over his head.

Though a thick fog clung to the ship, Kyler could see everyone. He found a place along the rail of the main deck beside Corbin. Farther down, Draven and Aeron leaned against the ship, and just past them, Novah stood stiffly, her gaze on the water below.

It was odd to see her out. Her jaw was set, and her sharp eyes trailed every one of the wave's movements. Like the rest of them, she donned a thick cloak, which matched the color of the clouds and concealed her armor and weapons.

Kyler reached a hand over his shoulder, ensuring his bow was hidden, and as he did, he met her gaze. Her eyes betrayed the anxiety she kept buried, and she quickly turned back to the waves.

Lieutenant Sorien stood over the helmsman's shoulder as he guided them through the dense mist. Kyler had his doubts at the start of the voyage, but the young lieutenant had done well captaining the ship despite the rocky weather they'd faced. He watched the choppy waters as they drew closer to the out-of-sight Islands.

Across the deck, the crew had become busy with preparations to unload. Though sea-colored scales hung from their ears, the faded capes they all wore resembled the one draped over Kyler's shoulders. At a single glance, one wouldn't notice the scales hidden beneath their hoods.

The crew began pulling barrels and boxes from the hold, hauling them on deck with practiced ease. The men worked quickly, and it wasn't long before the hold was emptied and the deck filled.

A large wave hit the side of the ship as its movement slowed, and the vessel began an easy turn. Sea mist sprinkled Kyler's face, much warmer than the rain but quickly cooled by the wind. The ship teetered slightly as the helmsman urged it to straighten, and Lieutenant Sorien descended the steps.

"We'll be docking in just a minute," he called out, the wind carrying his voice. "Good luck." He nodded to Novah before turning to his crew, his instructions to them drowned out by the sounds of the water.

Kyler steadied himself on the rail as Novah neared.

"You and I will go first," she said to Kyler. She pulled her hood over her head as she spoke, and the others moved closer to hear her. "Aeron will follow us, alone, then Corbin and Draven. The gate into the city will be heavily guarded, though most of the guards will be stationed above—on the wall. Their job is to alert their superiors of any suspicious entry into the city. Only registered tradesmen are allowed to pass through, so your goal is to blend in and act like you belong." She glanced up at the sky as the scattered rain began to thicken. "The weather works in our favor. We'll meet inside the inn."

Corbin met Kyler's eye, his face solemn. "See you there, Commander." He pushed off the rail and strode with Draven to the center of the deck. With their hoods over their heads and cloaks covering armor, they could've easily been mistaken for tradesmen.

Aeron's hood was still down, allowing his hair and scales to soak without care. He said nothing, moving toward the front of the ship as he concealed his scales.

Novah's face was hardly visible beneath her hood, and her sword bumped the rail as she leaned against it. She crossed her arms over her chest, taking a slow breath of the moisture filled air.

"Let me guess," Kyler said, rubbing a cut that was still healing on his palm, "you want to keep an eye on me?"

A tiny smirk tugged at her lips. "Excellent observation, Commander."

"Good. I'd like to keep an eye on you, too."

Humor danced at the edge of her words. "I'm as trustworthy as they come, but keep your wariness. I have no interest in proving anything to you."

Kyler dropped his hand with a *tsk* of his tongue. "You should. I can make your life miserable."

"You give yourself too much credit."

The ship lurched as the rudders turned, and the Middle Islands finally came into view. Fog rolled off the waves and onto the shoreline, where several sets of wooden docks stood on barnacle-covered legs, disappearing into the murky water. Two other ships sat in port, one much smaller and older than the ship they sailed, flying the white flag of the city of Potri, and the other was much larger, with the flags of southern cities waving from its many masts.

Through the haze, the gate of Potri rose above the port, much taller than Kyler had anticipated. Rainwater raced down the white stone and fresh golden paint. Three levels of open walkways overlooked the gate, giving the guards a clear view of the port below. The glint of their armor passed through the aperture as the guards made their rounds, pausing frequently to study the ships. White flags flapped from the tips of golden arches, striking against the dark sky.

Novah drew a sharp breath and rolled her shoulders, setting her gaze on the number of guards that covered the area.

The ship inched into port, water slipping down the hull as the bow cut through restless waves. The crew remained on deck, masking the five among their numbers. As they neared the dock, a young man made his way to the side of the ship. His dark hair had pulled free from its single plait, brushing against his small, rounded ears—unlike Kyler was accustomed to seeing. He held a leatherbound book, which looked much too heavy to be carried around.

Kyler moved to the side as Sorien pushed past, his thick jacket slapping his ankles as he descended the gangway. Kyler tried not to look too curious as Sorien shook hands with the man on the dock. The two exchanged a few words, and the man scribbled something in his log before waving a hand for the crew to begin unloading.

Sorien quickly made his way back to the ship, his voice muffled in the growing storm. "To the starboard side, gentlemen!" He strode past Kyler without a glance. "Carts are waiting to the east of the gate!"

At his order, the crew jumped into motion, passing cargo to the docks below. With so much movement, it was easy for Kyler and Novah to lose themselves, following the lines of soldiers like the cargo itself. Kyler stayed close to Novah's back, tugging the hood of his cloak farther over his head and keeping his face toward his boots.

The uneven boards of the dock were slick beneath Kyler's feet, and he stole another look at the wall as they grew closer. It appeared much larger from this angle, with its long silver gates opened wide within the center of the arch. Stone steps ran along the sides where guards paced the walkways. The entryway itself had no steps, but a ramp that ran into the sand and dirt of the port. Carts full of supplies traveled quickly in and out of the city, pulled by mules that were soaked with the stench of wet animal.

Mud splattered onto Kyler's ankles he followed Novah, weaving between crewmembers and traders all trying to keep their goods dry. Inaudible shouts passed between men, and Kyler shoved past trashmen who paid no mind to those who might be in their way. He shouldered around a group of sailors much too drunk for the time of day and tugged at Novah's arm as another cart nearly plowed through them.

Ahead, the gate loomed closer, and it felt as though every guard had their gaze locked on them. Two men were stationed at the entrance with chests draped in gray armor and white capes flapping in the rough wind. Though shielded by the arch, they too had hoods pulled over their heads, protecting their faces from the splatters of rain. They stood side by side, appearing uninterested in the business of the port. They joked back and forth, hardly taking note of those who passed them.

Several kinds of creatures filtered through the gate, and it was then that Kyler noticed how different this was from Sannir. His eyes skimmed past dwarves in coats larger than themselves and gypsies dripping in silver. Men with horns curved toward their chins pulled carts themselves, and the soft jingle of coins in pockets echoed off the stone walls. Every passerby reminded Kyler just how far they were from home—and how unwelcome they would be if their identities were discovered.

Novah urged Kyler to the right, leading them far from the guards just as tradesmen guided their barrels through the entrance. The opportunity allowed the soldiers to slip through the gates, using the large cargo to block themselves from view.

Kyler glanced back once they'd passed the threshold, finding the men still engaged in conversation. A deep breath filled his lungs with the heavy air, and he turned his sights to the city before him.

A path of water-slicked cobblestone marked the center of the city, with taverns, inns, and shops running along the sides. Buildings with curved rooves of brick and chimneys thick with smoke scattered down twisting alleys, hardly visible through the heavy droplets. To the west, mountains towered over the city, and straight ahead was the castle of Potri with its glass walls and pointed towers tipped in gold.

Kyler blinked against the wind. Water stung his eyes and soaked his clothes. Carts rushed past with no regard for travelers on foot, crossing roads and bumping over divots in the stone.

Novah took the lead again, bringing them to the side of the road and away from the crowds. The rain grew worse, pounding at Kyler's head beneath his hood and dripping relentlessly from his cloak. He wasn't sure how Novah found her way, but a moment later she halted beneath a sign streaked with water, making the name *Gray Lady* difficult to read.

Kyler looked over his shoulder, searching for Corbin, but Novah stepped quickly inside the inn, forcing him to follow.

Out of the cold and rain, Kyler fought the urge to remove his hood. The fabric was drenched and had begun itching against his hair, but he distracted himself from the discomfort by taking in the room.

Warmth filled the space, lit by a fireplace that crackled with glowing embers. The inn smelled of cinnamon and honey, and he wondered briefly if the keepers had scented the wood before burning. Large red couches made of velvet surrounded them and were joined by wooden tables topped with cards and reading materials. Along the right wall was a wooden stand stocked with fruit and pastries for guests, and the few people occupying the room seemed to be enjoying these amenities.

In the center of the foyer was a curved desk made of dark wood and brass knobs. It circled toward the back wall, which was almost entirely crafted of glass panes. It reminded Kyler of the windows in Sannir's castle, except these didn't have hinges. Rain slipped down the glass, which showcased the darkening sky beyond.

At the desk sat an older man, with round spectacles and a small book in his hands. His elbows rested atop the wood, and he moved only to lick his fingers and turn the page. Unlike the elves, his ears were large and round, curving at the edges in a somewhat floppy manner.

A grandfather clock pressed against the side wall, its ticking overpowering the conversations from the other guests.

Kyler stepped toward a vacant couch to take a seat as they waited for the others, but Novah grabbed his arm before he touched it.

"You're soaked," she chided, looking him up and down.

"So are you."

She held her grip, glancing at the man at the counter who was still oblivious to their arrival. "You'll ruin the furniture," she muttered.

Kyler sighed as he straightened and stepped away from the couch. "Will the others be able to find their way?"

"I hope so." She released his arm and turned away from him, trying to hide the concern that tugged her lips into a frown.

As if on cue, Aeron entered, ducking through the door, his cloak dripping with rainwater. His presence finally drew the attention of the innkeeper, who quickly set his book and spectacles aside.

"Come in, come in!" he urged, his voice light like a stringed instrument. "The weather's horrible today."

The man rose from his chair, circling out from behind the counter. Fur covered his bottom half and his small hooves tapped against the wooden floor as he approached. It was no surprise to see a satyr owning an inn—they had a knack for making guests feel welcome. Kyler had just never met one before.

The door swung shut behind Aeron, and the innkeeper reached out a hand for him to shake as he approached.

"Welcome to the Gray Lady. My name is Clide, and I'm the owner of this inn." He turned, offering the same welcome to both Kyler and Novah. He was quite short compared to the elves, with his forehead only rising to Kyler's chest, and Kyler found his hands to be rough, like the hands of a craftsman. His bright eyes smiled kindly, matching his gesture. "Just the three of you?"

Novah glanced at the door once more. "We're waiting on two others."

"They shouldn't be far behind," Aeron added, having picked up on her unease.

"Not a problem." Clide waved a hand. "I'll go ahead and check you in. This way." He turned and walked back to the counter, revealing a small tail that stuck out from beneath the hem of his shirt. It took him a moment to situate himself in his chair before he pulled out a large guest book.

"Name, please?"

Novah began to answer but Aeron cleared his throat, shooting her a look of warning. "Aeron Priamos."

The Middle Islands may have cared nothing for Sannir, but the name of the new general was bound to get around eventually. Novah pressed her lips thin as Clide scribbled the name down in his guest book.

"And there are five of you total?"

"That's correct."

The satyr hummed to himself as he turned to his left, pulling out a roll of fabric dotted with tiny stitches. It looked like an old piece, the stitches having been done over several times. His eyes scanned the fabric, and Kyler craned his neck to see the other side. It was a map of the inn, painted with black ink. Knots of thread had been stitched into several rooms, while others remained blank.

"I've got a room on the second floor. Three separate spaces and three beds. Will that work for you?" He looked up from his fabric.

Novah nodded. "That will be perfect. Thank you."

"It's my pleasure." Clide pulled out a ball of thread, the needle already attached to the end, and plunged it into the fabric, creating a mark over the rooms. "That'll be forty."

Aeron pulled out a coin sack from his pocket and passed the payment to Clide. The satyr accepted the coin, quickly counting it for himself before slipping into a drawer. He pulled out a bronze key and dropped it into Aeron's outstretched palm. "Enjoy your stay."

CHAPTER TWELVE

THE WIND WAS RELENTLESS, POUNDING WATER AGAINST THE
window as the storm raged on. Kyler lay on the bed, staring at the
ceiling above him. It was flat, with dark wood running in beams
across it, and it shook slightly with each rumble of thunder. A
small table was positioned against the wall across from the bed,
where Novah and Aeron sat in silence, and worn curtains stitched
in silver framed the windows, revealing the angry sky.

It'd been nearly an hour since they'd arrived in the city, and
there was still no sign of Corbin and Draven. Kyler assumed
they'd gotten lost in the storm, but as the minutes ticked by, the
fear began to creep in.

Kyler sat upright, no longer able to lay still as anxiety ate at his
skin. His movement caused Aeron and Novah to glance in his
direction; like him, they'd been watching the window. Aeron
dropped his gaze to the floor in thought, while Novah rested her
chin in her palm. Gentle creaks from the structure of the inn filled
the silence, accompanied by the drips of their hanging cloaks.

Finally, Aeron broke the silence. "Should we go look for
them?"

Novah didn't answer right away, though it was clear she'd been
thinking the same thing. "I'm not sure we'll be of much use. It's

bad out there."

Kyler looked once more to the window. "You don't think they ran into trouble?"

"They're smart," Novah assured. "I'm sure whatever's holding them up won't keep them for long."

She spoke with confidence, but Kyler didn't believe her. The clouds outside had become thick and threatening, blocking out the noon sun, as thunder rolled over the city and lightning crackled across the sky.

He threw his legs over the side of the bed, his laced boots colliding with the floor, causing Novah and Aeron to look up again. "I'm going."

Novah stood quickly, blocking his path to his hanging cloak. "I don't need three men lost."

"I won't get lost." He shouldered past her, pulling his cloak down from where it hung and tossing it over his shoulders. The damp fabric stuck to his dried shirt, chilling his skin.

"I wasn't asking, Commander."

Kyler paused, his fingers hovering over the clasps as she approached.

"Stay here. That's an order."

For a moment he stood frozen, every nerve begging him to defy her. "That's my lieutenant out there."

"And you're all *my* soldiers." She stepped closer. "I won't tell you again."

He set his jaw. His eyes met Aeron's, who watched with a look of caution. Novah's lips pressed thin in a silent threat to challenge her, and Kyler swore he could feel the tension buzzing between them. Finally, he pulled the cloak from his shoulders and tossed it to the ground.

"If something happens to him, it'll be *your* fault." He shoved past her, satisfied by the way she grunted when his shoulder thrust into hers, and reached for the chestnut door that led to the separate room.

"Commander."

He stopped, his hand still gripping the doorknob. Novah's footsteps neared, and a wave of anger rushed down Kyler's skin.

"We go together."

He kept his back to her. "Let me guess, because you don't trust me?"

"You haven't earned it."

He sighed and turned to face her. "I shouldn't have to. If you don't have to earn my respect, then I don't have to earn your trust."

Novah's hard features softened for a moment.

Kyler sensed her anger dissipating beneath the weight of his remark. He looked to Aeron once more, who watched their confrontation silently from his seat. The lieutenant observed with one elbow on the table, his hand mindlessly rubbing the scar on his neck.

Novah huffed, pulling Kyler's attention back to her. "You're right."

A smug smile rose to his face, but quickly dropped when she continued.

"But you still refuse to follow direct orders. You don't have to like me, Kyler, but my word is your law, and I expect you to abide by it."

The way she said his name was odd, much different from the harshness of 'commander'. She was reaching for peace, and Kyler chose to accept it.

He stepped past her, ignoring Aeron's watchful eye, and lifted his cloak from the floor. Then he pulled Novah's cloak from the peg she'd hung it on and offered it without meeting her eye.

She tossed it over her shoulders. "We'll be back in an hour, Aeron." She grabbed her sword from beside the table, quickly strapping it to her side. "If we're not, you have my permission to take whatever steps you deem necessary." She adjusted her hood and trailed Kyler out of the room.

Kyler dodged the droplets escaping from the leaks in the ceiling as they made their way down the wooden staircase and into the lobby. The lamps that lined the hallway flickered with the groans of the building as Novah stayed at his heels, following him back to the foyer.

In the hour that'd passed, most of the guests had returned to their rooms, leaving Clide to his reading. The satyr glanced up as the two reached the end of the steps and slid his glasses down his nose to see them better. "No sign of your friends?"

Kyler shook his head, straightening his cloak as he started for the door.

Clide frowned slightly, pressing his lips together. "I wouldn't recommend braving that storm. You may find yourselves just as lost. This city isn't very kind to newcomers."

Novah gave a thin smile. "Thank you for your concern. If they show up, would you send them to our room?"

He nodded curtly. "Of course. Stay safe out there and watch out for tradesmen's carts."

Kyler hardly heard Clide's warning as he stepped back outside into the pounding rain. It was nearly impossible to see more than a few feet ahead. The blanket of rain covered every street, and dark clouds blocked the sunlight from the city. Kyler's eyes shot to the sky. Flashes of lightning penetrated the darkness and illuminated the cobblestone road ahead of them. Novah led them slowly toward the gate, keeping a hand on the wall of the inn as the storm threatened to swallow them.

Wind yanked at Kyler's cloak, tangling it against his ankles and drenching its tips in puddles of murky water. Chills ran from his legs to his throat, and his fingers clutched his hood to keep it over his ears. He kept close to Novah, his eyes fixated on the back of her head. It was as if the storm were attempting to shove them from the city, ready to pick them up and toss them back to Sannir.

Kyler placed a hand on Novah's shoulder, halting her, and shouted over the wind. "We won't be able to see them in this!"

She scanned the narrow streets. "You wanted to look!"

He hoped the rain didn't mask his annoyance. "You insisted on coming!"

Novah muttered something as she turned back to the road. For a moment neither one of them moved as the heavy raindrops continued to beat against their heads. Water clung to Kyler's lashes, further blinding him and crushing any hope of finding Corbin in this city. He would just have to wait for the storm to pass.

Kyler gave a defeated sigh as he started back toward the inn, but Novah grabbed his arm. He followed her gaze to the corner across the street, where a glint of silver cut through the storm. Before he could stop her, Novah started toward it, rushing across the street with a recklessness Kyler hadn't expected from her. He followed, barely able to keep her within his sights.

Two figures were crouched between buildings, nearly hidden in the crooked shadows. Kyler recognized their cloaks immediately, but his eyes were drawn to the pale blood that slid across the cobblestone, washed by rain.

"Sannir's Saints," he swore.

Draven sat upright, gripping his leg just below his knee. His trousers were torn, revealing the deep gashes in his skin. His teeth barred as Corbin attempted to wrap his leg, fighting against the wind as it wrestled against the makeshift bandage.

Novah knelt at Corbin's side. She scrunched her nose as she examined the wound and helped Corbin keep the bandage in place.

Corbin glanced up as Kyler approached and relief flooded his face. "He needs Ponos!"

Kyler tugged a vial from his belt and squatted beside Draven as he pulled the potion free. The cork was slick, and he struggled for a moment before it opened with a pop, and he brought the glass to Draven's mouth. The kilder took the pain relief gladly, flinching from the harsh taste but refusing to choke. When he'd finished the vial, Kyler pocketed it and wrapped an arm around the kilder, hauling him to his feet.

Draven hissed in pain, keeping his right leg hovering above the road. The Ponos would take effect quickly, but that leg needed to be elevated and properly wrapped.

Corbin took Draven's other arm as Novah ducked out from between the buildings, leading them back to the inn.

Kyler's hands slipped as he gripped Draven's arm, taking as much of the kilder's weight as he could manage. Draven stumbled with each step, hobbling along as Corbin and Kyler kept Novah's quick pace. The wind tore Kyler's hood from his head, exposing his scales to the rain.

Novah reached the inn and pushed the door open, ushering them inside. Clide looked up from his reading with wide eyes and jumped from his seat as he spotted the limping Draven.

"Inside, quickly!" Clide rushed to the door, pulling it shut to block out the wind and rain.

Kyler coughed. His eyes trailed to the ceiling as the taste of fresh rainwater filled his mouth, clinging to his tongue. He shifted his hold on Draven, hauling him higher up on his shoulder to take more weight. Draven thanked him with a grunt.

"What's happened? Should I call a physician?" Clide looked from Draven to Kyler, pausing on the scales hanging from the commander's ears. Kyler didn't answer, locking his narrowed gaze with Clide's. The satyr quickly looked away.

Novah stepped in front of Kyler, blocking his scales from view. "Thank you, but we have supplies."

And potions. But their friendly host didn't need to know that.

The satyr glanced between the four of them. "Of course. Let me know if you need anything."

Getting Draven up the stairs was no easy feat, but Kyler and Corbin managed to do so with minimal struggle, pausing at the top to catch their breath. Kyler could still feel Clide's eyes on his scales as they disappeared into the hallway, and it wasn't until they reached their door that Kyler finally felt free from his stare.

He'd hardly stepped into the room when Aeron pulled Draven off him, and his shoulders slacked with relief. Kyler breathed a sigh of dry air, ripping the soaked cloak from around his neck.

Aeron brought Draven to the bed and began to unlace his boots before rolling the torn fabric away from his wounds. "Saints, Draven, what did you do?" His tone was humorous, but Kyler could sense his worry.

Novah watched over his shoulder, her brow knit with concern. "How bad is it?"

Draven hissed in pain as Aeron tugged off his boot. "He's been better."

"I've also been worse," Draven joked, his face strained with another grimace as Aeron repositioned his leg.

"We got stopped by the guards," Corbin explained as he began removing his cloak and armor. His shirt clung to his skin as he wrung out the fabric, allowing water to drip onto the carpet. "They questioned us. Wanted to know what business we had here."

"What did you tell them?" Kyler pressed as he knelt beside his potion bag. He'd brewed a good amount of Ponos, but he feared the soldier would need more than just pain relief. He began searching through his potions, hoping to think of something that might help.

"I don't remember. We came up with some story about meeting a friend—"

"Family," Draven grunted as he pushed himself upright, a smirk on his lips. "I told him our cousin was ill and we wanted to see him before it was too late."

Corbin snapped his fingers. "That's right. It was a bit of a stretch"—he motioned to himself and then Draven, exaggerating how different their features were—"but they bought it. By the time they let us pass, the storm had gotten so bad that we couldn't see more than a few feet ahead."

"Which is how I ran into a cart." Draven finished the thought and Corbin shrugged.

"I think the cart ran into you."

Draven gave a tight laugh. "Either way, it was incredibly painful."

Corbin slowly shook his head. "They plowed right through him. People in this city are brutal."

Aeron gave a sharp whistle, and Kyler turned. With Draven's pant leg rolled up, Kyler was able to get a good look at the injury. A massive bruise had begun to form along the shin bone, running from his ankle to just below his kneecap. Several gashes sliced his skin from where the cart must've caught him, and the wounds were still bleeding.

Kyler straightened. "You're lucky the rainwater washed those cuts clean. Otherwise, I'd have to use Moundi."

The potion drew out dirt and prevented infections, but the rain had done that already. On small scrapes, Moundi stung. On large cuts, it was brutal.

"You don't happen to have more Ponos, do you, Commander?" Draven asked with a small grin.

Kyler crossed his arms, leaning a shoulder to the wall. "That's all I can give you right now. You'll have to wait another five hours for your next dose."

"Four and a half?" he bargained, and Kyler shook his head.

"Five. And I'll be watching the time."

Draven gave a defeated sigh, laying his head back on the pillows.

"Kyler." Novah leaned close to him, her voice low. "Do you have anything to speed up the healing process?"

"If I did, don't you think I'd have given it to him by now?" He didn't bother to look at her and began wringing water from his clothes. It was clear she knew little of the limitations of alchemy. Ponos helped numb pain, but no elixir could alter the body's natural healing process.

He saw her jaw tighten from the corner of his eye, and his lips tugged upward at her annoyance. It was fascinating how quickly he could get under her skin.

"In that case, I'll need someone to stay with him tomorrow. That someone can be you, Commander."

He scoffed. "You need me out there."

"I don't *need* anything from you, Commander. It's about time you quit acting like it."

Kyler ground his teeth as he twisted the edges of his shirt a bit too forcefully.

Novah turned to Aeron. "Can you take care of him tonight?" When he assured her that Draven was in good hands, she stepped into the adjacent room and closed the door behind her.

Kyler's eyes traveled to the walls as frustration built in his chest. Apparently, she could aggravate him just as easily.

"Kyler."

He looked up to find Corbin unraveling a clean bandage.

"Help me wrap him up?" Corbin handed him one end of the cloth and took the other, wrapping it like a spool to make things easier.

Aeron had managed to clean up the blood, revealing more bruising and swelling along Draven's shin. He slowly propped the kilder's leg on a spare pillow, frowning at it as Kyler neared.

"You had to be difficult," Aeron scolded.

Draven shrugged. "I just like to keep things exciting."

Kyler studied the swelling. "I'm certain you broke something."

Draven cursed beneath his breath.

"The Ponos should bring down the swelling, but we need to clean this blood before we bandage you up. We can take another look at it in a few hours." Kyler gave a weary smile. "This won't be comfortable."

Draven grimaced, which turned into a pained groan as Kyler lifted his leg.

"Saints! Could you be gentler?"

"Hang in there." Kyler gently wiped the lesion free of blood and rainwater before tightly wrapping the area. "I'm almost done."

Aeron chuckled, crossing his arms. "You're whining, Draven."

Draven shot him a glare.

With one last tug, Kyler finished off the bandage, and Draven released a sigh of relief as his leg was laid back on the pillow.

"Imagine him with Moundi," Corbin teased lightly. "He'd faint."

Kyler chuckled, then pointed a finger at Draven. "Stay off that leg."

"You don't have to tell me twice," Draven mumbled, rubbing his hands down his face.

Kyler took the remaining cloth from Corbin and wrapped it neatly before stuffing it back into their bag.

"This will set us back a bit." Aeron ran a hand through his hair, eyeing Kyler's bag of potions.

Kyler scoffed. "It will if Novah keeps us locked in this room."

"Not *us*," Aeron snapped. "You."

Kyler straightened, waving a hand toward Draven. "We're one man down already. You think a petty punishment will do any of us good?"

If Aeron saw Kyler's point, he refused to admit it. Instead, he grabbed Draven's cloak from the floor and hung it beside his bed along with the kilder's armor.

Kyler pulled a fresh vial of Ponos and placed it on the table with a *clink*, pulling Draven's attention to him.

"Five hours." He tapped the cork. "I'll be back to give you more."

Draven gave a crooked grin. "Four hours and forty-three minutes."

Kyler stepped toward the room opposite of Novah's, bringing his soaking cloak with him. "Forty-three and a half." He winked, earning another smile from Draven before dipping into the room.

CHAPTER THIRTEEN

KYLER TUGGED HIS GLOVES OVER HIS FINGERS, TUCKING THE cuffs under his shirtsleeves to keep everything neat. The sun was up already, as were the rest of his colleagues, though no one had spoken much.

Draven had a rough night, and in turn, so did Kyler. The kilder needed as much Ponos as his body could handle, and Kyler had slept at the table across from his bed as Draven struggled to find comfort. Kyler's arms ached from the wood, and his stiff neck refused to loosen, making it difficult to put on his armor. He grunted as his breastplate landed against his chest, earning him a look from Corbin.

"That bad?"

Kyler huffed, tightening the straps. "Glad you got the bed to yourself while I listened to Draven cry all night."

"I was not crying!" Draven called from behind the cracked door.

"Tears are nothing to be ashamed of," Kyler teased, kneeling to tie his boots.

Aeron nudged the door farther open while tugging at the leather vambraces on his forearms. "I'd be crying too if I had to wake up to the commander's face every few hours."

Corbin laughed.

"Please," Kyler said with a smirk, "you *wish* you had my looks."

He crossed his arms. "You'd like to think that, wouldn't you?"

"Gentlemen." Novah appeared in the doorway, her armor in place and neat braids framing her jaw. She tossed her cloak over a chair. "As enjoyable as it is to belittle Commander Weylyn, we've got work to do."

"You're no fun." Kyler raised a brow as he stood, and Novah mimicked his expression.

"And you look like a nightmare." She turned from him and stepped over to the table, unfolding her map of Potri and flattening the edges.

Kyler came to her side, eyeing the map over her shoulder. She pointedly ignored him.

"We've got a lot of ground to cover today. We're down a man, so we'll have to adjust until Draven's back to normal."

Kyler shot a glance at Draven, who rolled his eyes in response. Draven's fingers interlaced on his chest as he watched them, tapping his thumbs anxiously against the buttons of his shirt.

"Aeron, I want you back at the docks. Watch the tradesmen and see if anything seems off. Corbin and I will split up and cover the south side of the city. Commander Kyler will stay with Draven."

"You can't be serious." Kyler cocked his head as she looked up at him.

"You thought I was joking?"

"I didn't take you to be so petty."

"And I didn't take you to disobey orders."

His jaw ticked. "I will if they're absurd."

Novah turned to face him fully. "You will *not*. Because if you do, you can say goodbye to your position, along with every single scale that decorates your ear. Understood?”

"Is that a threat?"

Her eyes danced between his. "Yes, actually."

His momentary shock seemed to satisfy her, and she turned back to the map, addressing Corbin. "We'll cover as much of the city as possible. I want to avoid overlapping or raising suspicion, so I'll stay to the west of the library. I want you toward the east."

Kyler dug his knuckles into the wood of the table. She was edging dangerously close to tainting his reputation.

Corbin nodded sharply, and Novah began folding her map. "We meet back here before sundown."

Kyler lifted his head. "And what do you expect me to do in the meantime?"

She looked past him to Draven. "Be an alchemist."

"I can be an alchemist *out there.*"

She tucked her map into her pocket and stepped over to the chair where she'd left her cloak. "You can, but that's not what I asked you to do."

Kyler kept close to her as she threw her cloak over her shoulders, fastening it in the front. She ignored him, which only infuriated him more.

"You expect me to sit here and do nothing?"

"No." She finally looked at him as her cloak snapped in place. "I expect you to stay with Draven and ensure he's getting the correct doses of potion at the correct time."

Frustration burned in his chest. "You want me to babysit."

Her shoulder brushed his as she stepped around him, strapping her sword to her waist. "Call it whatever you want, Commander. Your orders are clear." She turned to Corbin and Aeron, who stood ready with their cloaks on and weapons concealed. "Let's get moving."

Kyler caught a worried look from Corbin as he slipped into the hallway, and Novah closed the door behind them with a thud.

For a moment, Kyler stood there, staring at the closed door.

Draven cleared his throat. "Sorry."

Kyler turned to face him, finding a weak smile on his face. "It has nothing to do with you."

"I don't want to be here anymore than you do."

Kyler tore his eyes from the kilder. It wasn't his fault. "I know."

Draven was quiet for a moment, and Kyler could feel his gaze boring into him as he placed his belt on the table. He tugged potions from their pockets and pretended to be taking note of how much was left of each, even though he knew he hadn't used any but Ponos. His mind was far from potions.

Novah was toying with him. She knew Draven didn't need him; she just wanted to make an example out of him. It was spiteful and senseless, and yet, Kyler knew the game she was playing. If she couldn't have his respect, she would force his discipline.

In a way, it reminded him of Uriah.

"She's not kidding, you know," Draven said, shifting to sit up straighter. "Novah will take your scales."

Kyler set his bottle of Vothia down. "I don't need a lecture from you too. I've had enough of those."

Draven scoffed, shifting beneath the sheets. "This is a word of caution, not a lecture. I have known the general for quite some time. She does not let things go easily."

"No kidding." Kyler crossed his arms as he faced Draven. "And everyone's fine with that?"

This time, Draven laughed. "I'm not sure we have much of a choice. But that's why she is such a good soldier. She does not give in to pressure. In fact, I'd go as far as to say she embraces it."

"Huh." Kyler turned back to his potions, tracing the cork on the Ponos. "We'll see about that."

"That was not a challenge, Commander."

He chuckled. "How long have you known each other?"

Draven sighed, staring up at the ceiling. "Novah, Aeron, and I were buggers together. We were assigned to Commander Idar's troop back when he was just a kilder himself."

Ah. That was why she was so informal with her soldiers.

"I can understand your apprehension toward her." Draven continued. "I see how much you wanted that position, and I know Novah can be cold at times. But she feels things deeply, and I warn you to watch your tongue."

An idea had been forming in Kyler's mind, but Draven's words made him pause.

"Do not make her your enemy, Commander. Aeron and I are not the only ones who will support her without question."

"I'll heed your warning," Kyler stated, his hand dancing over the Ponos and landing instead on a similarly colored vial of Onys. He paused for a moment, letting the glass rest between his fingers. Draven *did* need sleep.

He could hear the sheets ruffling as Draven shifted again, attempting to find a comfortable position. He continued to tap anxiously along the wooden bedframe.

Draven sighed deeply, and his tone softened. "This may be the end for me."

Kyler kept his back to him, carefully hiding the potions behind his body. "End of what?"

He was silent for a moment, and the quiet rang in Kyler's ears.

"If this leg doesn't heal—" He stopped himself, and his hands momentarily paused of their tapping. "I may not be a soldier when we return."

"That's a lot of 'ifs', Kilder." Kyler swirled the potion, watching the color settle to a pale yellow. To anyone but an alchemist, it would appear to be nothing more than pain relief.

Draven only shrugged as Kyler passed him the vial.

"That's your dose for now. You get another in—"

"In five hours, I know." He smirked, tipping the bottle to his lips and downing the dosage. His nose scrunched as he swallowed and passed the empty glass back to Kyler. "You can't make it taste any better?"

Kyler grinned. "It's not my fault you got hit by a cart."

Draven grumbled, trying to hide his smile. "Well, maybe now we can both get a little rest."

Kyler nodded, bottling up his potions and strapping them back in place. "Maybe."

...

Kyler knew he should feel guilty, and maybe he did a bit. Draven's breathing slowed to a steady pace, the sleeping potion taking easily with his exhaustion. A part of Kyler envied his slumber, but it was outweighed by his eagerness to get out of that room. He didn't have much of a plan, but he knew where to avoid. It was a start.

Draven's breathing quickened into a light snore before fading back to its rhythmic rise and fall. He'd be out for several hours, just as long as the Ponos kept his pain down. Longer than that, the Ponos would wear off and the severity of his wounds would overpower the Onys.

Kyler grunted lightly as he tightened the guard around his forearm, giving it a good hit to ensure it was in place. It was a relief to drape his dried cape over his shoulders after the previous night's soaking, and with the flick of his hood, his scales were hidden from view.

He hesitated at the door, taking one last glance at Draven. He was perfectly safe and sound asleep. Had their positions been switched, Kyler was certain Draven would do the same. At least, that's what he told himself as he locked the door behind him and tucked the key into his trouser pocket.

The inn was mostly quiet, the only sounds coming from what Kyler assumed to be the kitchen; the clanking of metal pots and muffled speech filtered up through the carpets below his feet. His cloak brushed the steps as he descended into an empty foyer, and the previous night's events replayed in his mind. He instinctively tugged at his hood, feeling as though Clide's eyes still followed him. He hoped their friendly host wasn't a gossip.

However, there was no sign of the satyr this afternoon, and with the swing of the door and ring of the bell, Kyler was free from the confinements of the inn.

The storm had ushered in a new wave of cold that pricked his skin the moment he stepped outside. Though the temperature had dropped significantly, the sun was bright and provided a hint of warmth as he moved out of the shadow of the inn.

It smelled like earth; the scent of damp ground saturated the air. The weathered roads still housed small puddles of slick mud, which splattered as horses and carts cut through them. People flooded the streets, dodging each other as they hurried to and from the docks, and Potri soldiers patrolled the distant gate just as they had when they'd arrived. In the crisp light, Kyler could see their clean-shaven faces and shining blades.

He turned toward the castle and his breath fell from his chest as he took in its structure. The castle of Potri was an architectural masterpiece, constructed of white stone and crystal glass. Gold tipped each tower, matching the gate at the other end of the road, and Kyler could hear the white flags snapping in the wind. Massive windows graced the front of the palace, showcasing several stories of ballrooms and galleries, all decorated with glass chandeliers and golden tapestries.

The front of the castle was all for show; the royal family kept away from the massive windows, where onlookers couldn't observe them. Still, their absence did not distract from its beauty. A bridge arched over the narrow lake that separated the castle from the city, the gentle movement of the crystal waters reflecting off the walls of glass.

The chime of a bell pulled Kyler's attention from the castle to a large clock tower that shot up from across the road. It rang through the city in eight loud tolls. Just past it, the rounded roof of an observatory caught the light of the sun, with golden instruments visible within its glass windows.

Kyler stumbled to the side as a man in a gold-trimmed coat led his cantering horse down the center of the road. He hardly spared Kyler a glance, hurrying for the castle as if his presence was of the utmost importance. It wasn't until he'd passed that Kyler noted the markings that had been sewn across his clothes; the man was a king's messenger.

Kyler watched from the side of the road as the messenger crossed the river bridge, slowing only for a moment to address the guards before the gates were opened, and he continued his journey out of sight.

The urge to follow him rose. If the afi were in Potri, it was possible the nobility knew of it. But Kyler squashed the thought as he shook his head and turned down a split in the road. Even if that were the case, he wasn't there to see the royals, and he certainly wasn't about to announce his arrival. The point of the mission was stealth, and for that, he would need to obtain information subtly.

His eyes landed on an arena that came into view as he rounded a bend. It was constructed like the gate, with three stories of white stone and glittering gold flags. Men with ropes cinched to their waists hung from the walls as their watchmen on the ground directed them in the placement of large tapestries. Kyler quickly pulled the map from his cloak and unrolled the parchment. It was a crude copy of Novah's, since she'd given him so little time with her own, but it was accurate. Sure enough, a small pentagon marked the location of the arena.

"In need of directions, mate?"

Kyler turned to find an old face staring up at him. The man stood only to the commander's chest, with a thick gray beard and a nose as large as his leathery hands, which he rubbed together as he spoke. The dust of white stone covered his clothing, which must've been tailored to fit his short stature.

"I'm alright, thank you," Kyler answered, folding away his map and turning back to the arena. "Is there an event tonight?"

The man chuckled, brushing some of the dust off his legs. "You must be new around here."

Kyler chose his words carefully. "Just passing through."

The man nodded to the arena. "Every three months, the royal knights put on a show for us. At the end of the evening, one is crowned the season's champion by the king himself." He crossed his arms. "It's great fun, really. Jousting, swordsmanship, and plenty of mead. If you can spare the evening, I highly recommend it."

The men at the arena unraveled the final tapestry, revealing the embroidered shadow of a knight on horseback. His steed was reared and his sword raised—an image Kyler could assume brought excitement to the town. An event like this would present the opportunity to gather information in a crowd, and from the sound of it, the nobility would be present too.

"Thank you." Kyler turned back to the man. "I may take you up on your suggestion."

He smiled, revealing a mouthful of crooked teeth. "You won't regret it." He stepped past, making his way toward the arena. His body fell slightly as he walked with a stiff right leg, and before he was out of earshot, he glanced back at Kyler. "I'd ditch the cloak if I were you. The arena gets hot."

Kyler pursed his lips as the man turned his back, settling his gaze on the building before him.

CHAPTER FOURTEEN

THE BELL CHIMED ONCE AS THE DOOR SWUNG OPEN, AND AGAIN as it fell back against its frame. Kyler's nose filled with the smells of grease and burning coals mixed with the tang of fresh lime. The tavern was full of hard-working men and women pausing for a meal, and their chatter nearly drowned out the bell announcing Kyler's entrance.

"Take a seat anywhere."

Kyler turned to find a tall man at his side, stacks of dirty plates piled in his hands. His straw-like hair flapped against his forehead as he nodded toward a few empty tables just big enough for two. "I'll send someone to take your order shortly," he said before he dipped down a hallway.

The empty tables sat closest to the door, with their wooden chairs turned and shifted as if someone had abandoned them in a hurry. Kyler decided on a rectangular one that pressed against the wall and realized as he sat that the table legs were uneven; the whole piece tilted as he placed an elbow on the wood.

A moment later, he was approached by a boy who couldn't have been older than his buggers back home.

"Good afternoon, sir!" The boy greeted with a genuine grin that stretched the freckles on his face. "Can I offer you a menu?"

Kyler smiled, amused by the boy's enthusiasm. "That would be great."

The boy handed over a thick piece of parchment he had tucked under his arm and watched over Kyler's shoulder as the commander scanned it.

"The soup is a favorite." He pointed to the item, and Kyler stuffed a grimace as he read the ingredients. "And our smoked ham is really good."

"I'll take that." He handed the menu back to the boy. "And what have you got to drink?"

The boy paused for a moment, as if remembering his lines. "We've got all types of juice, water, and ale, but whiskey isn't served until evening."

"How about just water, then?"

He grinned again. "Anything else?"

"That will be all, thank you."

Kyler muffled a chuckle under his breath as the boy turned his back and hurried into the kitchen. He could hear him muttering the order to himself as he disappeared into the hallway, and Kyler leaned back in his chair to scan the room. He hoped to get more information on the event tonight, but he knew he'd have to be careful how he went about asking. Small talk could easily lead to answers when done correctly.

The boy returned with a glass of water, and Kyler nodded his thanks before taking a drink. It wasn't as fresh as the water from the wells and springs of Sannir, but his thirst overpowered the chalky taste as it slipped over his tongue.

"Excitable, isn't he?"

Kyler lowered his glass, finding company across his small table. The man was tall, even sitting down. His nose was long and sharp, interrupted halfway by a small bump, and dark curls piled on top of his head where he'd pulled them from his face, revealing high cheekbones. He watched Kyler intently, his pupilless eyes shining like mirrors of pale glass.

"Aren't all kids?" Kyler answered his question with one of his own, gently setting his glass down before him. He resisted the urge to turn from this newcomer's gaze. "To whom do I owe this pleasure?"

His name, however, was the least of Kyler's concerns. He was a celestial, a being whose ancestors traced back thousands of years before Sannir was inhabited. They mostly kept to themselves, and the sight of such a race set Kyler's nerves on edge, despite their history of peace.

"Ophir," the celestial responded, picking a knotted pill from his dark cloak. "I would ask you to remove your hood, but I see that would be unwise."

Of course he could see Kyler's scales. With eyes like theirs, celestials didn't need light to see the world around them, and the shadow of his hood was no exception. Though Ophir's knowledge made him uneasy, Kyler kept a calm demeanor. "It would be. I prefer not to draw attention to myself." He hoped the celestial would take the hint to leave him be, but Ophir responded with a small smirk.

"I've always wanted to visit Sannir."

Kyler lifted his glass again, keeping Ophir in the corner of his eye. "It's beautiful in the mountains."

"The mountains where the dragons dwell?"

Kyler set his drink down with a bit of force this time and leaned his elbows on the light wood between them. "I'm not inclined to inform you of the ways of my kingdom. Visit Sannir, if you wish, or pick up a book if you seek to gain knowledge."

Ophir stared for a moment, searching Kyler with his faded

gaze. "I'm simply curious as to what the commander of the Land Brigade is doing here, across the ocean and without his troops."

Kyler's mind stalled. "How did you—"

"You have a remarkable collection of scales, gracing such small ears in shades of green and brown. If it weren't for the lack of a white scale, I'd have pinned you as the general."

Kyler glanced around them to be sure no one had overheard and did his best to ignore the smile resting on Ophir's thin lips.

"I've read quite a few books in my day, *Sann.*"

Kyler knew the term. It was an informal name used for the elves of Sannir. The way he said it wasn't accusatory; he used it like a tease.

"Kyler," the commander corrected, turning back to Ophir. "And if you have any sense of dignity, you'll keep all of this to yourself."

He nodded slowly. "Alright, Kyler, what are you doing here?"

"Trade."

He raised his dark brows. "Fraudulency doesn't suit you well."

Their conversation was momentarily halted as the boy returned, a plate of steaming meat in his hand. He placed the meal before Kyler, but the commander's eyes never left Ophir's. When the boy was out of earshot, he leaned over his plate, ignoring the rising steam as it brushed his skin. He lowered his voice to ensure no one else heard him.

"Information does not equal power. If I say I'm here for trade, I am. And when I tell you I won't be in this city for long, I mean it." When he'd finished, he turned his attention to his plate of food, signaling that the conversation was over. Kyler still felt Ophir's unsettling eyes watching him from across the table, and he refused to meet them.

"If you're here about General Caligari, I might be able to help you."

Kyler stilled. What did this man know about Uriah? "*Former* general."

Ophir nodded, crossing his large pale arms. "He had secrets."

Had. "He's dead?"

The celestial didn't answer, his cloudy gaze revealing nothing.

Kyler bit his tongue, his mouth turning metallic. "Name your price."

The celestial stood slowly from his chair, taking his time as he pushed it into the table and readjusted his dark cloak. His thin fingers slid a piece of paper beneath Kyler's plate. "You know where to find me." With that, he turned, disappearing through the door with two chimes of a bell.

Kyler's hand settled on a slip of paper, the parchment dyed black as midnight and dotted with silver stars. He didn't need to flip it over to know where it pointed. He leaned back in his chair, squinting through the glass windowpane as he caught a glimpse of Ophir's dark cloak slipping through the busy street and towards the observatory.

CHAPTER FIFTEEN

THE HINGES OF THE DOOR LET OUT A CREAK AS KYLER reentered the room at the inn, his boots padding softy against the carpet. Draven's gentle breathing filled the space, mixed with the faint sounds of the city that slipped through the cracked window.

Kyler's thoughts were spinning, consumed by the information the celestial claimed to have regarding their missing general. What if Uriah *had* been involved in the attack? The thought pounded against Kyler's mind as he closed the door behind him.

He knelt, silently unlacing his boots, as images of General Uriah flooded him. There was a knot in his throat, the kind that made it difficult to swallow and even harder to breathe. The celestial had all but confirmed Uriah's death.

It was because of Uriah that Kyler had joined the ranks, and though those early memories brought bitterness to his tongue, he forced himself to dwell on them. Uriah—harsh and cruel as he was—had always been there. Haunting, distant, and angry, but there.

His thoughts muffled the sounds of Draven, who began to shift, and it wasn't until the kilder cleared his throat that Kyler broke free of his mind.

Draven attempted to sit upright, but Kyler rose quickly,

pressing a hand to Draven's chest. "Not yet."

Draven's hooded eyes blinked slowly as they came into focus, and Kyler waited until he relaxed to step back. The kilder glanced to the window, finding the amber light of late afternoon, and his voice croaked as he asked, "I was out cold, wasn't I?"

Kyler chuckled as he unlatched the cloak from his shoulders, tossing it over the back of the chair. "You were."

Draven furrowed his brow as he leaned against the pillow, his good leg shifting uncomfortably beneath the sheets. The sheen of sweat that had covered him through the night was finally gone, and he didn't complain when Kyler offered him a vial of Ponos. Perhaps he had needed the sleep after all.

No words were exchanged as Kyler recorked his potions, his mind still captured by thoughts of Uriah Caligari and the celestial who claimed to know him.

"Did you get any rest?" Draven broke Kyler's daze once more, and he snapped back to the present.

"Some." A deep breath filled his lungs. He forced his thoughts toward the arena and the event that evening. If he was careful with his words, he suspected he could talk Novah into attending.

"You're lucky I overpacked," Kyler called over his shoulder, hoping to lighten the kilder's mood. "Though, you certainly aren't leaving many potions for the rest of us." His smirk faded as he turned back to Draven, finding him studying Kyler's cloak.

"You left."

Kyler paused. He glanced at the mud on his shoes and wrinkles in his cloak before looking at Draven.

The kilder simply shrugged. "I know enough about Onys to recognize when I have been under its effects."

Kyler's throat tightened, but he feigned nonchalance. "I knew you needed rest, and I feared you wouldn't accept it if I offered.

I should've told you."

His eyes locked with Kyler's in a silent battle. "Yes, you should have. An alchemist can get himself in trouble for administering potions without consent."

"You know quite a bit about alchemy."

Draven allowed a smile to tug at his lips. "I do. My sister has been studying it for years. She is young but gifted. Alchemy was our mother's passion. Vera learned from her before she passed."

A pang of guilt snagged Kyler's chest. "I'm sorry for your loss."

Draven shrugged. "I was seven when we lost her. My brother was nine, and Vera was five."

Kyler pulled over a chair and seated himself so he faced the bed. "I've got an older brother too. He moved to a city in Xynack a few years ago. Not long after my father left us."

Draven nodded slowly, running a finger along the sheets, deep in thought. "The general won't like that you went against her orders."

"I didn't go far—"

"You've got dust in your hair, and you smell like ham."

Kyler snuck a whiff of his shirt. He did smell like ham.

"If you want to make allies out of us, Commander, you would be wise to assume us observant."

The comment came across as somewhat amusing, and Kyler let his shoulders fall in defeat. "Alright. I did leave, and I learned something." He leaned forward, propping his elbows on his knees as Draven sat upright in interest. "There's a large arena just down the road, and there's an event tonight."

Draven frowned slightly, as if this wasn't the information he'd hoped for. "A show?"

"The whole city is excited about it. Even the royals will be there. If the afi are here, this might be our chance to spot them while blending in."

Draven didn't answer right away. He frowned as he took in Kyler's words. "If we can blend in, so can the afi. I don't see how this will help."

"I'm more curious about the royalty. If the afi have domain in Potri, the nobility must know about it. This may be our only opportunity to lay eyes on them."

"Novah said we'd stay in tonight."

Kyler sighed, glancing toward the golden light of the window. Novah and the others would be returning soon. "She doesn't take me seriously."

"And you think she'll listen to me?"

"You said you were close." Kyler met his eye now, hoping his honesty would mask the questions about Uriah that still spun in his mind. "This isn't about me or Novah, it's about Sannir. Tell me you truly think this wouldn't be beneficial."

"I can't. I think it would be." Draven rubbed his forehead, a small scoff falling with his breath. "I like you, Commander."

Kyler lifted an eyebrow at his statement, but Draven continued.

"If I may be blunt, I think you're rash and horribly prideful, but I also think your tenacity is good for Novah. If you can find a way to work with her, I believe the armies of Sannir will thrive." Draven laughed softly to himself. "But if you cross her, you will find yourself buried beneath her flame."

His words sat oddly against Kyler's ears, like a puzzle that didn't quite fit together. "Was that a compliment, Kilder?"

Draven's small laugh turned into a grin, but before he could respond, a key turned against the lock of their door. Their conversation ended as Novah entered.

Her dark hair caught the light as she dropped her hood, rolling out her shoulders. Corbin followed closely behind her.

"Evening, gentlemen." She gave a curt nod.

Draven flashed Kyler a knowing look before addressing her. "Any news?"

It was Corbin who answered, shaking his head as he reached to untangle his scales. "Nothing. If the afi are here, they're well hidden."

"Same with the docks." Aeron's voice flooded the room as he entered, closing the door stiffly behind him. He looked to Novah with a sigh, dropping the hood from his matted hair. "Just the usual trade."

Kyler slid his tongue across his teeth, watching as the three hung their cloaks and removed their weapons. "Did anyone check the observatory?"

His tone immediately caught Corbin's attention, but Novah answered absentmindedly. "I passed by. It looks normal."

"What about the arena?"

Corbin lifted his chin, a curious look flashing across his face. But once again it was Novah who answered, her voice a bit breathless.

"No. Why do you ask?" She ran her fingers through her hair as she pulled out the chair beside Kyler to sit down.

"I spoke briefly with Clide. There's an event tonight—a large one, apparently." Kyler shot Corbin a look of warning, finding his lieutenant's jaw taunt. Corbin was onto him.

"I'm sure that'll be fun for people who enjoy that sort of thing." Novah shifted, tucking her hair behind her pointed ears. Her scales shimmered like fire, and Kyler's mind danced back to Draven's warning.

"The nobility will be in attendance. It may be our only chance to lay eyes on them. They could be working with the afi."

"Commander, this is not up for discussion."

Kyler pushed down the frustration as it boiled in his chest. "General, just hear me out."

"I have," she snapped. "The answer is no."

"General, if I may." All eyes turned to Draven, whose quiet voice cut through the tension in the air. "I understand your hesitancy, but this may be a well-timed opportunity."

Kyler pressed his mouth shut, not wanting to ruin the chance of a shift in the conversation.

"It would allow you to eavesdrop easily, and the commander has a point about the nobility."

Novah swallowed hard as Draven's words hung heavy between them.

Aeron broke the silence. "I can stay with Draven. If this event is that big, you're sure to pick up something."

Novah looked at Kyler, searching for a reason to decline him. Finally, she gave a curt nod. "Alright. We'll go."

A grin rose to Kyler's face, and he offered Draven a subtle nod of thanks. The kilder gave no reply as he rested his head back against the pillow, his gaze turning distant.

"Thank you, General." Kyler rose, pushing his chair back against the table, and tossed his cloak over his shoulder. "We should leave at sundown."

Novah barely acknowledged him, her hands folded in her lap and her sights focused on the carpet beneath their feet.

Kyler pressed his lips thin, the smile now fallen from his face as he turned toward the adjacent room with Corbin at his heels. As soon as they entered, Corbin shut the door.

"You left." The lieutenant's voice was low, and his gaze narrowed on Kyler as he crossed his arms over his chest. "Why?"

"I learned something about Uriah." Kyler clapped a hand on his lieutenant's shoulder, but Corbin brushed it away, a scowl etched across his mouth.

"That was foolish, and you know it. If Novah finds out—"

"She won't."

Corbin gave a frustrated sigh as Kyler reached into his pocket, revealing the folded paper dotted with painted stars and curved calligraphy. Corbin's anger quickly faded into curiosity as he took the slip. "What's this?"

"I met a celestial named Ophir who asked to meet at the observatory. He claims to know secrets about Uriah and his death."

"Death?" Corbin's eyes shot up from the paper.

"He knows something, Corbin."

"How are you going to lie your way out of this one?"

"I'm not bringing Novah into this." Kyler snatched the paper back from him, folding it once more and stuffing it into his pocket. "If we go to the observatory, we go alone."

Corbin stared up at the ceiling and shook his head slowly. "The more time I spend around her, the less I'm inclined to double-cross her. The general is smart, Kyler."

"So are we." He lightly tapped Corbin's chest. "If it turns out to be a real lead, we can let the others in on it. But for right now, let's keep this between us."

Corbin pinched the bridge of his nose. "Saints, I hate you sometimes."

"Trust me, Corbin."

He huffed, his shoulders dropping in defeat. "Fine. If you want to go to meet with your mysterious lead, I can stay and cover for you."

Kyler chuckled, bumping his shoulder into Corbin's as he tossed his cloak onto the bed just wide enough for the two of them. "I'll go tomorrow night."

CHAPTER SIXTEEN

THE FOLDED PAPER CRUMPLED IN KYLER'S FIST AS HE BALLED HIS hands inside his pockets. The smell of mead and mud wafted from the line waiting outside of the arena. Lamp posts shone overhead, adorned with banners of white and gold that flapped lightly in the evening breeze, and music hummed from the building before them. Kyler found himself studying the surrounding crowd, curious for a head of dark curls and empty eyes, but he found nothing apart from leather vests and assorted hooves. It seemed all of Potri had come to see the tournament.

Beside him, Novah flexed her fingers at her sides, and her spine stiffened every time a member of the boisterous crowd bumped her shoulder or brushed her elbow. She refused to look at Kyler and instead watched the fireworks that exploded above the arena in sparks of gold.

Kyler leaned toward Novah, keeping his voice low. "Everything alright?"

"Just fine, Commander," she whispered, muttering his title low enough that only he could hear.

Kyler strained his neck to see over the crowd, catching a glimpse of the colors that flooded from the open arena doors. "We're almost there."

Though she was nearly as tall as he, Novah made no move to look over the crowd. She gave a frustrated grumble as a dwarfish man shoved her into Kyler, and she tugged her hood farther over her head.

The man from earlier that day had advised Kyler to ditch his cloak. The suggestion had been disregarded, but the growing heat of the masses was already causing sweat to prick at his skin. He could only imagine how miserable the heat would be within the arena and instead chose to focus on the fireworks as the slow-moving attendees inched closer to the doors.

Corbin tugged at Kyler's cloak as he mumbled, "I hope for your sake we find some afi tonight."

Kyler noted Novah's rigid demeanor as they reached the open doors, where the sounds of clinking metal echoed from within the arena.

"Hang on."

Kyler tore his gaze from Novah to the man before them. His nose was slightly crooked, and his coarse hair was thinning at the crown of his head. His croaked voice barely rose above the arena's noise as he held a palm before Kyler's chest, a bored look plastered across his face.

"No weapons allowed."

Kyler opened his mouth to protest, but the man spoke first.

"Leave your weapons to the right. You can retrieve them afterward at the east entrance."

Kyler's hand found the pommel of his sword, his fingers brushing the leather grip. "Can't we—"

"No weapons, or I'll ask you to leave. You're holding up the line."

Before Kyler could think better of it, he tugged his sword free from his waist and tossed it to the grass beside the door. After a moment of hesitation, Novah did the same, her sword clattering as she dropped it atop Kyler's. Corbin was last, his lips pressed thin as he abandoned his sword and moved toward the door. He took a step but was caught once again by the man's hand.

"*All* weapons."

Kyler chuckled.

Corbin scrunched his nose and pulled a dagger from his boot, tossing it to the ground with a sigh. The man flashed a grin that revealed several missing teeth and waved a hand for them to enter.

The inside of the arena smelled like cheap whiskey and manure. Sweat dotted Kyler's neck, and the heat of bodies and lamplight suffocated his lungs. The crowd pushed through a tight hallway, and with nowhere else to go, Kyler followed. Novah and Corbin pressed to his back, attempting not to lose him in the hordes. After several turns and narrow stairwells, the group emerged under an open sky.

They were on the third of five levels, with rows of splintered wooden benches wrapping the slanted platform. The circular shape of the arena allowed the field below to be viewed from every angle, and fresh sand filled the center, disrupted around the edges by three gray stallions that trotted the circle. Riders donned heavy chainmail of flashing gold and held flags above their heads that matched the banners draped across their horses.

Corbin pushed Kyler down a row of benches, and the floor creaked as the soldiers took their seats among the crowd.

"The nobility isn't here yet," Novah noted.

Kyler followed her gaze to the row above them, where barriers blocked an empty private section. Armored guards dressed in fabric as gold as those below hovered near the vacant seats, open blades hanging from their sides.

Kyler leaned close enough to brush Novah's shoulder, his voice a low murmur. "Are you certain you're alright, General?"

Her eyes met his for a moment; a silent debate flashed across her expression. "Fine."

He signed and turned his attention to the surrounding crowd. Creatures with skin like fire and horns of ember traded coin for drink, and satyrs apologized as they stumbled over the feet of taller men. Merchants and tradesmen joked amongst one another while the fireworks continued to flash overhead, and the sound of trumpets joined in with the noise.

Below, more horses joined in the parade around the arena's edge, their riders waving flags of white. Heraldry had been stitched into each flag, and matching designs danced along the horses' hides. Polished armor reflected the golden sparks of the fireworks, and the stomping of hooves from nearly two dozen horses rose to the highest balcony.

Kyler felt a nudge from Corbin, who jutted his chin toward the empty section. A large group of guards had entered, their faces solemn and hands rested on the hilt of their blades. It wasn't until they reached the center of the blocked section that they fell back, revealing the royal family within.

It was the king who emerged first, his appearance leaving no question as to who he was. He wore no crown, but his cape was as white as the scales of Atlas, and his golden armor rivaled that of the knights around him. He stood with a straight spine, his steely eyes creased with wrinkles, and his rough skin was dotted with blemishes. His hair was thin and dark, combed away from his forehead, and his nose stuck out from his face, hooking towards his lip at the end.

Next to him, the queen stood, just as tall. Her face was long and cheekbones high, and curls of gray streaked with black had been pinned into place atop her head. Her lips, painted red, tugged into a frown as she eyed the crowd, her dark lashes flitting against the musty air.

And finally, there was the prince.

He was the perfect mix of his parents, having received only their best features. Gold and white reflected off his narrow chest, and atop his dark hair sat a simple circlet of gold. He looked only as old as Kyler, but he carried an heir of authority that his parents seemed to have left in their youth. His gray eyes scanned the arena with an edge of steel, and for a moment, they met Kyler's.

The prince knew who he was. Kyler could feel it.

Sannir's Saints.

This time, Kyler knew him too.

Though his face had been hidden by a helm, the familiar sensation of the prince's gaze dipped into Kyler's soul once more. Gold stitching ran across his white cloak, matching the design on the dark attire he'd worn the night that Sannir was attacked.

It was *him.*

Kyler tore his gaze away, but it was too late. From the corner of his eye, he saw the prince straighten, his nostrils flared and sharp jaw set.

"We have to go," Kyler breathed to Corbin, his heart pounding louder than the horse's hooves below.

Corbin frowned at the haste in his voice. "Why?"

The prince's golden threads disappeared into the staircases, and Kyler strained to catch sight of him once more.

"I was right. The prince was there at the attack." He faced Corbin. "I saw him in Sannir. He's with Orisis, and he knows we're here." Kyler's warning was drowned out by cheering as a knight was knocked from his steed, and the winner paraded around the arena's center. It was too loud. Too tight.

"Tell me you're joking."

"I wish I was."

Another string of shouts and cheers pulled Kyler's attention back to the show, and his pulse quickened. The prince now strode through the center of the arena with his hands clasped at his back and dust spiraling beneath his polished boots with every step. He looked like the center of a hurricane, moving calmly toward the knights as the arena around him turned fierce with excitement. This was something new, and the crowd was loving it. Gray eyes met Kyler's again, narrowed and sharp, sinking into him like the fangs of a serpent.

Kyler's skin burned as he looked at Novah, still feeling the prince's piercing gaze like the tip of a blade. Before he could speak, Novah stilled. "It's him."

"You saw him too." Kyler reached for his sword, only to find soft fabric. "It's like—"

"Like he can see through you," she finished, pushing herself to her feet. "We have what we came for." Novah turned her back to the arena's center and pushed her way toward the exit.

Kyler moved with her, the uneven planks beneath him shifting under the weight of his hurried steps. Spilled mead left slick spots along the floor, and people grunted as the soldiers shoved past. Cheers and gasps filled Kyler's ears, but he didn't dare stop to look. Corbin muttered apologies as he trailed close to Kyler's heels, following Novah toward the hallway where they'd entered.

A hand grabbed Kyler's forearm. Before he could shove it away, he found himself staring into eyes as clear as glass.

"You shouldn't be here." Ophir released his arm, his dark brows furrowed.

Kyler swallowed, stealing a glance behind him. The prince had placed himself atop a steed, his sword lifted in the air and drawing every eye to him.

"The prince is a distraction," Ophir pressed. "There are afi at every exit."

Kyler ground his teeth, his tone turning sharp. "You couldn't have warned me of this earlier?"

The celestial's jaw went taunt. "My help isn't free, Sann."

Ahead, Novah had slowed, watching the conversation that was taking place.

Kyler cursed. "Help us get out, and I'll give you whatever you want."

"Go up. There's a ladder near the north exit that will take you to the ground, but you can only access it from the top balcony."

"Thank you." Kyler started for the stairs once more, scanning the top floor.

Novah waited until he was beside her to catch his shoulder, balling a fist into his cloak. "Who was that?"

"The exits are blocked," he whispered, ignoring her question. "We can get out from the top floor."

"We'll deal with this later." She dropped her grip and scanned the two floors of seating that separated them from their escape.

It was then Kyler noticed the eyes that weren't on the prince. Spread throughout the arena were those who watched them with sharp looks. Many of them flexed their fingers, as though waiting for the order to move.

Kyler tugged his hood farther over his head, dipping his face to the floorboards as he shoved toward the staircase. He stumbled past drunkards, not caring who he pushed aside, as those who'd been watching started after them.

A hand reached for his neck, and Kyler shoved the larger man away, his run turning into a near sprint as the man fell onto the seats, cracking the wood beneath him.

Swordplay crashed from below. The ringing echoed in Kyler's ears as he took the stairs two at a time. Slick wood caused him to stumble, and his heaving breaths filled his lungs with musty air as he regained balance.

"Saints!" Novah swore. Kyler stole a glance behind him and saw a man in auburn robes grab her arm. He pulled her into him, thrusting an elbow into her side.

Kyler turned to help, but Corbin shoved him forward. "She can handle herself."

Though his stomach twisted, Kyler gripped the handrail and hauled up the steps. Sure enough, Novah was at his side a moment later, her breath heavy and knuckles raw.

As they neared the fourth floor, a woman with a cloak that nearly matched Kyler's scrambled to grab hold of his neck, and Kyler shoved a knee into her stomach, doubling her over.

"They're everywhere," Corbin gasped.

In the humidity of the stairwell, Kyler could feel the burn of his skin and the rush of his blood.

"They're going to cut us off at the top," Novah warned, fumbling with her cloak as it began to slip off her shoulders. Her steps wavered, and she muttered something to herself. "Wait."

Kyler halted, his chest rising and falling quickly as Novah unpinned her cloak, tucking it under her arm. The red of her scales was dulled in the low light, yet the single white one seemed to glitter even in the darkness.

"You're mad," he hissed over the drum of his heart. "They'll see your scales."

"They're not looking for scales, they're looking for hoods." She glanced back toward the fourth floor. "This way."

"Novah—"

Her gaze snapped to Kyler's. "Trust me for once."

With tense shoulders, Kyler ripped the cloak from his back, stuffing it into a ball. The sounds of clashing swords grew louder as Novah slipped into a row of seats on the fourth story, offering apologies as she pushed through the crowd.

Jeers and whistles filled Kyler's head once more, and he shook his hair over his ears in hopes of hiding the scales that hung from them. Blow, the prince's steely gaze flicked toward the seats above them as his sword cut through his opponent.

Corbin gripped Kyler's shoulder, his fingers digging into his shirt as they made their way to the opposite side of the arena. It was only when Novah began to turn down toward the lower levels that Kyler caught her arm.

"Ophir said the roof is our only exit."

"Ophir?" She jerked her arm free as her voice dipped to a warning. "You'd better have answers for me."

Before Kyler could come up with an excuse, Novah made for the roof, the pound of her boots causing the stairs to creak. To Kyler's relief, no afi blocked their path as they climbed closer to the stars. By the time they emerged at the top of the arena, he felt as though he could think again.

Novah was the first to spot the ladder Ophir had mentioned, finding its opening tucked behind the very last row of seats. She said nothing as she secured her cloak once more and began her descent to the empty courtyard below.

It was only when all three reached the ground that Novah spoke again, her voice clipped. "Corbin, get our weapons."

"Yes ma'am." He avoided Kyler's eye, slipping between them as he headed for the east gate.

When he was out of earshot, Novah stepped close to Kyler. "Who was that?"

Kyler struggled to catch his breath. "I think he's an ally."

"An ally?"

He cowered under the sharpness of her tone. The way she looked at him nearly rivaled the inexplainable way the Potri prince seemed to cut through him.

"Is that supposed to make me feel better, Commander?"

For a brief moment, Kyler felt the judgment of General Uriah. The same way he'd scolded and corrected his soldiers seemed to reflect in Novah's words, breaking the confidence Kyler had possessed just moments before.

When he didn't answer, she pressed her eyes shut, shaking her head slowly. "We have afi on our trail as we speak. I have many questions for you, *Commander*, but they'll have to wait."

CHAPTER SEVENTEEN

KYLER YANKED HIS FINGERS THROUGH HIS HAIR AS HE PACED around their small room at the inn, each tug harder than the last as his frustration built. "I got us a lead. Can't you just accept that?"

Novah sat calmly at the table, her elbows resting on the wood and hands clasped at her lips.

Behind her, Aeron's knee bounced lightly while he watched in silence, his gaze dark and chin dipped. He hadn't said a word, and neither had Corbin or Draven. Their gazes bore into Kyler, and he wished the general had chosen to have this conversation in private.

"No, I can't," Novah snapped. "Your lead came from disobeying a direct order and, as a result, has alerted the afi of our presence."

Kyler shook his head. "Ophir helped us *escape* the afi."

"He knows our identities."

"He's a celestial." Kyler paused, meeting her eye. "I couldn't have hidden it from him if I wanted to."

Novah stood, pressing her palms to the table as she did. "You could have, if you'd stayed here like I ordered."

Kyler inched closer. "The afi knew we were coming! This goes far beyond the celestial. You're a fool, Novah."

To his surprise, she gave a tight smile. "And you're on thin ice."

Before Kyler could move from her reach, Novah caught hold of his newest scale—the same one Corbin had knocked loose. He tried to dodge her, but she was faster. She tugged it free with a painful pinch and held it between her fingers. Dried blood coated the metal that had clung to his skin a moment before, and the dark green scale glinted in the low light of the room. Kyler's ear began to burn and swell as a bubble of blood rose to the raw surface.

"You've just lost a scale, Commander."

"Give it back." His voice was low and threatening, so much so that it caught him off guard.

Her eyes burned. "No."

"Novah, I swear to Sannir—"

"I said *no*, Commander!"

Her shout stole the breath from his lungs, angry and fierce and sharp enough to cut armor.

"And you're going to lose every one of those scales if you can't get yourself under control!" She dropped the scale from her grasp, and Kyler watched it fall to the carpet between their feet.

His voice was barely a whisper. "You wouldn't."

"I would." She shifted past, careful not to touch him as she left him staring at his fallen scale. "This conversation is over. Lieutenant Aeron, please inform our host that we'll be leaving tomorrow morning. We can't risk being tracked back here. I'll find us a new place to stay."

"You're a disgrace to Uriah," Kyler muttered, knowing he didn't need to be louder for his words to hurt.

She began to open her door but halted. "That makes two of us."

The metallic sting of blood tainted Kyler's tongue as he bit it, listening to her door fall shut. He could feel the eyes of the others boring into him as he bent to pluck his scale from the dusty carpet. Anger and humiliation flamed across his face, and he stalked to the opposite room, slamming the door behind him with more force than necessary.

The scale dug into his palm as he clamped his hand around it and leaned his back to the wall, tilting his gaze to the wooden beams of the ceiling. His opposite hand found his bleeding ear, trailing the remaining scales that hung like emerald armor. The skin above them was warm to the touch, tender and swollen and bare, and Kyler flinched as his rough fingers brushed it.

Draven had warned him, and Kyler now knew what he'd meant.

He dropped his hand and loosed his grip, glancing down at the lost scale. He could put it back on—if he wanted to defy her— but Novah's had made her point clear. Little by little, she would strip him of everything he'd earned.

In that sense, she was like Uriah. Kyler could picture him clear as glass, shaping and molding his men into the soldiers he wanted them to be. The former general was a heartless tyrant, a soldier with no equal.

And if Ophir was right, that tyrant had secrets.

The door creaked open as Corbin let himself in. He opened his mouth to speak, but Kyler cut him off.

"I'm going to see him tonight."

Corbin was silent for a moment. "I can't cover for you this time."

His words stung almost as much as Novah's had. Kyler straightened, pushing off the wall, and tilted his head. "You can't be serious."

"I won't help you lose any more of these." He pointed to the scale resting in Kyler's palm. "If you want to throw your position away for a shot at Uriah, I won't be responsible. You can ruin yourself." He shouldered past Kyler and dropped to a knee beside their bed to unlace his boots.

Kyler sucked a breath, tucking his scale into his pocket beside the crumpled parchment. "This is personal, Corbin."

"I know," the lieutenant snapped. "I'm well aware of your personal vendettas, and I don't want any part in them."

Kyler muttered a curse, stalking closer to Corbin. "What are you going to do? Run your mouth to Novah?"

Corbin grunted as he tugged off his shoes and tossed them to the corner. "No." He stood, shaking his head. "I won't say anything. Go if you want, but if she finds out then you're on your own."

The tension fell from Kyler's shoulders, and he nodded. "Thank you."

"Don't." Corbin turned his back, tossing aside the covers and laying down without another word.

. . .

Pale moonlight poked through the curtains of their room, brushing Kyler's skin in silver as he waited. The arm tucked under his head had begun to tingle, but Kyler lay perfectly still, letting his mind wander until he was certain the others wouldn't wake.

Beside him, Corbin's breath was slow and easy. Kyler wanted to be angry with him, to put him in his place as his commander, but he couldn't quite find the energy. Instead, he listened to Corbin's rhythmic breath, the sound mingling with the gentle groans of the old inn.

When the silence was full and moon high, Kyler shifted, softly brushing aside the bedsheets, and tugged his boots over his cold socks. The feather mattress hardly rustled as he stood from it, tossing his cloak over his shoulders. He then knelt, fastening his potion belt to his waist with the soft clink of glass bottles and secured his blade beside it.

The chill of the air outside of the inn seeped through the wooden walls as Kyler straightened, allowing his eyes to focus in the dark and fall on Corbin.

To his surprise, he found Corbin awake, his fingers laced over his chest and eyes fastened to Kyler. He said nothing, turning his gaze to the ceiling.

Kyler's boots sunk into the weathered carpet as he left Corbin to his thoughts, passing the shared bed where Draven and Aeron slept. Neither stirred, and Kyler continued past Novah's closed door and into the hallway.

The inn was dark, with a few oil lamps burning low to light the space, and the stairs let out gentle squeaks as Kyler descended them.

The fire that had crackled with warmth was now embers and ash, simmering low as if sleeping along with its guests. The armchairs and couches sat vacant, and the door hardly made a sound as Kyler pulled it open.

He was greeted with night air that pulled at him with its frigid breeze. The city seemed to be dreaming, and the sky itself dreamt along with it. Twinkling stars and warm streetlights brightened the shadowed roads. The crumpled paper in his pocket brushed against his lost scale with every step as he started across the slick cobblestone, his breath puffing in clouds before his face.

You know where to find me.

Kyler plunged his hands into his pockets to keep the cold from gripping them and turned east—toward the city gate. He had no need for a map as he strode through the darkness, thoughts of Uriah Caligari haunting his mind.

The sword at his side bumped his leg as he walked, a comforting reminder, though he felt bare without armor on his back or a bow across his shoulders.

The arching entry to the city glittered in the starlight. It was still stationed with guards, though fewer of them than when they'd arrived. Their low conversations and tired tones filled the night as Kyler drew closer, dipping between shops and alleys until he found a dirt road that led him far from their sight.

Every pebble seemed to crunch beneath his feet and every breath lingered in the air. He felt loud and uncoordinated, parading through the streets with his shining potions and emerald cloak. He was grateful he didn't need to go far. Ahead, the observatory light flickered.

There was a part of him that dreaded meeting those faded eyes and towering frame, but Ophir knew something. And, with the right persuasion, Kyler would soon know it too.

CHAPTER EIGHTEEN

❖

THE GATE WAS OPEN. THIN BARS OF STEEL TOPPED WITH miniature stars and crescent moons lined the perimeter of the observatory. Birch trees stood in rows along the brick path, their branches beginning to bare from the autumn chill, and warm light flickered through the observatory windows.

Fallen leaves scattered the brick, crunching beneath Kyler's steps as he reached the gate. The trees obscured his view of the sky, but as he drew nearer to the building they dwindled, leaving plenty of room for the telescopes to view the planets beyond. It appeared to be three stories, with the third comprised of nothing more than a domed glass ceiling that curved like a hat of crystal to give an easy view of the stars.

A figure stood within this dome, lean and dressed in a cloak of black. He disappeared just as Kyler caught sight of him, leaving the commander to wonder how long he'd been watching.

Before he could change his mind, Kyler stepped to the large glass doors and let himself into the quiet building. The first thing he noticed was the way it smelled—a mixture of lilac and a hint of rose, a familiar smell. It was almost identical to Aiyanna's perfume. Kyler tried not to dwell on the thought as he examined the space, finding every chair and chandelier to be circular. Even the walls themselves were rounded. Across from him, narrow stairs spiraled up to the second story, their dark metal blending in with the walls.

A counter of polished wood, engraved with more stars and crescent moons, sat to Kyler's right, and the man behind it caught Kyler's attention with the sound of ruffling papers. He seemed unaware of the commander's presence. His focus was glued to the pages of parchment he shuffled through. His weathered hands were thin, and his warm breaths were fogging his rounded spectacles.

Kyler approached the man. "Hello."

The man didn't so much as blink.

Kyler cleared his throat, preparing to speak a bit more firmly, but the old man grunted. "We close in five." His voice was thin and raspy, matching the bones jutting out from his thin skin.

Kyler sighed, growing quickly aggravated. "I'm meeting someone."

"Good for you." He finally glanced up, his gaze hollow. "We still close in five." He turned back to his papers just as the echo of footsteps descended the spiral stairs.

"It's alright, Sly," a familiar voice answered. "He's with me." Ophir paused at the foot of the stairs, his pupilless eyes making it unclear who he was looking at.

Sly huffed, muttering something to himself, as Ophir offered a thin smile. "Follow me."

Kyler started for the stairs as Ophir turned his back. The black metal was cold to the touch as Kyler gripped the handrail, leaving Sly to his parchment.

"I wasn't sure you'd come," Ophir said over his shoulder as they ascended, "but I'm glad you did."

Kyler gave no answer, attempting to read the celestial's

thoughts from the tone of his rich voice.

"The afi of Orisis have been in Potri much longer than people realize, and if something isn't done about it, we will all suffer the consequences."

"So you know about the afi." It wasn't a question as much as it was a statement. "How did you know they were at the arena?"

They reached the final step, emerging onto the second story of the observatory. This floor was full of tools for charting, mapping, and stargazing. Tables scattered the space, covered in maps of moon cycles and scribbled notes deemed irrelevant. Portraits of astronomers hung along the dark walls, their frames of bronze glowing in the candlelight. This room was darker than the foyer, and while Kyler struggled to see clearly, Ophir had no issue.

The celestial pulled his dark curls from his neck, securing them with a band as he strode to the far wall. "They're targeting Sannir." He turned, flashing a quick grin. "But you already knew that."

"Unfortunately, yes. But how did you?"

Ophir stopped at steps that'd been carved into the wall, resembling a ladder rather than stairs. "After you."

Kyler hesitated a moment. The celestial was avoiding his questions, but he needed answers, so he obliged. He scaled the ladder quickly and found himself on the third floor—the observation deck. Just as he'd seen from the ground, the deck was shelled by a glass dome that gave the viewers a seamless view of the sky above. Telescopes of brass and silver scattered the space, and for a moment, Kyler lost himself in the constellations.

"I can see it."

Kyler pulled his attention back to Ophir, whose glassy eyes shifted from the stars to the commander's face. The shadows of the sky cast across his sharp features, masking him in darkness.

"That's how I know. History states that Orisis cannot create, but who's to say he cannot control? The followers of Orisis often communicate through constellations, watching as their god shifts the stars at his command. I know the stars better than I know myself. I know who they are, and I know how they move."

Kyler faced the stars once more, allowing himself to get lost in their light. "What do they tell you?"

Ophir chuckled. "I don't know yet." His dark cloak brushed his ankles as he turned to one of the many telescopes. With his height, he had to bend over slightly to peer through the eyeglass. After a moment, he motioned for Kyler to do the same.

"The stars are moving." He angled the telescope toward the commander, and Kyler's vision was filled with the vibrant colors of the galaxy.

His breath caught, mesmerized by the intensity of the sky. It was like looking at a painting, falling into the blues and purples and dotted lights that shifted like cracked glass.

"That is what I see." There was a bit of pride in Ophir's voice as Kyler pulled away.

"Is this how you know about Uriah?"

"The stars hide nothing from those who know them."

Kyler straightened, his focus now on the celestial and the information he claimed to have. "What do you know of him? What do you know of the afi?"

Ophir leaned an elbow on the telescope, his fingers dancing across the divots in the brass as he spoke. "That information will come at a price, Commander."

"What about for the good of Potri?"

A look of amusement fell over his pale features, and Ophir let out a deep sigh. "I love this city, but it's not my home. My people do not often find themselves entangled in the wars of gods and men. We come from the stars, and to the stars we will return." He lifted a finger to Kyler's bleeding ear. "I want your blood."

Kyler's pulse quickened. Even in the darkness, the celestial could see through the shadows. Kyler removed his hood, allowing his scales to glimmer in the star's reflection like the telescopes.

At least, the scales that remained.

Kyler's ear burned under the watchful eye of the celestial, his skin still swollen and crusted in blood. "Why?"

Ophir chose his words carefully. He pressed his tongue against the inside of his cheek before he answered. "The elves of the kingdom of Sannir have magic in their blood, magic that is foreign to the rest of the realm. Pure magic of Adoni. A vial of Sann blood is the most valuable thing Sannir has to offer, especially when willingly given."

It was also dangerous. Blood, when given willingly, was potent, brimming with the power of the Dragon Pass. However, the longer an elf spent away from the Pass, the less powerful their blood would become until, eventually, their magic disappeared altogether. But that could take months—*years*. Kyler hadn't been away long enough. His blood was still rich with magic.

"You know the gravity of your request." Kyler stepped closer. "Name something else."

"There is nothing else you can offer me."

"Then we're done here."

Ophir dipped his chin in understanding, his mind clearly churning at Kyler's words. "I am not a martyr, Kyler. If Orisis tracks your knowledge back to me, there is nothing I could do to escape his wrath. I have no loyalty to Adoni or Sannir. You say the price I ask is steep, but what you ask of me is just as costly."

The way he spoke was smooth. Calculated. Almost as if he'd

expected Kyler to deny his request.

Kyler pinched his lips thin. There were things he needed to know about the former general, information that could mean the safety of Sannir. He shook his head slowly. "I need time to consider."

If his statement pleased Ophir, he didn't show it. The celestial simply nodded, lifting his sights once more to the constellations. "Take all the time you need. But we both know yours is limited."

...

Kyler took one last look at the observatory as he reached the end of the brick path. Ophir stood at the deck, his shadowed figure watching Kyler go. Cold once again hugged Kyler's skin as he pulled the metal gate closed behind him, its hinges squealing softly. The sun would be rising soon, as would Novah and the others.

Two days. That was what Kyler had told the celestial. In two days, he'd meet him at that tavern and give him either a vial of blood or a goodbye.

Kyler's sword felt heavier as he made his way back to the inn. The ghost of Uriah Caligari seemed to linger with him, taunting him with buried histories and threats of Sannir's ruin. Something had happened. Something caused the afi to attack and Uriah to disappear, and those answers could be unlocked with the key of Kyler's blood.

He sighed as the inn came into view. It was quiet and still, almost drowsy in the morning fog that had begun to roll in.

As Kyler reached for the door, someone grabbed his collar and slammed his back into the brick wall of the building. His head hit the stone with a grunt as the hands at his neck balled against his throat. Before he could get his bearings, Novah's sharp voice cut through, her face just inches from his.

"Where the *hell* have you been?"

CHAPTER NINETEEN

THE AIR FLED FROM KYLER'S LUNGS. HIS BACK ACHED FROM THE force of her shove, and he feared the fabric of his shirt would tear in Novah's grip as she dug further into his neck.

He forced a breath. "I can explain—"

"You'd better," she hissed. "Inside."

Novah ripped him from the wall, shoving him through the doors and into the quiet lobby. A few occupants glanced up from their morning reading, but Novah paid them no mind. Her grip remained firm at Kyler's shoulder, fingers digging into his skin as she dragged him like a stray animal.

"*Saints*," Kyler cursed, attempting to rip free of her grip. "What do you think I'm going to do? Run?"

She clutched the fabric of his shirt and cloak even tighter. "You seem to have a habit of running." She reached the door to their room and thrust him inside with enough force to make him stumble. The door slammed shut behind her, and Kyler looked up to find the eyes of the other three soldiers fixated on him.

"Explain," Novah seethed, drawing his attention once more. "*Now.*"

"Alright!" Kyler snapped back at her, adjusting his wrinkled cloak and shirt where she'd nearly ripped them.

A small scoff came from Aeron, who stood between Draven's bed and the chair in which Corbin sat. The lieutenant leaned a hand to Draven's wooden bedframe, his body tense and jaw taunt.

Kyler took a deep breath, checking his tone as he answered, "I was following a lead. I thought—" He stopped himself, deciding how much information he was willing to give. "I went to the observatory. The celestial believes he can help us track the afi."

"You *went to* him?" Novah gritted her teeth. "Kyler Weylyn, you've outdone yourself!"

"This will help us!"

"Help?" She almost laughed. "Commander, you've done anything but."

Kyler tossed his arms in the air, his frustration beginning to boil. "What else do you want from me?"

"Respect!" she spat. "And good judgment to go with it!" She turned her back to him, her fingers pressing hard into her temples. "How much does the celestial know?"

A tremor began to make its way across Kyler's limbs, a mixture of exhaustion, frustration, and nerves. He busied his hands, removing his sword from his waist and placing it on the table where Corbin sat. He avoided his lieutenant's eye as he steadied his breath. "I don't know. He figured most of it out on his own."

"Who is he?" Aeron's voice cut through the tension. His gaze narrowed.

"Just a celestial who works at the observatory. He claims the afi receive orders from Orisis through the constellations, and he can decipher them."

Aeron scoffed. "That's a bold claim."

"But not new." Draven shifted upright, causing even Novah to face him. "Astronomers have theorized that for a long time.

History shows that the movement of Orisis' armies correlates to planetary rotations."

Kyler nodded, swearing to thank Draven later. "Ophir told me they've been in Potri for a while now, targeting Sannir."

"We know that already," Novah shot back. "Give me something of value, Commander."

Kyler spun on her, his anger returning with a seethe. "The only reason you're general is because Uriah died with knowledge that we don't yet possess! If you were half the general he was, you'd forget your pride and listen to your soldiers for once!"

The room fell silent, and Kyler became suddenly aware of how loud he had shouted. Beside him, Corbin shifted uncomfortably in his seat.

Novah stilled. "He's dead?"

Kyler sighed, pressing his eyes shut and tilting his head to the ceiling. "Yes. And Ophir is willing to share everything he knows for a price."

"What price?" she asked through gritted teeth.

If she didn't hate him by now, he was certain she would despise him after this. "Elven blood."

A bitter laugh fell from her lips. "That's not happening."

"I didn't say we should give it to him," Kyler pressed, attempting to keep his aggravation down. "I'm just passing along the information."

"It doesn't help us."

"It does a little," Corbin offered, tapping his fingers lightly against the table. "We can learn to read the stars."

Kyler shook his head. "We don't have the time or resources for that."

"There's a library." Corbin glanced between the two of them. "We saw it yesterday."

"How can we be certain the celestial is telling the truth?" Accusation lined Novah's words as she looked at Kyler once more.

"We can't. But their kind has a reputation of peace."

She didn't seem to believe him, but for once she considered his words. "Let's say we learn to read constellations. What would we be looking for, exactly?"

"That's why we need him." Kyler lowered his voice. "We can learn to chart the stars, but deciphering their messages is another matter entirely. We can make an ally and end this now."

Novah's sharp gaze searched him for any kind of deception as she dissected his words. Finally, she spoke. "I could strip you of your title for this."

"You could certainly try." He held her stare, waiting for her reaction.

She stepped closer; her chin lifted. "You're lucky you're still standing before me with all of those scales."

The swollen skin of his ear began to burn again, and Kyler dipped his voice so only she could hear it. "You, Novah Elison, are not Uriah. And when you fail to return with information on the afi, you'll no longer be the general."

This time, he got no pleasure from saying the words. She didn't flinch or scoff. She didn't even appear hurt. Instead, Novah sighed, her eyes trailing his ears. "And you are no longer a commander." She held out her palm, her arm steady. "Pass over your scales, Kyler. You're relieved of your duty."

Kyler ground his teeth. The heat that flamed across his skin was nearly lethal, clouding his vision in hot sparks. "No."

She stood her ground. "That wasn't a suggestion."

"I don't care what it was. You didn't have the right to take one, much less all of them."

"That's where you're wrong."

He tensed, stepping closer. "If you want my scales, you can rip them from my ears yourself."

Novah's gaze darkened, and for a moment, Kyler wondered if she was about to take him up on his offer. His chest brushed her outstretched palm, so close he could smell the scent of pine that drifted from her skin.

"Scales or no scales, I will see you fail," he warned.

She held his stare. "You will see no such thing."

Before he could respond, a screech rose from beyond the walls of the inn, and the shake of the building sent Kyler stumbling into Novah. She grunted as she hit the carpet, shielding herself as Kyler rolled to the side to avoid falling on top of her. Sharp pain shot along his wrists as he landed, his head narrowly missing the legs of the table.

Kyler hadn't realized how haunted he was by the amphiptere's call until it ripped through the air again, chilling his bones to their core.

"Sannir's Saints…" Novah scrambled to her feet and stumbled to the curtains, ripping them away from the window.

The sunlight faded as a shadow blocked the glass, its scales of midnight sucking the life from the room. For a moment, none of them moved.

Then the window exploded into fragments of glass, knocking Novah to the floor once more. Corbin's shout of warning was inaudible as flames erupted in the streets outside. The beast slammed into the side of the inn, splintering the wooden beams and cracking the plaster walls. Kyler threw his hands over his head as shards of glass and wood sliced his knuckles.

Across the room, Aeron was hauling Draven onto his shoulder. A streak of red trailed down Aeron's temple. "Move!" he shouted, before his voice was drowned out by another explosion of fire.

Novah shoved to her feet, rushing toward the door with Corbin close at her heels.

Kyler hesitated, his instincts fighting against him. On the other side of the room, his potion bag sat lopsided beside his bow, full of valuable—and possibly life-saving—concoctions. He could hear the glass bottles clinking rapidly as the building shuttered.

He swore and pushed off the ground, running toward his potions. He barely kept his footing as a second beast collided with the wall. His fingers found the string of his bow, then the handle of his bag. Vials shattered at his feet as potions slipped from their places, the concoctions sinking into the carpet and glass mixing with the broken window.

Kyler's pulse drummed as he reached the door, finding Novah and the others already halfway down the stairs. The inn's guests crowded the hall, their screams and shouts frantic as the ceiling above threatened to collapse. Some wore nothing but sleep clothes, their shoulders bare and hands gripping one another as families and friends attempted to stay together. Sweat pricked Kyler's back as the heat of the flames seeped through the walls, and another jolt of the building let him know the amphipteres had struck again.

Kyler took the stairs three at a time. His knees throbbed from the impact of each step. He didn't bother with apologies as he stumbled through the stampede of guests before finally reaching Draven and Aeron.

The chandelier that'd hung in the center of the foyer was now in pieces, scattering the ground with metal. The cushioned furniture was torn and scratched, and the front door was nearly ripped from its hinges as people pushed their way through. Heat filtered through the cracked windows, and thick smoke filled the foyer.

While everyone else funneled through the door, Novah turned for the windows. The once-pristine glass that made up most of the back wall was now nothing but sharp edges, providing an escape to the alleyway behind.

Corbin started for the door, but Kyler caught him by his collar. "Windows!"

Corbin halted and spun to Draven and Aeron, turning them toward Novah.

Kyler reached the glass seconds before them, joining Novah in a search for a hole in the window big enough to fit through. When he found none, Kyler rammed a shoulder against the glass. Jagged edges caught his clothes and skin. His stomach rolled as he fell, and his bones rattled as he landed on his feet outside. The moment his balance returned, Kyler turned to catch Draven, guiding him through the glass with Corbin and Aeron at his heels. Novah was the last through, and she hardly touched the ground before shoving Kyler forward.

"Get us somewhere safe!" she ordered. "I'll watch our backs!"

Another screech pierced their ears, and Kyler shielded his head as the second story of the inn caved, sending wood pelting to the ground.

"You lead," he countered, drawing an arrow and aiming it for the sky. "I can handle this!"

She nodded, slipping past Aeron. Her eyes latched on his blood-covered temple, but she said nothing, hurrying them down the alley.

Kyler kept his arrow nocked as they slipped between buildings, the cries of the amphipteres still close. Flashes of wings and tails seemed to follow them, their cries returning just as Kyler hoped they might have lost the trail.

Novah didn't slow.

The general led them deeper into the city, watching over her shoulder to ensure her men were keeping pace. Aeron kept his grip firm on Draven, urging the injured soldier as fast as he could manage while keeping one leg hovered above the streets. They moved surprisingly quickly, but it was obvious by the sweat on Draven's brow that his strength was dwindling.

The sounds of chaos grew faint, yet Kyler kept his aim at the sky. His fingers trembled, but he refused to let his aching muscles ruin his shot. It was only a moment later that Novah made her final turn, dropping to her knees before a rectangular grate in the cobblestone.

"Corbin."

She'd hardly finished his name when Corbin fell to her side and took hold of the grate, combining their strength to pull it free. The iron, rusted and worn, squealed lightly as they tossed it aside, revealing a drain to the city's sewers. The sounds of sloshing water could be heard moving through the caverns below, and a metal ladder lined the wall.

Kyler stole a glance at Draven, whose face was pale and grimaced. Kyler lowered his bow.

"I'll go first." He passed his weapon to Corbin and placed his foot on the top rung of the ladder. "We'll have to help Draven down."

Corbin nodded and lifted an arrow to the sky, searching the clouds for any sign of the beasts of Orisis.

Kyler descended the ladder quickly—his years of scaling the castle wall proving useful—and his boots landed in a shallow stream that smelled of mold and feces.

Above him, Draven gripped the first step, one hand on the ladder and the other latched onto Aeron's forearm. He dangled for a moment, catching his good foot on the farthest step he could reach, and inched his arms to follow. Kyler kept close to the base of the ladder, ready to catch him should the kilder fall, but Draven made a slow and steady descent before landing with a small grunt at the bottom.

Kyler wrapped an arm around him. "Clear!"

Aeron and Novah followed quickly, and Corbin dropped the bow down to Kyler before pulling the grate back in place, sealing them in the darkness of the sewers.

CHAPTER TWENTY

THE ONLY SOUND THAT FILLED THE CAVERNS WAS THE STEADY stream of moving water, taunting them as it echoed in the darkness.

"Sannir's Saints," Corbin sighed, leaning against the mold covered wall.

Novah started deeper into the tunnel. "Don't rest yet. They're still searching for us."

Kyler slung his bow across his back and rested his hands on the potion bag that hung at his side. Corbin matched his stride as they followed the others deeper into the sewers.

Water sloshed at Kyler's shins, and he did his best not to imagine what might be in it. He focused instead on Novah's back, her cloak dotted with plaster and splinters. She'd dropped her hood and her scales burned red in the dim light that flooded in from the grates above. From here, the city seemed quiet. There was no fire, no screams, no collapsing buildings.

"You went back for your potions." Aeron's voice pulled Kyler from his thoughts, eyeing his leather bag.

Kyler tapped it firmly, hearing the crunch of broken glass inside. He'd have to check later to see how many potions survived. "I'm the closest thing you have to a physician." He nodded to Aeron's bleeding temple. "You're lucky I grabbed this."

Aeron's lips tilted in an almost playful expression. "Are you saying I can have some of that pain relief?"

Draven gave a *tsk* as they rounded a corner. "That's for me. Your thick skull is perfectly fine."

Before Aeron could retort, Novah halted, her palm landing on the pummel of her sword.

The prince of Potri stood in the center of the tunnel. His hands were clasped behind his back as if he'd been waiting for their arrival. Behind him, a handful of afi soldiers watched with narrowed eyes, each one with swords hanging at their hips.

The water beneath Kyler shifted as he came to Novah's side, smoothly drawing his bow and aiming at the prince's chest.

"Take it easy, soldiers," the prince quipped, his voice dipping with a light accent.

He was dressed in black—the same jacket he'd worn when Kyler had first seen him in Sannir. It buttoned down his chest and landed at his narrow waist. Black pants clung to his shins where the sewage water had soaked them, and his dark hair was combed neatly from his face. He lifted his hands to show they were void of weapons.

But the afi behind him had enough swords to make up for his lack thereof.

"I don't care who you are." Kyler's bow creaked. "Make one wrong move, and I'll pierce your throat."

He whistled lightly, taking a single step forward. His focus landed on Novah, studying her like one might a piece of art. "General Novah Elison. A force to be reckoned with, I hear." His eyes danced across the group before landing on Kyler once more, and something sparked within them. "Hello again."

Chills raked Kyler's skin, but he held his aim.

"Allow me to properly introduce myself." The prince held out a hand for Novah to shake. "Prince Elizus."

She didn't move, her white-knuckled grip tightening on the hilt of her sword. Elizus dropped his hand. "Orisis wishes to speak with you"—he nodded to Novah, and then to Kyler—"and you. The rest of you are worthless."

Corbin scoffed from behind.

Kyler jerked his chin. "Move out of our way."

"Let's not make this difficult," the prince said slowly.

Kyler pinched his arrow tighter. "I'm not asking a second time."

Elizus tilted his head, studying the commander's arrow. "Would it change your mind if I told you that Uriah Caligari said something similar once?"

Novah stiffened, and an easy smile fell across the prince's face.

Kyler loosed his arrow. It whistled past the prince's rounded ear, landing with precision on the exposed neck of one of the men behind him. The follower of Orisis released a gargled choke as blood exploded from his throat, and he collapsed to the ground with wide eyes.

Elizus sighed. "I guess we're doing this the hard way."

The words were hardly from his lips when the afi behind him rushed forward. They were disorganized, each one gripping their blade differently than the next, and fear flashed across their faces.

Kyler swiftly nocked another arrow, landing aim on the neck of another afi. Something bitter rose in his chest as his fingers pinched the feathers, his gaze lingering on the freckles that lined the afi's soft nose and the stains that covered his pale tunic.

This wasn't a soldier. This was a man.

The tip of the arrow pierced his throat, and just like the first, he fell, choking in the water.

Aeron mumbled an apology as he dropped his hold on Draven and pulled his weapon free. The kilder stumbled against the wall, catching himself against the stone.

Kyler lowered his bow and reached for his sword, only to find his hip bare.

"Sannir's Saints," he breathed. He'd left it at the inn.

A wide-shouldered man shoved past Novah, charging at Kyler with an outstretched palm. The commander dropped his bow, widening his stance as his feet slipped on algae. He caught the wrist of the afi, and the man grunted as he slammed into Kyler, sending them both tumbling into stone and sewage with a painful smack.

Water rushed into Kyler's mouth and nose, his body pinned beneath the larger man. He kept his grip on the afi's wrists, refusing to let his palms anywhere near the exposed skin of his neck. He'd rather drown than suffer Tophet.

The afi struggled, letting his blade clatter to the ground as he attempted to rip his arms free. Kyler's lungs trembled as he gasped water into them and, though muffled, a shout met his ears.

The shout was quickly followed by a scream as the afi slumped, and Kyler shoved the man off him.

He rolled to his knees, coughing up brown water. Aeron gripped his forearm, hauling him to his feet and shoving his bow back into his arms.

Only two afi remained standing, and behind them, Elizus' face twisted with frustration.

Novah drove her blade into the stomach of the afi nearest to her, and his disheveled cloak soaked in crimson as he crumbled at her feet. The final afi watched in horror, his young face full of fear. He hesitated, as if debating his fate. Then he turned and ran down a separate tunnel, disappearing into the dark.

"Some threat," Corbin muttered.

Kyler lifted his arrow to the prince once more, only to find him turning his back. Mumbled curses fell from his lips as he began an easy stroll, but one word came out sharper than the rest.

Snake.

He spoke it like a name he wanted to forget.

Kyler readied himself to land his shot, but Novah placed a hand on his forearm, urging him to lower his bow.

"He's right there," Kyler hissed. "I can get him, Novah."

She kept her hand steady. "Kill him now, and we make fugitives of ourselves. The satyr knows we're here, and if we kill the only heir to Potri, the entire kingdom will too. Let him go—this time."

Kyler lowered his bow and watched as the prince faded into the darkness of the sewers.

Aeron sheathed his blade. "They won't stay away for long. The prince was insistent." He strode to where he'd left Draven. The kilder grumbled something about how he would fight next time, which earned a chuckle from Corbin as he helped steady the injured soldier.

Kyler fell in pace with Novah as she led them down another tunnel, tapping across her sheathed sword as she thought.

"The prince knew you," Kyler stated, glancing at her from the corner of his eye.

She shook her head slowly. "I know what you're implying but no, we've never met." She took a deep breath. "I think he's an alithias."

A remnant of the war between Adoni and Orisis, alith was a magic so rare that most people didn't believe it still existed. It was more ability than magic, unhindered by the laws of Adoni and following no patterns or bloodlines. An alithias was born with the ability to see truth—to read a person's soul with nothing more than a glance. It was twisted and unstable magic, but effective nonetheless.

"Even if he possesses alith, he's with Orisis," Kyler reasoned. "An afi can't keep *any* type of magic, alith included. The prince would have had to trade it."

Novah's lips twisted in thought. "He might not be an afi. Maybe he doesn't possess the touch of death."

"Who in their right mind would serve Orisis while still subject to his destruction? He would have nothing to gain for his alliance with the god."

She shrugged. "I wouldn't say he is in his right mind. Either way, I'm more concerned with his implication about Uriah."

Kyler pinched his tongue between his teeth. That comment hadn't gotten past him either. He desperately wished he'd traded his blood for the knowledge from Ophir.

"I know you're not going to like this," he began slowly, "but I think we need to consider accepting the celestial's offer."

She puffed a breath, her churning thoughts evident from the furrow of her brows and shifting of her jaw. "You might be right. At this point, any move we make will involve some level of risk. This might be a risk worth taking."

Kyler narrowed his gaze with an edge of playfulness. "So, you're *not* going to slit my throat?"

A grin brought dimples to her cheeks, and she turned back to the sewers. "You're not out of trouble yet, Commander. But yes, your throat is safe. For now."

Kyler smiled, something that surprised him given their current situation, but he decided not to push her and fell in line beside Corbin once more.

They walked in silence, pausing occasionally for Novah to

listen for the sounds of footsteps. She led them with a certainty Kyler didn't possess, her keen sense of direction leading them farther and farther from the center of the city. Kyler supposed that the time she spent locked in her room with her maps had proven useful.

It was well past midday by the time Novah paused at another ladder, shielding her eyes from the warm sunlight that slipped through the iron as she gazed up. "This will do."

Kyler pulled the bow from his shoulders, passing it into Novah's hands, and reached for the ladder. "Watch my back."

She nodded, and drew an arrow with skilled ease, aiming above Kyler's head.

The metal grate was firmly rusted to the ground despite Kyler's efforts. It took him pushing with his shoulders to finally inch it out of place. The metal shifted with a groan, and Kyler risked a look around.

Novah had taken them to the edge of the city where buildings were scarce and the peaks of the castle were barely visible in the distance. Mountains walled them in, creating a barrier between the city and the ocean that wrapped around the island. Lanterns flickered in distant windows as the sun hung low between the mountains, and clear skies revealed hues of orange and yellow.

"Clear." Kyler hauled himself onto the cobblestone, turning back to offer Draven a hand.

"This won't be fun," Corbin mumbled, moving aside as Aeron brought Draven to the ladder.

Draven forced a laugh and took hold of the metal bars.

"Slow and steady," Kyler instructed, glancing up to the sky.

Corbin and Aeron lifted Draven as far as they could manage before Kyler took hold of the soldier's arms. Draven was surprisingly light as Kyler pulled him onto the cracked stone, and though he grimaced with discomfort, he didn't complain.

Corbin was next, then Aeron. When they reached the top, Novah shouldered Kyler's bow and scaled the ladder, passing his weapon back into his hands as she climbed out of the grate.

"I'm no surveyor." She looked to Kyler. "Will the mountains keep us safe?"

Kyler eyed them, studying the dying trees and dry grass that covered the rolling rock. "We'll want to make camp on the leeward side." He motioned to the right face of the mountains. "The wind will be less harsh."

He looked back to Novah, finding a small smile on her face. She almost looked relieved.

"Take the lead."

Usually, his pride would swell at Novah asking for his advice, but for some reason, the feeling never came. Instead, a lump sat in Kyler's chest, sending chills along his skin that he attributed to the cool air.

Kyler kept his steps light as he adjusted their course, heading toward the edge of the mountains. Wind ripped through the valleys and between the peaks, rustling their cloaks and making the potions at Kyler's side knock against one another as they walked away from the city. Kyler found himself looking over his shoulder, convinced the prince was following them in the shadows, but he saw nothing but trees and rocks.

He found a clear path quickly—a course with minimal elevation and few hazards. It would be a longer route, but with Draven's state, any steep inclines could leave them worse off than before. The scattered trees made for good concealment, and as Corbin finished covering their tracks, they finally came to a stop along a rounded plateau just out of sight of the city.

"We can make camp here." Kyler dropped his potion bag to

the ground, cringing slightly as the broken glass crunched.

Draven sighed in relief, and Corbin offered Aeron a hand as they eased Draven onto a patch of grass.

Kyler knelt beside his bag, tugging the straps free and lifting the leather flap to view the damage. He was glad to see a few larger bottles of Ponos still intact, their shimmering yellow sloshing within their vials. There was still some Zalis for headaches and Moundi for cleaning wounds, but several bottles had shattered, scraping the leather interior of the bag and soaking it with scents of basil and moss. He began to pick up the untouched vials from the mess, placing them on the grass beside him.

"Did any make it?" Novah came to his side, sitting on her heels as she watched him.

Kyler nodded to the pile beside him, which was much smaller than he'd hoped.

She frowned. "Enough for Draven?"

"I hope so." Kyler eyed the kilder, who joked lightly with Corbin and Aeron. He had spirit, that much was evident, but his leg needed to heal properly. Beside him, Aeron held a piece of cloth to his head, wiping the dried blood from his temple with a wince.

Kyler's gaze fell to Novah, finding her knuckles scattered with scrapes just like his own. He reached for the Moundi and tugged the cork free before passing it to her. "For your hands. Pour slowly, it'll sting."

She did as he said, dripping the silver over her raw knuckles. A soft hiss slipped through her teeth as the potion began to bubble, pushing the dirt and sweat from her skin and leaving the scrapes clean.

Kyler accepted the vial as she handed it back, dribbling the same onto his own hands before corking it once more.

"Are you able to brew more?"

"I should be." Kyler set the potion back down and continued his search for anything salvageable. "We haven't been away from the Pass too long. I'll just need ingredients, and I'll have to be precise with measurements."

Novah nodded slowly, her gaze settling on the grass at their feet.

"What are you thinking?" He didn't look at her as he asked, but he spoke low enough that the others wouldn't hear.

She released a frustrated sigh, shaking out her still-stinging hands. "I don't know. You're right, we need that information from the celestial, but not at the cost of our blood. I just don't understand how they found us. We were careful. We all were, even you."

He cracked a smirk. "I'm going to take that as a compliment."

Her face remained serious. "You might be foolish, but you wouldn't have allowed anyone to follow you back to our inn. And the prince was waiting for us in those sewers like he knew we were coming. Orisis must have eyes everywhere."

Kyler pulled the final potion from his bag. "Or he has one set of eyes that knew where we were staying."

"You think Clide fed the afi information?"

Kyler shrugged. "Who else?"

She dipped her head in thought once more. "He lost his inn. The amphipteres destroyed it."

"An inn in exchange for power over death? That seems like a fair trade to me." Kyler tipped his bag, dumping the glass at his feet. "Either way, I'm not sure how much longer we'll be safe in Potri. If you want my advice, I think we should get that information and get back home."

Novah gave a tight frown. "He was insistent on the blood?"

"'There is nothing else you can offer me'," Kyler repeated the words of the celestial.

Her gaze flitted in the direction of the city. "Can you take me to him?"

"To negotiate?"

"I think it's worth a try."

Kyler held her gaze for a moment, then nodded. "I can take you."

CHAPTER TWENTY-ONE

DESPITE THE STILL-FIERY SKY AND HANGING THREAT OF THE AFI, Kyler managed to doze off. His body was exhausted from so little sleep that even the rocks and roots beneath his back didn't faze him. It wasn't until the sun was hidden behind the peaks and the moon illuminated the ground that Novah woke him—with a kick to the ribs.

Kyler groaned, clutching his side as he caught the edge of her laugh.

"Sleep well?" she chided.

"A simple 'time to go' would have been acceptable." He propped himself up, his side throbbing lightly.

"I'll be softer next time." She passed him his potion belt, then strapped her blade to her side and tossed her cloak over her shoulders.

Kyler shoved to his feet, rubbing his side with an exaggerated grimace.

Novah rolled her eyes. "You're being dramatic."

He chuckled and tightened his potions to his waist. He tugged free another vial of Ponos, tossing it to Corbin who sat beside a sleeping Draven. "Give him that when he wakes."

Aeron shifted, his back against a tree and arms crossed over his chest. "Don't be gone long."

Novah flipped her hood over her head, watching as Kyler strung his bow over his shoulders. "No sword?"

"I left it. I'm a better shot than a swordsman, anyways."

"Swords are faster."

"Not from a hundred yards."

She lifted a brow. "You can make that kind of shot?"

Kyler cracked a grin as he covered his scales. "Underestimating me, yet again."

"I'll believe it when I see it." Though her words were condescending, her tone was light—almost impressed. She turned to Corbin and Aeron. "We'll be back by midnight."

Aeron leaned his head back against the tree trunk. "Don't worry, Draven will keep us safe in your absence."

"I heard that," Draven mumbled, revealing that he wasn't asleep after all.

Aeron let out a laugh.

"Give him that Ponos." Kyler pointed a finger at Corbin as he strode away.

Corbin tossed a lazy salute, and Kyler turned his attention to his footing as Novah trailed him down the same path they'd climbed before. The stars flickered in the dark, and Kyler thought of the telescopes back at the observatory that showed the colors hidden within the night.

"So, tell me," Novah began, pulling Kyler's focus back to her. "How did you become commander?"

"Are you *asking* me to brag?"

She grunted as her foot landed on the other side of a small incline. "I'm making conversation. It's clear that your favorite topic is yourself."

Kyler whistled softly. "Bold. But I could ask you the same,

General."

"Dragons," she said simply—simply enough that Kyler turned to look at her.

"That's not an answer."

She sighed, her gaze traveling to the moon above them. "What do you want to know?"

He thought for a moment before answering. "The Land Brigade doesn't interact with them nearly as much as the Regiment. What are the dragons like?"

She bit the tip of her tongue, and Kyler could tell her mind was being filled with memories. "They're incredibly gentle. Most keep to themselves, but a few enjoy the Regiment's company and will train with us. And they're wise. They can sense our intentions without even speaking to us."

"Can they speak? I thought their language was more…conceptual."

She maneuvered around a line of trees. "In a way. It's less with words and more with feeling. It's hard to explain without experiencing it. Their knowledge is like a pure version of alith, except it reveals more than just truth. It reveals character."

The thought of the dragons seeing good in Uriah made Kyler's chest clench, so he changed the topic. "What's it like in the Pass?"

Something warm brushed over Novah's face, a fondness Kyler hadn't seen her express before. "The Regiment's base is stationed at the entrance of the Pass, but you can't enter the Pass except on dragonback. You fly into the clouds, and after a moment of feeling disoriented, you're in the Dwelling of Dragons."

Kyler sat with this, picturing the golden arches and marble that were said to make up the Dwelling.

"You didn't answer my question," Novah pushed. "How did you become commander?"

Kyler kicked a stone from his path. "The same way you did. The commander before me chose me when he retired."

"That's not what I meant."

She was inching very close to a conversation he wasn't eager to have. "Then what *do* you mean?"

"Why did former Commander Calfner pick you above the others?"

Because Uriah told him to, the silent voice probed, but Kyler refused to accept it as truth. "I was committed to Sannir. He saw potential in me, and I'd already gained an impressive number of scales." He glanced sideways at her, hoping his answer would suffice.

Their conversation dwindled as they reached the city borders, the grass and dirt at their feet becoming stone once more.

"No sewers this time?" Kyler teased as Novah led them down a silent street, away from the main roads.

She chuckled. "Too dirty for you?"

"I still smell like mold."

Once again, Kyler found himself turned around in the numerous streets and alleyways, but Novah remained sharp. It wasn't long before the roads became familiar, and the observatory came into view.

It was much livelier than Kyler's first visit. Visitors occupied the grounds, making use of the tools and telescopes available to them. Charting equipment scattered the area, and figures moved within the observatory walls.

"Busy place." Novah voiced his thoughts.

"Hence the reason I made my visit just before closing."

"And how you got caught," she shot back, though it didn't have quite the edge Kyler was used to. "After you."

Kyler brought them to the entrance, weaving through the

scattered tents and equipment before entering the glass doors, which had been propped open.

The same *gentleman* whom Ophir referred to as Sly was at the counter. He appeared just as kind and welcoming as Kyler's first encounter, his scowl deep and dark eyes flickering with annoyance at the visitors that filled the first floor.

Novah studied the unique furniture and décor as Kyler approached the counter, forcing Sly to meet his eye. "I'm looking for Ophir."

His bug eyes glared at Kyler from beneath his spectacles. "We charge for entry."

"Just point me in his direction, and we'll leave you alone."

Sly's glare deepened.

A sigh fell from Kyler's chest. "I'm not here to use your equipment. We just—"

His argument was cut short by the clink of a coin as Novah slid it across the counter. "Keep the change."

Kyler pursed his lips, a bit annoyed that she'd given in to his request, but the old man seemed satisfied with the payment. "Second floor. Probably by the tapestries."

"Thank you," Novah said kindly, turning before she caught the snarl from Sly's lips. She waited until they reached the stairs to chuckle. "What a charismatic friend you have."

"I only met him yesterday." Kyler rested a hand on the metal railing as he ascended the spiral staircase, squeezing past several visitors on the way up.

"He seemed quite fond of you."

"The scowl radiated respect," he muttered.

Though his back was to her, Kyler could hear the laugh in her voice. "I thought everyone scowled at the sight of you."

"You're hilarious."

"Thank you."

The second floor was just as crowded as the previous, with nearly every table occupied and light chatter filling the space, but it wasn't difficult to spot the celestial.

He was a head taller than everyone else, his dark curls standing out against the pale tapestries as he studied at a table in the far corner.

"That's him?" The smile had fallen from Novah's lips. "Think we can get him alone?"

"Probably not," Kyler answered honestly and began making his way between people and tables. Thankfully no one paid the two of them any mind, but Kyler felt Ophir's stare the moment his glassy eyes fell on them.

His voice was low as he spoke kindly to a visitor, pointing the young girl in the direction of a completed map. He straightened in his seat as Kyler and Novah approached.

"I'm surprised to see you so soon, Kyler." Ophir set down his ink pen, folding his hands as he looked up at them.

Hesitant to have this conversation around so many ears, Kyler dipped his voice. "Any chance you could spare a moment?"

He sighed, glancing around the crowded room. "I suppose I could." He turned to Novah, his gaze unhindered by shadows of her hood. He dipped his head in a subtle bow. "General."

She didn't flinch, though Kyler wondered if the celestial's words made her as uncomfortable as they did him. She simply nodded, and Ophir stood.

"Follow me."

He guided them through the busy room, excusing himself as he maneuvered his large frame around people huddled beside telescopes and books. It wasn't until he came to a dark wooden door on the other end of the room that he stopped, pulling a silver key from his pocket and inserting it into the curved handle. The hinges swung without a creak, and he motioned them inside, shutting the door behind them.

The room was an office, neatly furnished and well-kept, with dark curtains and low oil lamps. A square desk made of smooth redwood took up most of the space, accompanied by two chairs of brown leather. A thick bookshelf full of various volumes and trinkets sat against the wall, and atop the dark rug was a globe that appeared older than Ophir himself.

The celestial strode across the room and took a seat in the desk chair, which sunk slightly under his weight.

"Please." He motioned to the leather seats. "I assume you've come to discuss my proposal?" Ophir folded his long fingers under his chin, his gaze staying mostly on Kyler.

"That's correct," Novah answered. To Kyler's surprise, she lowered her hood. "You have information we need, and we have the blood you want."

Ophir's eyes traveled across her scales, his face expressionless.

"You know what you ask of us." She stated it as a fact.

He nodded. "And do you know what you ask of me?"

Kyler leaned his elbows on his knees before answering. "We ask for knowledge that may mean the fall of our kingdom if not given."

"You must understand something." Ophir dropped his gaze to his desk. "I do not care for your kingdom in the way you do. What you ask of me is guaranteed to put a target on my back. Your blood is more valuable than anything you can offer me and is the only thing for which willing to risk my life."

His words hung in the air, filling the silence with his implication.

Novah's face revealed nothing of her thoughts. "How much?"

Kyler's brows dipped, unsure of her intentions.

Ophir took his time, playing with the cuffs of his sleeves as he thought. Finally, he nodded to Kyler's belt of potions. "Two vials. That size."

Kyler bit his tongue. "That's more than anyone needs."

Ophir watched Novah, waiting for a response.

"I can give you half a vial and a chest plate made in Sannir."

"I have no use for a chest plate."

"A knife, then. One crafted by the most skilled blacksmith our kingdom can offer."

"One *full* vial and the knife."

Kyler's pulse drummed, picturing the power a vial of elven blood would hold. Any magic Ophir attempted with the blood would succeed as if beneath the Pass—good or evil.

Novah's fingers danced along the seams of the armchair, her teeth digging into the side of her cheek in thought. "Alright."

"Hold on." Kyler shifted to the edge of his seat, looking Novah in the eye. "Are you sure about this?"

"That's the deal." There was a hint of caution in her voice, but if Ophir caught it, he didn't show. "What do you know about General Uriah?"

Ophir leaned back in his chair, his gaze flickering back to Kyler. "I understand your urgency, but I can't risk you disappearing without payment. I will need time to verify the constellations. I can meet you in two days with all the answers you seek, and that is when I want your blood."

CHAPTER TWENTY-TWO

KYLER WAITED UNTIL THE CITY WAS BEHIND THEM, WITH ONLY the trees to keep them company to question Novah. He placed a hand on her shoulder, bringing her to a halt, and spun her around to face him.

"Why did you give in to him?" he asked. She'd been so certain since the moment they stepped foot in this city—her decisions final and movements calculated. This wasn't like the general he'd come to know over the past few days.

Novah took a deep breath and pressed her eyes shut for a moment. "My blood may not be as potent as the rest of yours. A single vial won't be as powerful as Ophir expects, and by the time he realizes it, we'll be back in Sannir with all the answers we need."

Kyler dropped his hand from her shoulder, cocking his head as he crossed his arms. "What's that supposed to mean?"

"I haven't studied magic like you have. I've never wielded it." She turned and continued on the path toward their makeshift camp in the mountains. "We'll give him a vial of my blood."

"It doesn't work like that."

"It's the wisest option."

Kyler's steps were muffled by rotted leaves as he paced to her side once more, attempting to catch her expression in the light of the moon. "I still don't understand why you let him talk you into it. If your blood gets into the wrong hands, you'll be blamed for it. The king could strip you of your position. Saints, even the dragons could get involved."

"*Queen,*" Novah corrected, reminding him of how desperate their situation was. "And Ophir didn't talk me into anything, Commander. I made the choice. It was blood or Sannir, and our kingdom comes first."

"Why?"

She slowed. "Why Sannir?"

"Why take the punishment if it backfires?" Kyler rounded her, placing himself in her path and forcing her to come to a stop once again. "You're the general. You say the word, and any one of us would have to give our blood. You could force me to do it and save your own neck."

Novah was silent for a moment. Her mask of certainty was slipping, and Kyler saw something else beneath it—fear. She quickly steeled herself. "Because this falls on my shoulders. We knew this mission wouldn't be without sacrifice, and it's my job to take the brunt of the losses." A small smile tugged at her lips, though it seemed strained. "Besides, I don't think I could force you to do anything."

"Now you're catching on." Kyler smiled back, but it fell as quickly as it came. "One vial?"

She nodded firmly. "One vial." She began to move past him, but he caught her elbow, not quite finished with their conversation.

"You called me 'Commander'."

She pressed her lips into a thin line. "Yes."

He dropped his hold. "Does that mean I still have my

position?"

She sighed—though there was an edge of laughter to it—and faced him fully. "What you did was wrong."

"Which part?"

She tried to hide her humor but to no avail. "All of it." She tapped his chest lightly. "But in the last few hours, I've seen a change in you."

He raised a brow. "Oh?"

"You're not as insufferable."

Kyler chuckled and tapped her shoulder, mimicking her gesture. "And you trusted my judgment."

She pressed her tongue against her cheek as she studied him. "Your judgment isn't perfect, but perhaps you have some redeeming qualities." She turned back toward their camp once more, and this time, Kyler fell in stride beside her. "You're proving yourself trustworthy, Commander."

He smiled to himself, deciding to drop the teasing and enjoy the understanding they'd come to. They spent the rest of their walk in silence—the comfortable kind, acknowledging each other's need to be alone with their thoughts. When the trail became steep, Novah slowed to allow Kyler to take the lead, his skills as a foot soldier proving useful once more. Despite the darkness, he had no trouble finding their previous path, and before long, they reached their base in the rocks.

Corbin stood the moment they came into view. Aeron rose with him, and even Draven shifted to sit upright.

"Well?" The anxiety in Corbin's tone spiked Kyler's nerves.

Novah unclipped her cape, draping it over her arm, before addressing the men. "We've struck a deal with the celestial. A vial of blood and a Sannir-made knife for his help."

"You agreed to blood?" Aeron's brows lifted. "Whose are we

giving him?"

Before she could answer, Kyler spoke up. "The general wishes to give her own." He could feel all eyes shift to him as he placed his bow on the grass beside his potion bag. "It's her decision to make and hers alone."

The three of them traded glances, and Kyler knew their minds slipped to the previous morning—when Kyler had been eager to undermine her authority.

Novah cleared her throat, pulling their attention back to the situation at hand. "This may be our only opportunity, and we're going to take it."

"I'll do it," Aeron said, already pulling a dagger from his belt.

A faint smile rose to her face, but she kept her cool demeanor. "It's alright, Lieutenant. I've got plenty to go around."

He set his jaw, stealing a glance at Draven. "It's unwise, General."

She lifted her brow in silent defiance. "You've studied magic. I haven't."

"I rarely practice it."

She sighed, holding out her palm for him to pass over the blade. "Don't fight me on this, Aeron."

Draven scoffed. "Good luck changing his mind."

The look on Novah's face was almost playful, like she expected this sort of resistance from the two of them. "I just finished putting Commander Kyler in his place. I don't need to wrestle you too."

Aeron's voice dipped, so low that Kyler struggled to make it out. "Novah, if this gets back to you—"

"Yes, I've already gotten the lecture from Kyler. Now, please." She jutted her hand forward, urging him again to pass his dagger.

Aeron frowned, debating for only a moment before giving in,

and passed the knife into her hand.

"Thank you." She edged the tip of the blade into the pad of her finger, piercing the skin without so much as a flinch. A dot of red bubbled, and she kept her eyes fixated on the cut. "Kyler, a vial."

Kyler knelt to his potion bag, pushing bottles aside until he found an empty one, and passed it to her.

Novah's blood dripped in steady droplets. It caught the light of the moon, and for a moment, Kyler swore he could see the magic within, spinning in red and black as it pooled. She was careful not to spill as it drizzled into the vial. Once it was full, she corked the lid and lifted it to the light with a small frown on her lips.

"He has two nights." She tucked the bottle into her pocket. "Then we move."

. . .

Kyler struggled to get comfortable. The rocks and twigs bothered him more now that he was no longer aching for sleep. He flipped to his back, resting his head against his cloak, and let his heavy eyes meet the stars that poked through the trees. He tried not to imagine the messages that might be hidden in their shine, and instead let his mind wander back home.

The night was still young, and Salcon and Adri would have just finished a day of archery training with the buggers. They'd probably spend their night at the Lone Wolf for some well-deserved Apola. Salcon, of course, would skip the raspberry.

Kyler could practically feel the warm atmosphere despite the cold mountain air, imagining the enchanted lights and the band playing all their favorite songs. When they'd had their fill, his lieutenants would make their way back to the barracks, where the fireplace would be roaring in the common area and small beds with thick quilts awaited them. Then, they'd wake with the sun, eat under-seasoned eggs, and begin another day of training.

His mind shifted, filling with thoughts of Aiyanna—her laugh as he'd stumbled through her window, the feel of her head on his chest, and the sound of her voice as she'd describe the flowers she'd pressed and framed that day. He could smell her perfume, picture every curve of her face, feel her fingers in his hair.

Hear the tears in the shake of her words, feel her shove. *Selfish and arrogant.*

Kyler hadn't noticed the smile that'd crept onto his face until it fell. He shut his eyes and rolled to his side, burying his face in his arms. He needed sleep.

Despite his restless mind, sleep came. Kyler closed his eyes to darkness and stars and woke to warm morning light and pleasant conversation. It was well past dawn, the sun inching higher, and the clang of metal mixed with occasional laughter as Kyler pulled his groggy thoughts into reality.

"Faster, Corbin." Novah leaned a shoulder against the trunk of a nearby tree, the bark clinging to her cotton shirt. "You can't compete with his strength, but you can move quicker."

Before her, Corbin and Aeron stood with blades lifted, their steady steps crunching against the dry grass.

"Are you calling me weak?" Corbin teased through heavy breaths.

Aeron chuckled. "I think she's calling me slow."

Draven's voice came from Kyler's left as the commander sat upright. "You both are slow *and* weak."

"Watch it," Aeron snapped. "I'll bust your other leg."

Draven grinned, lacing his fingers behind his head. "I would like to see you try."

Aeron grunted as Corbin knocked the weapon from his hand, sending Aeron to his knees with a blade against his throat.

"Well done." Aeron accepted Corbin's outstretched hand, allowing the Land Brigade soldier to haul him to his feet. "You're stronger than you look."

"And you, faster," Corbin grinned.

Novah nodded. "Again."

"You're worse than Kyler," Corbin sighed, lifting his blade. Sweat glistened off his forehead, but his smile remained.

"And speaking of..." Aeron caught sight of Kyler as he approached, stopping at Novah's side to observe the training.

"Don't stop on my account." He waved a hand and crossed his arms over his chest.

Novah's brows lifted as if playfully scolding her soldiers for getting distracted. "Begin."

They resumed their sparring, and Novah turned to Kyler. "Sleep well?"

He rolled his shoulders. "Seeing how no afi tried to steal our souls, I'd say the ground wasn't terrible."

She hummed lightly. "I do miss those beds at the inn."

"I miss the beds at the barracks, even if they are horribly flat."

"If your celestial comes through, you should be back in your flat bed in just a few days."

Kyler cracked a smile, turning his attention to the match before him. He studied both of their fighting styles, watching their footwork and movement, and critiqued each in his mind.

Aeron was a brunt force with powerful swings, yet his steps were light and counters were smooth. Corbin's style was familiar, and Kyler knew his downfall was striking in even numbers. It was a subconscious habit that Aeron picked up on, throwing Corbin out of rhythm.

Corbin was disarmed a moment later, his lips curving into a frown. "I thought I had you."

Aeron chuckled. He retrieved Corbin's weapon from the ground and handed it back. "You attack—"

"In evens," Corbin finished, rolling his eyes in Kyler's direction. "Yes, I'm aware."

Kyler shrugged. "If you're so aware, why do you keep doing it?"

Aeron grinned at the ridicule, but Corbin's scowl only deepened. "Fine. I'll switch to only odds."

"And I'll disarm you just as quickly." Aeron spun his blade, lifting it to start again.

Novah straightened, an idea forming across her face. "That might work. Aeron, strike only if he moves on evens. Corbin, attack on odds."

The two glanced at each other before nodding and taking up position.

"Begin."

The clashing of blades filled the air once more, and this time, Corbin focused on his counting.

"He's a good swordsman." Novah's shoulder brushed Kyler's as she dipped her voice, low enough that Corbin couldn't hear. "He adapts quickly and can read his opponent well."

Kyler kept his eyes on the sparring. "He is, but he's even better without a weapon. His hand-to-hand is what advanced him so quickly through the ranks."

"And your hand-to-hand?"

Kyler glanced at her and shrugged. "Not awful. I prefer a weapon."

"How good are you with a crossbow?"

"I'm alright. We don't use them much."

She turned back to the fight. "The Regiment favors them over traditional bows. Easier to handle from the back of a dragon."

"I'd never considered that."

Corbin hesitated. His attack lingered on his fourth strike, and Aeron took his opportunity, battering Corbin's weapon from his hand.

"Saints!" Corbin cursed as his sword clattered to the grass.

Aeron's laugh filled the air, loud enough that it doubled him over. "Don't look so bitter, Corbin!"

Corbin huffed, crossing his arms like an irritated child.

"Don't be hard on him, Aeron," Draven teased. "He's learning how to count."

"Alright!" Corbin snapped. "One more try."

Novah interrupted, "Actually, Lieutenant, I hear you're excellent in hand-to-hand."

Corbin straightened, eyeing Kyler with a smile. "Some would say."

"I'd like to see for myself." She motioned for Kyler to step forward. "Commander?"

Kyler stilled. "Me?"

"That's right. Corbin needs a challenge, and you need improvement."

He sighed, running a hand through his disheveled hair. "I won't go easy."

Corbin set his sword against a nearby tree. "You never have."

"For Sannir's sake, don't hurt each other," Novah threatened as Aeron came to her side, "Or I'll set Draven loose on you both."

"I'm terrified." Corbin grinned at Draven.

Draven narrowed his eyes. "You should be."

Kyler positioned himself before Corbin and rolled his shoulders, taking note of the excited look in his lieutenant's eye. "Remember, I'm still your superior."

Corbin lifted his fists, his stance comfortable, and jutted his chin toward Novah. "And she's yours."

"And *she* said not to hurt each other." Leaves crunched under Novah's feet as she shifted. "Begin."

The word was hardly through her lips when Corbin struck, his left hand coming within inches of Kyler's face. The commander dodged, but not before Corbin landed a hit to his stomach, knocking the air from his lungs. A muttered curse fell from Kyler's lips as he stumbled and regained his footing, forcing a breath into his lungs.

Corbin laughed, but the sound was cut short as Kyler landed a hit of his own, his knuckles slamming against Corbin's shoulder as the lieutenant ducked. The small victory was short lived as Corbin caught Kyler's stomach once more, making him drop his hands with a grunt.

That was all Corbin needed. Kyler flinched as Corbin's knuckles paused just a breath away from his nose, his aim perfect enough to break it if he wished to.

"That would've knocked you out," Corbin teased, his hand still hovering.

Kyler panted. "You can't hit *that* hard."

"He has a point," Aeron called from the sidelines. "The commander's skull is quite thick."

Even Novah chuckled at that, and Kyler jabbed a finger at Aeron. "Watch it."

Corbin gave Kyler's shoulder a shake. "He doesn't take losing very well."

This only made Aeron laugh harder, and Kyler bristled. He wasn't going to let Corbin go that easy. He shot his lieutenant an arrogant grin before announcing, "Corbin's real name is 'Lovis'."

"I swear to Sannir—" Corbin's curse was cut off as laughter erupted once more.

"Lovis?" Novah sputtered.

Corbin scowled.

"That's payback." Kyler slung an arm around Corbin's neck, and his lieutenant shoved him off as he muttered another curse.

Kyler tossed him a wink, feeling vindicated as Novah reined in their laughter.

"That's enough for today, gentlemen." She shot Draven a look as he bit back another snicker. "The celestial won't have our information until tomorrow night, which means we can still search the city while we wait." Her hands moved to her hair, pulling it away from her face as she spoke. "Corbin and Kyler, head back into town. It doesn't matter where, just keep your hoods up. Stop by the inn if you get the chance and see if you can find anything that points back to us.

"Aeron, you're free to do what you'd like. I'll do a pass by the castle and then see if I can find some food so we won't be eating dried fruit for the next two days."

Corbin pressed his palms together in thanks, and Novah shook her head with a smile. "I want a report on everything you find." She turned to Kyler. *"Everything."*

He tossed a lazy salute. "You've got it."

CHAPTER TWENTY-THREE

DESPITE THE COVER OF CLOUDS THAT'D BEGUN TO ROLL IN, THE city was bright and bustling, a stark difference to the quiet night before. Kyler felt as though everyone they passed was attempting to catch a glimpse beneath his hood, searching for the scales that would draw the attention of amphipteres once more. But the cry of the beasts never came.

Corbin strode at Kyler's side, their cloaks tangling in the frigid wind that swept through the city. They weren't the only ones— nearly everyone they passed donned heavy fabric, with hoods high over their ears and coats draped around their shoulders.

Corbin shielded his eyes from the sun, looking up at the castle of Potri as they neared. "It must be amazing to live there."

While the castle of Sannir was made for functionality, the closer they came to the castle of Potri, the more evident it was that this structure was made for show. Pale sunlight cut through the glass walls, sending scattered rainbows to the street below. Tapestries were showcased along the walls and a large harp sat beside a piano so white, it rivaled Novah's scale. Farther down, rooms full of couches and chairs, which looked to have never been sat in, faced the city below, and hallways of portraits stared toward the docks.

Kyler searched the towers for a sign of Prince Elizus, but just as before, the rooms of glass were vacant. He dropped his gaze to Corbin, finding his lieutenant still studying the structure.

"Ask the prince for a tour next time we meet," Kyler quipped.

Corbin shoved his shoulder into Kyler's, earning a stifled laugh. But his laugh quickly fell as they neared the inn—or what was left of it.

The buildings that lined the cobblestone sat charred and torn, the bitter scent of smoke still tainting the air. Glass from the melted windows lay drooped against the brick and beams, and the structures looked so weak, it was a miracle the wind hadn't knocked the remnants down.

People slowed as they passed the line of ruin that marked death and destruction, standing out against the city like a fresh wound.

In the center of it all was a familiar satyr, whose usual smile was replaced with sorrow. The Gray Lady was nothing more than burnt wood and charred quilts flapping in the breeze. The look on the satyr's face made Kyler wince with guilt. He'd accused Clide of working with Orisis, but now the blame seemed misplaced. Clide appeared heartbroken.

Corbin sucked a breath. "Orisis is ruthless."

Kyler couldn't pull his eyes away from the ruins, his throat tightening the longer he stared.

Corbin was silent for a moment. "Do you think people died?"

Kyler didn't answer. He started toward Clide, who was rummaging through the ash. It wasn't until he was at Clide's back that the satyr turned, jumping at the sight of them.

Kyler placed a fist on his chest and dipped his chin, preparing to offer his condolences, but the satyr cut him off.

"Don't bother," he snapped. "Leave me."

Kyler stalled, his words halting on his tongue. "Clide, I'm so sorry you—"

"Look what you did!" he seethed, motioning to the place where his inn had once stood. "Your apologies mean nothing!"

"I swear to you, we did not do this."

His nostrils flared. "So, the twisted beasts that attacked my inn were hunting for another group of Sannir soldiers?"

Kyler glanced to Corbin, who was looking everywhere but at the satyr.

The commander sighed. "Yes, they came for us. But we had no intention of—"

"Save it." Clide turned his back.

Kyler lifted his face to the sky, his skin burning despite the cold. "Can I at least check for my sword?"

The satyr scoffed. "*If* your sword survived, it's mine. I think that's payment enough for the damage you've done."

"It was a gift from my father."

"It was valuable to you?" His tone was soaked in condescension. "I'm terribly sorry *you* lost something of value."

Corbin tugged at Kyler's elbow. "Let's leave him be."

"We didn't mean for this to happen." Kyler yanked himself free of Corbin's hold. "We're trying to hunt them down and rid your city of them. We're doing you a favor."

Clide lifted his chin, defiance dancing across his face. "Because they attacked Sannir, right? If they hadn't, you would still be tucked away in your kingdom, keeping magic to yourself."

The argument Kyler had prepared dissipated as the truth of Clide's words sunk into his chest.

The satyr continued, "You have the power of Adoni at your fingertips, and yet all you use it for is party tricks and enjoyment potions." He turned his back once more. "Leave me. I won't ask again."

This time, Kyler didn't argue as Corbin tugged him away.

They continued their walk in silence, the bittersweet smell of ash still dusting the air. The magic of Adoni was a gift. The elves and dragons were the only ones who stood by Adoni's side when he had declared war on Orisis, and because of that, they were rewarded.

But that was a thousand years ago. The elves of Eliab's army had long since passed from blade or arrow. The beings alive now were not the same ones that stood by Orisis or Adoni, yet all of them answered for the deeds of their ancestors.

Kyler hadn't earned a life with magic any more than Clide had earned a life without it.

He shook his thoughts away and focused on keeping up with Corbin, weaving through the crowds. Corbin took a few more turns, passing tailor shops and meat markets, and Kyler knew exactly where Corbin was leading him. The lieutenant was convinced that the library would bring answers or enlightenment, but Kyler had his doubts. In a city crawling with afi, he found it difficult to believe their secrets were simply sitting on the shelves for anyone to read.

The library was impossible to miss. It stood only two stories, but its height came from the statues that lined the flat roof. They stood along the edge with solemn faces, philosophers and writers preserved perfectly in gray stone, their books in hand. The building itself was long, constructed of the same stone as the statues and decorated with columns. Arched windows had been carved into every wall, and stairs stretched up to three sets of wooden doors.

"We won't spend long in here, right?" Kyler asked as they reached the steps.

Corbin grinned. "Is that an order?"

Kyler bit his tongue as they ascended, passing the columns and brushing past scholars who came and went, their noses dipped into book pages.

The first thing Kyler noticed as they entered was the ceiling. It was high and embossed, painted in hues of dusty blue and gold. The colors matched the weathered carpets that covered the pale wood floors and draped across steps, leading toward the differing sections. Wide windows filtered in cool light, enough that the interior lamps were unlit. Despite the countless people roaming the shelves, not a word was exchanged.

Corbin paused, scanning the map on the side wall, until he tapped a finger on the section labeled *Foreign Affairs*. "Let's start here."

Kyler scrunched his nose but followed, taking in the paintings and statues that accompanied the wall-to-ceiling shelves packed with books. Despite the apparent age of both the building and its contents, the library smelled fresh. Kyler trailed Corbin past several long tables scattered with people hunched over books. Quills scratched against clean parchment as students and scholars worked on their projects in silence.

Corbin stopped under a wooden sign that signaled they were in the right spot and turned down the line of books. His fingers ran along the spines, brushing leather and paper as he scanned the shelf. "I'm thinking we should look for anything on disputes between Sannir and Potri. Maybe that will reveal the ties between Potri and Orisis." He paused to tug a red hardcover from the shelf and tucked it under his arm.

Kyler studied the spines, some of the text faded and worn. "I doubt there are any. Sannir has had a long time of peace, and Orisis doesn't make political alliances."

He shrugged, adding a tattered leatherbound to his growing stack. "Maybe. But if that's the case, why is he working with the prince?"

Kyler sighed, his eyes trailing up the shelves. Corbin was right, but the information he sought was a sliver in a thousand years of history. They could spend weeks in the library, looking for a single page of a single book, and never find it.

"You head up to the second floor." Corbin had at least six books in his arms as he started for the tables. "There should be a section on religion. Grab anything you can find on Orisis."

Just as he'd said, Kyler found nearly a quarter of the upstairs area to be filled with religious texts and histories. The collection was expansive, with shelves containing countless authors and titles that Kyler had never heard of. After making it through three rows, his head was already spinning.

He stepped back, taking a breath. Corbin was right, they needed as much information as they could get, but without knowing where to start, he felt as though he were drowning in endless texts and jumbled information. He turned his back to the shelves, letting his mind settle.

Several other sections filled the second level, marked by matching signs to help navigate. There was an area for astronomy, which split into several smaller sections, a place for children's books, and an agricultural area that was blocked off by a glass door. But Kyler's attention was pulled toward a small corner labeled *Potions and Ailments*. Intrigued, he abandoned the religious texts and ducked between the shelves.

The first book he pulled was small and thin, nothing more than a picture book showcasing the easiest potions for beginners—potions he was very familiar with. Digging deeper, however, he found himself thumbing through volumes from across the realm. Alchemists from Xynack, the Middle Islands, Sannir and even as far as Midith and Junic—countries Kyler had never bothered to study—noted potions with obscure ingredients and curious effects. The authors had little skill with words, but Kyler was able to follow along easily as they revealed brewing techniques he'd never heard of and introduced potions with abilities such as hypnotizing and rapid healing.

Though Sannir received its magic from the Dragon Pass, it hadn't always been that way. There was a time early in Vellichor's history when every corner of the realm had access to the magic of Adoni, and some of these texts appeared older than the Pass itself. Others were more recent, and those were the books that Kyler found most intriguing. It seemed a few people had found ways to continue their practice of alchemy despite their separation from Adoni, scouring the realm for remnants of the war between the gods. Like a battlefield, Vellichor held pockets of history, housing ancient magic that desperate alchemists stumbled upon. The potions they brewed with this magic, however, were incomplete and resulted in crude twists and odd side effects.

Realizing he'd been gone awhile, Kyler grabbed whichever books would fit in his arms and carefully made his way back to Corbin.

Corbin looked up as he approached, eyeing the stack of books in his hands. He cleared a space for Kyler to set them down and grabbed the top book off his pile.

"Find anything good?" His curiosity turned to a frown when he read the title. "What's this about?"

Kyler pulled the book from his hands as he took a seat, scraping his chair against the wooden floor. "Potions for morphing and disguising."

"What about—"

"Don't worry about it." Kyler pulled a piece of parchment from the stack in the center of the table, as well as a quill from the jar beside it. "You do that, I'll do this."

"We're not here for potions."

Kyler flipped open a page and tapped the text. "Have you ever heard of a potion that can change the appearance of its drinker?"

Corbin hesitated. "No."

"Exactly. Imagine the advantage this type of knowledge could give us." He flipped open another book, pausing as a specific potion caught his eye. "See this? Pevoth. It's made with an herb common to the Middle Islands and can heal injuries up to twenty times faster than the body's normal speed."

The pieces began to click in Corbin's mind. "With that, we could get Draven on his feet in no time."

"This could change the way we deal with injuries entirely."

Corbin nodded, turning back to his own books. "I can work on this."

Kyler grinned, turning back to his book. "That's the spirit."

CHAPTER TWENTY-FOUR

IT WAS NEARLY DUSK BY THE TIME KYLER AND CORBIN LEFT THE library. Notes filled Kyler's pockets and ideas swarmed his mind as he and Corbin strolled through the streets of Potri. It seemed his knowledge of alchemy was actually quite minuscule, and there were dozens of brews he was itching to try.

There were weeds that could be brewed like Moundi, creating potions that slowed heart rate and boosted blood flow, and petals from flowers grown in Xynack that expanded the lungs of its drinker, allowing them to spend extended periods of time underwater.

The one that intrigued him the most, however, was a root whose history was vague at best. Its properties were unclear, but if brewed correctly, it caused any potion to become pain-inducing—though the results seemed to vary depending on what potion it was added to and how.

While Kyler's findings had been many, Corbin walked beside him with a knot between his brows and hands empty of notes. He'd torn through book after book full of information on Orisis and the afi but couldn't find anything that they didn't already know.

The afi were sworn to Orisis in a ceremony, trading whatever magic they once possessed for the touch of death. When magic was freely accessed in the realm, this trade had been costly. But now, the afi were made up of common men and women, all searching for some type of protection or power from Orisis. The trade cost them nothing, and it allowed Orisis to build his army, calling his followers to action whenever he needed them.

As for politics, Sannir had been uninvolved in the wars of the realm, watching empires rise and fall from a safe distance. The last recorded battle between elves and afi was several hundred years prior, when Alder, the general after Eliab, fought the battle known as the Battle of Sokota's Bridge, wiping out the last of Orisis' original army and securing Sannir's borders.

It seemed the Orisis and his afi had laid dormant since then. Until, of course, Novah's appointing.

Corbin kicked a pebble and watched it tumble down the busy street. "How is there nothing? Have the afi not shown their faces once since Sokota's Bridge?"

Kyler shrugged. "Why would they? Adoni crumbled Tophet, then Eliab and Alder rid the world of Orisis' followers."

"But they've rebuilt since then." Corbin dropped his voice, careful not to let curious ears overhear. "Sannir has been idle since that time, but Orisis hasn't. The afi's touch still curses a soul, which means Tophet still stands. They have power over royalty and strength in numbers—there must be something we're missing."

"Maybe you just weren't looking in the right place?"

Corbin scoffed, tossing a hand to Kyler's notes. "That's easy for you to say. I can't count how many useless pages I read today."

"That might be a good sign. If there's nothing else for us to learn, then they can't surprise us."

"Maybe." Corbin fell silent, disappearing back into his

thoughts.

By the time they arrived at their camp, Novah had returned, and the smell of cooked pork wafted from the smoke of the fire. Aeron stood over the flame, poking at the embers with the edge of a stick. When he caught sight of them, he grinned and pointed at a pot sitting in the fire. "Soup."

Kyler accepted a bowl from Novah, who was already finished eating. "General, you've outdone yourself."

"You can wait for the rest if you'd like."

Corbin was already mid-bite when he answered, "I'll start with this."

Kyler lifted a brow at him, and he swallowed.

"Thank you, General."

She smiled, but it was the tired kind that didn't quite reach her eyes.

Kyler lowered himself to the grass beside her. "Any news from the castle?"

She shook her head. "I watched for hours. Guard rotation is normal, messengers are normal. Saints, even the flower beds are normal."

"No sign of Elizus, I presume?"

"Unless we get inside of the castle, I doubt we'll find anything."

Kyler set his food aside, pulling the notes from his pocket. "I found something."

Her eyes lit up. "About Orisis?"

"Not exactly. About alchemy. Turns out, there are plants and techniques that can create potions I've never heard of. For example"—he flipped through the pages until he found his notes on Pevoth—"this one caught my eye. It speeds the healing process of its drinker."

Draven's eyes flashed to Kyler as he overhead, and Novah took the parchment from her commander's hands. She looked it over, scanning his scribbled handwriting. "You can make this?"

Kyler nodded. "It's similar to Ponos, but the key ingredient is an herb called 'tach'. It's native to the islands."

She looked at Draven before handing Kyler's notes back to him. "Can you brew it tonight?"

"I can. With the ingredients."

Her tongue pressed against her cheek as her eyes took in the setting sun. "Corbin?"

Corbin looked up from his soup. "Yes ma'am?"

"When you're finished, I want you and Aeron back in town. Kyler will give you a list of ingredients I want you to find." She turned to Aeron, who'd just pulled the pot out of the fire. "And, Aeron, don't put that out."

A moment later, the two of them started for the town. By the time they returned, Kyler was ready.

He sat by the fire, his sleeves rolled to his elbows as he warmed his hands with the flame. He'd created a makeshift brewing station before him—not nearly as efficient as his one at home, but it would do. The fire was split into three sections, each with varying levels of flame, and above the flames hung his brewing pot, suspended on a metal hook staked in the grass.

Kyler was once again grateful he'd grabbed his bag from the inn. His equipment was still intact, and he'd laid out a few empty vials to fill with new potions. The gentle smoke rose to the trees above them, mingling with the night as if greeting the stars.

"Did you find everything?" Kyler accepted the ingredients as Corbin handed them over, most wrapped in parchment or folded in strips of leather to keep them fresh.

"I think so. We had to rush. Everyone was closing for the evening."

Kyler wasn't fully listening. He studied the herbs and ingredients before him, opening each one up to inspect it. Things like limestone powder and bergamot oil he was familiar with, but the herb called tach was foreign to him. It was larger than he'd expected, made of flat, circular leaves and covered in a soft fuzz that clung to his fingertips. He gently tugged a leaf free, and his nose filled with a scent that rivaled cinnamon.

"Is it alright?" Corbin broke his thoughts.

"Should be fine." Kyler set the herb aside and took hold of the ingredient he was most curious about—the gallot root.

It was rolled in thin leather, heavier than he'd expected and dark brown. The shape and texture were like ginger, but when Kyler brought it to his nose, he caught hints of lemongrass and musk. He crinkled his nose at the scent and set it down with the rest of the ingredients.

How that root could corrupt a potion was beyond Kyler, and he wasn't sure how to test its effectiveness, as it was said to cause unexplainable pain. But, at the very least, he wanted to see how it would react when brewed in a potion.

"Was this difficult to find?"

Aeron sat down on the other side of the fire as he answered, "Not at all. It's apparently common here. Used for cooking."

Corbin knelt beside Kyler as the commander reached for his brewing pot and slowly and precisely measured out his ingredients. He hardly noticed the eyes of his companions as they studied his work, careful not to distract or disturb his craft. More than once, Corbin reached for an ingredient and Kyler swatted his hand away, hissing warnings that Corbin continued to ignore.

When Kyler added the tach, it popped and sizzled, dissolving into the liquid as if it were ice. He waited another moment, and as the bubbles began to settle, he removed the Pevoth from the heat.

The healing potion had a citrus smell to it, and soft steam rose from its surface as Kyler held it to the firelight. His notes stated that the potion was pale green, but even now it appeared a bit too dark for his liking.

"How's it look, Commander?" Novah asked, and Kyler realized he must've been frowning at it.

He checked his notes again, but his measurements had been exact. He folded the parchment back into his pocket and lifted an empty vial from the ground beside him, slowly pouring the potion in.

His anxieties settled as the potion hit the glass, cooling to a soft sage as the heat began to dissipate. It was more transparent than he'd expected, and it shimmered in the light of the flames.

"All yours, Draven." He flashed a grin, passing over the vial.

The kilder pinched it between his fingers, sniffing it lightly. His gaze narrowed. "This will heal me?"

"It's supposed to."

"And if it doesn't?"

Kyler sighed, cleaning out his brewing pot with a thin rag in preparation for his next potion. "We're outside of Sannir. There's a small risk, but it's well worth it."

Aeron twisted his lips as he eyed the mixture. "You've never brewed this before. It could have been written down wrong or measured incorrectly."

Kyler stood, brushing the dirt from his pants, and stretched out the ache in his neck from hovering over the fire. Before he could answer, Novah did.

"We need Draven on his feet. If Kyler thinks it's safe, so do I."

Aeron didn't look pleased with this, but he kept his mouth shut and turned to Draven. The kilder's dark eyes were trained on the potion, studying the way it spiraled as he swirled it lightly. Finally, he exhaled sharply and tilted the bottle to his lips, grimacing as it slipped down his throat.

"How's it taste?" Corbin pressed.

"Like citrus."

"Good." Kyler accepted the empty vial as it was handed back to him. "It's going to make you drowsy, so just keep your leg still as it heals and try to sleep it off. If all goes well, you'll be leaping down the mountain at sunrise."

"Leaping?" Corbin cracked a grin. "That'll be a sight."

"Free and wild." Draven winked, adjusting his seated position so that his injured leg was straight.

Novah pinched the bridge of her nose, hiding her playful smile behind her hand. "I'm going to set you all free and wild when this is over. You smell like horses and snore like gulls."

Kyler crossed his arms. "I don't snore."

"I don't think gulls snore either." Corbin sat beside Draven, lacing his fingers behind his head. "Your insult is invalid."

Kyler's lips dipped into a pout as he knelt by the fire once more. "It was still hurtful."

"Good," Novah quipped. "You could use some humility every now and then."

A branch snapped, and their banter dissipated like the smoke of the fire. Metal scraped against metal as swords were drawn. In a moment, Kyler had his bow in hand, an arrow nocked along the string and his blood humming wildly.

A figure stepped into the firelight, palms open and a dark hood draped over his head. Slowly and without sound, he pulled back his hood, and his glassy eyes caught the gold of the flame.

"It's Orisis," Ophir said softly. "He's moving. Tonight."

...

"How did you find us?" Novah hissed, her hurried steps even with Ophir's as he led them deeper into the forest.

The celestial moved quickly through the barren trees and rocky terrain, his long strides leaving Kyler breathless as he and the others followed.

Ophir shrugged. "You smelled of cedar when we spoke, and your fire was not difficult for my eyes to pick out. Much closer than stars."

Kyler was less concerned with how Ophir found them and more with the warning he'd given. If Orisis was moving, Sannir could be in his line of fire.

The hood of Kyler's cloak flopped against his shoulders, leaving his ears and neck exposed to the cold night air. Potion ingredients spilled from his pockets and bag, and he stuffed them down, attempting not to lose any valuable items on their trek through the mountains.

They'd taken everything from their campsite, leaving only ash behind. The sword that hung from Novah's hip knocked against Kyler's bag as he came to her side, maneuvering around knotted roots and fallen branches.

The general's jaw was stiff, her eyes as dark as the sky. Her fingers lingered on the hilt of her sword, and her brows creased with worry as Ophir led them farther from the mountains.

Finally, the celestial slowed at a clearing in the trees, just outside the city borders. "Here we are." His pale eyes searched the heavens as Corbin and Aeron caught up, their few belongings hanging from their waists and shoulders.

Draven was last, limping into the clearing with his teeth gritted. The Pevoth seemed to be working as promised, already beginning to seal his wounds, and Draven insisted he walk on his own despite his still-healing bones and heavy eyes. The effects of the potion made his movements sloppy, but he swatted away Aeron's hand, straightening as he came to a stop.

"I know I said I needed time," Ophir said, "but this information will be useless in two days. There." He lifted a finger to the sky as he spotted the constellation.

Kyler followed his gesture, attempting to pick out whatever it was he saw. The study of stars never interested him, but he recognized the scatter that Ophir noted. It was hard to miss, with a line of stars making three points that resembled a crown.

Ophir glanced at Novah. "Do you see how it's shifted?"

"Not particularly."

He dropped his hand, turning to face the group. He looked concerned when he caught sight of Draven's state, but he said nothing. "Anything involving the crown represents the castle. The crown's point is the prince."

Novah interrupted, "He's working with the afi, yes, we know. What does that have to do with tonight?"

Ophir motioned to the right of the crown. "See that triangle constellation?"

Novah looked just as lost as Kyler felt, but Corbin made his way to Ophir's side. "That's the Ilma mark. Astronomers have always struggled to chart its patterns."

Ophir flashed a grin. "You know your stars. The Ilma mark has been on the left side of the crown for the last four days. Tonight, it's on the right. They're moving."

"So, what do we do?" Corbin looked between Novah and Kyler for an answer.

Novah's voice was tight. "How long do we have?"

"A few hours. Maybe less."

"What *exactly* are they doing?"

Ophir frowned. "I don't know. It could be a simple change of position, or it could be an attack on your kingdom."

Sticks cracked beneath Novah's boots as she stepped back. "Commander, a word."

Kyler followed her away from the others and into the line of trees. The crooked branches above blocked the constellations from view, but Kyler wasn't watching the stars anymore. He kept his gaze fixed on Novah as fear crept along her face.

He dipped his voice so the others wouldn't hear. "Please tell me you have an idea."

She sighed, peeking over his shoulder at the celestial. "I do, but we'll get to that in a second. Do you trust him?"

Kyler hesitated, surprised by her question, and his stalling added urgency to her tone.

"Kyler, do you trust him?"

"I think so."

"Then so do I." She ran a hand through her hair, pulling the loose strands away from her face. "I think we can use the sewers to get into the castle. I want those three to flock it and act as our eyes while you and I enter through the servant's quarters."

"We're not prepared for a battle, Novah. There's five of us."

"We're not fighting afi tonight." The air was cold enough that her words puffed before her face like a cloud as she spoke. "We're going to take the prince as prisoner. Whatever they're planning, I'm certain it'll halt without him."

Kyler let her plan take form in his mind. "What about getting home? How far out do you think our ship is?"

She bit her tongue, shaking her head before he'd finished. "I don't know, but hopefully not far."

"Are you sure this is the best course of action?" He leaned

closer, ensuring the others wouldn't hear. "We were sent to gather information and we've done that."

"We don't have time to send a warning back home. If we're going to act, we must do it now."

Kyler was silent for a moment, his heart pounding in the quiet of the night. "At your word, General."

Her smile was tight as she stepped past him, rejoining their group once more. "Draven, can you make it to the castle?"

"Yes."

"Good." She turned to Corbin. "Give Kyler your sword."

Corbin tugged his blade free from his waist, trading it for Kyler's bow and arrows. The weight of the blade was unfamiliar to Kyler, but Corbin's weapon was well-balanced, and Kyler was glad to have something he could use to defend himself in the castle.

Finally, Novah faced Ophir, who'd been watching silently. She dipped a hand into her pocket, revealing the vial of blood. It glistened in the starlight, clinging to the inside of the glass in streaks of red. She passed it over without hesitation.

"You've been a great help. We'll meet you as planned for the information on Uriah. You'll have your knife then."

The celestial bowed his head, his expression flat. "Good luck."

CHAPTER TWENTY-FIVE

THE SEWERS SMELLED WORSE THAN BEFORE, IF THAT WAS possible, and Kyler did his best to ignore the stench. Darkness filled the tunnels, the only light coming from scattered streetlamps that shone through the various grates above them.

Kyler kept Novah's steady pace. The gentle run of the sewage water sloshed against their shins, but she moved with confidence, pausing only to listen, as they strode beneath streets and shops.

The passages created a network under the city, and if Novah's maps were accurate, they would land just past the castle gardens and well within the gate. From there, it would be simple to slip through the servant's hall and into the castle of Potri. The gamble was the prince himself—there was no telling where he might be, or who might be with him.

A conversation floated down between the grates, and Novah slowed, holding a palm to Kyler's chest to halt him. Laughter and slurred words drifted through the tunnels, mingling with the scrape of stone sharpening metal. Kyler kept his lips sealed and breath slow, assuming they must be beneath the soldier's lodging.

"Sluggards," Novah whispered, and Kyler caught the roll of her eyes.

He leaned closer. "Reminds me of the Regiment."

She gave a light *tsk* and dropped her hand before continuing down their path.

Kyler followed silently, waiting until they were distanced from the soldiers to tease her once more. "Don't take it personally, General. Every kingdom has its weak point."

"They do." She glanced over her shoulder. "Ours just happens to be six feet tall and covered in sewage water."

Kyler whistled. "I'm surprised you paid attention to my height."

"I was exaggerating."

Novah turned a corner, and Kyler's sleeve brushed the stone wall as he followed. As much as he wanted to offer a snide remark in return, the world beyond the grates had fallen silent, so Kyler did as well. His steps became lighter and movements smoother as Novah began to slow. It wasn't until they reached a rounded wall, marking the end of the tunnels, that Novah came to a stop and looked up at the final grate.

"We should be on the west side of the castle." Her voice was low, hardly a murmur, as she readied herself to scale the ladder. "There's a door a few yards from here that I saw the castle staff using earlier today. If luck is on our side, it will be unlocked."

Kyler sighed, catching sight of the dark sky beyond the grate. "I'm not sure luck has favored us since we arrived."

Novah placed her hands on the rims of the ladder, pausing to meet Kyler's eye with a grin. "It's had nothing to do with luck, Commander. Just your lack of common sense."

Kyler bristled, but before he could respond, Novah was climbing the ladder. She reached the grate and removed it silently, pausing to scan the castle grounds before she hauled herself out of the tunnels.

Kyler followed and emerged from the musty sewage into the

castle gardens.

Just as Novah had said, they were on the west side of the castle, with the sun far beyond the mountains at their back. Before them, the castle of Potri stood like a beacon, with white stone walls and starlight reflecting off of the glass windows. The gardens, full of poppies and oak trees, sat still, branches dark and silent but for the soft rustle of dry leaves. Ahead, a simple oak door was tucked into one of the pristine walls, nearly hidden by the shadows.

Novah moved silently, her cloak rolling behind her like waves as she stepped confidently to the door. She paused before it, brushing the wood, and listened. Silence. She turned the knob.

The flicker of golden lamplight illuminated the hallway from the cracks beneath the closed doors of a few of the adjacent rooms. Soft laughter and the crackle of a fireplace drifted into the gardens, warming even the lampless space that stretched before Kyler and Novah.

Novah stepped onto the wooden floorboards with Kyler close at her heels. She pressed a hand against the wall, her steps light and calculated, as she slipped past the lit rooms, slowing slightly as the hall turned and branched.

Kyler was hesitant to trust her lead, worried she would end up lost in the unknown quarters, but she moved too fast for him to question her. Before long she had led them to a set of wooden stairs.

"How did you know?" Kyler murmured, his steps nearly on top of hers.

"Sannir." She hurried up the stairs, not daring to glance behind her. "I couldn't sleep after the attack. Explored the servants' quarters instead. The layout is similar enough."

Just as she did with the first door, Novah paused at the top of the stairs and listened before cracking open the door, stealing a look at the room beyond it. She opened it wider and led Kyler into a short hall.

This part of the castle was rich and lush, with oil paintings, portraits, and golden tapestries. It smelled like spices as Kyler strode into the space, as if the fragrance had seeped into the stone and settled against the glass. Golden carpet lay along marble floors, and moonlight bathed the soldiers in silver.

The hallway let out into a large room—the one Kyler had seen from the ground. A wide armchair sat beside a grand piano that was made entirely of white wood. Beside it, a golden harp stood perfectly still, as if patiently awaiting a musician to tug its strings.

Novah stepped toward the massive window that overlooked the city, and Kyler came to her side. He could see everything from this height—the arena, the library, and even the charred remains of the inn.

"We're losing time." Novah scanned the room, finding separate doors that branched to different areas of the castle. She nodded to the one at her right. "Take that one. If you don't find anything in an hour, meet back here."

Kyler nodded sharply.

She turned from him and pressed her ear to the opposite door. When she'd determined it was clear, she slipped through it, leaving him alone in the darkened room.

The silence was nearly deafening. Kyler listened to the sound of his pulse as he moved to the other door—the one that seemed to lead farther into the castle. He wiped a palm on his shirt before twisting the knob silently and peeking past the dark wood.

Before him was another hallway, this one stretching nearly the length of the castle before curving. Doors lined the walls, each one shut.

Kyler waited until he was certain the hall was empty before

entering. His boots sunk into the golden threads of the carpet. He began cautiously down the hall, scanning the plates nailed beside each door.

Study One

Tearoom

Gallery

Outer Chamber

Observatory Tower

The final one made him pause. Ophir had been very clear about the afi's connection to the stars, and if the prince was one of them, he would be watching the stars too.

The door opened to a dark staircase. While the rest of the castle had smelled of perfume and spices, the entry of the observatory smelled of rust and coal. There were no golden carpets or painted portraits, just a narrow set of stairs that spiraled upwards. At the top, Kyler reached a plateau and found himself beneath a ceiling that was built partially of domed glass. The glass took up half of the space, while the rest was a painting of the night sky.

It was the painting that drew Kyler in, momentarily pushing the prince from his mind. It labeled every planet and constellation as if painted by an astronomer rather than an artist. Blue and violet spiraled like the view Ophir had shown him through the observatory telescope.

The room wasn't large, and every corner was stuffed with equipment and notes. Kyler pushed these aside as he maneuvered around the desks, placing himself beneath the glass and staring out into the sky above. The crown constellation was visible from here, as was the Ilma mark.

Kyler turned to the scattered papers, searching for something that seemed to have been written recently. His vision blurred the longer he stared at the parchment. They were disorganized and sloppy, and most of the handwriting was completely illegible. He gave up on the papers, deciding to examine the rest of the room.

Across from him, paintings hung from the wall, long and detailed and framed in gold. Labeled plaques hung above each one, the words etched into sheets as gold as the frames. Kyler inched closer, the pieces piquing his curiosity.

There were five total, but it was the second to the right that caught his attention. It was a painting of Potri, with its castle and mountains shadowed against the brilliant night sky. Each star was dotted with impressive accuracy, but it wasn't the detail that caught his attention.

The painting was moving.

At first, he assumed it was a trick of his tired eyes, but the closer he looked, the more certain he became. The stars were shifting, like the galaxy beyond the paint was alive. Along the surface of the painting, dust drifted, dancing past the stars and never straying far from the frame.

Kyler lifted a hand to the odd dust.

But the press of cold metal against his neck made him freeze.

"I was wondering when you'd show up again, Sann."

The air in the room became suddenly cold. The glint of a blade flashed beneath Kyler's chin, its edge scraping against his throat. He risked a swallow and turned slowly to face his captor.

Gray eyes, thick as thunderclouds and as bright as steel, greeted him, sinking into his soul like they had many times before.

Kyler forced strength into his voice, his body perfectly still as the prince's sword rested along the fragile skin of his neck. "Prince Elizus."

The prince's dark hair was combed and gelled, a single strand falling from its place and brushing his dark lashes. White and gold fabric draped his figure, topped with a coat lined in fur that fell to his ankles like a suit of armor across his back. No crown adorned his head this time.

The prince scowled, an expression that only seemed to darken his gaze. "Hello, Kyler."

Movement came from the doorway, but the prince didn't bat an eye. It seemed he had backup.

Kyler was out of time.

The commander drew his blade, slamming it against the prince, and drove him into a table. Elizus hit the wood with a grunt. His teeth bared, and surprise flashed across his face. He regained his footing and kicked at Kyler's legs as he shoved the commander's blade aside, swinging for Kyler's chest with enough force to pierce his bone if the prince's hit had landed.

Kyler tripped over equipment and tumbled into corners of tables and telescope poles. Parchment skittered to the floor, sliding beneath his feet and throwing him off balance, but Elizus seemed unphased. Every hit came harder and more precise than the previous, narrowly grazing Kyler's skin and sending shocks through his arms as he blocked the prince's blows.

"Any day now, Elizus," a lazy tone drawled from the observatory entrance.

In the fury of attacks, Kyler had forgotten about the other figure in the room. The voice pulled Kyler's attention, not because of what he said, but because the voice was familiar.

He leaned against the door frame, his figure tall and arms crossed over his chest. His face was dark, but Kyler could see his eyes clearly—white, as pale as stars.

"Ophir?"

The name was hardly through Kyler's lips when something very hard and very heavy collided with his temple.

CHAPTER TWENTY-SIX

OPHIR.

The name tumbled through Kyler's unconscious mind, mingling with the sting of betrayal. Pain pounded his head in sharp bursts, begging his eyes to remain shut and body to remain limp. He struggled against his muddled mind and, at last, forced his eyes to open. He winced as the room around him came into focus.

It was dark, but the low-burning lamps sent painful shards through his head. Kyler lifted his hand to his temple, feeling a warm trickle of blood beginning to dry against his hair. He tried to shift his feet, but the sound of chains knocking together stopped him.

Shackles were clamped around his ankles and secured to the cold stone wall that pressed against his back. The sword he'd borrowed from Corbin was gone, along with his cloak, potion belt, and the ingredients he'd buried in his pockets. Only his clothes remained, still smelling of sewage water and clinging to his skin.

Saints. Where was he? Where was Novah?

Before him, metal bars stretched from floor to ceiling, caging him in. Beyond them was a simple wooden desk as empty as the rest of the room, with a single chair tucked beneath it. The walls were bare, reminding Kyler of the cells beneath the castle of Sannir.

He pressed his palms to the floor, finding the stone damp, and tried to sit upright, but his stiff neck and sore back begged him to remain still.

He didn't notice the door to his right until it creaked open, and a figure emerged, shadowed by lamplight. It was a man—that much Kyler could tell—with a lean frame and a dark coat. He closed the door behind him, the soft jingle of keys echoing as he tucked them into his pocket.

"You're awake." His voice was easy and light.

The man began a slow pace around the room, his boots tapping against the stone as he reached a thin hand to each of the lamps, heightening their flame.

Kyler squinted at the brightness, struggling to keep his headache away. As light filled the room, the stranger slowly faded into view.

A scar began at his right cheekbone, trailed across the bridge of his nose, and finished at his opposing dimple. Hair the color of bone fell loose over his pointed ears, and his dark coat was stitched with spiraling designs of purple embroidery. Teeth as white as his hair filled his crooked smile, and his pale blue eyes flickered with something playful. He looked young, but he carried himself as though he'd been around for centuries.

His smile fell slightly. "Not what you expected?" He clicked his tongue. "You don't have to look so disappointed, Commander."

Kyler set his jaw. The tease in the young man's voice was maddening. If he was intending to provoke Kyler's anger, it was working.

The man circled the three exposed sides of the cage, dragging his cool gaze across Kyler's form. Finally, he paused. "I must admit, I expected more from you. Your name is highly praised, even here. The youngest commander with the most scales, the leader of the Brigade. You carry quite the reputation."

The taste of metal floated in Kyler's mouth. Whatever response this man was after, Kyler refused to give it. He locked eyes with the stranger and said nothing.

The man quirked a brow. "Defiance will get you nowhere, not here. You would be wise to cooperate."

"I don't even know who you are, and you expect me to cooperate?" Kyler spat.

His crooked smirk returned, satisfaction dancing across his features. "You have a lot to learn. Do you know what I like best about you, Commander?"

The way he spoke was like ink, dripping and pooling into a river of black. He stepped closer, cocking his head. "You are so easily fooled."

He leaned in, and as he did, his skin fractured like broken glass. The lamplight caught its translucence, and his features began to morph. His nose straightened into a near point, and his white hair darkened, curling into spirals. His eyes were the last to change, fading until his pupils disappeared entirely.

Kyler's breath hitched. It was Ophir.

"What are you?" He let the question slip, no longer worried about keeping his tongue reined. The man before him was so familiar—so honest. Kyler didn't want to stare, but he couldn't seem to tear his gaze away.

The man grinned, a look so far from the Ophir whom Kyler had come to trust.

He shrugged, as if he found the question boring. "Shapeshifter." He backed away, turning to glass and piecing his skin together again. It was like he tore himself apart piece by piece, rebuilding into someone completely new. The pale man was back now, amusement dancing across his face.

"I figured you'd give almost anything for my information, but blood…" He pulled the vial of Novah's blood from his shirt pocket, swirling it gently.

Anger rose in place of fear, and Kyler's gaze darkened. "You have no right to hold that."

The man looked from the vial to Kyler. "A deal is a deal, Commander. It just so happens that I need this."

"We made a deal with Ophir, not you." Kyler's words were sharp, intended to cut through this man's games.

Dimples formed in his cheeks. "Ophir is me, and I am him. Well," he said with a chuckle, tucking the vial back into his pocket, "at least that's how it's been for some time now."

"What have you done with the real Ophir?"

"You never knew him." The man leaned a shoulder against the bars of the cage, bringing himself teasingly close. "He died long before you stepped foot into this city."

"Who did I know?"

"Bricru."

"Bricru." Kyler said the name slowly, committing it to memory.

"Kyler." Bricru said his name with an authority he didn't possess. "We have some catching up to do."

He pulled the chair from the desk, the wood scraping against stone as he dragged it before the bars. With a sigh, Bricru sat down before the cage, resting his elbows on his knees. He folded his hands together. "Ophir was boring. You and I will have much more fun."

Kyler scoffed.

"Don't believe me? That's fine. We'll see how your general

fares."

Kyler tensed at the threat, and Bricru laughed.

"It seems I hit a soft spot. You have too many of those."

"Why am I here?"

"You're here because Orisis requested it, and as much as he likes me, he's far more interested in you." His lips tugged upward. "You, Kyler *Weylyn,* are very interesting."

The way he emphasized Kyler's name brought his blood to a rush. Kyler leaned closer, the chains at his ankles tugging in protest. "If this is about Uriah, I don't care anymore."

Bricru grinned. "You cared a lot the other day."

"What do you want with me?" Kyler hissed. "You have the blood. Kill me and be done with it."

"Orisis has another plan in mind."

"What plan?"

"Keep talking, and I'll tell you."

Kyler's jaw went taunt. "It seems to me you've already won. I don't need to know how."

He chuckled "You're right. But I'm not too prideful to admit that I still need your help."

"No."

He tilted his head, and the rough ridges of his scar turned to shadow. He reached a hand between the bars, his palm aimed at Kyler's neck.

A spike of fear jolted inside of Kyler, but he remained still. Whatever power Bricru possessed, Kyler would not cower before it.

Bricru hardly brushed Kyler's skin, and yet his touch already began to work. All at once Kyler's body was filled with ice, shards like glass digging into his lungs and stealing his breath away. Black spots filled his vision until all he could see was Bricru's twisted grin.

Kyler choked. "You can't." But he could feel his body giving in to the pull of Tophet within Bricru's touch.

An afi who kept his magic.

"You can't have both," he managed to grunt.

Both shapeshifting and the power of afi. Orisis could not create, he could only trade.

Bricru seemed amused by this. "Orisis *always* finds a way."

Kyler's muscles hardened and twisted around his bones, slowly squeezing the life from his body. His pounding pulse began to slow, and his blood ran cool. His eyes rolled, and just as Kyler prepared to lose his soul to the depths of Tophet, Bricru pulled back.

Kyler gasped, released from Bricru's curse. Life returned to him like a strike of lightning. His blood rushed hot and fast beneath his skin, burning and scalding like rivers of molten iron. The chains at his feet felt suddenly heavy, and the light of the room seemed so brilliant that Kyler feared he would never blink away the sunspots they caused.

Bricru leaned back once more, watching Kyler bite back the pain. "Just imagine what it would feel like if I allowed myself to send you to Tophet. You'd live in that torment forever." He wagged his fingers, staring at his hand. "Tempting."

Kyler's breaths came full and heavy. His ears still hummed as his body returned to normal, a tremor snaking its way along his limbs.

"You're unnatural," he whispered.

Bricru smiled. "You're learning."

Kyler hoped Bricru could see the anger in his eyes as he lifted his head, sweat dripping from his hair. "I'll kill you."

"Not if I kill you first."

"You won't." Kyler straightened, his strength returning once more. "If Orisis wanted me dead, I would be. You have no power Bricru. You're just a puppet."

His smile quickly turned into a snarl. "I am my own master. Your god keeps you weak—his magic binds you to the Dragon Pass. Mine does not. Mine gives me freedom."

"Yours gives death and false promises."

Kyler thought he'd bested the shapeshifter, but Bricru paused, and Kyler saw a new thought forming on his face. "Someone else said that to me not long ago. He believed it too, but when Orisis offered him power, he took it freely."

"Then he was a fool."

"You sound just like him."

"Do I?"

"The resemblance is uncanny." He dipped his hand back into his pocket, revealing the thin vial of blood once more. He dangled it between them, his eyes fixated on the swirling red. "You and Uriah are very much alike. Your general was almost finished with his project when he turned his back on Orisis, sentencing himself to misery."

Orisis. *Project.* What had Uriah gotten into?

"But the project is unfinished." Bricru shifted in his seat, fighting back a smirk as if he'd be waiting for the right moment to say, "And who better to finish it than his son?"

PART TWO

THE GENERAL

URIAH HAD BEEN MANY THINGS. HE'D BEEN A SOLDIER, THEN A general, who guarded the kingdom of Sannir and led its armies. He'd been a peace bringer, ensuring the people of Sannir were safe and the borders of the kingdom secure. He'd been simultaneously cruel and inspiring, leading with a cold fist and a sharp tongue.

But he'd also been a father.

Kyler was a child, no more than six, when Uriah was promoted to general. The young boy was enthralled with the idea. His father was *the* general. Fame and fortune would follow him wherever he went, and when Uriah returned home with a white scale on his ear, Kyler could hardly keep his eyes off it.

"Do you see how it shines?" Uriah lifted his younger son into his arms, holding Kyler against his armored chest. "It's from Atlas."

Fingers, round and rough, reached for the scale, and Uriah tilted his head to allow Kyler to grab hold of the piece.

"Gentle," he warned, his voice soft. "Atlas does not give them freely."

Small steps pattered closer as Kyler's brother joined them, his long face exaggerated by the slack of his jaw. Like Kyler, Evander stared at the scale as if it were the most priceless object in the realm.

And to them, it was. Not because of the color, but because it was their father's.

But the life of a general was not all they had hoped for. Their mother tried to hide it, but Kyler saw the red beneath her eyes and the tears that she tried to wipe away. He heard the shake of her voice when Uriah came home late, his jaw tight and eyes refusing to meet hers. On the nights when his family sat down to eat together, Uriah was no longer there. When Eliab's Eve brought liquid chocolate and the chiming of clocks, it did not bring Uriah with it.

One day, Uriah left. And he did not come back.

Weylyn was his mother's name, a name that meant peace and home to Kyler, and so he took it. While Uriah was leading and protecting, Kyler was growing, and his anger toward his father grew with him.

Kyler became a soldier—just like his father—under Commander Calfner, and soon enough, he was earning scales.

The ceremonies happened regularly. The soldiers lined up before the general to receive the scales they'd earned during their training. It was at these ceremonies that Kyler had to face the man he no longer called his father. Uriah said nothing, pressing scales of pine and emerald into Kyler's palm and dismissing him with the rest of the soldiers. But Kyler saw the way Uriah's eyes trailed his growing collection. The bitterness that slowly rose beneath Uriah's firm gaze was unspoken.

Until the night that Uriah caught him alone. It was after a ceremony, soon after Calfner had stepped down and Kyler had been promoted to commander in his place. Stars filled the skies of Sannir as Kyler strode through the silent courtyard, his mind wandering as it often did after facing Uriah. His newest scale sat curled in his fingers, tucked inside of his trouser pocket, as his gaze lingered on the budding lilies of the outer castle gardens.

He didn't notice Uriah until the larger man grabbed hold of his chest plate and shoved him against the side of the castle with enough force to steal the air from his lungs.

Kyler gasped at the impact, his armor digging into his sides, as the anger in Uriah's face caught in the starlight. The general riffled through Kyler's pocket, taking hold of the scale he'd just handed over.

Then he spat on it.

"You didn't earn this." The gentleness of his voice was gone, replaced with something far more crippling. "You're here because of me, and you won't even use my name."

Kyler attempted to tear himself free of the general's hold, but Uriah only pressed harder.

"I made you a soldier, and you disgrace me." He tossed the scale to the dirt and scuffed it with the heel of his boot.

"You did not *make* me," Kyler snapped, finally shoving free of Uriah's hold. "I made *myself.*"

The sneer on Uriah's lips remained as he studied his son's collection of scales. "Take your scale from the dirt and slink back to your barracks. But remember, Kyler, you are nothing without me."

That had been their final conversation, a threat in the darkness of the castle shadows, but Kyler never forgot it. Uriah avoided him from then on, taking frequent trips into the Dragon Pass and distancing himself from his soldiers. When word reached Kyler nearly a year later that General Uriah had disappeared, Kyler did not mourn. He knew he was going to take his place as general and prove to his father that he had *earned* that position.

Now, as Bricru spoke, Kyler felt those memories resurfacing. They reached for his throat like hands, ready to press against his neck and suffocate him.

"Kyler Caligari. Son of Uriah Caligari. Don't worry, he told me everything." Bricru drummed his fingers along his kneecaps.

"How your mother remarried, and brother moved away. Somewhere in Xynack, no?"

Bile rose to Kyler's throat, his teeth grinding so hard they began to hurt. "He's not my father."

"But he is."

"He's dead. He's rotting in his grave where he belongs."

Bricru pursed his lips. "Do all children treat their fathers with such disrespect?"

"If they're monsters, yes."

"Men are not monsters unless we make them into such things." Bricru paused. "And I never told you he was dead. Uriah is very much alive. How much do you want to know about your father, Kyler Caligari? I can relay his fears and temptations. I can recite to you his final pleas before his soul was damned to Tophet, if you so wish."

Then, in a way, he was dead. Tophet was a place worse than death, and there was no return.

Kyler could taste the bitterness of his words as they fell from his tongue. "Uriah is finally getting what he deserves."

Despite his confidence, Bricru seemed to see through the commander's façade. "You don't mean that. He loves you, you know."

"He loves himself."

Bricru laughed. "He does. But there's love for you too. His youngest son—the brilliant alchemist, the commander. I think deep down, he's even proud."

Heat burned Kyler's eyes and rushed through his blood. He wanted to retort, but the mixture of anger and hate choked his words, so he said nothing.

The shapeshifter stood and dragged the chair back to the desk, tucking it into place. "It was a pleasure to meet you, Kyler

Caligari, as we both truly are—not wearing our masks. I look forward to our future conversations." He straightened his shoulders, brushing nonexistent lint from his clothes and tugging at his collar. "Until next time."

He strode to the door without another glance, and the sound of metal gears clicking into place faded to silence as Kyler was left alone once more.

He waited until the footsteps retreated. Silence roared in his ears, empty and void and yet terribly powerful. The chains that bound him to the cell clattered as Kyler began to pull at them, each wrench more forceful than the last. Blood rose to his palms as the metal scraped against his skin and stung his hands. He knew the chains wouldn't give, but he wasn't truly trying to free himself. He had nowhere to go.

"Bastard!" His head knocked against the stone as tears blurred his vision, clinging to his lashes like ice. His breath came in labored gasps, rough and desperate, like the air in the room was made of salt and brine.

Uriah had betrayed him again.

Kyler cursed his god. Then he cursed Bricru and Uriah and Aiyanna and anyone else he could possibly blame.

But when there was no one left to curse, and his voice was as raw as his hands, Kyler Caligari cursed himself.

CHAPTER TWENTY-SEVEN

THE PAINTING DANCED TO UNHEARD MUSIC, THE STARS AND planets humming gently beneath a thin layer of dust. Above, the pale light of dawn cast the castle observatory in a blanket of blue, like the sky itself was waking with the city below.

Bricru pressed his eyes shut, attempting to calm his mind. He'd done it. Elven blood sat secure in his pocket, and not only that, but Uriah's son was in his hands. It was because of Ophir—because of him.

Yet the fear of failure still clung to his chest.

"Going back so soon?"

Bricru turned and found the prince in the doorway. Like him, Elizus was dressed in fabric as dark as his combed hair, though his coat had been stitched with the gold of his kingdom, mocking his royal attire. The prince paused in the center of the room, his steely eyes boring into Bricru in a way the shapeshifter hated.

"How's the new general?" Bricru ignored Elizus' question, asking one of his own instead.

Elizus shook his head slowly as his eyes drifted over the scattered papers before rising to the open sky above. "She won't talk."

A smirk curved the corners of Bricru's lips, which he quickly hid by turning back to the painting of stars. "Change your tactics, prince."

"Watch your tongue, *snake*," Elizus spat, pushing off the wall. His steps were steady as he maneuvered around the mess left in the observatory. "Just because you succeeded once doesn't mean you will again. Orisis will not forget your previous failures."

Bricru scoffed, but the prince's words only heightened the fear simmering in his chest. "I knew I could gain his trust, and I did. Just like I did with Uriah." He turned, lifting his chin slightly to meet the prince's iron gaze. "Orisis doesn't play favorites, Elizus. Don't think yourself special."

"I'm not special." Elizus brushed past Bricru, stepping to the painting. "But neither are you." His words faded as the painting swallowed him, leaving nothing but a puff of dust in his wake.

Bricru fixed his gaze on the shifting of stars. It was as if Elizus knew the exact words to slice his pride, cutting away bit by bit until he could no longer trust his own instincts.

He ducked his head and sank into the painting, allowing the soft buzz of magic to fill his mind. Darkness engulfed him, brushing his skin and swallowing his thoughts, and the gentle pressure urged him through the gateway.

When Bricru lifted his head, he was met not with charts and parchment but dust. Tophet smelled of ash and tasted of sorrow, as if the tears of those trapped within tainted the air. Spiraling towers as black as Bricru's coat rose into the void above, the tips of their spires brushing the wings of amphipteres who circled the sky. Before him, the keep sat like a stronghold amid the destruction.

This was not the true entrance to Tophet—that gateway lingered in the Sea of Hermon—but with the help of Uriah Caligari, the followers of Orisis now had ways to reach their home from anywhere in Vellichor.

Well, *almost* anywhere.

Elizus was already walking toward the keep, dust clinging to his ankles and spiraling around his cloak. That was one thing Orisis could not rid his home of—the dust. It was all that remained of Adoni's siege. The battle still lingered in the dust that hovered along the ground of Tophet, reminding its residents of the history that had happened there.

Soot spun at Bricru's boots as he trailed after the prince, his eyes sweeping the landscape. Afi soldiers walked the twisted roads between crooked buildings, unphased by the tormented cries that echoed from within each structure. Screeches of amphipteres danced from the void to the dust, and though no sun filled the space, light still dwelled, like the sky just before sunrise.

It was the only home Bricru had ever known.

He reached the doors of the keep just behind Elizus, coming to the prince's side as the afi before them hauled the doors open.

While the keep consisted of dark brick like the other structures, it was one of the few that didn't spiral to a point. Instead, it was flat and square, only five stories tall and split into sections connected by straight bridges. Windows pressed into the brick, mostly blocked by heavy curtains of gray or plum, and the doors had been crafted of smooth ebony.

"Don't expect praise," Elizus mocked, his heeled boots echoing on the floor.

Bricru said nothing, keeping the prince's pace as they strode through the entryway.

While the castle of Potri was lush and glowing, the keep was cold and ghostly. A few shelves of tattered books sat crooked against the stone walls, and several chandeliers of iron dripped wax onto the wooden floorboards. The afi strode freely through this level of the keep, the sounds of their armor clanking in the branching halls and light chatter adding warmth where there was otherwise ice.

The conversations drifted as afi stepped through gateways, emerging into parts of Vellichor that Bricru had often wished he could witness. There were dozens of them, made of silver arches, that filled the surrounding hallways. But there were even more that remained unfinished—metal arches without dust or light that sat vacant, abandoned.

The prince and shapeshifter reached the large set of stairs that rose to the second story, leaving the hall of gateways behind.

Bricru's hand mindlessly drifted to his coat pocket, where the elven blood was tucked beneath layers of cotton. The glass was cool to the touch, yet he felt as though the blood itself hummed beneath, alive and brimming with magic.

The uneven stairs stopped at the dark carpets of the second floor, this hall much cleaner than the first story. Closed doors sat undisturbed, their silver knobs free of fingerprints. Oil lamps illuminated the space, and the floor beneath Bricru's feet creaked slightly with each step.

Elizus straightened his shoulders as they drew closer, his iron eyes wandering slightly as if captured by thought. His mindless teasing had stopped, and while Bricru was no alithias, he could feel the tension seeping through the prince's bold exterior.

At the very end of the hall, an open doorway revealed black spiral stairs.

It was before these stairs that Bricru paused, his teeth digging into his tongue and filling his mouth with metal.

Elizus paused as well. "You got a second chance, Bricru." He spoke quietly, the cruel edge no longer clipping his words. "Don't ruin it. I will not save you."

Bricru straightened his coat and flexed his hands in the cold air. His voice was nothing more than a murmur. "You couldn't save me if you wanted."

"Good thing I *don't* want to." Elizus started up the steps, their conversation fading to silence once more.

Bricru felt his blood coursing through his veins, his heart racing in his ribcage. The air seemed to grow thinner with each step, like the oxygen was slowly draining from the room.

At last, the stairs ended.

The room was small, about the size of the castle observatory, and it housed no halls or windows. The low ceiling felt as though it was falling, ready to crush those within at the snap of a finger. A single gateway, coated in dust, was in the center of the room, filling the space.

It stood as tall as Elizus did, made of nothing but a silver frame and elven magic. Images flashed within the curved structure, glimpses of white oak and marble pillars; yet, these images were faded and fleeting, like a dream slipping from a waking mind.

And before the gateway stood the god of destruction.

Bricru dipped into a bow, his right hand pressed firmly to his chest to keep it from trembling. It'd been so long since he'd been in the presence of Orisis that he'd forgotten the weight the god carried with him. It nearly suffocated Bricru, swallowing his body in darkness and ruin.

There was a soft shuffle as the god turned to face his alithias and shapeshifter. He strode toward them, his steps tapping rhythmically on the stone floor.

Bricru struggled to keep his eyes shut. His lashes fluttered open to see the polished boots had stopped before him. He felt a hand on his chin, cold and demanding, and Bricru slowly lifted his head.

His eyes drifted past silver buttons and black cotton. Dust clung to the fabric, spiraling and dancing. It filled Bricru's breath as he lifted his gaze and met the face of Orisis.

Eyes as black as ink studied him, drifting along Bricru's scar as his fingers remained pressed against his chin. A frown was etched across the god's thin lips, and his dark hair had fallen against his furrowed brow. Pale skin starkly contrasted the solid black of his coat, and his pointed ears were decorated in cuffs of silver.

Orisis tilted Bricru's face slowly, as if seeing him for the first time. "I feel it." When he spoke, his voice dripped like honey, smooth and gentle, yet laced with poison.

Bricru swallowed. He no longer bothered to hide the tremble of his hands as he reached into his coat, revealing the vial of red, and passed it into Orisis' hand.

The god's lips parted slightly as he lifted the vial, studying it much like he had Bricru's face. For an agonizing moment, the god seemed to forget Bricru was there, his attention fully transfixed by the magic he held. But then he turned, his midnight gaze falling on Bricru once more.

"Welcome back, child."

For nearly six weeks, Bricru had ached to hear those words. He'd gathered the information, killed the celestial, initiated the attack on Sannir, found Uriah's son, and now he'd brought Orisis the one thing that could reverse the damage Uriah had done.

A chilled breath fell from Bricru's lips, though the tremors still shook his hands. "Kyler Caligari is chained beneath the castle, as is the new general."

Orisis raised a brow, accompanied by a small smirk. "You've outdone yourself. And the alithias doubted you."

Elizus bristled, though he said nothing.

"Well done, both of you." Orisis popped the cork on the vial, bringing it to his nose and inhaling the scent. He smiled.

Then Orisis stepped to the gateway. The dust within the curved metal frame came alive, jumping with excitement. It spun faster, more violently, as Orisis neared. Tendrils of dust reached for his clothes and brushed the vial.

Bricru set his sights on the flashing images that began to solidify within the dust. The white brick of Sannir's castle, the blue sky dotted with spots of pale clouds, became crisp as Orisis lifted the blood, presenting it to the gateway as one might an offering. Blood dissipated into the dust as Orisis tipped the vial, the smile on his face growing wider with the giddy excitement of a child.

And when the final drop of blood had slipped from the glass—

Bricru froze as the dust swallowed the gateway once more, covering the images of Sannir and locking it behind a layer of mist. The images within grew distant and faded once more.

For a moment, no one spoke. In fact, Bricru was certain no one breathed. The smile had fallen from the face of the god, now replaced with something far colder. He lifted a hand to the gateway. His palm came to a halt as he pressed into it. Just as it was before, the gateway to Sannir remained locked.

Orisis slowly dipped his chin, his dark hair falling across his cheekbones as his hand remained firm against the dust. "Elizus?"

"Bricru speaks truth," the prince answered quickly, his voice pinched. "It's elven blood. You felt it—"

"I know what I felt!" Dust leaped into the air as Orisis shouted, stinging Bricru's cheeks as it whipped around him. The empty vial shattered. Glass skittered across the stone and crunched beneath Orisis' feet as he stalked toward Bricru. He gripped the shapeshifter's chin once more.

This time, his touch was angry, violent, like the edge of a knife pressed to Bricru's throat. The pads of his fingers dug painfully into the shapeshifter's jaw as Orisis held him, his dark gaze somehow darker.

"What did you do, snake?"

"I did nothing—"

"You did nothing!" He threw Bricru's face aside, his teeth bared and breath quick. "I ask for the key, and you come back with *nothing!*"

Tears burned Bricru's vision, but he didn't dare let them fall. His mind spun, recalling every move he'd made, every piece of knowledge he'd gathered. He must've missed something. The blood was supposed to unlock the gateway.

His gaze fixated on the stone floor, blurred and searing.

"And you, *alithias*"—Orisis turned to Elizus, the pride that he'd once taken in the prince now cracked—"who fails to see truth!"

Elizus filched slightly, but his chin remained high. "I will find you truth."

"Yes, you will." Orisis pulled a deep breath into his lungs, the anger on his face slowly fading, and the dust that trailed him calmed to a soft swirl once more. "Elizus, speak to Uriah. Do not let me see your face again until you've uncovered every last secret that man is hiding. Am I clear?"

"Yes, my lord." Elizus dipped into a bow, his form practiced and flawless, as smooth as his voice.

"Bricru."

Bricru lifted his head, finding something soft in Orisis' gaze once more.

"I do not wish to cast you from my side." He spoke so plainly, yet his words held the power to shatter Bricru. "It was you whom Uriah came to trust, you who guided him to open the gateways of the realm. It is you who will break young Caligari."

Ori stepped closer, staring down his nose at the shapeshifter. "If Kyler is anything like his father, then he should crumble just as easily."

Bricru dropped his head, his practiced bow tarnished by the fear that gripped his chest. "Yes, my lord."

CHAPTER TWENTY-EIGHT

THE LOCK ON THE DOOR CLICKED.

Kyler raised his head, his lashes dotted with salt and mind still dragging. He wasn't sure how long he'd been alone, but it was long enough that he'd been able to gather his thoughts and think logically. The chains were thick and the bars heavy. Even if he could free himself from the shackles, the bars would be impossible to slip through.

His best bet was to play Bricru's game.

The stone at his back had dug painful rivets into his skin, and the clean braids he kept at his temples had begun to unravel. The stray hair brushed his face as he blinked at the light that slipped through the open door.

He recognized the shadow that entered. The shapeshifter, dressed in the same dark cloak, met Kyler's cold gaze as he sealed the door shut behind him. His steps echoed as he strode calmly to the desk, dragging the chair out once more and seating himself before the bars.

Kyler's jaw ached with tension, and the weight of the chains at his ankles hung heavy over his boots, but he made no move to reposition. He simply lifted his chin, waiting for Bricru to resume his teasing.

Bricru pursed his lips and leaned forward in the chair. His gaze dropped to the floor, and his voice was lower than before—more calculated. "Whose blood did you give me?"

A smile urged its way to Kyler's mouth.

The shapeshifter glared at him. "Answer."

Kyler closed his eyes and rested his head against the stone. It seemed whatever Bricru had wanted with the elven blood hadn't worked. Novah had been wise to give hers.

Bricru rose from his chair, slamming his hands against the bars that separated them. "Answer me, Caligari!"

"That's not my name." Kyler looked up at him.

Bricru's eyes were wild. The calculation Kyler had seen previously was now replaced with a look of chaos. His chest fell with a frustrated sigh, and he raked his hands through his hair. With each tug, his hands began to fracture, flashing like broken mirrors in the light, as his aggravation grew.

He backed away from the bars, swallowing his emotions. "Alright. I propose a deal."

"A deal?" Kyler lifted a brow. "Last time I made a deal with you, I ended up in chains."

"For every question you answer, I'll answer one in return."

There was a desperation in his eyes, the kind that made him look more elf than afi. His tousled hair fell against his lashes and brushed his burning cheeks, as if attempting to calm whatever raged within him. He looked the way Kyler felt—foolish and alone.

Despite his better judgment, Kyler sat upright. His palms dug into the stone as he pushed himself up from his slouch. "No lies."

Bricru sat down, the chair creaking lightly as he did. "No lies." He straightened his shoulders. "Whose blood did you give me?"

"Novah's."

His lips twisted slightly, but he didn't push further.

It was Kyler's turn. "Where is she?"

Bricru's fingers tapped his kneecap gently. "Worried about your soft spot, Caligari?"

"Answer."

"She's in a cage, like you. Alive, last I saw her."

The knot in Kyler's chest loosened slightly.

"When was the last time you spoke to your father?"

The harsh memories rushed into Kyler's mind like a cold mountain wind. That was a conversation he wished desperately to forget, and yet it resurfaced over and over. Kyler held the shapeshifter's eye. "Nearly a year before he disappeared."

"What did he say?"

Kyler clicked his tongue. "One question at a time, shapeshifter."

Bricru scowled but remained silent.

"Why is Orisis keeping me alive?"

This question made Bricru lift his gaze to the ceiling, his thumb rubbing the inside of his palm as he thought. "I don't know."

"That's not an answer."

He shook his head slowly, still staring at the dips and cracks in the stone above their heads. "I have my assumptions, but keeping you alive was nothing more than an order. Orisis wants you alive, so you'll stay alive."

Kyler tilted his head, his tangled scales knocking against his jaw. "So, you *are* just a servant."

This time, it was Bricru who chided. "One at a time."

"That wasn't a question."

The shapeshifter leaned closer, lacing his fingers together. "What was the last thing Uriah said to you?"

Kyler knew the words. They danced through his mind, the very tone Uriah had spoken them in engraved in his thoughts like the embossing on his armor. As he opened his mouth to repeat them, they seemed to stick on his tongue. "'You are nothing without me.'"

Bricru slowly leaned back in his seat, his face betraying thoughts unspoken.

"My turn." Kyler's voice was rough as he forced out his next question. "How long has Uriah been working for you?"

The shapeshifter took his time answering, tallying the dates in his mind until he was certain they were correct. "About two years."

Two years. All that time, all those harsh words and cold stares, Uriah had been serving Orisis. He was the general, and he was a traitor. Perhaps that was why Uriah had become so distant.

Fear crept through Kyler's blood. Uriah had access to information beyond that of the commanders—information on the Pass, on the kingdom, on the dragons.

"Go ahead," Bricru interrupted his thoughts. "I see you have another question. I'll play nice."

Kyler chose his question carefully. "What project was he working on?"

"I don't think that's my place to answer."

Kyler's gaze narrowed slightly. "This is your game, shapeshifter. If you want my answers, give me yours."

Bricru scrunched his nose, and his fingers resumed their anxious tapping. "I think Uriah will want to tell you that himself."

"He's in Tophet." The chains at Kyler's ankles clanked as he shifted. "He's not telling me anything."

"It seems you don't know the rules of Tophet. Uriah may be imprisoned, but he is very much conscious. A tortured soul is still a soul."

"Take me to him."

Something sparked across Bricru's face, his eyes lighting in a way that made Kyler regret his request. "That can be arranged."

If the shapeshifter could hide his thoughts, he didn't bother trying. His fidgeting grew faster as the frown dissipated off his face. Kyler could see an idea was forming in his mind, which he wished the shapeshifter would voice.

He stood, lightly kicking the chair to the side, and straightened his jacket. "Give me time."

Kyler looked at the iron bars. "I'm not going anywhere."

"That humor is familiar." Bricru gave a tight smile, the first expression he'd made that resembled Ophir, and he disappeared into whatever lay beyond that door.

...

There was a part of Kyler that hoped Bricru wouldn't return. He watched the door, expecting the shapeshifter to deny his request, and yet when it finally opened once more, Bricru entered with chains in his hands.

"Elizus isn't happy about this." The chains clamored as he untangled them. He gave a deep sigh as he dug a key from his pocket, shoving it into the lock on the iron bars. He struggled for a moment, the lock clearly not used to being opened and closed. When it finally released, it let out a rusted squeal as he swung open the cage.

"I'm expecting you to behave, Commander."

Kyler wanted to retort, but he was too engrossed in thought. He hadn't spoken to his father in years. He stood slowly, his head spinning and legs aching. The shackles at his ankles rattled as he faced Bricru, eying the iron in his hands. "Is this necessary?"

Bricru shrugged. He joined Kyler within the bars, clamping the chains around his wrists and giving them a firm tug to ensure they were secure.

The shapeshifter was shorter than he seemed. From this angle, light caught the scar that ran across his nose, the skin pale and disfigured, as crooked as the shapeshifter's soul.

"You don't look excited," Bricru stated, kneeling to free Kyler's ankles.

Kyler twisted his wrists, attempting to ignore the way the chains dug into his skin. "I just want answers, not a reunion."

The chains at his ankles released with a click of the lock.

"I'm not certain your father feels the same."

"I don't care what he feels."

Kyler rolled his shoulders as Bricru took hold of the chains, guiding him like the prisoner he was through the bars and out of the small room.

Beyond the door was a hallway of stone, lit by the same low lamps that burned in Kyler's cell. Doors of oak ran the length of the hall, and several turns branched out into new hallways and corners. Damp air clung to the stone, heavy and smelling of mildew, and low conversations mingled with the sound of footsteps.

Kyler kept the shapeshifter's stride, his chains the only thing distinguishing him as a prisoner, and he studied the doors they passed.

"If you're looking for your general, you won't find her."

Kyler's gaze snapped back to Bricru. "You said—"

"The dungeon is vast. She's here, just not close." He brushed a hand down his coat as they neared a set of wooden stairs. "I hope you know how much convincing this required."

"You want information, don't you?"

Bricru frowned but said nothing as he led Kyler up the stairs and into a room of gold and glass. Tapestries hung from the walls, vaulted ceilings had been painted in white and silver, and the prince of Potri stood, waiting, with a scowl on his face.

The moment Elizus laid eyes on Kyler, his scowl deepened, a wrinkle curling up his straight nose. "Gods, he smells horrible."

Kyler smirked. "A dungeon will do that."

The edges of Bricru's lips tugged upward, but Elizus didn't seem to find it humorous. He gave a deep sigh and pressed his fingers to his temple. "Don't touch anything, Sann."

Kyler lifted his bound hands, his chains clinking as he did, and this seemed to be answer enough for the prince. He started across the room and guided them through another twisting hall.

This one was familiar. Golden knobs and golden plates adorned every door, and just as before, Kyler found himself walking the curved stone stairs that led to the castle observatory.

Curiosity flooded him, overpowering the feeling of dread that threatened to surface.

Rays of vibrant sunlight cut through the half-glass ceiling, illuminating the scattered papers and bronze equipment. Spots of white dotted Kyler's vision as Bricru led him across the room, stopping before the painting of moving stars.

"I hope you know what you're doing, Bricru." The tone Elizus used now was different than his usual sharp arrogance.

Bricru straightened, keeping his sights on the painting. "Come on, Caligari."

Kyler had no choice but to follow as Bricru stepped into the painting, and the observatory disappeared.

The first thing he heard were the screams—desperate and ragged, filled with an agony only Orisis could offer. Cool air brushed his skin, much colder than that of the castle, and when Kyler opened his eyes, he was met with scattered pale light and spires that reached toward a starless sky. The clang of shifting armor surrounded him as afi soldiers patrolled the streets, their boots sinking into the dust. Most had their helmets removed, their hair tussled and voices gentle with pleasant conversation.

Dust clung to his shoes and danced up his legs, as if it were alive. There was *so much* of it, covering every surface, and it swallowed his shoes like sand.

"Welcome to Tophet." Bricru flashed a grin, his voice carrying despite the lack of wind. The whole world seemed to echo, voices drifting into the void above only to be swallowed by it.

Before them, a structure that resembled a fortress stood sturdy, its walls square and level as opposed to the rest of the long buildings. This was where most of the afi lingered, pacing in and out of the wide wooden doors.

Bricru nodded his chin to the structure. "That's where your father's creations dwell." He turned from the keep, and Kyler followed without him having to tug on the chains.

He wanted to ask questions, but Tophet drew out a certain reverence from him, the kind of reverence reserved for tragedy. This was a place of death.

Uriah would answer his questions soon enough.

Kyler kept his sights on the spires, catching glimpses of amphipteres twisting between the structures. Their calls filled the dust-covered streets, mingling with the muted cries that fell from each spire they passed.

Bricru led him to a gate, the bars nearly as tall as the spire they enclosed. Spiked arrows tipped the metal, running along its length and pointing up to the void, and before it was a man dressed unlike any of the afi Kyler had seen.

He appeared unarmed, his attire subtle, yet elegant. Like Bricru, he wore a dark coat stitched in designs, but the thread was the same black that made up the fabric. The man was tall and thin, with skin as pale as moonlight, sharp cheekbones, and dark hair combed from his face. Kyler struggled to place his age. His ears stretched to a point, and silver cuffs ran along them in rows of metal.

The man watched Kyler with a gaze that rivaled the alithias, his dark eyes studying every step until the commander stood before him. He seemed to judge every curve of Kyler's face and freckle on his skin, and when he was finally done, he turned to the shapeshifter.

"Thank you, Bricru."

Bricru stood still, the playfulness gone from his face.

The man turned back to Kyler. "Kyler Caligari, I'm thrilled." The monotone way in which he spoke contradicted his words. "You may address me as Ancelin."

Kyler lifted his chin, forcing himself to meet Ancelin's dark gaze. "You may address me as Weylyn."

A smile rose to his lips, creasing the edges of his mouth. "You *are* a stubborn one. Runs in the family." He spotted Kyler's chains, and his smile fell. "We can't have that. Bricru, please."

Bricru reached for Kyler's chains, fumbling with the key for a moment before releasing their hold and letting them drop to the dust. Kyler clamped his fingers around his sore wrists, rolling them slightly as the ache subsided.

Then he lunged at Ancelin.

His hit landed against Ancelin's sharp cheekbone with a crack that echoed in the silent street. Ancelin stumbled against the metal gate, barely dodging Kyler's next swing. It missed, and Kyler hardly caught his balance before dust curled up his arms, halting him.

Stronger than chains, the dust tugged his hands to his sides, locking his muscles in place despite his attempts to free himself from its hold.

Ancelin blinked in surprise, his fingers mindlessly brushing where Kyler had caught his face. The shock slowly shifted into amusement as he straightened. Nothing but a faint red blotch marked his skin.

Kyler's brow furrowed. He swore he'd hit the man hard enough to draw blood. He tugged against the hold of the dust, feeling it curl along his torso and brush against his neck.

This man had unnatural power.

"What are you?" Kyler asked through gritted teeth.

Ancelin shrugged. "Your enemy."

The dust slowly loosened its grip, falling like sand from Kyler's clothes.

Ancelin ran his hands down his coat, tugging the cuffs of his sleeves straight with a sigh. "We don't have all day. Let's get on with it."

He turned his back to Kyler, and the gates swung open of their own accord, as if summoned by some unspoken command. Dust spiraled as Ancelin strode through the gates, and Bricru followed, urging Kyler to do the same.

Before them, an open door offered entrance into the spire. Kyler found himself studying the buildings, his eyes raised to the crooked edges of black stone and metal that curled upward. Ancelin stopped at the door and motioned Kyler inside.

The room within was bare, without windows or candlelight, yet even as Ancelin closed the door behind them, Kyler could see fine. The same pale light that filled the streets filled the room as well, illuminating the low ceiling and gray walls.

Just like the room Kyler had been caged in, this one was sectioned off by bars, the area within them so small that it fit only a vacant wooden chair. It smelled like decay and blood.

Kyler's breath puffed before his face. He felt oddly warm despite the cold air that surrounded them. The heels of Ancelin's boots echoed in the space as he stepped toward bars, pressing his eyes shut and mouth muttering words unheard.

Then, he snapped his fingers, and the dust rose.

The bars filled with gray and brown, spinning hard enough to sting Kyler's skin even as he stepped away from the swarm. A gentle hum rose from within the flurry, and when it finally settled, the chair was no longer vacant.

There sat a man. He looked weaker than Kyler had ever seen him, his once harsh demeanor now lifeless and hollow. Dark bags hung beneath his eyes and sweat dotted his skin. His dry lips parted as his faded gaze fell on Kyler. His voice was ragged, scraping against his throat as he spoke.

"You shouldn't be here."

CHAPTER TWENTY-NINE

KYLER SAW HIMSELF IN URIAH. IN THE WAY HIS FATHER'S BROWS furrowed and jaw shifted. Uriah was broader, with a square chin, dusty hair, and eyes so blue they rivaled the sky, but his wide hands looked just like Kyler's when bound in chains, and his expressions failed to mask the defeat that plagued Kyler's own mind. Scales of emerald dangled from his ears, their shine all but gone, except for the lone bone-colored scale that hung on the right.

Uriah's gaze shifted to Ancelin. "I said—"

"I don't think you're in a position to be making demands, General." Ancelin tilted his head, his brows lifting.

"Leave us," Kyler said evenly. His pulse drummed fiercely beneath his skin, yet he kept his voice steady.

Bricru hesitated, but Ancelin seemed to have expected this. He dipped his head with a nod, guiding Bricru toward the door with a hand on his back. "It seems you have unfinished business with your father. I suggest you say your goodbyes."

And with that, the door fell shut, locking Kyler in with the man he hated most.

For a moment, neither of them spoke. Kyler stared at the closed door, his mind rushing as fast as his blood.

It was Uriah who broke the silence with a single word. "Kyler."

Kyler turned, his vision clouded and blood hot. He slammed a fist against the iron bars, hard enough to make his bones rattle, and Uriah flinched at the sound.

"This is your fault," he spat, his face inches from the bars. "You should be dead. You *are* dead. You are nothing but a corpse."

"Kyler, please," His voice was raw, struggling to surpass a whisper. "I can fix this."

"Please?" he scoffed. "Tophet's changed you. Since when do you have manners?"

You are nothing without me. You are nothing.

The words pounded through Kyler's skull.

He pushed off the bars, beginning a slow pace around the room. His steps echoed in the space between them, and his fingers dug through his tangled hair, catching in painful knots.

"I need you to listen to me."

"You did this!" Kyler's shout filled the room. "This is *your* fault, Uriah!"

"Let me make it right."

"You can't!" He paused as the words left his mouth, the truth of them leaving a bitter taste on his tongue. It was only then he noticed the way his hands trembled and lungs shuttered with every breath. He was terrified.

Uriah shifted in his chair, his chains tapping against one another as he did. "Orisis wants Sannir. He plans to enter it and lay claim to the kingdom."

"He already entered Sannir," Kyler snapped. "He doesn't need help with that."

"If it were that simple, neither of us would be here."

Kyler forced a breath and faced his father once more. "Why am I here, Uriah?"

His gaze remained steady, the muscles of his neck tensing at the question.

Kyler stepped toward the bars once more, crouching to meet the former general's eye. "What were you doing for them?"

He paused before he answered. "The afi are children of Orisis, trading themselves for his touch. They can no longer create, so they need someone to do it for them."

Kyler sighed and closed his eyes. "They want me to finish what you started." A dry laugh escaped his lips. "And what did you start?"

He swallowed. "Gateways."

Kyler stilled, recalling the painting they'd used to enter.

Uriah continued. "They have access to nearly every edge of Vellichor, but the gateway to Sannir is different. Sannir and Tophet were never made to mix. Orisis and his followers are locked out of it—I ensured it."

The pieces slowly secured themselves in Kyler's mind. He stood, refusing to meet Uriah's eye. "You gave them direct access to our kingdom?"

"I did."

"Sannir's Saints," Kyler groaned, running his hands down his face.

"But it's sealed. They need elven blood to open—"

"They have it."

Uriah's head snapped up, his eyes wide. "Whose blood?"

"Does it matter?"

His voice rose. *"Whose blood?"*

"Novah's." Kyler snapped. "The new general."

Uriah released a breath, nodding slowly. "Of course the dragons chose her."

Anger burned within Kyler's chest, as bitter and hot as flame, but Uriah spoke again before he could gather his thoughts.

"Her blood won't work for them. They haven't succeeded yet. I can only assume that's why they brought you."

"Why?"

Uriah straightened in his seat. "Because I used my blood to lock the gateways. That means only I can unlock them."

"They think one look at me will make you fill their vials with crimson in exchange for my freedom? At least they got one thing wrong."

The look on Uriah's face softened slightly, as if the words cut deeper than the chains around his skin.

Kyler caught the look. "Don't tell me you care all of a sudden."

"Kyler." He stopped himself, pinching his tongue between his teeth. "You're my son."

A hollow laugh rose from Kyler's chest. "I can't believe I'm hearing this."

"We share blood."

"Ah, so you don't care." Kyler knelt by the cage once more, his hands still shaking and mind finally coming to terms with the situation Uriah had placed them in. "I can unlock those gateways just like you can."

"Only willingly. Novah's blood didn't work, and when they realize why, you will know no peace," the former general said, without expression. It was as if Tophet had ripped him of whatever humanity he had left, leaving only a shell of the man he once was.

"You're a wretched man, Uriah Caligari."

Uriah blinked, his gaze dropping to the floor. "I'm sorry—"

"And I'm not your son!" Kyler's voice ripped from his throat, full of the rage he'd harbored since that final conversation in the castle courtyard. "You left. You chose to walk away from

Evander and me, and now you've chosen to walk away from Sannir. You're a vile man, Uriah. Do us both a favor and save your love for yourself. Adoni knows you need it down here."

CHAPTER THIRTY

ORISIS PRESSED A GENTLE HAND BETWEEN BRICRU'S SHOULDER blades, his cool touch seeping through the thick fabric of the shapeshifter's coat. Wails and cries filled the air, but Bricru's focus was latched to the presence of the god. Dust clung to his shoes like ants, crawling up to his hands and tugging at his clothes.

Orisis said nothing, his touch firm as he guided them out of the gate and into the twisted streets. It was here that Orisis finally dropped his hand, pausing with his chin tilted to admire the spires above.

"I hope you're right, Bricru."

Bricru calmed his mind, focusing on the god's face. There was no anger in it now, just a soft curiosity, which was almost as terrifying. His skin still pricked red where Kyler had hit him, though the color was quickly fading.

Bricru followed Orisis' line of vision toward the peak of the temple, which rose through the shadows.

"Walk with me."

It was not a suggestion as much as a command. Bricru fell in stride beside the god of destruction, fear and pride swimming in his chest. He found himself stealing glances at Orisis, wondering what filled his mind and guided his steps.

The mind of a god was a mystery that enchanted Bricru.

"I take great pride in you, Bricru," Orisis began, his words slow and easy. "You, of all your brothers, have risen well. Your mind is sharp, and your magic is powerful." He took hold of Bricru's hand, pausing in the middle of the dust and flipping Bricru's palm upward. His thumb traced the lines that ran across the shapeshifter's skin, his touch light.

"Shift for me."

Bricru obeyed, turning his skin to glass. Fragments caught in the pale light, casting rainbows into the dust as the shards rolled across Bricru's arm. This was a familiar sensation. His body felt light, and his arm was numb to Orisis' touch. The shapeshifter kept his mind steady, his arm remaining mid-shift as Orisis studied it. He brushed the fragments, his eyes fixed on the transformation.

"Incredible, as always." His voice was merely a breath. "Even now, your magic remains potent."

The words did not please Bricru in the way they did Orisis, but the shapeshifter didn't dare voice this. He held his arm steady until Orisis released his hand, then allowed his skin to return to normal.

Orisis reached for Bricru's face, running the tips of his fingers along the scar that danced across Bricru's nose and cheek. His lips parted as he studied the mark, a furrow set between his brows. Finally, he met Bricru's eye, and his hard expression softened. "I have missed you, child."

Bricru did not doubt the truth in his words. Even as a boy, he had known the desire Orisis had to be close with his chosen. To cast Bricru away must have hurt the god as much as it hurt the shapeshifter, and Bricru clung to this thought as Orisis resumed their walk, strolling slowly beneath bridges and between spires.

"Unfortunately, my love for you is not enough. The three that came before you had to earn their place at my side, and you and Elizus must do the same."

You and Elizus. Not the Sixth. That one was different, and Bricru couldn't help but wonder why.

Orisis clasped his hands behind his back, studying the spires once more. "I advise you to work with the alithias, Bricru. I know how you two quarrel, but you must assist one another if you are to find a way to complete the gateways."

Bricru pursed his lips, recalling the previous few weeks. "I could not allow Elizus to resolve my failures."

Orisis said nothing, making one final turn before coming to a halt just outside of the keep. The swirling dust gateway that led back to Potri's castle greeted them with images of stars and parchment spinning beyond, its metal arch standing alone in the center of the street.

The god did not look at Bricru. His dark gaze lingered on the gateway as if studying the castle within. "I will send young Caligari back to you when I am done with him. Do whatever you must to get me what I want."

Bricru dipped his head, stepping through the gateway without another word. Orisis' touch still lingered on his skin—a threat as much as it was an endearment. Orisis would get what he wanted. If Bricru couldn't do it, Orisis would find someone who could.

Parchment and astrolabes greeted as Bricru stepped back into the castle observatory and found Elizus sitting atop one of the crooked tables.

His hands gripped the edge of the wood, ankles crossed and lips pursed in thought. He glanced up as Bricru entered. "Where is he?"

Bricru sighed, taking what felt like his first breath since

speaking with the god. "With Uriah. Orisis will send him back."

Elizus' dark brows only dipped deeper. "Orisis doesn't get his hands dirty."

"He does this time." Bricru combed his fingers through his hair, leaning against the table opposite the prince. "I know how to persuade the commander."

Elizus tilted his head, his hair falling from its combed place as he did so. "Do tell."

"You won't like it."

The prince's smile grew. "Now I'm intrigued."

"Move him and the general from their cells. Let them stay in the castle."

Elizus scoffed, but Bricru spoke before he could counter.

"Uriah was easy to manipulate once I'd earned his trust. His son will never cooperate until we treat him—and his general—kindly."

A small laugh fell from Elizus' lips. "You're right. I don't like that."

"I can break him, Elizus." Bricru caught the gaze of the alithias.

For a moment, neither of them spoke. The prince and the shapeshifter sat in a silent war, the lingering magic of alith filling the space between them.

"You really believe that." Elizus finally broke the silence. "Then you should know what I've just learned." His gold-stitched coat shifted as he leaned closer. "The blood didn't work. If Uriah had simply abandoned his project, it would have, but he didn't. He locked those gateways intentionally, so they must be opened *intentionally*, using the blood with which they were locked."

Bricru leaned back against the table, his eyes lifting to the star-clad ceiling. "We don't need elven blood, we need Uriah's blood."

"No," Elizus corrected. "We need *Caligari* blood."

CHAPTER THIRTY-ONE

WHEN THE DOOR FINALLY OPENED, KYLER DIDN'T SAY GOODBYE.

He lifted his head as dust rolled into the room, carrying Ancelin with it.

Ancelin looked at Uriah, then Kyler. "I'm sorry to interrupt."

"You didn't interrupt anything." Kyler shoved off the wall, brushing past Ancelin and stepping into the cool air of Tophet. He could feel Uriah watching as he left, but the former general gave no argument.

Kyler's tongue stung from the bitter words he'd uttered to Uriah, and he said nothing as the door shut behind him, resigning Uriah to his fate once more. He'd hoped the heaviness in his chest would subside once he was away from his father's gaze, but it only seemed to grow.

Kyler turned to Ancelin. The man was alone this time, without the shapeshifter at his side.

"I hope your conversation was insightful," Ancelin said plainly, crossing his arms over his narrow chest.

Uriah's voice still clutched Kyler's mind, the rough edge of his warnings lingering like the dust around him.

He met Ancelin's eye. There was something unnerving about the way he carried himself—the way he spoke as if his words held some sort of strength he didn't want revealed.

Kyler turned his attention to the world around him, full of destruction and chaos. "What did Tophet do to him?"

A tiny smirk tugged the afi's lips, but it dissipated as quickly as it'd come. "Tophet is a slow pain, the kind that rips a man apart, piece by piece, until nothing of him remains." He began to walk slowly, guiding Kyler away from the building and away from his father. "Uriah is losing himself day by day, and soon enough, he will lose his mind. He will exist as a shell of a man, tormented by his own thoughts for as long as Tophet stands."

Kyler stared at the spiraling dust, imagining the man he'd once admired as nothing more than a living corpse. "And what if he were to escape?"

Ancelin hummed with amusement. "The twisted magic that binds Tophet is powerful, Caligari. Uriah will not be escaping anytime soon."

"I don't answer to that name."

He paused, his dark gaze falling on Kyler once more. "Orisis sees you as you truly are, and he doesn't care. The name 'Caligari' may have held power in Sannir, but here, it is nothing. To you, it means rejection. To me, it is a means to an end, nothing more." He shrugged, and the dust seemed to rise and fall with his shoulders. "But, if it holds that much power over you, then so be it. Your name is the least of my concerns. There are a few more things I'd like to show you while you're here."

Ancelin motioned him out of the gate. Kyler found himself studying the dust, losing himself in the way it spun and danced beneath his steps as if it were alive.

"It is our constant reminder," Ancelin said, noticing the way Kyler watched the dust. He paused and knelt, combing his fingers through the rough specks that climbed along his hands as he touched them. "When your first general, Eliab, led his armies into Tophet, he left it in ruins." He looked up at Kyler, dust clinging to his touch. "These are the ruins. We may rebuild, but we cannot erase our past."

Kyler knelt beside him. The callouses on his hands caught the dust as it slipped through his fingers. It did not cling to him the way it did Ancelin. Where the afi seemed to bring life to the ruin, Kyler seemed to make it cower.

"What do you think of it?"

Kyler's brow furrowed. "You mean Tophet?"

"Very few outsiders visit. I'm curious what one who simply passes through might make of our home."

Spiraling buildings reached toward the void above. Ruin lined the streets. "It's unnatural."

There was a snag in Ancelin's smile. "To you. You're accustomed to the laws of Adoni's creation. You view the world through him. You know up from down, right from wrong, light from dark. Think of Tophet as an in-between. There is no true definition of these things. We are separate."

"But you face the consequences of the gods." Kyler grabbed a handful of dust, watching it drizzle back to the ground. "You cannot create, so nothing you do is truly your own. You've separated yourself from magic."

"No." Ancelin grew suddenly serious, as if something Kyler had said was like the tip of a blade to his heart. "We are *free* of magic. If magic were a gift, it would not have limits." He stood suddenly, the dust following his rise. "The alithias and shapeshifter have yet to face the consequences of the afi. Their magic remains, untethered to the Dragon Pass."

Kyler's jaw shifted in thought, and he rose slowly to meet Ancelin. "They must've sacrificed something. Afi power comes with a cost that must be paid."

Ancelin dipped his chin in a nod. If he knew what they'd paid, he did not share it. "You should know that there is a way to free your former general from this place."

Despite his will, Kyler found himself staring back at the metal gate, picturing the tired eyes of his father. "How?"

"Orisis will free anyone for the right price."

Kyler's head snapped back to Ancelin, his gaze now sharp. "I am not Uriah. Don't fool yourself into thinking I will bend as easily as he did."

He lifted his palms in surrender. "My apologies. I thought it was only fair you understood the way things work. Uriah has put himself in this position, and I should not assume you wish to be his savior."

"He is past the point of saving."

Ancelin's lips pressed thin, as if wishing to argue those words, but he chose to drop the matter and resumed his stroll. "Can I ask you something?" He curiously watched the afi that passed as he spoke. "What makes the call of Adoni so appealing?"

"I could ask you the same about Orisis."

He thought for a moment. "The freedom, I suppose. Orisis challenges the law and makes his own truth. He keeps his followers from being blinded by good and evil, allowing us to decide for ourselves what we believe to be true."

Kyler listened, allowing Ancelin's words to etch themselves into his mind. "You call the rules of Adoni binding, but they are just." He mindlessly reached for his waist, where the shadow of his potion belt seemed to linger.

Ancelin noticed this. "You are an alchemist. I saw the potions you carried. I must admit, I was impressed. Your skill was evident in everything, from your brews to your notes. You should be proud."

An odd warmth curled around Kyler's chest.

"It's funny," he continued, "how different we are, and yet we desire the same things. Respect. Appreciation. Peace." He slowed as they reached a rounded building, its pointed tip rising like a steeple. Unlike the rest of the spires, this one was open, its ceiling nothing but walkways that seemed to welcome the void. It glistened of black stone, and just like everything else, dust danced along its surface, catching in the unknown light.

Ancelin started up the steps. "This is what I want to show you."

The interior of the building was dark, yet Kyler could still make out the singular item that sat in the room's center. A chalice rested atop an elegant metal pole, engraved with images of amphipteres. The beasts spiraled up the chalice, their shapes shifting in shadow as Kyler inched closer. His shoes thumped against the polished floor, and he noticed quickly that there was no sign of dust within this hall.

"What is this?" Kyler's voice echoed in the emptiness, carrying to the vaults in the open ceiling.

Ancelin remained at the doorway. "We are in the Hall of Transformation, where those who chose to devote themselves to Orisis drink of the cup and are gifted with his power."

Kyler's reflection caught in the silver liquid that filled the cup. Though no wind of movement touched it, the liquid rippled lightly, twisting the faded freckles on Kyler's face until he hardly recognized the man staring back at him.

He lifted his gaze to Ancelin. "Is this some kind of potion?"

"No." He strode closer, while keeping his distance from the cup. "It is all that remains of the original afi—the only thing Eliab did not destroy. When Orisis saw he was losing the battle, he stole away with the cup, keeping it safe until he could rebuild his army once more."

Kyler backed away from the chalice, his skin beginning to burn beneath his cotton shirt. "Why are you showing me this?"

"I want you to know what we offer." His voice floated through the empty room. "I am not Bricru or Elizus. I won't threaten you with my power or trick you into talking, and I won't feed you false hope as Adoni does so often. You won't choose this, I know that, but I want you to see it."

Kyler stood his ground as Ancelin neared, his face close and voice low. He smelled of ash and metal, his presence cooling the very air Kyler breathed. "Your god keeps his dragons sheltered. He hides knowledge from you and drops you into enemy hands. This is war, Commander. Though we may be on opposing sides, it's not a fair battle unless both are fighting freely. You will choose Adoni, and I will choose Orisis. But now, the field is leveled. Your choice is not your father's. Your choice is your own."

Silence filled the hall, as empty as Kyler's chest. He stared at the man before him, those words sinking into his skin. He had no rebuttal or challenge. He wasn't sure he wanted one.

"Thank you." The words fell out of his mouth before he knew what they meant.

Ancelin dipped his head. "Bricru will be waiting at the painting for you."

He turned to leave, but Kyler halted him. "One more question."

Ancelin met his eye once more, curiosity brimming in his dark gaze.

"Who are you to Orisis?"

He offered a tight smile, and the darkness of the room seemed to curl with his lips. "I said before that I was your enemy, and I hope for both our sakes that remains true. Without a battle to fight, we soldiers are nothing."

CHAPTER THIRTY-TWO

"DID YOU GET THE ANSWERS YOU WANTED?"

There was a playful edge to Bricru's words as he pushed off the table he'd been leaning on and folded his arms as Kyler emerged through the painting. The dust fell from Kyler's clothes the moment he entered the small observatory, as if the painting were sucking the destruction back into Tophet.

He watched it tumble into the painted stars. "I assume you're going to shackle me again?"

The shapeshifter eyed Kyler's hands, then clicked his tongue. "Not anymore. In fact, I have something for you."

He turned to the table behind him revealing cotton clothing and polished armor. It was neatly folded and recently cleaned, embossed with dragons as if mocking the chalice within Ancelin's hall. The sight of it made Kyler momentarily forget the afi.

"Why are you giving me this?" Kyler asked as he took his familiar armor into his hands, running a finger along the polished surface. It hung heavy in his arms, the soft fabric draping over the sleeves of his dirty tunic and the bright silver shifting in his hold.

"It wasn't right to keep you in a cage. You are a highly esteemed commander, and you should be treated as such."

A frown etched onto Kyler's face. "Don't play kind, Bricru. I'm still a prisoner here."

He shrugged. "A prisoner who will receive a bed and hot food. And who desperately needs a bath." Bricru uncrossed his arms, motioning Kyler to the door. "I'll show you to your room."

Kyler hesitated, his mind tugging back to Ancelin and Uriah. But exhaustion clung to his bones—and a bath *did* sound incredible—so Kyler followed. Gold and white greeted him once more as Bricru guided him deeper into the castle. Portraits as tall as Kyler hung from the walls, and staff in polished suits passed them without a second glance.

"Elizus is an alithias," Kyler said, refusing to waste this time with Bricru. "Did he keep his magic like you?"

Bricru glanced back at him, his eyes dancing between Kyler's for a moment. "Yes. Though, he faced the least consequences of any of us."

"There are more of you?"

"Are we playing another game, Commander, or am I to answer your questions with nothing in return?"

Kyler bit his tongue in frustration, deciding not to push.

At last, Bricru came to a stop at a wooden door, this one without a plaque. He opened it, leading Kyler into a bedroom fit for a lord. Large windows draped in golden curtains filled the space with light, the sun's rays rolling across the wooden floor and illuminating the pure white bedsheets. The bed itself was made of dark-stained mahogany, its posts nearly reaching the ceiling, and was topped with a mattress wide enough for two. Against one wall sat a bath, blocked by a curtain for privacy, and against the other stood a mirror made of glass so clean, it rivaled the windows.

"The castle is yours," Bricru stated. "Aside from the royal chambers and, of course, the gardens." He flashed a smirk. "You are still a prisoner, after all."

"Thank you." Kyler faced Bricru, sincerity pressing into his words.

The shapeshifter paused with his hand on the doorknob. "You're welcome." He left swiftly, shutting the door.

Alone and finally away from that wretched cage, Kyler strode toward the bed. His feet dragged, as if still being held down by the dust of Tophet's ground. Beside the bed, on a nightstand as white as the sheets, was a platter of food. Steam wafted from it as Kyler removed the silver lid, and his stomach rolled at the sight.

He was hungry. He was *exhausted.* But his mind refused to settle. His thoughts raced, searching for a solution to the gateways, and their intensity made him dizzy. He wanted to lie down and rest, but he knew rest wouldn't come—not until those gateways were closed and he was certain Sannir was safe.

He reached for the small glass of water that accompanied the tray of food, his hands shaking. It soothed his throat and tongue as he drank, but the tremor in his limbs grew until he could no longer control it.

Kyler placed a hand on the bed to steady himself and attempted to place the empty glass back on the tray, only to miss. It shattered on the floor at his feet. Tears, hot as embers, filled his eyes and slipped down his face, despite his will to slow them. He balled his fist against the blankets and gasped against the hollowness in his chest.

He was supposed to hate Uriah. But the more he tried to ignore his father, the more Kyler ached for him. He remembered the man Uriah once was, gentle and kind. Was Bricru right? Had Uriah actually been *proud* of him?

A dry sob fell from his lips, choked and pained. Each breath wasn't enough. Every tear was followed by another, angrier and more bitter, full of hurt and hate.

The pleas of Uriah, his eyes dead and voice ragged, sent Kyler to his knees. A sharp pain shot through his bones as he met the polished floorboards, his grip on the sheets dragging them down with him.

It wasn't fair. None of it was.

Kyler remained on the floor, his fists against the wood and hair clinging to his damp cheeks until the last tear had fallen. He cried until his tears ran dry, and numbness replaced the pain.

When his breath became steady and his arms had stilled of their shaking, Kyler pulled himself from the ground and caught sight of his armor once more.

Soft light cast gently across it, brushing the images of dragons. Bricru couldn't have known the comfort those designs brought Kyler. He missed Sannir. He missed Corbin and the others. He even missed Novah, who felt as distant as Sannir despite how close she was.

Kyler slowly peeled the shirt from his back, folding it neatly and placing it at the foot of the bed. He did the same with his trousers before stepping toward the bath, finding several buckets of water waiting for him, along with a single sponge. The water was comfortable, and Kyler took his time scrubbing every inch of grime away, until he finally felt rid of the dust of Tophet.

He moved slowly, the rhythmic routine of donning his armor like a dance he'd almost forgotten. His wet hair caught in his scales as he braided it, framing his face, which no longer felt like his own. He found it difficult to stare at the mirror, seeing Uriah in the bags beneath his eyes and clench of his jaw. Even the armor, a symbol of Sannir, felt like a piece of his former general lying heavy across his chest.

No longer wishing to remain in the room, Kyler stepped into

the hall, surprised to find his door unlocked despite what Bricru had told him. His mind slipped back to his game with the shapeshifter, his question about Novah resurfacing.

The castle was quiet, the hush of evening filling the halls. Kyler studied the portraits as he passed them, seeing the same dark hair and sharp nose that Elizus possessed in many of the artists' renditions. He passed tapestries and curtains, pausing before open doors to admire the studies and ballrooms. It seemed chandeliers and embroidery were a passion of the Potri nobility, and even the glimpses Kyler caught of the libraries and spare rooms contained at least one notable piece that shimmered gold.

At last, Kyler wandered into a familiar hall. His steps quickened, filling the silence as he reached for the door that would lead to the dungeons, only to find it bolted shut.

Saints.

He rattled it softly, a poor attempt at breaking in, and sucked a deep breath. His forehead fell against the wood, the bitterness of exhaustion and frustration tightening his throat.

The shapeshifter would come looking for him eventually, and Kyler would play whatever game was needed if it would get Novah out of those cells.

He peeled himself from the door, the ache in his bones only growing, as he forced himself to continue walking the castle. He scanned every piece of furniture, picture frame, and candle for signs of Orisis. He ran his hands along the metal of the harp and the curve of bookshelves, wondering what secrets the god of destruction might be hiding in this castle of glass.

Yet not a single speck of dirt clung to his fingers, much less a secret of Orisis.

Noticing the sun setting behind the curtains, Kyler began searching for his room once more. The empty castle seemed to swallow his thoughts, and it wasn't until he heard his name that he realized he wasn't alone.

"Kyler."

Kyler stilled, the voice familiar and light. He turned and found the face of the general shadowed in the light of the castle hall.

General Novah.

Like him, she wore her uniform, the leather and steel looking like it'd just been cleaned. A small cut curved along her cheek, still red but beginning to scab.

"Novah." He started for her, not caring that his voice caught as he spoke her name. Her armor scraped against his as he pulled her into a hug. Novah's scales brushed his cheek, and her chest fell with a sigh of relief. The scent of pine mingled with the leather, as if she'd just come from the mountains at the opening of the Pass.

Novah held her left arm stiffly against her side, and Kyler quickly realized her shoulder was wrapped in cotton, not armor.

"What happened?" He reached for the bandages, tugging at them gently to ensure they were fresh and secure.

Her chuckle was strained. "The prince stabbed me."

"Bastard," Kyler muttered. He tilted her arm. "How did they clean it?"

"Herbs of some kind." Light humor graced her tone, but Kyler was too focused on her bandages to notice it.

"Moundi would have been better. When they rewrap—"

She laughed again, tugging her arm free of his hold. "It's fine, Kyler. I'm fine."

"Are you certain?" He caught her eye, his throat still tight and lips pressed thin.

"Yes." The humor fell from her face as she studied him, her gaze making him feel as though the fire Draven had warned him about was catching his shirt. "Are you alright?"

"I'm fine," he said quickly, straightening. "No stab wounds."

Her head tilted to the side and the neat braids at her temples brushed her jaw. "You don't look fine."

He didn't answer, holding her gaze for entirely too long.

Finally, she dropped it. "You can tell me later, Commander. But right now, we need to get word to the others. I don't know why they've moved us to the castle, but it was foolish."

"Not foolish." Elizus' voice drifted from down the hall, pulling Kyler's attention from Novah. The prince's hands flexed at his sides as he walked, as if uncertain he should be inserting himself. "Respectful. Kind. I hope we can come to terms with one another. I've invited you into my home in hopes of working something out. A political gamble, if you will."

Elizus came to a stop beside Novah. The easy way in which he spoke was contrasted by the displeased look on his face.

"This is your offer for an alliance?" Kyler asked. It was a pitiful attempt at gaining their trust.

He gave a sharp scoff. "Absolutely not. Potri isn't interested in an alliance of any kind with Sannir. We are, however, interested in cooperation. There are gateways that need opening, and people in my kingdom who wish for the magic you hold. Orisis gets what he wants from you, Caligari, and my people get what they want. The only thing in our way is your stubbornness."

The second half of his statement went unheard. Novah's face shifted. Her lips parted slightly as she mouthed the name she knew well.

Caligari.

Her head snapped to Kyler. "Caligari?"

A wicked grin spread across the prince's lips. "My apologies. It seems I've said too much." He winked at Kyler and turned on his heel, starting back the way he'd come. "I think you two have some catching up to do."

Novah studied Kyler as if seeing him for the first time, her eyes glazing along his jaw and nose. Kyler's looks had always favored his mother, but anyone could see Uriah if they knew to look for him.

With the way Novah was looking at him now, Kyler knew she'd found his father.

"You're his son." She said it plainly, and yet it made Kyler stiffen.

He refused to confirm what she now knew to be true.

"Kyler Caligari." The name sounded gentle on her tongue. Not an insult or a curse, as Kyler had grown so used to it being. "Is that why the position of general—"

"Don't." He stopped her from finishing her question, his voice soft. "Please don't."

She sucked a breath, glancing behind her to ensure Elizus was gone. "I need to know what's going on."

"It was Ophir. I'm sorry, Novah. I thought we could trust him."

Her smile snagged, but her voice was steady. "I know. I thought we could too."

Something about the way she said this gave him pause. Kyler blinked, stunned by how gently she was speaking to him. "You're not going to threaten my position?"

"What good would that do, Commander?" She waved a hand to the darkening hallway around them. "We may not be in cages, but we're as trapped as ever."

"You're welcome. I think they moved us because of my charm." His joke felt forced, but she laughed anyway, and for a moment the darkness of the castle felt a bit less dim.

"Perhaps you can convince the prince to let us go. You can try flirting with him, like you do everyone else."

"I do *not* flirt with everyone."

"You'd flirt with a tree if it gave you attention."

A smile rose to Kyler's face, creasing the edges of his mouth and lifting the pressure on his chest. "You're cruel, Novah."

She brushed past him and her armor scraped against his. "That's *General* to you, Commander. Now, I think you have some answers I need."

Kyler had expected her to be angry or afraid, yet Novah was smiling. She made him feel light. She made him feel *good*. After the day he'd had, he didn't think that was possible.

He hurried after her, motioning for her to stop at the door to his room. "I do have answers," he said. "But I don't think you're going to like them."

CHAPTER THIRTY-THREE

NOVAH SAT ON THE EDGE OF THE BED, HER HANDS CLASPED AND elbows rested on her knees. Kyler sat beside her, recalling all that he'd learned of Tophet, the gateways, and the shapeshifter. He spun the tragic tale as he spoke, leaving out only the things that tugged at his heart—the words of Ancelin in the Hall of Transformation and the words of Uriah that night at the castle.

Novah didn't need to know the depths to which he hated his father. Those thoughts were his, and he was not anxious to share them.

By the time he was finally finished, the moon of Vellichor had draped the room in silver, and the rest of the castle was deep in slumber.

Novah sat back and stared up at the vaulted ceiling. "We have to ensure that gateway never opens."

Kyler shrugged. "That shouldn't be a problem. Uriah is a stubborn man. He won't change his mind easily."

Novah frowned, meeting Kyler's eye in the darkness. "He turned his back on Sannir. I don't think he's as stubborn as you believe."

She had a point, but Kyler knew his father better than that. He'd seen his face in the confines of Tophet and heard the desperation in his voice. Uriah would not yield anytime soon.

"You have a brother, don't you?"

Kyler sighed. "Yes, but he's in Xynack. If Orisis knew how to reach him, I think he'd be trapped in this castle with us."

"They have gateways, Kyler, and an alithias. If they haven't found him yet, they will soon."

"I'll write to him when we get back to Sannir." He looked at her, hoping this would alleviate her worries.

She sat upright once more. "Aeron, Draven, and Corbin are sure to be working something out. In the meantime, we can rest and hopefully return soon with more information." She paused. "This isn't easy for you, is it?"

Kyler refused to look at her. "It's not easy for any of us."

"Of course not," she said softly, studying his face in the darkness. "But for you, it's personal."

He pinched his tongue between his teeth, not wanting to open this conversation with her.

After a moment of silence, Novah stood. "I'll leave you be. Find me in the morning."

Kyler didn't want to talk. But more than that, he didn't want to be alone. Not with his thoughts.

He stood with her as she turned to leave. "Stay here."

Her brows lifted at his request. He quickly grabbed one of the blankets and tucked a pillow under his arm. "You can have the bed."

Her shoulders fell. "Kyler, I'm not making you—"

"Please." It was the second time he'd pleaded with her that day, and just as before, his throat seemed to catch. "Just stay. And don't ask questions."

He was haunted, his mind at war and soul tangled in the dust of Tophet, and he didn't care if she could see it.

"Alright."

The tightness in his chest eased a bit, and Kyler tossed his pillow and quilt to the floor. "I'll try not to snore like a gull tonight."

She chuckled and unstrapped her armor, placing it at the foot of the bed. The bedframe creaked lightly as she lay atop it, turning to Kyler with a soft smile on her lips. "I was joking about the snoring. You do talk a bit, though."

He grinned, grateful for her teases again. He removed his own armor, allowing the cool castle air to sink through his cotton shirt. "Do I?"

"Yes. Mostly about how wonderful I am."

"Now I know you're lying." He lowered himself to the ground, pulling the quilt over his chest. "I would never call you wonderful."

She smiled down at him, the moonlight brushing the scattered freckles that lined her jaw. "Goodnight, Commander."

He laced his hands across his chest and closed his eyes. "Goodnight, General."

...

The halls of Potri's castle were silent but for the gentle tap of Bricru's shoes on the polished floors. The wind tugged at branches on the other side of the windowpanes as Bricru passed them, scraping gently against the glass. He could see the observatory from here, its round dome and trimmed grounds distant yet visible in the light of the moon. Soon enough, the sun would rise, and the silver of night would be replaced with the gold of dawn.

The shapeshifter stared up at the constellations, his mind wandering, thinking of the way the stars had come alive in the eyes of the celestial. To view the world with so much light was incredible—every secret revealed in the pupilless eyes that didn't truly belong to him.

Kyler Caligari had caught on quickly. Bricru had faced the pain of tainted magic, and it was something he did not allow himself to dwell on. Of course, there were others whom Orisis had formed—the six soldiers he had crafted with destruction whose magic remained intact. It seemed the commander had a knack for asking the right questions, and unfortunately for him, they were the questions Bricru cared not to answer.

Bricru stopped before the door to the study, the gentle scent of bergamot and limestone drifting from within. He unlocked it and stepped into the cramped space, which contained a simple desk shoved between overflowing bookshelves.

He closed the door behind him, relying only on the little light poking through the curtains of the short window above the desk. Glass bottles scattered the desk's surface, each one filled with different liquids. Some glittered silver, the potions within seeming to move even as they sat still, and others were so green that they rivaled the forests beyond the city. As thick as blood or dark as mead, each of Kyler's potions had been brewed to absolute perfection.

Bricru stepped toward the desk and rested his palms on the dark wood, studying the concoctions in the moonlight. The vials were small, only a single dose of potion per glass, and he could smell the distinct roots and herbs the commander had put in each one.

Beside them, Kyler's scribbled notes had been piled, the parchment refusing to lay flat after being stuffed into his pockets. A few herbs and roots lay on the loose papers to hold them in place. Across the back of the chair hung his leather potion belt, void of its contents.

Bricru reached for the notes, taking the crumpled paper into his hands, and flipped through them yet again. It was fascinating, the way these ingredients would interact when combined by one who knew the magic of Adoni. Simple herbs and oils became potions of healing, change, and ability when brewed. Potions that had the power to bring a kingdom to its knees if one knew how to wield them.

Glass clinked softly as Bricru carefully lifted a vial from the desk, holding it up to the moonlight to admire the golden liquid within. According to Kyler's notes, it was a pain reliever, made from limestone and brewed until the surface bubbled. Now, it sat almost translucent in the vial, without a single speck of limestone lingering on the bottom of the glass. He wondered what it might taste like, if the bitterness he smelled would stick to his tongue or dissipate with the sweetness of pure magic.

His gaze shifted to the large root he'd pushed aside when taking hold of the papers. The plant was crooked and smelled of lemongrass, and according to Kyler's notes, this root would cause immense pain, twisting potions into something they were never meant to be.

Not unlike Bricru—twisted into something he was never meant to be. He could kill and taint and bury, but Bricru could not create. Whatever ancient magic had fallen upon him as a child was no longer his, shattered by the will of Orisis and rebuilt into something he wasn't certain he liked.

Like a potion mixed with gallot, he too was tainted with destruction.

Bricru set the vial of pain-numbing potion onto the desk a bit harder than he intended, forcing his eyes away from the root. He scanned over the next page of notes, containing untested theories for potions that Kyler seemed to be excited about. His writing became sloppier the more interesting the topic, as if he were afraid the theories would slip from his mind if he did not write them down fast enough. Where his father had been cautious and traditional, Kyler seemed to thrive off new ideas, willing to keep an open mind.

There was passion in these potions. Each one brewed with so much intentionality that it was clear his alchemy was not a simple pastime. Kyler put time and effort into each one, and that was all Bricru needed to know.

He set the papers back down as he noticed that the sky had turned from the color of ink to lavender. The soft chatter of castle staff filtered through the door, which meant Bricru had work to do.

The shapeshifter ensured the door was locked behind him before starting down the hall, passing the occasional man in white or woman in gold. The black that draped Bricru's lean form starkly contrasted that of the castle, but Elizus had a way of charming those around him. If anyone in the castle had questions about the man with the scar across his face, they went unspoken. In fact, some even met his eye with a nod as he strode past.

At last, Bricru came to a stop at Kyler's door and tapped his knuckles against the dark wood.

"Come to see me already?"

Bricru spun at the sound of Kyler's voice, finding the commander with a shoulder against the wall behind him. His armor lay even across his chest, every fold of the fabric and leather beneath the steel perfected and clean. Two neat braids hung from his temples, and the dark circles that had lingered beneath his eyes had faded into a soft purple.

Kyler jerked his chin to the door. "Kind of you to knock.

Though, I suppose a commander of my *esteem* should be treated as such."

The edges of Bricru's lips curved into a smirk. "Good morning to you too. Have you eaten?"

Kyler lifted a brow. "Am I on your good side now?"

"I don't have a good side." Bricru tucked his hands into his pockets and leaned against the door frame. "However, I do have a kitchen full of pastries that you're welcome to partake in, and a room full of potions that I'm very curious about."

The commander frowned and his gaze narrowed. "My potions?"

Bricru shrugged. "They're fascinating."

"They're just potions."

"Potions I could never recreate, even if I had Adoni's magic. Uriah was right, you are extremely skilled."

A small scoff fell from Kyler's lips, but Bricru saw the way his eyes brightened at those words. The commander craved his father's approval.

Bricru tucked this knowledge away as he smoothed a hand down his crisp coat. "Will you tell me about them?"

Kyler twisted his lips, his gaze flickering to a room just down the hall—the room Bricru had assigned to Novah Elison. "If you insist."

Bricru tilted his head, his words lightening to a tease. "Do you need to ask permission from your general first?"

This time, Kyler quirked a smile, though it didn't quite reach his eyes. "Don't patronize me, shapeshifter. We both know you're the one who can't act without permission."

Bricru bristled, the words striking a spot he tried very hard to ignore.

Kyler pushed off the wall, uncrossing his arms, with the smirk still slung on his lips. "After you."

Bricru bit his tongue and started down the hall, without checking to see if Kyler followed. The sound of his armor was confirmation enough, shifting and scraping softly as the commander trailed.

"Are the new accommodations to your liking?" Bricru called over his shoulder.

"I prefer the cage."

"Hm." Bricru paused at the study door once more. "Spoken like a true follower of Adoni."

This time, Kyler did not seem to find humor in the tease. His face hardened as he followed Bricru into the small room, his sights landing on his potions lined up along the desk. He stared at them for a moment, as if making certain every one of them was present.

When he was finished, he moved to the desk. "You didn't drink any."

Bricru pursed his lips, coming to Kyler's side. "No. We don't know what most of them do."

Kyler took a vial of light silver and lifted it between them. "This one is called Moundi. It's poured over wounds to cleanse them."

"I thought all potions were made to be consumed?"

"You thought wrong." He swirled it gently. "You should have used this to clean Novah's shoulder."

"Seeing as how I wasn't the one who stabbed her, I don't think that was my responsibility."

Kyler didn't respond. He set the Moundi back where it'd laid and picked up a new potion, this one a deeper silver. "Zalis," he explained. "For headaches."

Bricru tapped the glass as Kyler held it up to him. "That one might be useful."

"Try it." Kyler popped the cork, filling the room with the scent of honey. "It won't hurt, and it tastes decent."

Bricru accepted the glass as he passed it over. The potion inside was slightly chilled. The scent intensified as he brought it to his nose, breathing in the herbs before tipping his head and allowing the potion to roll down his throat. It tasted bitter, yet there was a soft edge of something almost floral that made it enjoyable.

"I give that one to my soldiers when they hit each other too hard." Kyler's face softened slightly as he spoke of his men. "They won't stop complaining until I hand over the Zalis."

"They trust your potions?"

"Of course."

"And Uriah? Did he ever taste your brews?"

Kyler's jaw went taut, his gaze shifting back to the spread of potions before him.

Bricru slowly set the empty vial down, a soft buzz beginning to fill his mind. "I understand why you hate him."

Kyler's hands tightened around the edge of the table.

"I had the displeasure of getting to know Uriah Caligari very well. He is not a kind man, that much is clear."

"No. He never tried my potions." Kyler answered the question, his tone hard. "He never cared to."

Bricru allowed his mind to fall back to Uriah's final moments before Tophet consumed him. For the first time, the man had looked scared and lost, like a child without a home rather than a general. His voice had been desperate, ragged and shaky, yet what surprised Bricru most was the words he'd spoken.

"'Not my sons,'" Bricru said lowly. "'Not a hand on my sons.'"

Kyler glanced at him as he continued. "Those were Uriah's final words before I grabbed hold of his neck and cast him to misery. He didn't fear for himself. He feared for you." Bricru held Kyler's eyes, finding a storm raging behind them.

The commander dropped his gaze to the floor. "You didn't listen."

"Of course not. Would you? He'd turned his back on his promise to Orisis, and I was to be punished for it. It was time to move on."

"You were punished?"

Bricru's shoulders stiffened. "I was in charge of overseeing Uriah's work."

Kyler's emotions did a poor job at staying hidden. "How?" he asked finally. "How did you get him to work for you? He's the most stubborn man I've ever known."

"I learned him." Bricru studied the designs on his sleeves, needing to focus on anything but the commander. "Not unlike 'Ophir' did with you. I was patient, showing him the things Orisis could offer until he was practically begging for more. His final months in Sannir were full of fortune and greatness—far more than the position of general could give him. He was a greedy man, though; nothing was ever enough."

"And when he turned on you, you trapped his soul in Tophet," Kyler finished.

Bricru chuckled. "When you say it like that, it sounds terrible."

The commander offered a tight smile. "Maybe because it is. Is eternal torture kindness to you?"

"War is gray, Commander. You know this. What has become of those whose ancestors turned on Adoni? He's never given them a choice. He left them to fend for themselves. Your god promises strength to his men yet denies life-giving magic to those who have done him no harm. Orisis' punishments may be severe, but at least he offers a choice. Even he will assist those who ask."

Silence filled the small room, with only muffled footsteps and distant conversation floating in from beyond the closed door.

Finally, Kyler broke it. "Gray indeed."

The words were hardly through his lips when the Zalis Bricru had taken turned on him. The shapeshifter's stumbled, his mind stabbed with a pain so violent it rivaled the edge of a blade, and he screamed.

CHAPTER THIRTY-FOUR

KYLER REACHED FOR BRICRU AS HE COLLAPSED TO THE FLOOR, but the shapeshifter shoved him away.

"What did you do to me?" Bricru choked, hardly finishing his question before his words were swallowed by another scream. He balled his fists into his hair and sank to his knees.

"I don't know!" Panic inched its way up Kyler's throat. He forced out the words as Bricru screamed again, loud enough to leave his ears ringing.

Kyler was certain the shapeshifter couldn't hear him. He scrambled for the vial of Zalis, a few drops of the silver still lingering in the glass. It looked normal—sparkling silver and the smell of honey. He tossed the glass aside, kneeling before Bricru, and wrestled his hands away from his face. "I need you to tell me what you feel."

The shapeshifter swore, sweat dotting his skin, as tears ran rampant down his face. "You said it wouldn't hurt."

"Saints, Bricru, I'm trying to help!"

A sob ripped through Bricru's throat, violent and raw. Kyler dropped his wrists and stood once more to frantically search his potions. He lifted each vial, not caring as they toppled over one another. The clinking glass was muted by the cries of the shapeshifter.

Kyler finally grabbed hold of his Ponos, the pale yellow mixture sloshing as he tugged the cork free. "Drink this."

He lowered the glass to Bricru as the shapeshifter's bloodshot eyes met his. "You're going to kill me."

"Drink it!"

"No!" Bricru cried out once more, his sobs turning desperate.

Kyler crouched beside him. He gripped Bricru's arms and tried to pull his fingers from his face, but Bricru fought back, slinking farther onto the floor as if hoping to disappear into the castle. His cheeks were blushed and hot, and his teeth ground between each cry. He dug his nails into his scalp, scraping and pulling in a useless attempt to remove whatever pain filled his head.

To Kyler's surprise, no one came. The door to the study remained closed; no one was alarmed by the cries raging between the crooked shelves.

Kyler tried to swallow, to breathe and think, but all he could hear were Bricru's screams. Not a single person had ever been slain by a mixture of his, and yet a sip of Zalis was enough to tear the shapeshifter apart from the inside out.

Kyler looked to his potions once more, hoping something would come to his mind, and it did. He caught sight of the gallot, the root that claimed to cause pain.

He gripped Bricru's shoulders. "Did you add anything to that potion?"

"No!"

"Did you touch that root?"

Bricru choked, blood sputtering from his lips.

Kyler snatched the root, snapping it in half and filling the room with its earthy aroma, so strong that it brought tears to Kyler's eyes. Perhaps the gallot could counteract the pain?

He shoved the root in Bricru's face, pressing the bitter insides to his blood-stained mouth.

"Come on, Bricru."

The shapeshifter choked again, his cries weakening.

The tears in Kyler's eyes now were no longer from the root. His ribs ached from the pounding of his heart, desperation clawing at his chest and clutching his lungs.

Bricru's sobs slowed. His body fell still, and the room went silent. The only sound was Kyler's racing pulse.

He hadn't meant to—

The door to the study burst open, sending Kyler's notes skittering to the floor beside him. Silver armor and scales as green as Kyler's caught in the fragmented light.

"Corbin?"

Corbin's shoulders fell. He hurried to Kyler as the commander stood, their armor clashing as Corbin embraced him. "Saints, I thought that was you screaming."

Kyler gripped him tightly, the ache in his chest still suffocating. "I'm fine. How did you get—"

"We need to go. Now. I'll explain later." Corbin gripped the back of Kyler's head, his calloused hands pressing into his neck. He gave Kyler a small shake, as if trying to pull him from the daze that clouded his mind. His sights dropped to the shapeshifter for a moment, and his brows furrowed slightly. "What—"

"Later," Kyler repeated. He tucked the remainder of the root into his pocket and grabbed his potion belt from where it lay across the back of the chair. He could feel the presence of Bricru behind him, as if begging him to stay. Kyler pushed the shapeshifter from his mind.

They hurried from the room, leaving Bricru to his fate.

Kyler's armor rattled as he sprinted after Corbin through the castle halls. Corbin watched every corner, keeping his sword raised and ready to strike. There was no sign of life, no chatter or laughter, and even the portraits seemed to watch with glassy eyes as Kyler stumbled after his lieutenant, guilt creeping up his neck.

He hardly noticed Draven until they were in front of him, the kilder's breaths heavy and sword drawn.

"Glad you are all right, Commander." Draven stepped toward Kyler, and lightly jostled his shoulder. He looked well, his face no longer pained and pale, yet his steps wobbled.

Kyler caught his elbows and stared down at his leg. "What happened? Did the Pevoth work?"

Draven gave a crooked grin. "Yes and no. Don't worry about it right now."

"Draven, I—"

"He said don't worry about it." Corbin cut him off, tossing a spare sword into Kyler's hand. "Where's the general?"

Draven started back the way he came. "With Aeron. The sooner we get out of here, the better."

Kyler flexed his hand around his blade. Shouts echoed from one of the many hallways, and Corbin urged them to move, his haste returning as the rustle of Potri soldiers' armor grew louder. The golden curtains and tapestries snagged Kyler's arms as he raced past them, stealing a few glances over his shoulder to catch glimpses of flashing blades and edges of angry shouts.

"Novah!" Corbin nearly slammed into the general as he turned a corner, catching her by the shoulders with a small laugh. Beside her, Aeron's scales tangled in his hair, and his scarred neck reminded Kyler of the shapeshifter he'd left behind.

Kyler shoved past Draven, pulling Corbin's hands from Novah's shoulders. "Easy, she's injured."

Novah sucked a breath, offering a tight smile to Corbin. "I'm all right." She turned to Kyler, her face growing solemn. "The screams—"

"Bricru."

"Later," Aeron urged. He started down an adjacent hall, his steps hurried. "There's an exit down—"

The words were hardly off his tongue when more shouts filled the castle, this time much closer. Aeron halted as soldiers donning golden chainmail and the crest of Potri came into view with swords lifted and crossbows aimed at the elves' heads.

Aeron swore, yanking Draven's arm as the kilder struggled to keep up. "Never mind," he muttered, turning their group around.

Kyler followed his soldiers down a different hall, the colors blurring and sounds muffling in his ears. He could see the blood on Bricru's mouth, hear the rasps of Uriah. He found himself staring at Novah's bandaged shoulder, expecting the wound to burst open and blood to coat her skin as well. He couldn't save them—could he save her if he tried?

Corbin's shouts were drowned out by Kyler's thoughts. He felt as though he were walking on clouds, each step too slow and every voice muffled.

But this hall was familiar.

Kyler stopped, scanning the doors and plaques until he found the one he recognized. "This way!" He ripped the door open and started up the stone steps, breathing in the musty air. At the top, sunlight filled the small observatory, making the air warm and instruments blinding.

It was a reckless move, and Kyler knew that. Yet, there was something in him that urged him to disregard the risk.

Corbin was right behind him, scanning the small space, and the others followed closely.

Kyler started for the painting, shoving past tables and toppling the brass telescopes.

"Kyler—" Novah started, but the look he gave her made her stop.

"Trust me. Stay close." He pressed a hand to the stars, and it disappeared into the artwork. Kyler closed his eyes and stepped into darkness.

The cold of Tophet greeted him with a dry wind, and dust brushed his boots the moment he stepped foot into the destruction. Before him, the keep seemed to urge him inside, its doors open and streets bare. Spires curled up to the void, and the distant calls of the amphipteres above the soldiers teased with how foolish this was.

Kyler pushed the fear away, turning to the others.

"Bricru said the gateways are in that keep." He sheathed his blade, hoping to steady his breath as he made for the building.

"Where are we?" Corbin's voice was barely a whisper. His breath caught as the cries of amphipteres filled the sky.

Kyler kept his sights on the keep, praying desperately that his risk would pay off.

Inside, they were met with a wide room, its floors coated in candlewax and the gray stone illuminated with the candles in the chandeliers.

In the center of the room stood the prince of Potri.

Kyler was before him in an instant, his blade lifted to the prince's throat. "Tell me where it is."

Elizus refused to flinch, even as the edge of Kyler's sword scraped his throat. His steel gaze drifted across the soldiers as his lips tugged into a frown.

Kyler pressed closer. Close enough to force Elizus to take a step backward. "Talk, Elizus."

The prince scoffed. "No."

He slammed the hilt of his sword into Elizus' ribs, making the prince gasp. "Try again."

Elizus stumbled, his words strained. "If you think you can play with me, Commander, you're sorely mistaken."

Kyler drove his hilt again, this time hard enough to thrust him against the stone wall. "This isn't a game," he spat. "The gateway to Sannir—where is it?"

Elizus choked a swallow, his glare deadly. "I don't think you want to go there."

Kyler pressed the sharp edge of his blade into Elizus' throat, bringing speckles of blood to the surface of the prince's perfect skin. "If you tell me, alithias, I will let you live."

"Ah," Elizus rasped, a loose grin rising to his lips. "The commander does not lie."

Kyler didn't move.

"Take the stone stairs at the end of the hall above, and you will find the gateway at the top. But you will not escape."

"I'll take my chances." Kyler pulled back his blade. Then, he thrust it into Elizus' shoulder. The prince gasped in pain, a grimace replacing his smirk. "Now we're even," Kyler muttered. He pulled his blade free with a jerk and headed for the stairs.

Corbin was at Kyler's side in an instant, his jaw locked in a way that let Kyler know they'd be talking about this later. He could see the fear in Corbin's eyes. His heavy breaths filled the staircase as they ascended. Behind, Novah and Aeron hurried Draven along, and Kyler did his best to ignore the kilder's grunts as the steps of the keep rose higher.

At last, Kyler reached the top of the stairs and threw open the door, emerging into a small room.

He came to a halt. His heart pounded so heavily that it was painful.

The dust swallowed him, blocking the others from view as it formed a wall, thick as stone. It coated his tongue like dense honey, trying to force its way down his throat. It danced between his fingers and curled into his hair, alive and swarming and separating him from his men. Kyler could no longer hear the groans of Draven or curses of Aeron. It was just him and the dust, endless and distant, filling every one of his senses until Kyler felt as though he were dust himself.

A voice broke through the destruction, smooth and heavy and dangerously familiar. "Hello, Kyler."

Kyler blinked against the grain, attempting to wave the dust from his eyes, only for it to cling to him once more.

Footsteps neared, steady and calculated. "You continue to surprise me. I must admit, I'm impressed."

If the dust wasn't already choking him, Kyler might have forgotten how to breathe. His lips parted slightly, a name falling from them. "Ancelin."

Dust skittered away, revealing the man who stood before him. He looked ethereal, the dust gripping to his form as if worshiping his very being, and his eyes landed on Kyler with a darkness so deep that it chilled him to his core.

"You take me as a fool, Kyler Caligari."

"What is this?" Kyler tossed a hand to the dust, his breath still struggling to steady. "What are *you?*"

He knew the answer even ask he asked the question.

Ancelin's jaw shifted. "I told you I was your enemy."

Kyler's eyes began to burn as ash and ruin filled them. "Orisis."

"That is one name, yes." Orisis stepped closer, his head tilting to one side. "Do you fear that name?"

"No."

"Oh, I think you do." He waved a hand before Kyler's face and the dust fell at his command. The specks joined the wall that closed Kyler in with the god, trapping them both in a cage of dust that spun so fast, it shook the scales at Kyler's ears.

"But Ancelin, you do not fear," he continued, studying Kyler as if he were a work of art to be admired. "Ancelin will not hurt you. Ancelin is just a man."

With the same hand he'd used to wipe away the dust, he offered an invitation to Kyler, his palm open and voice soft.

"Speak with me, Kyler, as a man, not as a god."

"You let me leave Tophet once," Kyler challenged. "Will you let me again?"

A sad smile rose to Ancelin's lips. "I can't. It seems we've come to a place that leaves us without many options. However, I may have a solution from which we can both benefit." His hand inched closer, a gentle plea to take hold of him. "Take my hand, Kyler. I truly do not wish to see you fall."

CHAPTER THIRTY-FIVE

THE MOMENT KYLER'S HAND TOUCHED THE GOD'S, THE ROOM changed. The dust rose and twisted, swallowing him whole like a wave of the sea and drowning him in its salt. He sank into a cloud of gray as the dust settled at his boots and muffled his breath. When it finally stilled, Kyler found himself in a void, the specks of dust falling still in the darkness.

"Do not let it frighten you." Ancelin dropped Kyler's hand, his voice crisp and clear. He motioned to the world around them and took a silent step backward. "What you see now is time, the best way I can show it to you. Endless in every direction, with room for a thousand things to take place."

Kyler lifted a finger to the dust, plucking a speck out of the air. His chest felt light, like his burdens had been momentarily lifted.

Ancelin took a deep breath. "Do you remember what I told you in the Hall of Transformation?

"You told me a lot."

"About knowledge."

"That Orisis doesn't hide it." Kyler paused. "That *you* don't hide it."

"I was not lying. What I am about to show you is something I have allowed few to witness. You've grown on me, Kyler. I can see your yearning for the success and skills that most only dream of. The events that have brought us to this moment cannot be undone, but I hope we can redirect our future."

Kyler flexed his fingers at his sides, mulling over what the god said. "I will not become your slave, Orisis."

"I have no slaves," he said simply. "I have children, and it seems you are missing a father." He shrugged, his eyes gentle with hope. "But I understand. Before you cast me away, let me show you what your future could look like."

The dust began to shift, forming into something new. Color sparked from within, casting light into the void, as Kyler turned to face the scene taking place.

At first, the images were blurred and speckled by dust, until they slowly materialized.

"Do you recognize this?' Ancelin asked, coming to Kyler's side.

Kyler couldn't tear his gaze from the scene. The grounds of the barracks and mountains of Sannir brought a knot to his throat. He was drawn toward it, the vision of home welcoming him like a dream he wished to never wake from. The haze solidified, and before he knew it, Kyler was no longer standing in dust but in the soft grass of the barrack grounds, surrounded by the scent of pine and the distant sounds of swordplay.

"I'd miss it too."

Ancelin stood at Kyler's side, his dark eyes catching sight of the Pass above the mountains.

"You worked very hard to get where you are. You should be proud."

Laughter danced from the barracks as Corbin and Salcon emerged into the courtyard, their armor reflecting the afternoon sun and scales of green rivaling the grass.

"I am," Kyler answered softly.

A voice called from behind, "Lieutenants!"

Corbin and Salcon stilled, struggling to suppress their grins, and Kyler was met with his own face. It was odd to watch himself from the outside. He never realized how stiff his shoulders were as he walked or how sharp his nose was from the side.

Kyler remembered this; it was a memory. A glad one.

"Care to share what's so funny?" The commander asked as he reached them, crossing his arms and lifting a brow.

"Nothing," Corbin answered, with a wink.

Kyler rolled his eyes. "Salcon, you're late for training, and Corbin, I need you at the docks."

Salcon gave a quick salute, his dark hair brushing his cheeks as a light wind picked up. He flashed Corbin another grin before he hurried off toward the arena.

"What's happening at the docks?" Corbin asked, falling in stride beside his commander.

Kyler slapped a hand across his back, hard enough to make the lieutenant grunt. "Nothing. I just want in on the joke."

Corbin's laugh lifted to the sky, and Kyler found himself smiling as the scene began to fade.

"Good joke, then?" Ancelin asked as the fog surrounded them once more.

"Always."

The pleasant look on Ancelin's face faded as the next scene began to form around them. "I'm afraid this memory is not so friendly."

Kyler's breath hitched as the castle of Sannir came into view, its gardens illuminated by the stars. The soldier that stood before them looked nothing like the man Kyler was now, and yet he recognized himself all too well.

"I don't want to be here," Kyler whispered.

Ancelin didn't look at him, his sights set on the lone figure who trekked through the gardens with a faint smile on his face and his hands buried in his pockets.

His ears were barer then, and his face softer. The freckles that dotted his nose and jaw almost disappeared in the darkness.

He had nearly reached where Kyler and Ancelin stood when a pair of heavy footsteps thumped toward him.

"Worthless boy." Uriah caught his son by the collar of his armor and shoved him hard against the brick of the castle. Kyler's head slammed on the stone, forcing a grunt to slip from his lips, but Uriah didn't relent.

Kyler stared at his father with wide eyes, his face filled with shock, as the general dug the scale from his pocket and spat on it.

"You didn't earn this." His voice was just as nasty as Kyler had remembered. "You're here because of me, and you won't even use my name."

Kyler attempted to tear himself free of the general's hold, but Uriah only pressed harder.

"I made you a soldier, and you disgrace me." He tossed the scale to the dirt, scuffing it with the heel of his boot.

"You did not *make* me."

Kyler felt a stab of pain as he listened to the anger in his voice, hard and sharp and yet utterly broken.

"I made *myself.*"

Uriah stared at him, his lips still curled and gaze dark. "Take your scale from the dirt and slink back to your barracks. But remember, Kyler, you are nothing without me."

Kyler had let those words capture his mind many times since that day, but hearing them from Uriah's mouth again nearly suffocated him.

Kyler had forgotten what happened next.

Uriah turned and strode from the gardens. His single white scale shone like a star itself as he disappeared around the castle wall.

This younger version of Kyler knelt slowly to the dirt. He lifted his scale, carefully brushing the earth and saliva away with his sleeve until it shone like his armor once more. His chest rose and fell quickly, and he attempted to hold his emotions together.

It didn't work.

Tears broke through his lashes, angry and hot, as he fixated on the scale resting in his palm. The sobs that broke free were pitiful, but he made no effort to stop them. His shattered gaze lifted to the night above, silver reflecting off his damp cheeks as the scene began to face to dust once more.

Kyler swallowed, the sound of his sobs echoing in his mind even as the memory dissipated.

"He was a cruel man," Ancelin said softly. "You deserved much better than him."

"He is paying for his crimes."

Ancelin nodded slowly. "That was the past. Now, let me show you what can be."

Another scene began to form, taking the shape of the castle courtyard, this time in the light of afternoon. Snow covered the grounds, and Kyler shivered as his boots sunk into a thin layer of ice.

"Go on." Ancelin nodded to the path before them, which led into the largest ballroom.

Kyler started slowly, snow crunching beneath him as the path curved. Soft chatter filled the crisp air, and behind the glass walls, guests filled the ballroom, draped in clothing of blue and silver. Excitement seemed to bubble over like a potion mid-brew.

"Kyler!" Corbin emerged from the ballroom, his cheeks pink

from the cold and a wide smile across his face. He clasped a hand on his commander's shoulder as he stopped in front of Kyler, meeting his eye.

His touch felt real. Solid.

"Are you ready?"

Kyler stole a glance at Ancelin, who stood silently behind. It seemed this version of Corbin had no awareness of the god who watched from the shadows.

A laugh fell from his lieutenant's lips. "Don't tell me you're nervous. Novah won't let you hear the end of it."

"Novah?"

"Commander!" Salcon poked his head out from the ballroom. "It's time!"

Corbin's grin grew wider, and he shoved Kyler toward the open doors. "If you happen to vomit, try to aim for Advisor Cadmus. Saints know he deserves it."

Kyler snuck another glance back at Ancelin, finding a genuine laugh resting on his lips. No one acknowledged the god as they entered the ballroom. All eyes were fixated on Kyler.

The chatter hushed as Kyler started down the aisle of chairs toward the familiar marble staircase. He halted when he reached the base of the steps.

Aiyanna stood on the balcony. She was dressed like a queen, her hair pulled away from her face and falling in ringlets down her back. Silver and blue draped her form like starlight and sky, and beaded crystals fell from her clothes, sending rainbows spinning across the marble floor.

To her right, Advisor Cadmus watched with a steely gaze, his peppered hair topped with a silver circlet, and his usual scowl seemed a bit less harsh.

To Aiyanna's left was Novah. The general wore the same silver armor, dancing with dragons. Her shoulder was no longer wrapped in cloth, and her smile formed soft dimples in her cheeks.

Another man stood on the balcony, his ears void of scales and chest bare of armor, but Kyler recognized him regardless. Uriah was behind Novah, his hands clasped before him and jaw tight.

"Commander," Aiyanna spoke, pulling Kyler's gaze from Uriah. "For bringing former General Uriah from the depths of Tophet and successfully leading Sannir into a time of peace, it's my honor and privilege to appoint you as Kyler Weylyn, General of the Armies of Sannir."

It was then that Kyler noticed that Novah no longer donned her white scale.

The audience erupted. Kyler's heart jumped to his throat as Novah applauded along with the others, her smile radiant. She wasn't angry or envious, but proud.

It seemed Uriah was, too. He dipped his head, a fist pressed to his chest. He'd been put in his place—no longer a general, no longer fit to lead, but alive and away from the torture of Tophet. Kyler Weylyn had made himself the general.

Sannir was safe.

And then the scene faded, leaving Kyler in the dusty air with Ancelin at his back.

Kyler closed his eyes, willing the images to fade from his mind, but they simply refused. His breath felt cold as he steadied it, and although Ancelin's steps were silent, Kyler knew the god now stood before him.

"That is what I can offer."

Kyler opened his eyes, looking at Ancelin no longer as a man, but as the powerful being he was. "For what price?"

He swallowed, his eyes dropping. "I would give this to you

freely if I could."

"The price, Orisis."

His jaw tightened. "Finish what your father started, and this will be yours. Complete the unfinished gateways and open the one Uriah locked."

Gateways to Sannir. To the Pass. The realm would be thrust under Orisis' rule, his magic tainting that of Adoni and his gateways reaching every corner of the realm.

"You will be my general," Orisis continued, "and the trade will be our secret. I will tell no one of your choice, and you will return to Sannir as a hero. I will allow you to succeed in all you do, and Sannir will remain standing."

Kyler released a shaky breath. "They would never know?"

"I swear it."

"Uriah would come home?"

"Just as he was taken, he will be returned."

"Novah—"

"I will not harm those under your protection, Kyler, I swear it. I want only the magic that I have been denied." He stepped closer, his eyes damp. There was something deeper in them, something that reflected in his voice. "I love this realm more than you will ever understand. I wish only to create as you do."

Kyler ran a hand down his face. "And if I refuse?"

The dust around them shifted once more, and Kyler didn't need it to settle for him to recognize what he saw. Novah covered in blood, a fever burning her skin as her mind slipped away. Corbin in a cage, his eyes white with blindness and his silent screams falling on deaf ears. The castle of Sannir coated in flames that lifted embers to the night sky. Armies advanced as the flag of Sannir caught in the flames, and scales covered the ground, the blood of soldiers splattered across their surfaces. The Temple of

Adoni crumbled to dust as the Pass closed, separating Sannir from their magic.

And then there was Bricru, his skin pale, lying where Kyler had abandoned him.

The scene froze.

Ancelin stared. His eyes widened. He lifted a hand to the image, his dark brows dipping and breath falling still.

"What have you done?"

Fear gripped Kyler as the world spun back into focus and the dust fell like lead, revealing the small room with walls of stone. Behind Ancelin, a single arch flashed with white oak and stained glass, the misty shapes all too familiar to Kyler.

The gateway to Sannir.

The god's eyes burned as his chest rose and fell quickly, and angry tears glossed his eyes. "What have you done, Caligari?"

CHAPTER THIRTY-SIX

NO SOONER HAD THE WORDS FALLEN FROM THE MOUTH OF THE god than Corbin lunged for him, his sword raised to strike.

Kyler stumbled back, slamming into Novah, as dust rushed into the air, catching Corbin and thrusting him against the side wall with enough force to make him shout. Novah steadied Kyler as the god's gaze narrowed on him once more, his eyes like coal.

"Caligari!" He shouted the name like a curse as he reached for the commander, dust shooting from his fingers like arrows.

Novah shoved Kyler to the ground and fell on top of his chest, shielding his head with her own. Dust sliced through her hair, exploding against the stone wall behind them. Kyler was hardly able to catch his breath when Aeron leaped over them, swinging at Orisis, only to be tossed aside like a doll as the dust caught his clothes. He grunted as he landed beside Corbin, his blade skittering across the floor. Corbin stood and scrambled for the weapon.

"Get to the gateway!" Kyler shouted, his voice picking up in the wind that surrounded Orisis. He reached for his own blade as Novah hauled him to his feet.

There was no fear in her gaze, just a burn like fire and whiskey, as she flexed her grip around the hilt of her sword. She placed herself between Kyler and Orisis. Draven made for the gateway, urging Corbin and Aeron to follow.

Orisis ignored them completely, his anger fixated on Kyler alone.

Novah didn't move. "Go, Kyler."

"You're delusional," he spat, lifting his weapon and staring Orisis in the eye. "You want me, Ancelin?"

Orisis didn't answer. Instead, he called the dust to him in an unspoken command, a shout rising from his chest as he thrust his destruction at the general.

Novah swore. Dust slammed into her, and though Kyler tried to brace her fall, her body went flying into the stone with a deafening crack. She cried out as Orisis threw her again, crushing her injured shoulder against the wall. He watched, with thrill in his eyes, as she crumpled to the ground.

Before Orisis could throw her again, Kyler charged the god. He swung wildly at his face, scratching his cheek with the very tip of his sword. Blood dribbled onto Orisis' dark cloak, and a sneer fell from his lips. "Special indeed, Caligari."

Dust stung Kyler's eyes as it shoved itself down his throat and into his lungs. His sword fell from his hands, and he gripped his neck as air refused to fill him. Minerals coated his tongue, grainy and bitter, and even through the blinding storm, he could see the smile that rose to Orisis' face.

"Do you want to live?" He stepped closer, taking hold of Kyler's chin and forcing their gazes to meet. "I will destroy you all, one by one, and in the end, your blood will be mine."

Kyler struggled to answer, but all that emerged was a weak choke. He fumbled for his weapon, searching blindly for the sword that had fallen at his feet. The world was becoming spotted. Darkness crept into the edges of his vision.

Corbin swung at Orisis, only to be tossed aside. Draven struck and missed.

The cold metal of his blade sliced Kyler's hand, drawing blood, as he desperately grasped for it, but Orisis kicked it out of reach.

Kyler was growing weak.

He gripped Orisis' wrists, his blood smudging across the god's skin, and the scent of burning flesh sparked between them.

Orisis stumbled back, and the dust freed Kyler of its hold. Ragged coughs raked Kyler's body as he straightened, finding Orisis clutching his arm, a look of utter surprise in his eye. The smear of blood bubbled black against his skin.

Kyler didn't linger. He rushed to Novah's side and hauled her to her feet. Images of pale marble and blue tapestries blurred within the arch, and the moment Kyler touched his bleeding hand to them, the images solidified.

Before Orisis could stop them, Kyler leaped into the gateway, pulling Novah through with him.

There was a crack—louder than the split of an axe. His lungs burned. Nausea climbed his throat as darkness surrounded them, and a moment later, the darkness was pierced with silver light and cool air.

Kyler stood in the center of the great hall. Blue curtains and silver chandeliers hung undisturbed, and nothing but a faint roll of dust remained of the gateway through which they'd come.

"Saints," Kyler swore softly. He urged Novah away from the dust.

Blood soaked through the bandage at her shoulder, and her arm hung limp. Her usually warm skin was as pale as the marble floors, and the grimace that sat on her features tightened as Kyler gripped her.

"You're all right," he said softly, brushing the tangled hair from her face. "We're home."

Another snap echoed as Corbin stumbled through the gateway, Aeron and Draven close at his heels.

"Can he follow us?" Corbin asked, his sword still drawn as he turned to face the dust.

Kyler swallowed. "I don't know."

Aeron shoved past, his sights on the blood that now smeared Novah's silver armor. "Physician!" he shouted, his voice echoing in the empty hall. "Draven, get—" He paused, seeing Draven gripping his poorly-healed leg.

"I've got him," Corbin said quickly, wrapping an arm under the kilder's shoulder. "He'll be fine with rest. Get her help."

Aeron hurried down an adjacent hall as Corbin helped Draven toward the spare rooms in the west wing.

Novah hissed as blood continued to flow. She dropped her head to Kyler's shoulder.

"No," he muttered into her hair, urging her upright. "Breathe, Novah. You're all right, just breathe."

The pound of racing footsteps grew louder as Aeron returned, the advisor at his heels. "The physician, Cadmus," Aeron seethed, shoving the advisor as he paused, grimacing at the blood.

"This way." His cool tone was edged in worry as he started for an area of the castle that Kyler had never explored.

Blood drizzled down Kyler's hands and soaked into his sleeves as he held Novah close, guiding her sloppy steps quickly down the curves and corners of the castle halls. His muscles ached, and his lungs still burned from the dust. He was nearly ready to collapse with her when Novah was lifted from his arms, and they both were ushered into a large room.

Three thin beds sat vacant in the small infirmary, and a single desk made of oak sat before a wall of shelves packed with potion bottles. The physician was at Novah's side in a moment, shouting instructions to his assistants as they lowered her to one of the beds. He quickly rolled his cotton sleeves, tossing aside his spectacles, and began to cut away the bloodied bandage.

Dust clung to her skin, soaking into her wound. Kyler knelt at her side as the physician demanded a bottle of Moundi.

Kyler offered her a gentle smile, his voice steady. "They're going to clean you up, okay?"

Her brows were furrowed, but there was no fear in her eyes. She took a shaky breath. "That's the one that stings, right?"

Kyler didn't answer. He grabbed a clean rag from a nearby stack and rolled it tightly, slipping it between her teeth. "Bite down."

She did, and her eyes squeezed shut as the physician uncorked the potion, tilting it toward her gaping wound.

Kyler gripped her hand. "It'll be over before you know—"

He wasn't finished speaking when Novah released a gut-wrenching scream through the cloth. Her hand crushed Kyler's, turning his knuckles white, as the potion buried itself between muscle and tissue, dragging the dust to the surface. The scent of burning blood filled the room, its potency bringing water to Kyler's stinging eyes. Red mixed with the white bubbles of the Moundi, and the physician began to wipe the dust away.

It wasn't until her screams quieted and a bottle of sleeping potion was brought to her lips that Novah loosened her grip, the mix of pain and potions finally taking over. Stitches were strung to seal the wound as Kyler rose on shaking legs, allowing himself to be guided to one of the other beds.

The moment he touched the mattress, coughs erupted from his chest. There was so much noise, so many people, and so much light. He could hardly hear the head physician giving orders, his deep voice no longer panicked. Kyler felt like he was back in the dust as every sound became muffled and his eyes glazed over.

A hand pushed him flat to the mattress, and a cold potion filled his mouth. Then, Kyler slept.

…

Gentle chatter of familiar voices filled Kyler's mind. Soft light filtered through his resting eyes, and the slow dripping of clean water met with the shifting of sheets as Kyler stirred beneath them. His aching body had sunken into the thick feather mattress, swallowing him as he dreamt.

Kyler turned his head and blinked, finding Corbin and Zale standing nearby. The Sea Force commander had his arms crossed over his wide chest, and a frown sat on his face as he listened intently to Corbin's low voice.

Discomfort rolled across Kyler's body as though he were covered in a thousand bruises. Maybe he was. The smell of lemon zest let him know he'd been washed, his hair and skin free of dust and sweat.

And Novah—

Kyler jolted, his head pounding from the movement, and his sights fell on the general. Relief flooded him when he saw her in the bed beside him, a fresh bandage on her shoulder. Her chest rose and fell steadily, and clean clothes and fresh sheets had replaced the bloodied ones.

"Easy," Corbin warned, placing a firm hand on Kyler's shoulder. "You've been under Onys."

He should have been able to recognize the dizzying effects of the potion, but it seemed Kyler's mind was still pulling itself from the fog.

"The gateway—"

"It's fine." Corbin pressed down firmly, forcing Kyler to rest his head on the pillow. "Orisis never came through."

A few scrapes scattered Corbin's forearms and jaw, but he appeared otherwise unharmed. His armor was clean, and a dark green cape was slung over his shoulders.

Kyler focused on the wooden beams above his head as tears threatened to fall. They were tears of relief—Novah was okay, and the gateway was still closed—but they were also bitter. They were filled with hurt for Uriah and Bricru.

"You've been through a lot," Corbin said gently, pulling Kyler's attention back to him. "You need to rest. Physician's orders. Salcon and I are handling the Brigade."

Zale chuckled. "You've been through more than a lot. I hear your trip was successful."

Kyler laced his fingers across his chest, a sigh falling. "More than Corbin knows."

Corbin quirked a brow. "I'm intrigued, but we can talk about this later. Go back to sleep."

"No, we'll talk about it now." Kyler pushed himself into a seated position, trying to ignore the headache that returned the moment he sat upright. "How's Draven? Is he alright?"

Zale's lips twisted, but it was Corbin who answered, "He's fine. Just that cursed leg of his."

Kyler bit his tongue. "I thought that potion would work."

"It did. But then Ophir found us, and he started running on it." Corbin shrugged. "He doesn't blame you."

He knew it was meant to be comforting, but Kyler still felt a prick of guilt.

"When you didn't return, we tried to follow you in the sewers, but they'd been blocked off. We thought it was a trap—"

"It was," Kyler interrupted. "Ophir was a shapeshifter working for Orisis. Those screams you heard in the castle were his."

"The white-haired one." Corbin nodded. "But why were you in the castle?"

Kyler took a breath and started his story from the very beginning. The prince, Tophet, and Uriah all sat fresh in his mind, memories he was sure would not leave him for a long time.

"The prince and the shapeshifter both found a way to keep their magic, and Bricru implied there's more than just him and Elizus. But their magic wasn't enough to make the gateways. That's why they had Uriah do it. After some time, Uriah had a change of heart and sealed the gateway to Sannir. They need his blood to unlock it."

"His blood, or your blood?" Zale asked.

Kyler stiffened.

The Sea Force commander shrugged. "Corbin told me of your relation."

Kyler's eyes snapped to his lieutenant, but Zale waved a hand. "He did not betray you—I pulled it out of him. I'm not sure when you were planning to tell us, and if I'm honest, Commander, I think you've caused more harm than good in keeping this a secret. But, if it's that important to you, I won't share."

Kyler changed the subject. "That gateway felt different than the one to Tophet. It was painful to cross, like the connection was shattered."

"Sannir and Tophet were never meant to mix," Zale said slowly. "We are of Sannir, and our blood will always lead us home. It's possible Orisis didn't follow because he cannot. He is not welcome here."

"Uriah never finished the gateways." Kyler met Zale's good eye. "That's why they wanted me. There were dozens of them he hadn't opened yet. But the gateway to Sannir was separate."

"If Orisis wants to get into Sannir, he will." Corbin sucked a breath. "The man in the room, that was him, right?"

"It was, but he calls himself Ancelin."

A smirk rose to Corbin's mouth. "And you say you landed a good hit on him?"

A soft laugh rose from Kyler's raw chest. "I did."

"You need more sleep," Zale said with a grunt, turning for the door. "Leave him be, Lieutenant."

Kyler huffed. "I'm fine."

"You just fought a god."

"And I won."

Zale chuckled. "I'm not going to argue with you. That potion is getting to your head."

It definitely was, but Kyler wasn't going to admit that.

"Rest, Commander." He waved Corbin after him, and the lieutenant gave a small shrug.

"The barracks miss you." He flashed a grin. "So do the taverns."

CHAPTER THIRTY-SEVEN

KYLER SLEPT FOR A LONG TIME. EVERY INCH OF HIM WAS ACHING and sore, and each time he awoke, he found he hurt more than he even knew possible.

But Novah never stirred.

"She looks good," the physician stated one afternoon. He stood over her bed, his wide hands hovering above her.

Behind him, one of his assistants watched in silence as he worked, her pen pressed to the blank pages of her journal. She was younger than Kyler, with thick, dark hair tied hastily from her face. Her sloped nose hooked at the end, and every time Kyler had seen her, she carried a leather bag that echoed with the clinking of potion bottles as she walked.

Healing in Sannir came mostly in the form of potions, but some learned a magic that could read the body, helping guide them in the healing process. Many alchemists studied both, becoming proficient in understanding the way potions interacted with the body.

"It won't be long until we can take her off the Onys." The physician faced Kyler, his round face splitting into a grin. "And how are you feeling, Commander?"

Kyler chuckled. "I've been better."

The man waved a hand over Kyler, and his limbs tingled. "Drink more water. I will not send you back to the barracks until I'm certain you won't pass out along the way."

Kyler reached for the cup at his bedside, lifting it to the physician as if giving a toast before taking a long drink. "I have a question, if you don't mind."

The physician shrugged, waiting for the girl to finish scribbling whatever notes he needed into the journal before passing it back to him. "Go ahead."

"Do you know what might cause the body to reject a potion?"

He thought for a moment. "I suppose if they've developed some sort of intolerance to the ingredients. But even still, magic masks most brews. What type of rejection are you referring to?"

Kyler set his glass back on the table and let his head fall softly on his pillow. "There was a shapeshifter in Potri. I let him try Zalis, and it killed him."

"Zalis?" The physician looked up from his notes. "That should be harmless."

Kyler gave a weak chuckle. "That's what I said. But then he gripped his head, screaming, and collapsed."

The physician was silent for a moment. "This shapeshifter belonged to Orisis, yes?"

"He did."

"I can only assume his body rejected the magic."

Kyler thought back to the root, the way he'd thought Bricru had mixed it with the potion. "What do you know of a root called gallot?" He stole a glance at the assistant, only to find her watching him with intrigue.

The physician answered, "I've never heard of it."

Kyler nodded slowly. "I figured. That's all. Thank you."

The physician gave a small smile and motioned the girl from

the room. He paused at the doorway. "From one alchemist to another, know that your potion was not what did him harm. He sentenced himself to death by partnering with Orisis."

Kyler nodded. "Thank you."

Those words lingered long after the physician left, and Kyler didn't mind the silence of the room. He felt a bit at home with so many potion bottles surrounding him and the smell of lilac filling the castle. Courtiers brought warm broth as the sun began to set, and the aches in Kyler's body finally felt as though they were easing.

The slow *tick* of the clock attempted to lull Kyler's mind to sleep, but he'd slept so much in the past few days that his thoughts weren't ready to give in. The mystery of both Bricru's reaction to Zalis and the gallot root consumed his mind, as if replaying the moment over enough times would reveal the answers he sought.

The shuffle of sheets finally pulled Kyler from his thoughts, and he turned his head to find Novah opening her eyes.

She stared at the ceiling, and Kyler knew she was trying to clear the fog that came after such large doses of Onys. Her fingers instinctively reached for her shoulder, running along the tight bandages.

"You didn't break anything."

Her head snapped to Kyler, and when she saw him, a small smile rose to her face. "Of course not. I've never broken a bone."

Kyler grinned, his gaze flickering around the dark room. "This is much better than Potri."

Novah sighed, as though breathing in the air of Sannir would heal the wounds she'd gained. "What happened?"

He wanted to wait—to tell her to go back to sleep and they could talk in the morning—but something about the way she looked at him made him answer. "We escaped through Orisis' gateway to Sannir. Everyone is fine. Draven's leg is a bit messed up, but Corbin thinks he'll manage. And Orisis never followed."

Silence filled the room as Novah studied it, and the ticking clock filled the lull in conversation.

"I've missed Sannir," she said finally.

Kyler laced his hands across his chest. "Me too."

She fell silent again, then whispered, "Thank you."

His brow furrowed. "For what?"

She nodded to her bandaged shoulder, and Kyler chuckled.

"Anytime. Just try not to get stabbed again."

"I'll do my best, so long as you try not to talk in your sleep. I don't need you telling me how wonderful I am."

"We've been over this, Novah."

She chuckled and closed her eyes with a satisfied smile. "Don't be embarrassed. I don't think you're so bad either. Maybe not *wonderful,* but tolerable."

Something buzzed in Kyler's chest at her words, but he simply shook his head with a sigh. "Then it seems we can finally agree on something."

Neither of them spoke after that, and soon enough, Novah's gentle breathing floated across the room.

Kyler, on the other hand, didn't have such luck. His mind continued to tumble back to Tophet, filling with Uriah and Bricru, death and destruction.

Finally, exhaustion took over, and Kyler plunged into a nightmarish sleep.

He wasn't there for long.

At first, he thought he was back in the cage, his still-tired thoughts trying to make sense of what was happening. When he finally came to, however, Kyler was in the same feather bed, and though darkness surrounded him, his eyes adjusted quickly.

Someone was crying.

Novah.

He sat up, his heart pounding as he tossed the sheets back. He saw Orisis' threat, the wound splitting and darkening, burning her with fever.

His feet hit the cold floor, and a moment later, he was beside her bed. He reached for her face, expecting to be met with a fevered burn, but instead he found her skin cool and dotted with sweat.

"Novah." He inched closer, brushing his thumb across her brow. Her eyes were sealed shut. It seemed he wasn't the only one haunted by nightmares.

He tried saying her name again, combing gently through her hair as he attempted to break the ghostly spell.

Finally, she gasped, her eyes meeting his as the dream slipped from her mind.

"Easy. You were dreaming."

She released a breath, closing her eyes as her shoulders relaxed. "Thank you."

Kyler prayed she couldn't hear the way his heart was pounding, from both the scare she'd given him, and from the way she seemed to lean into his touch.

"I have them too," he whispered.

She swallowed. "That's what you talk about."

He pulled his hand away from her hair, wondering what she meant.

"When you talk in your sleep, it's from nightmares."

"Something else we have in common then." He stood, pulling the tangled sheets from his bed, and tossed his pillow to the floor beside her.

Novah said nothing as Kyler laid on his back. The floor felt cool against his skin, and he pulled the sheets over him. "Goodnight, Novah."

Her voice was softer than the cotton sheets. "Goodnight, Kyler."

...

Kyler woke to warm sunlight as it slipped through the glass windows, masking the room in gold. For a moment, he forgot where he was. His back was stiff from the floor, and a cold shiver ran over him from the thin sheets, but his heart stuttered when he looked up.

Novah lay on the edge of the bed, her hair tumbling off the mattress and tangling in her scales. This time, she slept without the pressure of nightmares, and her expression had softened.

Kyler studied her. Freckles danced along her jaw, some darker than others, and a few spotted her nose and brow. Her mouth was gentle, and small dimples sat against her cheeks even though she wasn't smiling. He liked it.

He reached for her hair, his fingertips tangling in the strands as he brushed them from her face. He gently moved to her jaw, finding her skin warm but not uncomfortably so. No fever. He let his touch linger there, pressed against her scattered freckles until she woke, the light catching her eyes that burned like whiskey.

"Good morning." He offered a smile that she didn't immediately return.

She stared down at him, her eyes landing on his mouth for a moment. She quickly turned, and Kyler's hand fell back to his chest. The cold of her absence hit his skin, pulling him from whatever daze he'd let himself fall into.

"It's getting late," he said, sitting upright. He was being foolish, letting himself revel in her like that. He knew better. "They'll be in soon to redress that wound."

Novah stared at the ceiling. "You act as if I've never been wounded before." Her voice was slightly rough, like the roll of salt against a ship's hull.

"You act as if you've had a million."

"Maybe I have."

Kyler chuckled, tossing his pillow back onto his own bed. "I find that very hard to believe. You'd lose count at some point."

He wasn't in his bed but a moment when the door creaked open, and the physician entered.

"General!" he greeted, setting his journal on the desk, and approached Novah's side. "Happy to see you awake. How does it feel?"

She answered his question, and his next one, explaining the soreness and allowing him to feel her shoulder.

But Kyler's mind was far from their conversation. All he could think about was her—the way his hands had tangled in her hair and her gaze had locked with his.

He needed to get out of that room.

CHAPTER THIRTY-EIGHT

KYLER WAS RELEASED THAT AFTERNOON AND ALLOWED TO walk himself back to the barracks—back home. He was grateful. It gave him something to do and something to think about that wasn't the general.

The castle was full of life, with silver décor being strung from the ceilings and candles lining the halls. The weather was growing cooler, and Eliab's Day was quickly approaching. Excitement filled the castle as Kyler moved through the halls, the scent of fresh bread and warm chocolate floating after him.

Even still, there was a hint of worry that grew as Kyler passed the great hall, his eyes scanning the open space for flickers of dust. Soldiers had been stationed nearby, their chainmail ringing as they shifted, and their pleasant conversation carried through the room. Kyler caught the end of their words as he turned for the castle doors—they spoke of the queen's coronation.

He ventured toward the west wing, where the afi had previously toppled its walls. The west wing was standing again, fully rebuilt and smelling of fresh paint and wood.

Soldiers paced the grounds as Kyler descended the steps to the courtyard, the chilled air sinking into his skin despite the armor that covered him. His cloak tangled in the sharp breeze as his boots met cobblestone, and the voices of noblemen and women walking the grounds floated around him like clouds, too foggy to understand but too thick to ignore.

"Commander."

Kyler paused at the unfamiliar voice, turning to find the physician's assistant descending the castle steps.

Wind tugged at her hair, the strands catching in her lashes as she brushed them from her face. Her dark skirt, the color of deep sea, had been hiked up to reveal worn boots, and even though she wore a cloak, she was shivering as she reached Kyler.

"Did the physician change his mind?" Kyler asked.

The girl shook her head, one hand gripping the strap of her potion bag. "Here." She handed him a folded piece of parchment, a page clearly ripped from her journal.

Kyler frowned as he took it, unfolding the page to find a few lines of scribbled notes. Her writing was slanted and sloppy. There was one word, though, that he made out immediately.

Gallot.

"That's everything I could find."

Kyler looked back up at her. There was something familiar in her face. "Thank you…"

"Vera."

He nodded, tucking the paper into his pocket. "Thank you, Vera."

She turned to reenter the castle, but Kyler placed a hand on her shoulder, stopping her. He suddenly realized why he recognized her.

"You're Draven's sister."

It was obvious now, as they shared the same sloped nose and round eyes.

Vera tucked her hands into her pockets, a small grin rising to her face. "How'd you guess?"

"The resemblance is uncanny." He paused for a moment. "If you see him before I do, tell him I'm going to fix his leg."

Her smile fell, the humor dissipating from her face. "Commander, I don't know if that's—"

"It was my potion," he interrupted, "and I'll be the one to undo its damage."

She pursed her lips, her gaze lifting to the castle behind her. "I can help." She faced him again. "We'll fix his leg and figure out your mystery root."

Kyler thought for a moment. There was an unbreakable determination in her gaze.

"Alright," he said finally. "We can start after the queen's coronation."

Her chin lifted, a look of satisfaction dancing across her face as she gave a firm nod. "I'll see you then, Commander."

"Kyler."

"Thank you, Kyler." She turned and hurried up the castle steps.

Leaves crunched as Kyler started toward the barracks once more, the gardens now a full blaze of orange and red as autumn hung in the air. From here, he could see the smoke that billowed from the barracks' fireplace. As he grew nearer, its sweet smell filled his nose.

The moment Kyler walked inside, he was bombarded with cheers and claps on his shoulders. The common room was so packed with soldiers that they were piled into the adjacent hallways. He startled, momentarily forgetting potions and coronations, and laughed as his soldiers surrounded him.

"Commander!" Salcon flung an arm around Kyler's neck, pulling him in. "It's good to have you back!"

Kyler grinned at his lieutenant, wrapping him in a hug. "Saints,

I missed you." He pulled back and placed his hands on Salcon's shoulders. "Glad to see you kept the place standing."

Salcon's knuckles collided lightly with Kyler's chest as Adri squeezed through, gripping Kyler's hand so tightly that it made his knuckles turn white.

"Easy," Kyler scolded, jerking his hand away with a playful scowl. "I didn't survive Orisis just to have you crush me."

Adri only grinned wider, giving Kyler a good shake.

"What's the news?" Salcon asked, his question causing the chatter to quiet.

Kyler scanned the men, his gaze finally landing on Corbin. His lieutenant stood near the fireplace, arms crossed over his chest and lips pressed thin. It seemed he hadn't told them anything.

Kyler took a breath and faced Salcon, his voice low. "Not here." He turned to the rest of the men. "You will all be filled in shortly. But right now, I'm just happy to be home amongst friends. I believe the kitchens are waiting for us?"

A collective cheer rose as the soldiers started for the dining hall, the smell of cooked meat racing through the barracks.

"We'll talk later?" Salcon came to Kyler's side.

"Of course."

Salcon stayed close to Kyler's side as they trailed the men into the dining hall.

The kitchens were already alive, and before long, food filled the counters. Kyler loaded his plate with rice and chicken and found a seat beside his lieutenants, hardly able to take a bite before being swarmed with questions.

"Did you find the afi?" Lieutenant Aantho pressed. He was a tall, thin elf, with pale skin and paler hair. Three lengths of green scales dangled from each ear, and he'd begun to grow a beard in Kyler's absence.

"We did, though not in the way we expected."

Adri scoffed. "You can't say something like that without sharing the story."

This time, it was Corbin who answered, a sly smirk on his face. "Kyler got kidnapped."

Salcon choked a laugh. "You did not."

"And then I escaped." Kyler pointed a finger around the circular table. "Keep that in mind."

"That's good," Adri reasoned. "We have an advantage now. You know their inner workings, no?"

"Exactly." Kyler took another bite, hoping the questions were finished, but Corbin spoke up again.

"They have a shapeshifter and an alithias, both full afi who somehow kept their magic."

Adri whistled and Aantho's eyes widened. "How?"

Corbin shrugged. "Don't know."

"But we'll find out," Kyler finished, taking another bite of rice.

"And what of the general?" Salcon changed the topic. "How is she faring?"

At the mention of Novah, Kyler's mind flew back to the previous night, and Salcon misread his change in demeanor.

"You can be honest, it's just us. She's in over her head, isn't she?"

Corbin met Kyler's eye with a look of warning, but Kyler was already answering. "She led our team well in Potri. She's adjusting, but she's done alright."

Aantho smirked. "Are you certain? I'm pretty sure you just mentioned a kidnapping."

His jab brought another round of laughter, and although Kyler joined, it wasn't genuine. He fell quiet as the conversation drifted, thankful the topic was no longer focused on Novah.

. . .

The evening came, cool and lively, and talk of what was to come had begun to spread throughout the barracks. His men had been informed of the threat—of the gateway that was at risk of opening and the powerful afi on the other side—but the prospect of war was nothing but a fanciful idea of heroism to Kyler's soldiers.

When Kyler at last retreated to his room, he found his clothes cleaned and folded at the foot of his bed. The scent of old wood and faint herbs brought a sense of comfort that Kyler hadn't realized he craved. A knot formed in his throat as he found his potion belt beneath his clothes, the leather oiled and shining.

Kyler ran his fingers along the belt, his thoughts wandering to Potri, before he caught sight of what lay beside it.

The gallot root lay atop his quilt, its brown texture as dark as the leather of his belt. Even from here, he could smell the odd aroma it released, the same smell that'd filled the study when Kyler had broken it open.

He took hold of the root, lifting it to the warm light of his lamps. There was so little knowledge of it. The plant seemed ordinary, but Kyler couldn't help but wonder what secrets were hiding within.

What are you?

Kyler's door swung open, and he grabbed the first object he could find—his potion belt—and sent it flying toward the doorway.

Corbin ducked with a curse, the belt barely missing his head. It slammed into the wall behind him, falling to the floor in a heap of leather.

Kyler scowled, setting the root on his desk, as Corbin retrieved his belt. "Knock."

Corbin gave a playful glare. "I didn't know you could throw that well."

"I'm going to pretend you didn't just insult me." Kyler glanced to the door he'd left open. "Close that."

Corbin did and took a seat on the mattress as Kyler pulled out his desk chair, sitting backward on it to face Corbin. "How are you?"

His lieutenant shrugged. "I've been better. I'm just glad you're alright."

A soft smile rose to Kyler's lips, but it didn't quite reach his eyes. Corbin noticed.

"I saw how you stalled with that shapeshifter." He folded his hands, leaning his elbows on his knees as he met Kyler's eye. "You didn't mean to kill him."

Kyler pursed his lips. "No."

"You can't let this get to you."

Kyler tilted his gaze to the ceiling, his scales brushing his neck as he did. "It's not just him. My potion hurt Draven too. And Uriah—"

"Uriah isn't your problem." Corbin's tone was sharp. "Draven will be fine, and sometimes people need to die. You're a soldier, Kyler, and not just that, you're also our commander. The good of Sannir comes first. Always."

Kyler sucked a deep breath, hating that Corbin was right. He reached behind him, plucking the root from his desk, and held it between them. "You don't know anything about this, do you?"

Corbin took it, studying it from every angle before passing it back. "Not a thing."

"It's said to cause pain, which was exactly what happened when Bricru drank Zalis. I think he's tied to this somehow."

"Do you know it's origin?"

Kyler dug the folded parchment from his pocket, scanning over Vera's notes. "No. Just that it was first discovered in Xynack."

"Evander is there. You could ask him what he knows."

Kyler sighed at the mention of his brother, remembering the promise he'd made to Novah. "I can try."

Corbin chuckled. "Don't sound so excited."

"I'm not sure he'll even answer." Kyler faced his desk and pulled out a piece of parchment. "Is there anything else I should know?"

Corbin folded his hands behind his head, lounging back against Kyler's pillow. "Aiyanna's coronation is tomorrow night, and we've been invited to spend Eliab's Eve at the castle. They're planning to celebrate as usual."

Eliab's Day marked the building of the Temple and the opening of the Pass. Just like Kyler had seen inside the castle, silver décor—and melted chocolate—were staples of the holiday, and all of Sannir stayed awake until the twelfth chime of the clocks on Eliab's Eve, releasing fireworks and dancing late into the night.

"That's good. The people need stability."

Corbin was silent for a moment. "So, Aiyanna…"

Kyler groaned. "Don't do this."

"Easy, Kyler. I was just going to tell you that she was asking for you. She wanted to hear that you were alright."

He bit his tongue, wishing Corbin would talk about anything else. "You can tell her I'm fine."

"I did, but I think you should tell her yourself."

"Corbin."

"I'm serious." Corbin sat upright, his hands gripping the side of the bed. "I know things didn't end well with you two, but she's your queen. She still cares, and I know you care, too. Just talk to her."

Kyler ran a hand through his hair, his words laced with sarcasm. "I didn't realize you were the one giving orders."

Corbin grinned, and the bed let out a small squeak as he stood. "When you and Novah disappeared, we thought you were dead. Someone had to step up."

"Unfortunately for you, I'm still alive. You follow my orders."

"If your orders are 'Corbin, you can have my room', then I won't argue."

"You're a nuisance."

He grinned. "You missed me."

"Get out."

His fingers brushed his temple as he turned to leave. "Of course, Commander. Whatever you say."

CHAPTER THIRTY-NINE

KYLER RAN HIS HANDS DOWN HIS EARS, ENSURING EVERY SCALE hung even and straight. Dark green cotton poked out from beneath his silver armor, its color matching his scales and making his eyes look as dark as the pine trees that filled the forests of Sannir.

When he was satisfied with his appearance Kyler stepped away from the mirror and secured his potion belt, filled with fresh, colorful elixirs, around his waist. The brews had kept him up well into the night.

That, and he hadn't been able to sleep.

Every time Kyler had closed his eyes, he could feel the burn of the gallot root, and his body jolted awake, as if he'd been the one about to die from the potion.

So, while the moon still sat high above the mountains of Sannir, Kyler had sat at his desk brewing potion after potion, keeping the flame burning low and steady. The smell of bergamot and peppermint still lingered as the sun finally rose.

He gave the belt a tug, ensuring it was secure, before leaving his room. He trailed through the barracks and stepped into the cold Sannir air. There was no sign of Corbin yet, so Kyler leaned a shoulder against the outer wall of the barracks, studying the dry leaves that masked the grounds in brown and yellow as he waited.

A shadow cast over the training field, and Kyler lifted his eyes to see the dragon, Atlas, followed by three others as they emerged from the Pass. He wondered, briefly, if the Pass felt like the gateways Uriah had built—if flying through those clouds would produce the same sensation as when he entered Tophet.

Shades of golden rays covered Atlas as he curved toward Sannir's castle, his horns cupping his jaw and pale scales reflecting the morning sun.

"I think they're going to beat us."

Kyler turned to find Corbin dressed in the same pine green as him. A smile crept onto his face as Corbin fell in stride beside him, his lieutenant's attention locked on the dragons. Kyler plunged his hands into his pockets and chose to let the silence between them linger.

As they reached the courtyard, Kyler was surprised to see it already bustling with people. Nobles spilled from their living quarters that sat at the outskirts of the castle grounds, and everyone funneled into the castle entryway. Through the crowd, Kyler caught sight of the dragons already inside, their massive forms nearly as tall as the castle itself.

It wasn't until they rounded the castle that Kyler spotted Aeron. His maroon cape swung from his shoulders as he turned at the sound of their approaching footsteps.

"Commander." He offered Kyler a gloved hand.

"I never got the chance to thank you," Kyler said, accepting the gesture, "for getting us out of Potri."

Aeron clicked his tongue lightly. "Now we're even."

Kyler dropped his hand. "How so?"

"I saved your life in the Potri castle, and you saved Novah's."

Something in Kyler's chest tweaked, but he ignored it. "Of

course. She means a lot to you, I can tell."

"She means a lot to Draven as well, and now that she's the general, she means a lot to Sannir. We need her."

Kyler nodded, turning to follow the crowd. "If you don't mind me asking, what do you think of Aiyanna as queen?" He was curious of what the other soldiers thought of her. Did they respect her in the same way that they revered the king?

Aeron was silent for a moment, falling in stride beside Kyler and Corbin. "I hope she'll do well. The circumstances, however, are unfortunate."

"Very." Kyler nodded to the passing soldiers as they entered the foyer.

A man approached Aeron, and Kyler recognized him immediately as the newly appointed commander of the Sky Regiment. His gray beard had filled out since Kyler had last seen him, and the dozens of scales that hung from his ears well surpassed Aeron's.

He greeted his lieutenant with a smile that brought wrinkles to his eyes before turning to Kyler and Corbin, offering a hand. "Commander, it's good to have you back." He spoke kindly, much less formal than Zale tended to be.

"Commander Idar, correct?"

He laughed. "Still getting used to that, but yes. Thank you for looking after our general."

Kyler whistled softly, stealing a glance at Aeron. "It seems the entire Regiment would fall without Novah Elison."

"She was a great commander," Idar said with a shrug, "and an even better general."

His words trailed off as the guests were ushered into the great hall. Strips of silver cloth fell in spirals to the marble floor, dancing between the pillars like a canopy above Kyler's head.

Chairs of matching dark wood sat in rows that stretched the length of the room. Instead of a table, a small stand sat before the windows, topped with the same silver crown that Kyler had seen the king wear many times before. Its intricate twists of diamonds rose to a point, with a sapphire at the center. The dragons had positioned themselves around the edges, watching every person that entered.

Kyler felt Atlas' eyes on him as he found his seat at the front. The row was draped in dark fabric, marking the seats as reserved. One of the chairs was already occupied, and Kyler smiled when he spotted Draven.

His hair had been trimmed and his beard cropped, and in one hand he clutched a cane carved from dark wood. A dragon head had been whittled into the head of his cane, and his fingers rested on it, rubbing the detailed scales and curved horns.

"Look who's up and walking again," Kyler teased, pulling Draven's attention to him.

The kilder laughed, using the cane to push himself to his feet. "I could say the same about you."

He caught Kyler eyeing his cane and lifted it off the ground, passing it into the commander's hands. "It is beautifully made. The healers are working on a more permanent solution, but this will do for now."

Kyler gave a tight smile and handed the cane back to him. "I think it makes you look intimidating."

He chuckled, which helped to ease the pinch in Kyler's chest. "I will take your word for it."

Corbin rounded Kyler's side and took a seat beside Draven. Their conversing faded from Kyler's ears as he caught sight of red scales and a flash of white.

Novah slipped into the great hall, her hair braided at her

temples and armor reflecting the light of the chandeliers. She wore a burgundy cape over one shoulder, and a sword sat secure at her hip. She smiled thinly at those she passed, and Kyler was sure he was the only one to notice the way her left arm shifted stiffly as she walked.

He made his way toward her, and his chest hummed when her thin smile turned genuine. "Out of bed already, General?"

She scoffed. "Remind me to never get stabbed again."

He chuckled as he reached for her cape, adjusting the fabric so that it fell neatly over her uninjured shoulder. "The kidnapping was never part of the plan."

She lifted a brow as if to argue, but the doors behind her began to close. Kyler motioned her to their seats. Zale and Idar had already made their way to the front, and Aeron slipped into their row just as Advisor Cadmus reached the front of the hall. The soft chatter fell silent.

The advisor wore a coat as dark as the sapphire and trimmed in silver, which brushed the marble as he walked. His dark gaze floated across the hall as every eye fixated on him. He took a deep breath and welcomed the guests, beginning the ceremony.

Kyler found himself lost in the jumble of words, his mind wandering. He recalled the scene Orisis had shown him—a crowd, like this, gathering to watch him become general. He snuck a glance at Novah. The white scale dangled from her chain of red and orange. Were the scale on his ear, he would look like Uriah.

He didn't like that thought.

It wasn't until Aiyanna strode to the front of the room that Kyler focused once more, his breath stilling at her appearance. She was dressed like a queen, her hair pulled away from her face and falling in ringlets down her back. Silver and blue draped her form like starlight and sky, and beaded crystals fell from her clothes, sending rainbows spinning across the marble floor.

She looked just as she had in Orisis' vision.

Aiyanna faced the audience, her soft eyes resting on Kyler's. Her face didn't change; her chin remained high, and her gaze flickered away after a moment.

Cadmus motioned for everyone to rise, and his voice echoed across the room. "Kingdom of Sannir, I introduce you to your new ruler, the only heir of the Late King Ouxileous Ascian, Queen Aiyanna Ascian."

Applause filled the room, and Kyler joined in as Cadmus lifted the crown from its pedestal and placed it atop Aiyanna's head. The queen smiled warmly, her face beaming in a way Kyler knew would capture the hearts of the people. As the applause settled, Novah stepped away from the seats. She took her place at Ayanna's side, a symbol of her support and protection.

Novah muttered something to the queen that made her chuckle, the two sharing some joke that made Kyler wonder how they'd gotten so close.

Cadmus' voice rose again. "Hor d'oeuvres will be served in the foyer, and you all are invited to congratulate the queen. Stay as long as you would like. Today, we are all friends."

With that, the doors were pulled open, and light conversation once again filled the great hall.

Corbin nudged Kyler with his shoulder, jerking his chin in the direction of Aiyanna.

"Now?" Kyler hissed. "Absolutely not."

Corbin rolled his eyes. "Not for that. Just go give your congratulations. The people need to see your support."

"She has my support," he muttered. Reluctantly, he stood from his seat and made his way toward her.

Lords and ladies approached the queen one at a time, pressing kisses to her hands and wishing her well, but when Kyler reached her, he found it difficult to meet her eye.

He pressed a fist to his chest and dipped into a bow. "Queen Aiyanna."

"Commander Kyler." There was a light edge to her voice that made him look up, relieved to find a smile on her pink lips. "I'm glad to hear your mission was successful."

Kyler stole a glance at Novah. "I suppose you could say that."

"The general has filled me in on most of the details, but I'd like to hear from you as well."

He struggled to decipher what it was she was asking for.

"Thank you for serving Sannir well." Her brows lifted slightly as she spoke, her tone level and her eyes boring into him.

Kyler nodded and slipped away before he lost his wits under her gaze. It seemed Corbin had been right—she wanted to talk.

In the time the ceremony had taken place, the entryway had been transformed. Pub tables filled the room, stretching from wall to wall and draped with navy tablecloths. Platters stacked three plates high had been packed with miniature pastries and crackers with cheese. Kyler made his way to one, watching the room around him as he leaned an elbow on the table.

"Novah looks well." Zale came to Kyler's side, crossing his arms as he watched the guests mingle.

"She didn't look well a few days ago. That injury could've been worse."

"I think she blames herself." Zale sighed, facing Kyler with a frown. "I understand the events that took place in Potri were no one's fault. She seems like the type to take the blame whenever she can."

Kyler straightened and looked through the open doors of the

great hall, hoping to catch a glimpse of Novah. Instead, he saw the brilliant scales of the dragons as the room began to empty.

"I'm going to look for Idar," Zale changed the subject. "Let me know if you run into Cadmus. I'd like to speak with him as well."

Kyler nodded, his mind still stuck on Novah, as Zale disappeared into the crowd.

Chatter filled the room like the soft hum of the tides beyond the castle, and Kyler lost himself in the gentle noise. It was pleasant, a comfort he'd forgotten.

The soft tap of scales and claws joined the noise, and from where he stood, Kyler watched as the dragons began to rise from their seated positions. The great hall was empty now. Even Novah and Aiyanna had left its confines, and something made Kyler set his plate of food aside.

No one paid him any mind as he returned to the great hall, the voices fading behind him, and all four dragons turned their fierce gazes upon his lone form. Embarrassment flamed across his skin as he halted, realizing how foolish he must look, wandering into their presence like a lost child. He opened his mouth to speak, still unsure of what had drawn him back in.

"Sorry." The word slipped. He couldn't force another, and yet couldn't find the will to leave.

After a moment, Atlas cocked his head, his horns brushing the drapes of silver. Ink-black eyes locked on Kyler, and smoke puffed from his nose as he straightened.

Before Kyler could think better of it, he asked, "Why did you choose Uriah?"

If a dragon could laugh, Atlas did. Another stream of smoke filled the air, and his body shifted as he lowered his face to Kyler.

"I don't know if I want to free him."

Saying it out loud felt different somehow, but the words didn't faze the beast. Atlas dipped his head toward Kyler, and the commander swallowed as his horns drifted closer. Kyler kept his feet planted and squeezed his eyes shut as Atlas' cool scales pressed firmly against his forehead.

The moment they touched, a low rumble filled Kyler's thoughts, like a song he could almost understand. The language of dragons rattled his bones, unknown yet wonderfully familiar— as if his blood understood. No words were spoken, and yet Kyler *felt* what the dragon was trying to communicate.

Disappointment toward Uriah. Hope for Novah. Fierce anger toward Orisis.

Kyler shook his head against the scales. *I don't understand.*

Patience toward Kyler.

He took a breath, willing his thoughts to accept those of Atlas. Slowly, an image came into view. A plan for elves to thrive and a general who would bring peace, not just to Sannir but to all of Vellichor. Dragons and elves living together, and the creatures of Orisis trapped in their prison of Tophet.

Kyler pulled back, his blood racing. "Orisis offered me something similar, and I almost took it. Are you saying I should have?"

Atlas' gaze darkened as he rose to his full height. No. Kyler had been right to turn Orisis down. But from the look the dragon gave, it seemed there was more that perhaps even he didn't fully understand.

Kyler nodded slowly, backing away from the circle of beasts. "I want that too. But right now, my job is to protect Sannir."

Atlas gave no sign of his thoughts as he squared his shoulders, turning his gaze to the windows.

With a pounding heart, Kyler returned to the gathering, his

mind once against numbed by the gentleness of pleasant conversation.

"You look nervous."

Kyler spun, finding Novah leaning on the table behind him. Her fingers tapped the table as she eyed the dragons. "You know, you're supposed to ask the general for permission before you speak with them."

Kyler reached for a glass of Apola as it passed. "I do now. I hope you don't mind, *General.*"

He brought the drink to his mouth, and his tongue was quickly assaulted with the bitter herbs of unflavored Apola. His face twisted in disgust, and Novah ducked her head to hide her laughter.

"Saints, that's horrible," Kyler sputtered.

She took a glass for herself, sniffing it lightly before taking a slow sip. "It's expensive."

"It's repulsive."

"I said expensive, not good." She pursed her lips as the Apola settled in her mouth, but unlike Kyler, she was able to keep from showing her distaste. "How's Corbin doing?"

Kyler scanned the room, finding his lieutenant in conversation with Zale and Cadmus. "I think he's happy to be home."

"I'd like him to be part of our meetings going forward."

"Meetings?"

She shrugged, swirling the glass in her hand. "We need to work together. All of us." Her gaze flickered to Cadmus. "This gateway poses a real threat, and until Uriah is out of Tophet, there's a chance Orisis will find a way through."

Those words were more acrid than the aftertaste of the Apola. "Uriah can't be our priority. We should focus on destroying the gateway."

A knot formed between her brows. "And leave Uriah to suffer? He's our general."

"Uriah is not our general."

She paused, taking a slow breath as she stared at her Apola. "Alright."

The silence that fell between them made Kyler's stomach sink. He gripped his glass, and despite the taste, he took another sip. Novah didn't understand his complex relationship with Uriah— she couldn't. He'd kept that part to himself. "There's more about Uriah I didn't tell you."

Novah met his eye, her face hard.

"I'll tell you everything. Just not here."

She rolled her bad shoulder, wincing slightly at the movement. "I don't understand you."

Kyler chuckled. "That's what makes me so charming."

"That's not the word I'd use." She straightened, humor dancing on her lips, as she brushed past Kyler, and he lost sight of her in the crowd.

CHAPTER FORTY

THE FIRE CRACKLED, SENDING SPARKS FLYING AGAINST THE brick chimney. The flames warmed the barrack's common area, yet Kyler was still cold as he flipped through the pages of a worn book. A deep chill had swept in overnight, and the thin walls of the Land Brigade's living quarters did little to block it out.

The circular table at which Kyler sat was occupied only by himself and Corbin, his lieutenant silent but for an occasional sniff or turn of a page. Between them, stacks of leather and clothbound books lay lopsided, several of them splayed open with scribbled parchment tucked between their pages.

Kyler's vision blurred the longer he stared at the text, the history of various plants and herbs jumbling his mind and making him dizzy. Corbin, on the other hand, was fixated on his volume. He traced the parchment with his finger as he read each line, fully intrigued by the contents of the book.

"Gateways aren't inherently complex," Corbin said out loud, pulling Kyler's focus from his own reading. "Vellichor is practically built on them. The Pass and the entrance to Tophet are both gateways, so opening a gateway is natural."

Kyler sighed and turned back to his page, rereading the same paragraph for a third time. "I'm glad you're enjoying this."

Corbin shifted, pushing the scattered volumes aside, and set the book between them. "To close the Pass, one would have to destroy the Temple of Adoni." He tapped the parchment, waiting for Kyler to look up again. "The Temple is what ties the Pass to Sannir. To close the gateway Uriah made, we just need to figure out what he used to tie it to Sannir and then destroy it."

Kyler set his book aside and leaned across the table to get a better look at Corbin's claims. "Uriah's gateway is different. It let us into Sannir, but there's no way back to Tophet. It's like it's one-sided."

Corbin shrugged and pulled the book back to himself, quickly flipping to the next page.

The door to the barracks creaked open, letting in a rush of cold air that caused the fire at Kyler's back to flicker.

"Saints," Vera swore as she shoved the door shut behind her. She shivered beneath her heavy cloak, which was lined with wool the color of Atlas' scales, and she pressed her cold fingers to her face as the warmth of the barracks greeted her.

"You're early." Kyler waved her over. "Vera, this is Lieutenant Corbin. Corbin, meet Draven's sister, Vera."

Corbin glanced up from his reading, flashing her a grin. "Draven's talked about you."

The young alchemist stalled for a moment. It seemed Corbin's smile had caught her off guard.

"Good things, I hope," she answered quickly.

Corbin chuckled. "Mostly."

Vera scrunched her nose, and Kyler tried to hide his smile as he pulled out the chair beside him. He passed the book on herbs into Vera's hands as she sat. "See what you can find on gallot."

She frowned. "Why? I already gave you what I found."

"We're still missing information."

She stole another glance at Corbin, so fast that Kyler almost missed it. "It's an unknown root. I'm not sure what else you expect to find about it."

Kyler sighed and leaned back in his chair, crossing his arms over his chest. "We know that gallot causes severe pain when added to a potion. We know that the shapeshifter was in pain after drinking Zalis." His eyes rose to the ceiling, trailing the dark beams over their heads. "My theory is that gallot root and Orisis have something in common. If we can figure out what, we might be able to use it to our advantage."

Corbin gave a light scoff and flipped to the next page of his reading. "You came up with that from such a small similarity?"

"I get it." Vera tucked her hair away from her face as she began to flip through the book. "Alchemy is a science. The similarities between the two may be few, but that's an incredibly strong and specific reaction."

Kyler snapped his fingers and pointed at Vera as he shot Corbin a smug look.

His lieutenant pursed his lips, falling silent once more.

Satisfied in proving Corbin's skepticism invalid, Kyler stood. "The two of you stay busy. I have a meeting." He lifted his cloak from where he'd hung it over the back of his chair.

Corbin clicked his tongue. "With whom, Commander? The queen?" He looked up just in time to catch Kyler's glare.

"The general."

"Aren't I supposed to be part of these meetings?" He slammed his book shut and grabbed his cloak. "General's orders."

Kyler rolled his eyes. "Fine. Vera, don't move."

She scowled. "You're just going to leave me here?"

Corbin brushed past her chair. "It was either me or you, and I've done more than enough reading on his behalf."

Kyler offered Vera a small shrug as he slipped through the door, closing it firmly behind him.

The cold air bit at his bare hands, and Kyler stuffed them into his pockets to keep warm.

"Good thing the castle isn't far," Corbin mumbled, ducking his head against the wind as they started for the castle.

Kyler glanced at him from the corner of his eye. "That was risky, mentioning Aiyanna like that."

"I'll stop bothering you when you stop pouting about your princess."

"Queen," Kyler corrected. "And she's not mine."

Corbin lifted a finger and tapped Kyler's temple, despite the commander's attempt to dodge his hand. "Don't lose your head. Just settle things, for everyone's sake." He picked up his pace as the wind grew sharp, and Kyler almost didn't hear his next jab. "Besides, I saw you with Novah yesterday."

Kyler's head snapped up.

Corbin laughed. "Don't look at me like that."

"I don't know what you're talking about."

"Just be careful, Kyler." He bumped Kyler with his shoulder. "Deal with Uriah and these gateways, and then we can talk about the general."

"There's nothing to talk about."

Corbin pinched his tongue between his teeth, a small laugh resting on his lips as they neared the castle.

The doors to the meeting room were already open and the voices inside carried across the great hall as they neared. Kyler veered as he reached the spot where the gateway had opened, sidestepping the area as if touching it might reactivate the gateway. His gaze lifted from that area to the meeting room where Novah, Aiyanna, Zale, and Cadmus were already waiting, hovered around scattered parchment.

Kyler tapped his knuckles against the doorframe as he and Corbin entered. "I hope we're not late."

"You're on time." Novah motioned them inside. "Aiyanna?"

The queen stared at the parchment with twisted lips, her hands gripped to the side of the table and her hair spilling over her hunched shoulders. "I've just discovered these in my father's belongings. I think they're notes of Uriah's."

Kyler's brow dipped. He came quickly to her side, recognizing the clean handwriting immediately. The notes were incomplete, compiled of half-finished thoughts that seemed to continue elsewhere, but one word appeared on every page.

Gateway.

"Where did you find these?" Kyler took one of the papers into his hands and flipped it over, finding more writing on the back.

"They were in my father's desk, hidden neatly between pages of various books," Aiyanna answered. "That's not my father's handwriting, though."

"Of course not. It's Uriah's."

"How can you be certain?" Cadmus asked, his gaze narrowed on the paper.

Kyler hadn't missed the advisor during his time away. Cadmus always spoke to him with a condescending tone.

Kyler chose to ignore the question completely. He was too fascinated by the parchment before him, filled with drawings, measurements, theories, and facts all surrounding the creation of gateways.

Footsteps approached, announcing the arrival of Commander Idar and Aeron, whose heavy cloak swept the floor with each step.

"I'm not sure I like the look on your face." Aeron came to

Kyler's side immediately and spread out the parchments to get a better look at each piece. There were only five pages, but it was enough to make him pause. "What are these?"

"Hopefully, our answers." Kyler finished reading and looked up to find Aiyanna watching him with a curious eye. "Are there any others?"

She shook her head and crossed her arms, eyeing the paper. "Not that I could find. Uriah's room has already been cleaned out. If he had more, we should have found them then."

"I don't understand," Novah said. "Why were these in the king's possession and not Uriah's?"

"Because Uriah hid them," Kyler answered without looking up. It was something his father had done in Kyler's youth. When he didn't want something discovered, Uriah would tuck it away beneath carpets or in hollowed-out books. Kyler and Evander often made a game of it, searching for Uriah's secrets while he was away. "He didn't want anyone finding these, so he must've stashed them in various places. No one was supposed to find them."

"My father did." Aiyanna dug her nails into the table. "Just before the attack, he shifted my studies to focus on gateways. I thought it was just because of the Pass but—"

"But it wasn't." Novah finished. "He found some of Uriah's notes and was trying to decipher them." She tapped a hand against the table. "He was onto something. Kyler, where might Uriah have hidden the rest of these?"

"Try his office first." Kyler was already moving toward the door. "Check anywhere he frequented or had regular access to."

Aiyanna's shoes clicked against the marble as she hurried to Kyler's side, the others at her heels. "He had access to the whole castle."

"Then check the whole castle."

"Commander!"

Kyler slowed at the sharpness in Advisor Cadmus' tone, turning to find his heavy glare. "Pardon my apprehension, but why should we trust your word on this?" He looked at Novah, his question directed at her as much as it was at Kyler.

Kyler's ears rang, adrenaline rushing through his blood. Everyone waited for his response, and when he looked at Novah, he found her lips pressed shut. Even Corbin was silent, his eyes flickering between Kyler and Cadmus.

The commander's jaw shifted, the words like metal on his tongue. "Because I'm his son."

For a moment, no one spoke.

"Uriah had a son?" Cadmus asked, his voice low.

"Unfortunately, yes."

"When where you going to share this?"

"I wasn't," Kyler snapped. "But now, it comes into play." He spun on his heel, the eyes of those behind him boring into his back as he stalked across the castle hall. "Split up. Look for anything that could hide folded or rolled parchment. Uriah wouldn't crumple it."

"I don't believe this," Cadmus muttered.

"Watch your tone, Advisor," Novah reprimanded. Her shoulder brushed his as she slipped past, pausing beside Aiyanna. "Keep searching your father's things. You might find more." Then she turned, trailing after Kyler.

When they were out of earshot of the others, Novah released a heavy sigh. "You handled that well."

Kyler kept a quick pace as he headed for the general's study. "I never wanted to claim him."

"But you're right, it comes into play." She caught his eye. "Not just with this. Uriah might bend if he thinks you're in danger, and Orisis can use that as leverage."

"You don't know him like I do. He won't bend for me."

Kyler reached the study first, the golden knob cold in his palm as he opened the door. The study wasn't a deep room, but it was long. Bookshelves lined the far wall and paintings hung from the others, accompanied by a collection of various trinkets and tools. Books were scattered across the wide desk, its dark wood chipping at the corners. Half-burned candles sat unlit beside the large window, and the smell of sweet soap mixed with hints of leather filled the air.

"The study contains items from every general in the history of Sannir," Novah explained, starting for the massive bookshelf. She grabbed a random volume and quickly flipped through the pages. "Each one left their belongings, building a collection of personal items that date back to Eliab himself. I don't know which were Uriah's."

Kyler scanned the room, glancing over brass sextants and leather journals. A model ship sat tucked away on a shelf, with white sails and brown rope, and Kyler's mind flew back to late nights and the scent of cinnamon. Uriah had kept that ship in their dining room. It had sat above their fireplace, the bow pointed toward the grandfather clock in the corner of the room. He wasn't sure when the former general had taken it to the castle. He reached for it, careful not to drop it.

Kyler pushed aside some of the books that occupied the desk and placed the ship down firmly, running his hands along the hull.

"This was his?" Novah came to his side, leaning her palms on the corner of the desk.

Smooth wood and brass buttons brushed Kyler's fingers as he searched the ship. "He's had it ever since I was little."

She tilted her head, admiring the piece. "It's beautiful."

"He took good care of his belongings." Kyler gave a satisfied grunt as he caught hold of a dip in the wood, just large enough to hook his thumb into. "Got it."

The wood snapped as Kyler popped open the side of the ship, revealing three pages of parchment neatly rolled up inside.

Novah let out a low whistle and took hold of the paper, flattening it against the desk. "Well done, Commander."

"Anything new?" He glanced over her shoulder. The notes were covered in numbers, each seeming to reference a line or page in various books.

Novah turned to the bookshelf once more, scanning the endless spines. "These books are probably here."

"Good." Kyler joined her, tilting his head as he read the titles of each volume. "Sounds like Corbin has some more reading to do."

Novah chuckled, and for once, Kyler was glad to have known Uriah like he did.

CHAPTER FORTY-ONE

WHEN KYLER RETURNED TO THE BARRACKS LATE THAT EVENING, he found the fire smoldering and the table empty. Vera had marked several pages, leaving her thoughts scribbled on ripped journal pages, but Kyler's mind was too full to bother reading them. He grabbed whatever would fit in his arms and carried them back to his room, setting them down on the floor with a thump.

Everyone else's search had come back emptyhanded. Kyler's extensive rummaging of the general's study produced no other hidden pockets or folded parchment. The notes they had were full of information, but without the rest of his studies, Uriah's information was less than helpful. It was still unclear what he used to build the gateway to Sannir, and his methodology was confusing at best.

Corbin trailed him into the room and dropped the final stack of books at the foot of his bed, letting out an exasperated sigh. "Salcon and I are going out."

Kyler had nearly forgotten the Lone Wolf. He missed its lively music and flavorful potions—especially after that dreadful excuse for Apola he'd had at Aiyanna's coronation. Outside, the sun had nearly set, and stars would soon be poking through the canopy of night.

"I have something I need to do first." Kyler avoided Corbin's eye, but he still caught the knowing grin that tugged at the edges of his lieutenant's mouth.

"We'll meet you there." Corbin tapped the doorframe as he left, leaving Kyler alone.

Kyler took his time removing his armor, setting it neatly beside the stacks of books, and combed his fingers through his wind-tossed hair. It'd been a long day of searching the castle, but as much as Kyler wanted to rest, there were still things that needed his attention. He slung a heavy cloak over his shoulders and began the familiar walk out the back door and toward the castle gardens.

His breath lingered in the air, creating puffs of white before his face, and the chill eased the burn of his skin as he neared the castle walls.

He pressed a palm to the cold stone, letting his hands slide along the textured surface until he bumped the metal ladder hidden by shadow. Above, Aiyanna's window illuminated the silver curtains that flapped from within, the glass opened to the night.

Kyler hesitated at the bottom, his throat tightening. Was she going to scold him? He felt he deserved it, but that didn't mean he *wanted* to face her wrath.

He stepped on the first rim before he could change his mind. The metal was frozen beneath his fingers, numbing his hands at the touch. He didn't slow until the warm light brushed his cheeks, making him squint as he grabbed hold of the windowsill.

His boots landed once more on soft carpet, and Kyler found himself face-to-face with the new queen of Sannir.

Aiyanna wore the same simple gown from earlier, her shoulders covered by a decorative coat and her hair a bit tangled from the wind outside. She looked to have been pacing, stopping only when she caught sight of him.

Her chest fell with a breath as she stared at him, swallowing hard before saying, "I wasn't sure you'd come."

Kyler waved a hand to the open window. "I know my signal."

Her room was the same, with flowers pressed and framed and pale blankets draped over her furniture. The small hearth sparked orange with a low fire, and Kyler instantly smelled the familiar lilac he'd grown to associate with her.

Aiyanna's jaw shifted as she studied him, her dark eyes searching his face as if looking for answers hidden beneath his gaze. "I was cruel to you."

A gentle squeeze tugged at Kyler's chest. "I was worse." He stepped closer, away from the cold of the window and toward the warmth of the fire. "How were things while I was gone?"

She shrugged. "The people of Sannir are shaken. They want answers and security, and unfortunately, I can't give them either of those right now."

"That isn't your fault. No one has answers."

"You did." She lifted her chin. "You never told me you were his son."

Kyler suddenly wished for scolding. That would be more comfortable than this conversation. "I'm not really. We share blood, but nothing else."

Aiyanna was silent for a moment. Then she stepped forward, wrapping her arms around Kyler, and buried her face in his shoulder.

Kyler froze, unsure of what to make of her move, but he quickly softened. He pulled her close, dipping his nose into her hair. "I'm sorry, starlight."

Aiyanna pulled away slowly, her voice steady. "You are a good commander. I think you'd have made just as good of a general."

"I think we both know Novah was the right choice."

Her dark brows lifted slightly, but she said nothing.

"You make an incredible queen. The soldiers agree."

"I hope Sannir agrees." Aiyanna dropped her hold on him, tucking her hair behind her pointed ears. "I have a duty to them now."

"You always did." Kyler studied her face. He wondered how all of this had changed her view of the world, her memories now stained by death and ruin.

Aiyanna gave a tight smile, noticing him staring. "You can go now."

Kyler chuckled and turned for the window, catching hold of the curtains as they swung in the wind. "Don't let Cadmus tell you what to do. If Sannir is in your hands, I don't fear its future."

The last thing he saw as he left her room was her smile—genuine and bright and something Kyler was grateful for.

The road to Leida was quiet, the streetlamps and stars guiding Kyler's path. He enjoyed the silence as he entered the town. Carts lined the streets, filling the air with the smell of citrus, and music hummed as Kyler neared the tavern. The bell on the door chimed as he swung it open, immediately greeted by a crowd of people talking, laughing, and singing to one another.

"Kyler!"

He spotted Corbin waving him over, with Adri and Salcon at his side. Drinks scattered the counter before them, two glasses already empty and the others swirling with colorful potions.

"Glad you made it." Corbin wrapped an arm around his shoulder, urging him to sit. He waved a hand at Maeve.

She made her way over, grinning at Kyler as she neared. "Well, look who's back." She leaned her elbows on the counter, loose strands of ebony spilling over her shoulders. "It's been boring without you, Commander."

"Is that so?" Kyler grinned, glad for the familiar face. "It's a good thing I'm back then."

"I didn't say that. It was nice."

"You're bluffing."

"I am. Raspberry?"

Salcon made a noise, and Kyler laughed. "Please."

Maeve winked and stepped away to pour his Apola as Salcon bumped his shoulder. "The commander has some stories I'm certain he'd love to share."

Adri took a sip of something that smelled strongly of citrus. "Let's hear it then. What tales can you tell?"

A few of those around them began to swivel their heads, their conversations halting as curiosity took over.

"The lieutenant is bluffing." Kyler shot Salcon a look.

Salcon rolled his eyes. "*The commander* owes the people a story."

"Salcon."

"Come on! I'm sure there's something you can share."

Kyler caught his glass as Maeve slid it across the counter. Even she hovered, her gaze lingering in hopes of hearing a tale from his latest endeavor.

Kyler took a large sip of his Apola. "We were attacked by amphipteres."

Corbin grinned. "That's right. They burned an inn to the ground."

"I thought I was telling the story?"

Corbin's smile only widened as he turned to his drink. "Go on then."

"They'd somehow found out where we were hiding and battered the inn, trying to flush us out. We barely escaped through the sewers."

Adri shook his head. "Those beasts can do a lot of damage."

Kyler pictured the street, scarred with scorches and marked with destruction. Clide's entire livelihood had been crushed in minutes. People had died.

The raspberry suddenly tasted bitter.

"Anything else?" Salcon pressed, but Kyler shook his head.

"I'm going to step outside for a minute." He tossed Corbin an easy smile. "I'll be right back."

Corbin didn't look convinced, but he remained seated as Kyler headed for the back door. He slipped through the crowded tavern, muttering apologies as he brushed arms with those he passed. It wasn't until he reached the cool air that he felt he was able to breathe.

Kyler rested his back against the brick outer wall of the tavern, the music and laughter from inside now muffled. His chest ached with something he couldn't quite identify, and though he tried to chase the feeling down with more Apola, it simply refused to budge. He let his gaze drift along the empty street—this corner of the city was quiet and more unfamiliar than ever.

He should feel good. The mission had been successful in the end—they knew more about Orisis now than they ever had, and all his men had made it home alive. Aiyanna wasn't angry with him, Sannir was stable, and they'd uncovered the first of Uriah's secret notes.

All was well, and yet Kyler felt nothing of the sort.

It wasn't until a shoulder brushed his that Kyler realized he had company.

"A bit crowded in there," Novah said, taking a small sip of ginger Apola.

Kyler turned to face her. "What are you doing here?"

She shrugged, glancing back at the closed door of the tavern. "Same as you."

"It's late. Shouldn't you be resting?"

Novah chuckled. "Sorry, Commander, I didn't realize you were my keeper."

"Fine." Kyler leaned back against the wall, letting their shoulders brush once more. "Maybe next time, I'll let you bleed out."

She laughed, and her head tapped the stone as she lifted her eyes toward the stars.

Kyler swirled his drink, watching the red spiral. "It feels weird to be back."

"I know what you mean."

He looked at her, surprised by that answer. Her scales caught his eye, the same red as his potion, and Kyler reached for them without thought. His touch lingered on the single white scale. He'd once thought the scale to be more valuable than a thousand colored ones. But now, he knew it wasn't about the scale but the soldier who donned it.

Kyler dropped his hand and quickly tipped his glass, letting the ice fall against his tongue. His chest hummed in the quiet, and he blamed it on the Apola.

"I think the dragons chose wrong." Novah's voice was barely a whisper.

Kyler's brow furrowed. "Why do you say that?"

She continued to stare at the sky. "I don't know what to do. I don't know how to close that gateway or lead these soldiers. The dragons chose wrong."

Kyler shifted so that he faced her fully. "No, they didn't."

"For once, don't argue with me."

"You clearly don't know me very well," he retorted. "I saw how you led us in Potri. You're brilliant, Novah."

She was silent for a moment. "You haven't always believed that."

He wanted her position. He wanted her to fail. At least, he *had* wanted those things. Kyler became suddenly aware that he wasn't sure what he wanted anymore.

He stood close enough to smell the pine that always seemed to float from her, his thoughts and emotions tangling together in a mess that surrounded Novah Elison.

"I hated you," he said finally, gentle and soft. His knuckles brushed hers. "Even before you were general, I thought you were stuck up and naïve and a horrible commander."

Novah's gaze steadied on him in a way that made his already racing pulse jolt even faster. "What do you think of me now?"

Kyler swallowed, his voice nothing more than a murmur. "I'm not sure what to think of you."

Whatever she was about to say next was interrupted as the tavern door swung open. Kyler backed away, dropping whatever had just happened between them.

"Ah, General." Corbin nodded as he caught sight of them. "Feeling better?"

She smiled, recovering much faster than Kyler did. "I am, thank you. I should be heading back." She passed her glass to Kyler, half of her potion still swirling within. Her fingers brushed his once again, and her touch seemed to scald his skin. "I'll see you both tomorrow." Novah tugged her cloak tighter as she disappeared around the corner of the building.

Kyler's hand felt hot against her glass, his mouth dry and mind still reeling.

Corbin crossed his arms and leaned a shoulder to the wall, lifting his brow. His lips pulled into a smirk, that made Kyler scowl.

"Shut up." Kyler shoved past him, dipping into the tavern once more.

...

That night, Kyler's dreams were vivid. He could smell the sweat on Uriah's brow as his father screamed for help, his voice slowly fading to a whimper as his eyes turned to glass.

Kyler just stood there, watching Uriah lose himself in his personal torment. Then his face shifted, and Kyler no longer stared at Uriah, but Corbin.

Panic flooded Kyler's bones as he shouted, reaching for his lieutenant, only to find shackles clamped around his wrists, holding him back. Kyler's wrists turned raw as he shook the chains, his arms aching, until the restraints finally broke loose, and he reached Corbin's side.

But he was too late.

Corbin stared into nothingness, his screams permanently silenced and eyes white with blindness. Kyler screamed his name, only for his voice to fall on deaf ears, and he dropped to his knees beside Corbin.

"It's all right," he whispered, knowing his words were for his own comfort. "I'm getting you out, okay? We're going home."

"Home?" The word came from Corbin's lips, but the voice wasn't his.

Kyler pulled back as a twisted grin split Corbin's cheeks, and his skin fractured like broken glass.

"Bricru." Kyler tried to stand, but his legs refused to move. "You're dead. I killed you."

"You can't kill me, Caligari." Bricru's face was his own now—his hair tussled and skin horribly pale. "I'll always find a way back to you."

Bricru lifted a hand, the dagger in his grasp shining like the glint of his smile, and drove it forward.

Into Novah's throat.

Kyler didn't fall back asleep that night.

CHAPTER FORTY-TWO

THE HALLS OF THE CASTLE ECHOED AS KYLER PASSED THROUGH them, not entirely certain of where he was headed. He scanned every chest and couch as he walked, wondering if Uriah's notes might be tucked within. Kyler had seen maps of the castle before, and Aiyanna had gone into length explaining how the staircases spiraled and ceilings domed, but walking the areas was much different.

He hoped to find Novah in the general's study, but the room had been vacant when he stopped by. Now, his limited knowledge of the castle layout left him wandering the empty foyers. He'd promised Novah answers, and he intended to keep his word.

That, and he selfishly wanted to see her again.

Golden beams stretched above Kyler's head, catching every drop of sunlight that soaked through the glass windows. Framed pictures hung from the walls, mostly of dragons. Their scales were every shade of green, blue, and red, and their flames appeared as real as fire as Kyler's shadow passed by.

Other paintings tried to capture the image of Adoni, and while this art was stunning, it seemed his face was never quite right. In fact, most of them had simply covered his face in veils of light, foregoing any attempt at humanizing him.

There were portraits of royalty, nobles, and generals dating back hundreds of years. It seemed every inch of this wing was full of history just waiting to be brought back to life.

Kyler's steps faltered as he reached the end of the hall. A painting of Uriah stared down at him with a hollow gaze, his face void of warmth. While this picture was striking, it wasn't what caught Kyler's attention.

Beside it was a portrait of Novah. Unlike Uriah, her face seemed to glow with life, from the pink of her cheekbones to the glint in her eyes, their color as sweet as honey and as rich as soil. Her mouth lay without a smile, but it seemed the artist managed to capture her kindness without a tilt of her lips. Even the small dimple in the corner of her cheek had been shaded to perfection.

He shouldn't have stared.

Footsteps made Kyler drag his eyes away from the painting.

"Looks just like her, doesn't it?" Aeron grinned, rounding the hall with confident steps, his hands tucked into his pockets.

Heat flamed at Kyler's neck, but he tried to ignore it with a sigh. "I wasn't expecting to see you here."

Aeron came to a stop at Kyler's side and blinked up at Novah's picture. "I'm incredibly proud of her."

Kyler stayed quiet, letting him continue.

"She went through hell and back to get to where she is, and now she's facing it again with these afi."

"We all have stories."

"Yes, but hers has been a difficult one. She brushes things off with more grace than I could ever manage, but those of us who know her well have seen the toll it takes." He nodded to Kyler. "Novah is a good soldier, but she'll carry weight that's not her burden to bear. Make sure she knows you're here to share those burdens."

He knew what Aeron referred to. Kyler glanced at the portrait once more before stepping back. "Understood. You don't happen to know where she is now, do you?"

"Go down the next flight of stairs and turn left. She's in the old training room."

"Thank you."

"And, Kyler"—Aeron grabbed his shoulder—"if you're going to stare at her portrait, make sure no one catches you." He gave Kyler's shoulder a slap, hard enough to make him wince, and strode down the hall before Kyler could come up with an excuse.

Sannir's Saints.

Kyler pinched his brow, attempting to shake off the embarrassment, and started for the old training room.

The gentle echo of easy swordplay reverberated down the hall as Kyler neared the open door. He paused at the entrance, expecting to find Draven or Zale with her. But Novah's blade swung gently toward someone Kyler had never expected to see with a sword in hand.

Aiyanna moved with light steps, following Novah's instruction as she met hit after hit. Instead of silver skirts, the queen wore gray trousers. Her curls were pulled from her face, slicked with beads of sweat.

"Counter," Novah instructed, her sword in a single hand. The other she kept tucked behind her back, careful not to agitate her still-healing shoulder. "Deflect, then strike as you circle."

Aiyanna did as she said, rounding Novah's side and swiping her blunt blade across the general's torso.

Novah grinned. "Do it again."

She did, this time with more confidence, and Novah lowered her sword with a laugh. "How do you feel?"

Aiyanna's face was bright, beaming from Novah's approval.

"Exhausted."

Kyler stepped into the room, and the two turned at the sound of his boots. "You're a natural." He turned and nodded to Novah. "I didn't mean to interrupt."

The general sheathed her blade. "We're wrapping up. Cadmus asked to meet with the queen." She dipped her head in a bow to Aiyanna. "Tomorrow?"

Aiyanna passed her blade into Novah's hands. "Please. Thank you again."

"Remember, Aiyanna," Novah advised, addressing her informally, "Cadmus does not rule this kingdom."

She gave a small smile and hurried from the room.

Novah began resetting the space, placing Aiyanna's training sword against the wall and dragging the wooden dummies back into place. The former training room was once used regularly by soldiers. Before they were split into three branches, soldiers lived on castle grounds and used the room to hone their skills. It was small, compared to what Kyler was used to, but clearly it was still efficient.

"You're teaching her to fight?" Kyler asked.

"She came to me." Novah brushed her hair from her face. "She wants to be able to defend herself in case of another attack, and with Cadmus breathing down her neck, I think she needs a good escape." She grinned. "You know what that's like."

Kyler scoffed. "Cadmus breathes down everyone's neck, especially mine. I don't think he's ever liked me."

Novah raised a brow and reached for a cloth, using it to wipe her face and neck. "You're not always the most likable."

"I'm not sure where you get that idea."

She stifled a laugh, tossing the rag into a basket. "I hope you didn't seek me out just for this."

"Not at all." Kyler glanced at the room around them. "I'm not sure this is the best place."

Novah nodded and led him from the training room and up a flight of stairs to the study. She closed the door behind them and moved to her desk, piling the papers that scattered its surface. She set them aside before hoisting herself onto the wood. She motioned for Kyler to sit in the desk chair across from her.

The leather sunk beneath Kyler's weight. He caught sight of engravings along the desk surface as he sat, and he ran his fingers across them.

E.A.B.

The initials of Eliab.

He gently brushed the others, the markings of every general—Uriah's included—until he reached the newest one.

N.S.E.

Novah S. Elison.

"Did you know he was in Tophet?"

Kyler looked up to find Novah watching him as she perched on the desk.

He pulled his hand into his lap. "No. We weren't close, especially not after I became commander. He despises me."

"Orisis doesn't seem to think so."

Kyler's gaze fell to the ground, his fingers picking at a loose thread on his pants. "He's my father, but—"

"But not really a father." Novah finished. "I understand that." Her eyes drifted to the bookshelves. "If it were my father, I wouldn't want to free him from Tophet. But this isn't about whatever Uriah did to you. This *must* be about Sannir, and what's best for this kingdom."

"It is." Kyler leaned forward, resting his elbows on his knees. "I know him. Once Uriah has made up his mind, he won't change it. Uriah will not open those gateways. Orisis will be after me now."

"And your brother."

"I already wrote to him."

Novah nodded. "What do you propose?"

Kyler was silent for a moment, allowing himself to think. "If we can find out what Uriah used to connect that gateway to Sannir, we can close it. That gateway we came through is open, and sooner or later, Orisis will find a way to use it. We need to close it before he can do that."

She chuckled. "Cadmus won't like this. He was fond of Uriah and is weary of me. He wants Uriah out of Tophet."

"Is that why you're working with Aiyanna?"

"The queen has been in other people's shadows for too long. She rules Sannir, and Cadmus is going to have to accept that."

Kyler grinned. He laced his fingers behind his head, leaning back in the chair. "It's about time someone put him in his place, General."

"You're next."

"Novah Elison, you run a tight ship."

She dropped her voice, a smirk quirking her lips. "And you, Kyler Caligari, are in my chair. Get back to work."

CHAPTER FORTY-THREE

TWO DAYS HAD PASSED, AND DESPITE THEIR EFFORTS, THERE WAS no sign of the rest of Uriah's notes. In the midst of their search, the castle came to life for Eliab's Eve, a needed reminder of stability for the people of Sannir.

Excitement bubbled through the air like Apola on the tongue, tasting of sweet sugar and warm coffee. Cups of liquid chocolate were given to the guests as the great hall began to fill with laughter and silk gowns. Crystals hung from the chandeliers, dancing to the rhythm of the flickering candlelight and filling the hall with illuminations as warm as the chocolate. They cast fractured light onto sheets of silk, coating the room in shades of silver and blue.

Of course, no one was completely at ease. Soldiers stood stiffly along the edges of the room, their eyes sharp and blades open. No movement had been detected from the gateway, and yet Kyler still found himself jumping at the smoke that drifted from the candles, its form too similar to Orisis' dust.

Kyler nodded his thanks to a server as he offered a tray of glasses filled to the brim with chocolate. The commander took one, swirling the liquid but not yet drinking it. Steam rolled off the chocolate, sending wafts of the rich scent through Kyler's nose. He glanced down at his chest, where silver buttons twinkled like the crystals, and resolved to take extra care not to spill the dessert on himself.

Everyone dressed up for Eliab's Eve, and being part of the castle festivities meant that invited soldiers were expected to dress with exceptional taste. Kyler had returned to his room after the day's search of the castle to find a tailcoat waiting. It was deep green, the same shade that hung from his ears, with detailed stitching spiraling and swirling down his chest. Silver buttons engraved with miniature dragons folded the front of the coat, catching the light even more than the embroidery did.

Kyler tentatively brought the chocolate closer, fearful of burning his mouth.

"It won't bite," a familiar voice teased, accompanied by the rhythmic tap of a cane.

Draven's coat was like Kyler's, but instead of green, he was dressed in deep burgundy. Similar trails of silver raced along his chest and arms, though his were more intricate, with tighter spirals and looping turns.

Kyler chuckled, looking down at his chocolate once more. "I've burned my tongue enough times to know when I should let it cool, Kilder."

Draven accepted a cup of his own, bringing it to his lips immediately. Kyler expected him to wince from the heat, but he hardly blinked as he took a large sip.

"My brother and I used to challenge one another every Eliab's Eve to see who could drink it the fastest. I've built up somewhat of an immunity." He winked. "And it's *lieutenant* now."

Kyler lifted his glass. "Congratulations, Lieutenant. You've earned it." He blew lightly on his dessert. "I take it your sister was never in on your games?"

Draven laughed. "Oh no. We stopped challenging her because

she beat us every time."

Kyler grinned and took a sip. It was rich and lightly sweetened, with a bitter aftertaste that left him wanting more.

The taste brought back memories of his years celebrating the holiday in the barracks. While a large portion of soldiers took the evening to spend time with family, not all of Kyler's men had family to go home to. So, the barracks were brought to life with singing, dancing, and more liquid chocolate than any man should ever consume in a single night. They filled the halls with laughter, and as midnight approached, they'd file into the courtyard to watch the fireworks that filled the sky.

Kyler could hear them already, the distant booms and crackles from the surrounding towns. He was sure the castle had plenty of fireworks that were being reserved for the later chimes of the clock.

That was something else Kyler loved—the clocks. There were four of them in the foyer alone, each one set to chime in unison so that at the stroke of midnight, no one would be left to wonder what time it was.

"Enjoy yourself tonight, Commander," Draven said, breaking his thoughts. He patted Kyler's shoulder and strode off to join Aeron across the room.

Kyler caught sight of Zale, and the Sea Force Commander smiled as Kyler approached. His deep blue tailcoat blended nicely with the décor, as if he were dressed to match the curtains and beads. His scales gleamed so vividly that Kyler could almost see his reflection in their shine.

"Commander Kyler, it's good to see you." Zale turned, inviting Kyler into the conversation he was having. He motioned to the men before him. "Allow me to introduce Lord Greyson and Lord Bloud."

"A pleasure to meet you both."

Lord Greyson offered a smile that was too large for his face, pulling his thin hands from the pockets of his silver coat and extending one to Kyler. "You as well, Commander. Your record precedes you. Is it true you are the son of former General Uriah Caligari?"

Kyler's teeth dug into his tongue. "It is."

Lord Bloud was as tall as Zale, with pale skin and shoulders wider than the length of a short sword. He shook Kyler's hand with a firm grip, his dark eyes sparkling like the chocolate. "I can see the resemblance. It's good to know Uriah had an heir, as I assume you will lead the Brigade as well as he did."

Kyler's mouth tasted like iron. "Of course." It seemed the depths of Uriah's faults hadn't yet reached public ears.

A flash of green caught Kyler's eye, and his gaze faded from Bloud to Corbin, who stood a few paces behind the lord.

"You are truly making history." Bloud grinned.

"You're very kind."

A round of excited chatter sounded from Kyler's right, and he turned to see Aiyanna entering, her arm resting in Cadmus' hold. The advisor wore a tight smile, and a coat that looked to be made of water hung from his shoulders. The blue shifted from the color of the sky to the depths of the oceans as he walked, his chin high and steps purposeful.

It was Aiyanna, however, who drew every eye. Silver skirts trailed behind her as if stitched with moonlight, and silver brushed her cheekbones making her appear almost ethereal, unsuited for a world this broken.

"Ah, there's the general." Zale turned his head, and Kyler followed his gaze across the great hall.

Saints.

Novah stood by Commander Idar, her smile bright as she laughed at something he'd said. Folds of red draped her frame, twisting across her chest and hanging from her shoulders like a cape of silk. The fabric clung to her waist before dropping to the floor in crimson trails so warm, they rivaled her scales.

Kyler's eyes raked every inch of her, dancing along until Zale cleared his throat.

"If you don't want to start rumors, I'd suggest you stop looking at her like that."

Kyler spun, finding a smirk on the older commander's lips.

"I wasn't—" His throat tightened, cutting his defense short. He swallowed. The knot wouldn't budge.

"Breathe, Kyler," Corbin teased, appearing at his side.

His neck warmed. "I'm breathing just fine." He took another sip of chocolate, red filling his vision. The music was suddenly too loud, and he struggled to put together a single coherent thought. His eyes skirted around the room, desperately trying to focus on anything but her.

Corbin laughed, bumping Kyler with his shoulder. "Talk to her."

"I don't need to."

"Scared? It's just Novah."

"Fine," Kyler snapped.

He started toward her, and Corbin caught his arm. His voice was too low for the others to hear. "*Just* talk. And maybe dance. But nothing too—"

"I've got it." Kyler yanked his arm away, shooting Corbin a glare.

Corbin winked and turned back to the others.

Kyler brushed out the wrinkles in his sleeve and began weaving through endless skirts and intricate coats. Every step felt heavier than the last as the music seemed to fade behind him. He traded his nearly empty glass for two full ones, the dessert warming his palms as he drew closer. He felt her gaze the moment it landed on him.

"For you." Kyler passed her the drink.

She smiled. "Thank you." Her eyes scanned the design of his coat in a way that made Kyler burn beneath it.

"Novah, you look stunning."

She laughed, and the sound was contagious. "So do you." She tapped her glass lightly against his. "Happy Eliab's Eve, Commander."

"Happy Eliab's Eve." He took a sip, his tongue curling from the heat. "How are you?" As he asked this, Kyler caught sight of her shoulder.

The bandage barely poked out from beneath her silk drapes, white cotton wrapped tightly over her skin. She instinctively reached for it, tugging on the silk to cover her shoulder.

"Fine. I'm tired of these bandages."

"Why? They suit you." Kyler teased, making her chuckle once more.

Their conversation was cut short as Novah's attention was grabbed by others, and Kyler was left wishing that her eyes were on him and it were his words causing her laughter.

He told himself she would find him when she was free and decided instead to admire the music and chocolate.

The clocks ticked slowly along as midnight drew nearer, and after his third drink, Kyler put his chocolate consumption on hold. He found himself among nobility and political leaders whose faces he struggled to put to names. At one point, trays of salted pastries were passed out, relieving the sweetness of the chocolate with their light crunch.

It wasn't long before the dancing started, and the musicians followed the tone of the crowd, shifting from song to song with ease. Kyler watched the spin of skirts as he leaned against a column, admiring the way that silver seemed to glisten on every gown and coat. One by one, noblemen took the hands of women, filling the floor with chatter and laughter beneath the canopy of blue drapes. Aiyanna spun from hand to hand, kindly accepting anyone who offered her a dance, and even Cadmus had found some unlucky partner to join him.

The pleasant smile on Kyler's face fell.

Aeron guided Novah onto the floor, taking her hand gently in his own. His face was light as he laughed at something she said.

Kyler tried and failed to watch anything but them. It seemed he'd missed his chance. She looked comfortable, allowing her soldier to guide her through the dance. Kyler wouldn't disturb that.

A low whistle came from Kyler's side, and he glanced over to find Corbin leaning a shoulder against the same column, with Draven trailing behind him. "You look like you drank some bad chocolate."

Kyler ignored him, staring at the floor.

"You think too much." Corbin brushed crumbs from his jacket, sighing deeply. "You don't know Aeron's intentions."

"I think they're clear."

Draven shook his head with a smile. "I am sure anyone would be glad to have the general's eye, but Aeron is not the jealous type." He jutted a chin toward the two of them. "He was not going to leave her partnerless, or worse, subject her to a dance with some prudish lord. Look."

Kyler lifted his gaze, against his better judgment, and found Aeron watching them from over Novah's shoulder. He lifted a brow, tilting his head in a subtle invitation.

Corbin shoved Kyler forward.

The commander crossed the floor, his skin burning and heart pounding. He couldn't look at Novah, focusing instead on Aeron's scales. "Mind if I cut in?"

"Not at all." Aeron grinned, passing Novah's hand into Kyler's. He gave an exaggerated bow, a playful look in his eye as he backed away.

Kyler's fingers brushed Novah's wrist as he took Aeron's place. Her hands were calloused—the hands of a soldier—and yet her touch was feather soft. His other hand found her side, and eyes like fire latched with his as he pulled her closer. She smelled like forests and burned like coals.

"I didn't know you could dance," Novah teased, following his steps.

Kyler gave a gentle *tsk*. "I can do many things, General. It would do you well to stop underestimating me."

She chuckled and shook her head, causing her scales to jingle. "You think too highly of yourself."

"Me?" He spun her gently. "You clearly haven't spoken to these noblemen. All they talk about is themselves."

Novah lifted her chin. "As if you don't do the same."

"I think I'm quite interesting."

"I think you're full of yourself."

"I think you like it." He bumped his forehead against hers, making her laugh.

Kyler's pulse pounded, watching the dimples that pressed into her cheeks. He let himself linger for a moment, holding her as close as he dared. Her breath caught as he dipped his face beside hers, his scales brushing her cheek. He closed his eyes.

"People will talk," she whispered, making no move to distance herself.

"Let them," he murmured.

He could feel her every breath, the gentle brush of her fingers against his, and the soft hum of her touch.

The music slowed. Kyler stepped back, just enough to look her in the eye. "The fireworks should be starting." A playful grin rose to his face. "Care to join me, General?"

Novah squared her shoulders and released his hand to adjust the silk over her bandages. "After you, Commander."

Kyler led her past the dancers and toward the doors that opened to the gardens, stepping into the brisk night air.

The garden lamps flickered just as bright as the lights in the great hall, and the music continued to float past bushes of seasonal flowers and trees that still clung to their autumn leaves. The gardens were far from empty. Several other guests strolled the walkways, their laughter and talk filling the grounds. Fireworks cracked overhead, creating constellations of rainbows in their wake.

Novah rubbed her arms, and Kyler quickly undid the buttons of his coat. "Here."

He tossed his jacket around her, not minding the cold that sunk into his shirt. His grip lingered on the collar, just inches from her skin, as the words he wanted to say tangled his tongue. What *did* he want to say? The explosions flashed across her face, lighting her eyes in flashes of orange and indigo.

It was then that the clocks began to chime, their sound hushing every voice. All of Sannir seemed to still as the bells rang in the darkness, echoing across the kingdom, and every soul held their breath.

The moment the twelfth chime struck, the silence erupted into shouts and cheers. From the palace to the courtyard to the cities at the edges of Sannir, no one was quiet.

"Welcome to Eliab's Day!" The phrase danced across the gardens, rising above the explosion of fireworks.

Kyler's gaze lifted from Novah's for only a moment, catching sight of the explosions that painted the night sky.

"Welcome to Eliab's Day." Novah's easy tone pulled all of Kyler's attention back to her.

"Welcome to Eliab's Day," he repeated, his voice low enough that only she could hear.

For a brief moment, there was nothing but her. He could practically taste her, like sweet honey mixed with the burn of Apola. She stood there, wrapped in his cloak, which he clung to as if letting go would undo everything that'd just happened.

Another sound joined the booms and crackles of fireworks, but this one brought neither beauty nor joy.

A crack echoed from inside the ballroom, accompanied by screams that set Kyler on edge. The moment between them vanished in the dust that tumbled into the gardens.

Kyler bolted through the doorway, the general at his heels.

The screams quieted as they pushed through the crowd, which had split around the billowing dust. Kyler briefly caught Zale's eye across the room, his chest rising and falling with a fear that Kyler wasn't used to seeing on him. Aeron pushed his way closer, his wide eyes fixated on the center of the room.

Standing there was a man, dressed in a black cloak that was so worn and frayed it appeared gray. His bone-white hair was matted with dirt, and blood trailed down his temple like a crimson snake. A scar ran from his right cheekbone, cutting across the bridge of his nose, and finished at his opposing dimple, which dipped as he offered a breathless grin.

"Well, I certainly know how to make an entrance."

Bricru's eyes rolled to the back of his head, and his body collapsed onto the marble.

CHAPTER FORTY-FOUR

THE FIRST THING BRICRU FELT WAS PAIN, RIPPING THROUGH HIS limbs like fire that burned him from within. This pain was familiar, something he'd learned to both adore and despise. It was Orisis' greatest secret—a power even Bricru couldn't understand.

Bricru hardly heard his own screams as life was thrust back into his body.

And then, there was darkness. Consuming and cold, wrapping his consciousness in a fog so dense that he couldn't tell if he was truly alive. It wasn't until Elizus' voice broke through the darkness that Bricru was certain he was still among the living.

"The snake returns," Elizus chided.

Bricru blinked his eyes open, crust clinging to his lashes. The prince stood at the foot of his bed, arms crossed over his black coat and dark hair brushing his cheekbones.

Bricru's body felt heavy, and though he tried to sit upright, his muscles wouldn't budge.

"Take it easy. You won't be moving for a while."

"Gods." His voice was rough, scraping against his throat like sand. A series of coughs erupted, shaking his chest in painful throbs. Blood clung to his tongue and sprayed from his mouth as hot tears rose at the lingering pain. "What—"

His question was cut short by another round of coughing, and Elizus loosed a laugh.

"Quit talking." The prince rounded the bed, brushing the quilt made of heavy cotton, and it was then Bricru realized he was in his own room.

Shelves lined the far wall, dark wood stretching from floor to ceiling with books and trinkets Bricru had collected. His personal array of weapons sat in a disorganized heap beside the books, and above them was a window overlooking the jutting buildings and gray dust.

Elizus lifted a glass of lukewarm water to Bricru's lips. He squirmed as it dribbled down the shapeshifter's cheek, turning brown as it mixed with the blood.

The water soothed Bricru's aching throat, and his head sunk into his pillow as Elizus placed the water back on his bedside table.

"You were nearly dead. Orisis brought you back."

Bricru had assumed that much. He flexed his fingers beneath the sheets as feeling began to return to them. "What of Caligari?"

"Which one?" Elizus scoffed. "Uriah is where he belongs. The young commander escaped."

Bricru's limbs fell cold, and his heart began to race within his weak chest.

The prince stole a glance at him, his lips pressing into a thin line. "He blames you."

Salt burned Bricru's eyes as he closed them, trying to slow his quickening breaths. "Orisis saved me." He wanted desperately to believe that the god saved him purely out of love, but Bricru knew better than that.

"For a purpose." Elizus leaned his hands on the foot of the bed, his steely gaze falling level with Bricru's. "Sleep. You'll need it.”

He did. For days, Bricru rested, brushing blood from his lips and drinking broth as it was brought to him. Each time his door opened, the shapeshifter expected Orisis to enter, but it wasn't until the bleeding had finally stopped and his strength had begun to return that the god showed his face.

Bricru knew it was him the moment he touched the doorknob, the heavy presence of Orisis flooding the room like the dust that followed him.

He sat upright, the sheets wrinkling beneath him, as chills raked his skin. Pale light flooded through his curtains, flashing across Orisis' dark robes and catching in his ebony gaze.

“Hello, Bricru.”

Orisis walked slowly, his steps silent as he strolled nearer. When he was close enough that Bricru could taste the dust, Orisis came to a stop. He stared at Bricru, his gaze unreadable. Then, he slipped a hand into Bricru's hair and pulled the shapeshifter against his chest. “I thought I'd lost you,” Orisis whispered, resting his chin atop Bricru's head.

Bricru didn't dare move, his cheek pressed against the embroidery of the god's cloak. Orisis' hands were cold, and his fingertips pressed into the shapeshifter's scalp like pricks of ice. Bricru choked on his words. “I'm sorry.”

“I know.” Orisis released him, cupping his chin like he had so many times before. “You're growing soft, Bricru. You're making mistakes. I did not raise you like this.”

“I can fix them.”

Orisis' grip on his chin tightened. “You don't have a choice.” He gave a deep sigh, leaning closer to study every inch of Bricru's face. “Kyler Caligari has opened the gateway, yet it will not let me through. But you...” Orisis tilted his chin, forcing Bricru's eyes to meet his. "Your bloodline traces back to Sannir." His dark gaze flickered to Bricru's pointed ears.

Bricru was silent.

"You will be my way maker. You will pass through the gateway of Sannir, and if you succeed, it will accept me as well." A smile rose to his face. "I have set my sights on something greater. I will have more than Sannir—I will have Adoni himself."

He finally dropped Bricru's face and straightened, allowing his shadow to swallow Bricru entirely. "You are Sannir and Tophet. You are my greatest work. Adoni will not close Sannir to those whose blood it gave birth to." Orisis turned, pacing to the foot of Bricru's bed. "Get up, snake."

Bricru tossed the quilt away, sliding off the bed until his bare feet hit the floor. His pant legs fell against his ankles, which buckled under his weight the moment he stood. He caught hold of the bedframe before he fell, white knuckles gripping the posts as he steadied himself.

"Get dressed." Orisis turned for the door and shut it behind him without so much as a glance at the shapeshifter.

Numbness ate at Bricru's limbs, but he forced himself to stand, using the bedpost like a walking stick to straighten himself. Light caught his hands as he held the wood, and it was only then he noticed what had changed.

The veins that ran beneath his skin were no longer blue but pale as snow. He tilted his wrists, studying the way they wrapped his fingers and traveled up his arms like scars. His pulse pounded gently within them, the life that now filled him somehow marked by the death he'd almost faced.

Bricru quickly dressed himself. The heavy cloak with spirals of purple felt heavier than it ever had and gaped in places where it used to be snug.

I am alive, Bricru told himself. *I am alive.*

But he didn't *feel* alive. He felt like a skeleton. He felt like nothing more than skin and bones that Roark had brought to life with the twisted magic Orisis had bestowed upon him. Bricru hesitated for a moment, his fingers hovering over the buttons of his coat. He wasn't a resurrected puppet of his third brother…was he?

Bricru rolled his shoulders and shook the thought from his mind. Roark was off doing the bidding of Orisis in the southern lands of Midith and Abernyn.

His boots seemed to drag across the floor as he reached the door and found Orisis waiting patiently on the other side.

He wasn't alone. Elizus stood by him, his solemn gaze revealing nothing of his thoughts.

Orisis turned without a word, guiding them down the hall and up the staircase that Bricru knew very well. The shapeshifter stumbled on the stone steps, catching himself with his palms, and brushed off the gravel that clung to his skin. His head still felt light and legs uneven, but he forced himself to continue forward, slowing only as he entered the room with the gateway.

The arch spun with dust, but it was different this time. The image within was clear, filled with blue and silver as the great hall of Sannir's castle prepared to welcome Eliab's Day.

Orisis pressed a palm to the gateway, and immediately the scene faded, covering his touch with dust and bringing a frustrated scowl to his face. "Sannir does not accept me."

Bricru ground his teeth, ignoring the pounding of his skull that was worsening from the dust. His fingers shook enough to make him clench his fists, and his skin grew clammy.

"The blood of Caligari is powerful, more so than we originally believed." Orisis circled the gateway. "Adoni will not stay silent forever. Crush his kingdom, and he will come running. Break his soldiers, and he will save them."

The god paused. He lifted the knuckle of his thumb to his lips and dug his teeth into the skin until crimson bloomed. Then, he brushed Bricru's hair aside and smeared the blood across Bricru's temple.

"You bear my mark. If the gateway accepts my blood that you carry, then we can move forward."

Bricru had no knowledge of what his god had in mind, but he didn't dare question. His shoes scuffed the stone floor as he stepped to the gateway. Dust spiraled along his coat and tucked itself against his skin as if longing for his touch.

His pulse quickened as Orisis placed a hand on his shoulder, his voice low and chest brushing Bricru's back. "Earn his trust, as you swore you would, and you may yet again earn my favor."

Before he could change his mind, Bricru stepped into the gateway.

A scream ripped free of his chest, so unhuman that he hardly recognized it as his own. Every inch of his body burned and stung, as if he'd been cut by a thousand knives and thrown into the sea. His blurred vision spotted with red and black. He couldn't breathe.

Then, the pain halted, and a deafening crack filled his ears. The dust before him faded like wisps of shadow touched by sunlight, and he was met by the familiar face of Commander Kyler Caligari.

CHAPTER FORTY-FIVE

"EVERYONE, OUT." NOVAH'S VOICE WAS INCREDIBLY CALM, cutting through the shock that clung to the hall. "Commanders and lieutenants, stay. Everyone else, leave."

Her steps echoed as she hurried to the center of the room, her gaze sweeping over the guests as they began to file into the courtyard. Their anxious whispers filled the air and eyes flickered toward the figure who lay unconscious on the marble.

Kyler couldn't move. His mind began to race and his breath turned quick as he stared at the shapeshifter's fallen form. Bricru looked as horrible as he had when Kyler had left him—his skin gray and blood staining his lips.

I killed him.

"Zale, take him downstairs. Check for a pulse and keep him chained. Aeron, go with him."

The command was hardly off Novah's lips when Zale knelt. He pressed his fingers against the shapeshifter's neck. "He's alive," Zale affirmed.

"Kyler." A firm hand gripped his shoulder as Corbin came to his side. "Easy."

"He's dead." Kyler's voice was soft, and it seemed to stick in his throat. "I killed him."

Novah set her jaw. "Zale, get him out of here. Now."

Zale hauled Bricru onto his shoulder. The shapeshifter hung limp in his arms, his bloodied head slumped as Zale started for the dungeons beneath the castle.

Kyler felt as though his lungs would collapse beneath his ribs. Sweat coated his palms as he ran them down his face and neck. His skin was burning. He began to pace the foyer, willing his mind to still and his breath to ease.

"Corbin, I want eyes on this gateway at all times," Novah said.

"Done." Corbin gave a sharp whistle, catching the attention of the castle soldiers that still occupied the room.

An order like that would've gone to Kyler, but his thoughts were spinning too fast to register what Novah had said, much less act on it.

"Breathe." Novah was before him now. She placed her hands on his shoulders to halt him.

"I killed him."

"I need you steady."

He sucked a shaky breath, and then another, attempting to regain control of whatever gripped him. "I'm fine."

"You're not." She took hold of his wrists, pulling his fingers from his hair. "Breathe, Kyler."

Tears burned hot against his lashes, but Kyler blinked them back. His mind finally began to slow.

Her voice was level, and her touch was firm. "Bricru is alive, and this might be our only chance to get some answers." She gave his wrists a tight squeeze before releasing them. "Take a minute. I'll meet you in the foyer when you're ready."

Corbin returned as Novah left, having finished giving orders to the castle soldiers. "What happened in Potri?"

Kyler swallowed, staring at the spot that had beheld the

gateway just moments before. It was bare now, nothing but flickering candles and spilled chocolate. "I gave him Zalis. He said he wanted to try it. He was fine at first, but then he started screaming. I tried to help, but he collapsed and stopped moving. Then you showed up."

"Did you check for a pulse?"

Kyler's memory felt distant, like a dream. "I don't remember. Maybe?"

"That's alright." Corbin guided him away from the other soldiers as they took their positions around the gateway. "You're shaking."

"I'm fine," Kyler lied again. "Novah's waiting."

Corbin caught his forearm as he started for the doors. "It's not your fault, Kyler."

Kyler shrugged out of his grip.

When he reached the foyer, Novah had her back to him, her arms crossed and face to the floor. Her fingers tapped anxiously against her arms as Kyler approached.

He cleared his throat to get her attention. "What's the plan, General?"

She was silent for a moment. "Come with me."

They walked in silence, the pounding of Kyler's heart mixing with the step of his boots, before they came to a stop at an oak door. Sannir rarely kept prisoners in the castle. Most unlawful citizens were placed in smaller prisons scattered throughout the towns, so their families could visit. It'd been decades since a citizen of Sannir had committed an act against the crown, so the cells held nothing but cold stone and rusted iron.

Kyler followed Novah through the narrow, twisted hallway to the very end. Zale stood before the small cell, his brow knotted. "He's still out cold."

Kyler slipped past Novah, forcing himself to study the shapeshifter.

Blood ran like scarlet ribbons down his face and hands, the worst of it pooling from a spot on his temple. His body had been propped upright against the back wall of the cell. Chains clamped his wrists, and his head slumped against the jagged stone.

Kyler bit his tongue. "He's of no use to us right now."

"Zale, did you search him?" Novah asked.

Zale nodded. "No weapons."

Kyler turned from the cell, his shoulders rigid. "Coming through that gateway cost him a lot of blood. I'd rather we spend our time ensuring he's the *only* one passing through."

Novah pulled a breath. "You're right. Zale, I want eyes on him at all times, and I want to know the moment he wakes up. Both of you get changed. We may have another attack on our hands."

. . .

Corbin strode at Kyler's side, his armor crisp and cape snapping behind him. The morning air and lingering shadows only heightened Kyler's nerves, making his steps brisk and eyes sharp. It was the morning of Eliab's Day, yet no one was celebrating.

"Nothing south of the castle?"

Corbin shook his head.

"Any news from Salcon?"

"Barracks are clear."

Kyler spotted the sage cloak of Adri, who was guiding several dozen soldiers on yet another sweep of the castle grounds. In the distance, Zale's ships rolled slowly over the choppy waves, their silhouettes like flags of warning to any ship that tried to draw near. Dragons dipped from the sky with Regiment soldiers on their backs, watching Sannir from above.

From where he stood, Kyler could make out Commander Idar sitting atop Atlas. His heavy cape snapped in the wind, and smoke rolled from the mouth of the dragon.

"Anything from Novah?" Kyler asked.

Corbin sighed, a puff of cold forming before his face. "Nothing, Kyler."

They crossed the bridge and reached the palace doors, which had been propped open since Bricru's arrival. The last thing they wanted was to lock the afi in with the queen and nobles if the gateway reopened.

Kyler spotted Aiyanna immediately, her silver gown now traded for a loose skirt and laced boots. Her hair had been pulled from her flushed cheeks, and purple sat beneath her eyes. Despite her exhaustion, she was quickly giving orders to castle staff, sending them across the grounds with supplies, healing potions, and weapons to be distributed in case of a breach. She faced Kyler and Corbin as they approached, and she relaxed as she laid eyes on them.

"How are things looking?"

"Clear." Kyler came to a stop before her. "Take a break, Aiyanna. You need rest too."

She eyed him. "I could tell you the same."

She was right—no one had slept. Nerves were high, and every vein in Kyler's body buzzed.

"You give orders well." Kyler said, watching as staff rushed past with arms full of fresh linens for the infirmary beds.

Aiyanna shrugged, crossing her arms over her chest. "My father did better."

"He taught you well."

She nodded as Cadmus approached.

"Commander, Lieutenant, any news from outside these walls?"

"Everything is clear. How's our prisoner doing?"

"Awake." A new voice joined as Aeron hurried toward them. "Just came to. And he refuses to speak with anyone but *Caligari.*" Aeron tweaked a brow at the name.

"Fantastic," Kyler grumbled. "Find the general. She comes with me."

Aeron gave a stiff nod, and a few moments later, he returned with Novah at his side.

She'd changed from her dress; leather and metal engraved with spiraling dragons now replaced the silk gown. Her hand rested on the pummel of her sword, and she didn't say a word as she trailed after Kyler, following him through the stairways and halls until they reached the castle dungeons.

"Are you certain you want to talk with him?" Novah asked as they neared his cell, her voice low.

Kyler didn't slow. "If we want answers, I don't have a choice."

She pressed her lips thin but didn't argue. Kyler was grateful for that. He didn't have the energy to oppose her.

Just as Aeron had said, Bricru was awake.

And he looked terrible.

His eyes were glassy and drooping, like he'd been awake for days. He tried to hide it, but his face still twisted in pain with every breath. Blood continued to bubble slowly from his temple.

Kyler stood before him, separated by nothing but bars of metal. It was oddly familiar. The hall felt like a tomb—small, dark, and filled with the stench of death.

Kyler looked Death in the eye. "Talk."

Bricru's nose scrunched, his gaze falling to the chains at his wrists. They were already beginning to rub raw. "Good to see you too, Kyler." His voice was rough, like gravel against rock, and a labored wheeze coated his words.

"You don't get to play your games here, Bricru. What is Orisis planning?"

"Did you try to kill me?"

Kyler ground his teeth.

The shapeshifter watched him without expression, his question lingering in the damp air between them.

"Why are you here?" Kyler pressed.

Bricru swallowed. "I don't know."

Kyler's fist collided with the bar, hard enough to make Bricru jump. "No, Bricru!" He steeled himself, pushing back the anger that rose to his chest like boiling water before he continued. "No, I wasn't trying to kill you."

"I don't know why I'm here." Bricru struggled to speak, his words breathless. "All I know is that you're going to lose."

Kyler closed his eyes. "Novah, will you get Moundi and some bandages?"

"No more potions," Bricru said quickly. "Please."

Kyler nodded. "Fine. Just bandages and clean water."

Novah hesitated before she started down the hall. Her shoulder brushed Kyler's as she left him alone with the shapeshifter.

Kyler crouched, eye-level with Bricru, and hoped whatever understanding had been built between them could be salvaged. "I watched you die while I tried to save you. Now, I'm asking that you try to save me."

"Honestly, I don't know anything. I'm not in Orisis' favor."

"Then put yourself in mine."

Bricru's chest rose and fell in trembles, and his nails dug into his palms at the pain. "The plan was to use the gateway created by your father to gain access to Sannir and finally crush your kingdom to the ground. But now, there's something more." He met Kyler's gaze. "'I have set my sights on something greater,' he said. 'I will have Adoni himself.'"

Kyler leaned back on his heels, letting the threat sink in. "What's changed? Why has Orisis shifted his focus?"

"That's what I'm unsure of. All I know is that your blood is powerful, and Orisis will stop at nothing to make you spill it for him."

Kyler shook his head slowly, the braids at his temples brushing his jaw. "How do I close the gateway?"

"You don't," he said simply. "As long as Uriah's bloodline remains, the gateway stays open."

Understanding rushed the commander. Gateways needed something to ground them. "That's what he used to link the gateway to Sannir. The same way he locked them. He used his blood."

Kyler's blood was to the gateway what the Temple was to the Pass. *He* was Orisis' link to Sannir.

Bricru nodded. "Uriah's blood links the gateway between Tophet and Sannir, but Orisis wanted it to be different than the others. He had Uriah make it so that only a creature of Tophet can pass back the way they came. You can't get to Orisis, but he can get to you."

"That's brilliant." Kyler raked his finger through his hair. Orisis had thought of everything.

"Except, he can't get to you. Or at least he couldn't. I was a *test,*" the shapeshifter spat, using as much energy as he could muster. "He needed to see if Sannir would accept me."

"And did it?"

"Well, I wasn't bleeding in Tophet."

"But you're here."

Bricru shrugged and grimaced from the movement. "I don't have the answers you want. You're going to have to ask Orisis himself."

Kyler rose and looked down on the shapeshifter once more. "Someone will be in to clean you up. And no potions."

Then, he turned and left Bricru to the cold of his cage.

CHAPTER FORTY-SIX

SILENCE THROBBED IN BRICRU'S EARS. ROUGH STONE DUG INTO his back, forming bruises he was much too tired to worry about. Every inch of his skin seemed to burn, yet it was cold to the touch, like he was made of rainwater and glass.

Bricru forced himself to breathe slowly, his ribs tightening with every gasp, and blood tainted his tongue. He could feel the blood on his temple too, hot and fierce, as if Orisis' mark had split his skull open. When he closed his eyes, Bricru found the darkness to be just as miserable as the warm light that filled his cell.

He wasn't sure how long he'd been alone, but eventually a soldier arrived. He held a handful of cotton strips and carried a bucket of warm water that sloshed as he walked. He scowled down at Bricru before opening the bars and set the bucket down with enough force to make the water spill over the rim.

"Clean yourself." He tossed the rags into Bricru's lap and crossed his arms. Green scales hung from his ears. Despite the pounding of his head, Bricru recognized the soldier's face. It was one of the soldiers that had been in Potri. In fact, if Bricru's understanding was accurate, this soldier was close with Kyler Caligari.

That was useful information, but Bricru was far too tired to do anything about it. He could hardly move the bucket as he dragged it closer and took a drink. The soldier grimaced but said nothing.

"Corbin," a new voice called from down the hall, accompanied by quick steps. "Let me handle him."

Corbin's brows knotted. "What do you mean?"

The girl stopped as she reached the soldier, coming into Bricru's view. She was dressed simply, and long curls spiraled down her back. She was shorter than the soldier and had to lift her chin to meet his gaze, a silent command in her eye.

"I just need a moment," she assured.

He bit his tongue, dropping his arms with a nod. "I'll be down the hall. Be careful with him."

She gave a kind smile and waited until he strode away to finally look at Bricru.

The girl had soft eyes, the kind that looked at him as if unbothered by the blood and dust. Light freckles dotted her nose, and pink dusted her pale skin. Bricru assumed her to be a noble of some kind, from both the way she carried herself and the way the soldier had obeyed her command.

The girl stepped into the bars, taking a knee at Bricru's side. She pulled the cloth from his lap and wrapped it neatly before dipping it into the bucket.

"I've heard stories about you, Bricru." Water dripped back into the bucket as she squeezed the cloth. "Kyler speaks as though you're the most deceptive man to walk the realm."

A tiny smirk pulled at his lips. "He speaks so highly of me?"

The girl didn't respond. She gently pressed the warm cloth to Bricru's head, and he winced at the touch. The scent of lilac soap rolled from her skin, reminding Bricru of the observatory he'd spent time in as Ophir.

She pushed his hair aside and noticed his pointed ears. "You're an elf," she said.

"I am."

She dipped into the water once more, washing the blood away. "Have you ever lived in Sannir?"

"No."

"But you come from here." Her touch was as gentle as her voice. "All elves have bloodlines that trace back to Sannir, no matter how distant their relation."

He caught her eye. "You seem to know a lot about me."

"Very little, in fact." She sat back on her heels, her face firm. "Uriah trusted you, for some reason or another, and I want to know why."

"I manipulated him."

"I think he saw something in you. Something he deemed trustworthy."

"I'm good at my job." Bricru looked down at his hands, the only weapons he possessed clamped in iron. Tiny crescents marked his palms, the result of clenching his fists against the pain.

"That's why you're here, isn't it? Orisis gave you a job to complete."

He stayed silent.

"You may belong to Orisis, but you belonged to Sannir first. You may be as dangerous as they say, but you're a Sann just like the rest of us." She stood, her arms full of bloodied cloth and the water bucket now murky. "My name is Aiyanna, by the way."

Aiyanna locked the bars as she closed them. "Do me a favor. Don't tell Kyler I was here."

Bricru almost smiled. "Why? Do you answer to him?"

She chuckled. "No. He will scold me though, and I've had enough scolding in my lifetime." She lifted her chin, taking one

final look at him. "It was nice to meet you, Bricru."
He didn't return the sentiment.

CHAPTER FORTY-SEVEN

KYLER TRIED TO SLEEP. HE SPENT HOURS TANGLED BENEATH the sheets, his mind refusing to still and muscles tensing at every sound. Dreams of Uriah tormented him, the former general dressed in tattered armor that barely covered his sick flesh and jutting bones. He begged for Kyler to save him with every gasping breath, and each time, the commander refused.

It was still dark when Kyler ripped off the blankets. Sweat drenched his hair and slicked his skin, and the cold air chilled it. He tossed his feather pillow to the floor with a frustrated grumble and lay on the wooden floorboards—like he had beside Novah. He wrapped the lopsided sheets over his chest and buried his head into his arms. Lying on the ground, he could almost imagine she was in the room with him.

It was only then that Kyler slept.

Much too soon, the break of dawn woke him. Kyler blinked up at the ceiling, his back sore and mind groggy. He tossed his forearm over his eyes. A headache began to pulse at his temples.

He needed every soldier sharp. He needed answers and he needed a way to close that gateway. And he *desperately* needed more sleep.

He rolled to his side, shoving himself to his feet before he dozed off once more. Messy braids fell into his eyes, and heat burned against his ears as he tugged at the tangle of hair and scales. Beside his makeshift bed, Kyler's armor sat piled atop itself, leather straps and silver steel he'd left without bothering to keep it organized.

His body seemed to move as if underwater as he began to dress himself, washing his face and fixing his hair. His fingers fumbled with the laces of his boots, and the familiar armor suddenly felt heavy.

All he could see was Uriah's crooked face.

But Uriah would have to wait.

Kyler clung to this thought as he followed the halls of the barracks to the common room, finding one table covered in potion bottles and a familiar head of dark hair hunched over them.

Vera's back was to the fireplace, and her knee bounced against the table leg as she poured over a textbook. Several vials of Zalis lay scattered before her, their silver sheen reflecting light onto the barrack wall. She didn't look up as Kyler approached, her eyes glued to her page.

"You're here early."

She startled at his voice. "I thought you'd be at the castle."

"I was headed that way." He pulled up a chair beside her, stealing a glimpse of the page she was reading. It was instructions on the various ways to brew the headache-curing potion and what each method resulted in.

Other things begged for Kyler's attention, but he welcomed the distraction of potions.

"You make yours by adding the bergamot before the herbs." She lifted a vial, its color and texture identical to all the others. "Herbs first will lead to a stronger flavor."

"And?"

She sighed and set the vial down with more force than was necessary. "Nothing. I thought the brewing technique might affect the way it interacts with the gallot, but the result is the same. The root expands when added to the potion and then slowly shrivels."

Kyler shifted in his seat, his interest peaking. "What do you mean?"

Vera reached into her bag and pulled out the gallot root, letting it rest between her fingers. "I tried to find research on it, but there's so little. We know that brewing it into a potion changes the mixture, so I tried to reverse it."

"You mean instead of putting the root into a potion, you put a bit of the potion onto the root?"

"Exactly." Her dark eyes skimmed the root's surface. "But it's about what I would expect. The root just dies. It puffs up, then hardens and crumbles into dust."

Dust. Kyler's mind reeled.

Dust like Tophet. Like Orisis. He took the root from her hand, breaking off a small piece and pouring the Zalis over it. Just as Vera said, the root began to expand, but a moment later it deflated, crumbling in on itself until it was void of all moisture. Kyler pinched what remained between his fingers, and sure enough, it flaked into dust.

Vera frowned. "I don't get it."

"When the root encounters magic, it turns to dust. Just like Tophet turned to dust when it came in contact with Adoni." He stood quickly, his knees bumping the table as he did. "Come with me."

Vera quirked a brow and looked up at him from her seat. "I'm not sure I like the way you said that."

He paused. "What way?"

"Like whatever you're about to do is going to get me in trouble."

Kyler shrugged. "If anyone is going to face the general's wrath, it'll be me. I assume you've heard about the gateway?"

She narrowed her gaze. "I'm here for alchemy, not gateways."

"Saints, you're a pain. Just answer my question."

"Of course I have. I think all of Sannir has."

Kyler tapped the table. "Great. How would you like to meet a shapeshifter?"

She stood, gripping the strap of her leather bag. "As long as you call it alchemy training, I'm in."

"I knew I liked you."

Vera rolled her eyes. "I don't like asking for permission. But between the two of us, this doesn't sound like something the general would approve of."

"Definitely not. We'll run it by her first." Kyler ushered Vera into the courtyard and started quickly for the castle. "Thankfully, I'm on Novah's good side."

"According to Draven, you were more than that on Eliab's Eve."

Kyler bit his tongue, his pace slowing, and a sly smirk crept onto her face.

"So the rumors *are* true?"

"Rumors aren't to be trusted."

She hummed to herself, her steps lightening to a tiny skip as they neared the castle. "I suppose I'll let you do the talking then."

"Of the two of us, I am much more qualified."

"Of the two of us, I think the general likes you more." She winked.

Ridiculous girl.

Kyler swung open the castle doors and strode through before her. He let the door fall closed behind him and gained some satisfaction as Vera narrowly missed being hit by it.

"Alright, I'll stop," she grunted, though the glint in her eye said otherwise.

"Good. Now, follow me, and don't touch anything."

"I'm not a child." Vera scowled, trailing after him.

Kyler hurried her through the hall of portraits and stopped when they reached the open doors of the old training room. Just as he'd guessed, Novah was there with Aiyanna, but this time, Draven was with them.

He leaned on a single leg, his other hardly brushing the ground, and sweat matted his hair to his forehead. His training sword swung wide with each slow strike, throwing off his balance, but he managed to keep himself upright.

Before him, Aiyanna met every attack, blocking and dodging his blade at the instruction of Novah, who stood close enough to touch them.

Draven was the first to spot Vera and Kyler. His focus wavered, and with it, so did his balance. He swore as he lost his footing, and Novah caught his arm just before he hit the floor.

"You should have let him fall," Vera teased.

Draven grinned, steadying himself. "At last, Kyler has met his match in wit."

Amusement passed over Kyler's face. "Lieutenant Draven, I had no idea your entire family was as difficult as you."

"Difficult? Nonsense. Vera is charming."

Vera crossed her arms. "I'm a delight."

"General, could I steal you for a moment?" Kyler shouldered past Draven, earning a laugh from the lieutenant.

Aiyanna dropped her weapon, releasing an exhausted sigh.

Novah placed a hand on her shoulder. "Take a break." She turned from the others as Kyler urged her out of earshot.

He took a deep breath, readying himself for her stubborn refusal of his request. "Before you say no, hear me out."

She lifted her brows.

"I'd like to take Vera to see Bricru."

Immediately, her lips parted with an argument, but Kyler silenced her. "What did I *just* say?"

"If you knew I'd say no, why bother asking?"

He glanced back at Vera. "She's onto something with that root, and possibly Tophet. She's smart. Let her examine him."

"You think a student will be able to find something our physicians couldn't?"

Kyler pursed his lips. "Maybe."

The tap of a cane made Kyler turn, and Draven came to his side with narrowed eyes. "I heard enough of that to know you're trying to involve Vera in something she has no business being a part of."

Novah nodded to him as if this proved her point.

Kyler's voice dipped. "All of Sannir is involved in this, whether we like it or not. Your sister is sharp, Draven. She's innovative and is already thinking outside of the box when it comes to this root. Just let her question him. She doesn't have to get near him."

"She will *not* get near him," Draven said forcefully.

"She won't. Why don't you come with us?"

He frowned, deep in thought, and rubbed his hand the engravings of his cane. "Just to question him?"

"That's all."

"You exhaust me." Novah sighed, pinching the bridge of her nose. "If you think it's beneficial, then do it. But Draven, you have the final say."

He frowned at his sister, who had managed to convince Aiyanna into letting her hold the training sword. "Fine."

Novah gave a sharp nod. "The three of you go together. I'll finish up with the queen and meet you in my study when you're done." She started to turn away but paused, as if a new thought had bloomed in her mind. "Don't let her talk you into anything."

Kyler tilted his head in confusion. "…Bricru?"

She dipped her chin to Vera. *"Her.* She's got a will stronger than that sword in her hand—I can see it from here. Don't be pushovers. You're soldiers."

Kyler opened my mouth to argue, but Draven clamped his shut, giving Kyler a look that told the commander she'd talked him into one too many things.

"That's an order," Novah added.

"Yes ma'am." Draven gave a mock salute and pulled Kyler after him.

A moment later, the three reached the dungeons, leaving Aiyanna and Novah far behind. The stone walls dripped with condensation as they snaked through the halls, and Vera scrunched her nose as she studied the rugged stone and dim lights.

"You couldn't have made this place any nicer?"

"We didn't build the castle," Draven said.

"And it's a dungeon," Kyler reminded. "It's not meant to be pretty."

Oil lamps flickered as they passed, and Vera shivered.

The gentle clanking of chains rose from the final cell. Bricru's hair fell into his eyes as he lifted his head at their arrival. The blood had been cleaned from his head and hair, though some still crusted along his coat, blending in with the black cotton.

"Oh, good," he said dully. "Company."

Kyler stepped to the bars, his tone hard. "Make one wrong move, and I'll lodge a knife into your throat."

Bricru lifted his faded gaze to Vera, studying her for a moment. Then he sighed, leaning back against the stone, and laced his fingers across his chest. "This should be interesting."

"Keep your distance. You're going to answer her questions, nothing more." Kyler faced the young alchemist. "Go ahead, Vera."

She stepped toward the bars, taking in every inch of the shapeshifter.

Bricru shrugged. "Ask away."

CHAPTER FORTY-EIGHT

"WHAT DO YOU REMEMBER?"

Bricru felt her gaze digging into his skin. He'd expected her to be wary of him, or at least a bit uncomfortable, but she showed nothing of the sort. Vera pinched a quill between her fingers, and on her knee rested a leatherbound notebook with frayed seams and ripped edges. Behind her, a soldier that Bricru immediately recognized leaned against a wooden cane, his leg clearly not healed from when Bricru had last seen him in Potri.

But it was Kyler who watched him intently, as if daring him to move. Not that Bricru had anywhere to go. His wrists burned from the chains, and his body was still incredibly weak.

"Your commander offered me a potion. I drank it," he answered her question simply.

"What did it taste like?"

Bricru sighed, already growing annoyed. "Like flowers and honey. A few minutes later, I could hardly breathe."

She scribbled that down. "Describe what it felt like."

Bricru's eyes flickered to Kyler. "It felt like my head was expanding, cracking my skull from the inside out."

Vera's eyes sparked with excitement, but when she caught sight of Bricru's face, the excitement fell. "That must've been horrible."

"It wasn't enjoyable."

She bit down on her tongue, her next question coming out hurried. "What next?"

"Next?"

"After the expanding?"

Bricru frowned. "I don't know."

"How did you counteract the reaction?"

This time, Bricru lied. "I don't know."

Her dark eyes stayed heavy on him. "You can't give me anything?"

He felt the need to squirm beneath her stare, like she knew the answers he wasn't giving and just wanted him to say it. "Nothing."

"What about after? Did you notice anything different about the way you looked? Felt?"

"No."

Vera inched closer, studying him.

"Vera." Kyler caught her by the shoulder.

"I just want to examine him."

"No." He held her firmly. "That's an order."

She shrugged out of his grasp. "I'm your apprentice, not your soldier."

"*Vera.*" Kyler's voice was cold. Demanding. Beside him, the other soldier glared at her.

Bricru almost laughed at the frustration on her face. "I won't bite."

Kyler set his jaw. "Just ask your questions, Vera."

She scowled. "I'm done."

The one with the cane straightened. "Good." He motioned Vera out before him.

Kyler gave Bricru one final look before trailing after them

without another word.

Bricru closed his eyes and leaned his head against the stone as their footsteps faded. When he was finally alone again, he released a slow breath, eyeing his hands that lay laced across his chest. White veins still spiderwebbed across his arms—the mark of Orisis' power.

She'd been close.

...

The skitter of rats and dripping water became Bricru's source of comfort. The hours crawled by, and he was never quite certain of the time of day. Food that tasted like parchment came often, and he liked to remind the castle soldiers that he'd fed their commander and general much better.

At some point, Bricru fell into a deep sleep. It was the type that sunk his mind into darkness and left him feeling empty when he woke, but it was the best he'd slept since stepping through that gateway.

However, it wasn't the skitter of rats that woke him this time, but the undeniable sensation that he was being watched.

Bricru peeled his eyes open. The darkness retreated from his mind, and he realized that he had company standing on the other side of the bars.

Vera.

She watched him with a shifting jaw, her hands gripping the strap of the leather bag that hung from her shoulder. She was alone.

Bricru didn't move. "Are you allowed to be here, alchemist?"

"I'm not."

Bricru pushed himself upright, and his heavy chains dragged against the stone. "Go."

"You're a filthy liar, Bricru."

His brows lifted as she continued.

"You're an elf, which means your family line originated in Sannir after the battle of Adoni and Orisis. Except I can find no record of a *Bricru*." She spat his name as though it were poison.

Bricru couldn't help the grin that rose to his face. "Clever girl. But I wasn't born here. You'll find no record."

"Not clever. Observant."

There was something about the way she watched him that piqued Bricru's curiosity. "It's just us. Ask your questions, alchemist."

She straightened. "What's your surname?"

"Borealis."

"Lies."

Bricru stilled. This was familiar. He forced himself to meet her dark gaze and he held it. His tongue clicked lightly as he recognized the sensation. "Alith."

Vera gave no response, which simply confirmed what he suspected.

Bricru's smile remained. This was a game he was very excited to play. "No one is supposed to know, are they, *alithias?* You see the truth and yet you hide it. Why?'

"Tell me how that potion was counteracted."

"What makes you think I'm willing to cooperate with you?"

Vera bristled, her frustration showing in the clench of her fists and grit of her teeth. "I will expose your lies, shapeshifter, and when I do, I will make the rest of your short life absolutely miserable."

"And then what?" He leaned forward, meeting her steady gaze with one equally as hard. "Your alith is a secret it seems you've kept well. Expose me, and you'll fall by my side."

"A minor sacrifice." She lowered herself so that their faces were even, her knees brushing the metal bars. "I will not see my brother fall at your hand. You can play the fool, but you cannot lie. Not to me."

Bricru's voice dipped to a low hiss. "I'm not your puppet."

"You're not my ally either. Were you given a different potion to counteract it?"

Bricru clenched his jaw.

"Did the pain wear off on its own?" She tilted her head, studying his face. Then, she dropped her sights to his arms and hands, where they lingered much longer than he was comfortable with.

Bricru resisted the urge to squirm under her stare, and she noticed.

"You don't like that."

He mentally cursed the strength of her ability. Even compared to Elizus, this girl was incredibly attuned to her alith.

"Let me see your hands."

He worked his jaw.

"Your hands."

"Find someone else to torment."

"No." She inched closer.

Bricru waited in silence for her to piece things together, watching her mind work on the other side of the bars.

"This wasn't the healing of another potion," she said finally. "This was another kind of magic. Your veins are white."

He lifted his chin. "And what can you conclude from that, little alithias?"

"There is someone in Tophet who healed you. Some kind of *magic* that brought you back."

"There's that cleverness again."

She stood slowly, her form shadowed in the darkness of the cell. "Kyler says there are more under the power of Orisis who have managed to keep their magic."

Bricru leaned his head back against the stone, his lips curved in amusement. "Goodnight, alithias."

"I'm not done."

He closed his eyes. "I doubt this will be the last time we speak."

CHAPTER FORTY-NINE

KYLER'S BONES RATTLED AS CORBIN BLOCKED HIS HIT, THE SHARP
ring of steel-on-steel floating across the grounds. Kyler adjusted
his stance and swung again with a grunt. Corbin dodged his blade
and attacked, sending Kyler into defense.

"Watch your back!" Adri shouted.

Kyler spun, meeting Salcon's sword with his own and throwing
him backward. The lieutenant stumbled on the dry grass, a playful
sigh falling from his lips as he caught his balance.

Adri's deep voice rose again. "Faster, Commander!"

Kyler huffed.

"Tired already?" Corbin teased, shaking out his arm and lifting
his weapon.

Kyler lunged at him, throwing a series of attacks that sent
Corbin tripping over his own feet. He quickly knocked the sword
from his hand and laughed as Corbin cursed.

Adri whistled and clapped slowly as Kyler struggled to catch
his breath. "I'm not sure what kind of critique you're looking for,
Commander. That was impressive."

Corbin's sword hung limp as he rolled his shoulder, wincing
slightly. "I think he just wanted to show off."

"I wanted to clear my head." Kyler passed his training sword back to Adri, accepting a cool cloth from him. Despite the brisk air, sweat clung to his skin, and heat radiated from beneath his armor.

"I assume that means you haven't gotten anything out of Bricru?" Corbin asked.

Kyler shook his head. "He's being difficult."

Salcon shrugged. "Did you expect anything different?"

"Not really." Kyler took a moment to readjust his armor. "Any news from the castle?"

"Still clear."

Through the thick trees and bare branches, the white brick of the castle rose to the sky. It was calm, yet Kyler could almost feel the dread that coated everything like a fog. Soldiers patrolled every inch of the kingdom, and the flicker of red marked the Sky Regiment who watched from their stations in the mountains. Ships loaded with cannons rolled along beaches, and physicians and alchemists filled the castle halls. The Pass above Kyler's head was more active than usual, as the dragons frequently soared through to check on Sannir below.

Kyler sheathed his blade as Adri handed it back. The grip of this sword wasn't as comfortable as the one he'd grown up with, but he was starting to get used to it.

"Rotate out troops seven and nine," Kyler instructed Adri. "And give Aantho a break. He's been out all night."

The lieutenant tossed a quick salute and headed in the direction of Leida. Salcon gave Kyler's shoulder a firm shake, a gesture meant to reassure him, before he made for the barracks.

"We're fine." Corbin motioned to the soldiers in the distance. "Sannir is ready. Don't you have a meeting with the general?"

Kyler finished tugging at his breastplate. "I do."

"Go." He tossed an arm around Kyler. "Meet your lover."

Kyler shoved him. "Shut up."

"You haven't been subtle about it!"

"She's not my lover."

"Then what is she? Because she's not just your general."

Kyler scowled. "She's *our* general, so I'd suggest you keep your mouth shut."

He crossed his arms. "People talk. Your dance on Eliab's Eve didn't go unnoticed."

"That's all it was."

"You're a bold-faced liar."

"Enough, Lieutenant."

"Don't 'lieutenant' me." Corbin raised his brows. "I saw how you looked at her."

Kyler pressed his palms to his eyes with a groan. "Nothing happened, okay? Just drop it."

"Nothing *can* happen. You know that. You can flirt all you want, but don't forget who she is."

Kyler couldn't forget that. There were unspoken rules they'd both become subject to when taking their positions. Rules he was beginning to think he would happily break for her.

"Stop that," Corbin snapped.

"Stop what?"

He motioned to Kyler's face. "I know exactly what you're thinking right now, and I'm telling you to stop it." He inched closer, jabbing a finger at Kyler's chest. "You can like her all you want, but I told you not to lose your head."

"I have a meeting with *the general.*" Kyler brushed his hand away. "Go find something to do."

Corbin stepped back, amusement dancing across his face. His shoulders rose and fell with a defeated sigh. "Yes sir."

He turned for the castle, giving Corbin's shoulder a good slap as he passed, "Worry about your own relationships."

"I don't have any!"

Kyler laughed.

Soldiers draped in the green of the Brigade paced the castle grounds as Kyler neared, their armor clinking as they walked.

Inside the castle was no different. Soldiers from every branch were stationed around the great hall and spread throughout the surrounding rooms. Even as Kyler reached Novah's study, he was met by two Sky Regiment men leaning against the frame of the door.

The soldiers straightened as the commander approached, but Kyler eased them with a nod. He knocked twice on the wooden door before he let himself inside.

He'd expected to find Novah. He didn't expect to find Zale, Vera, and Bricru with her.

Kyler immediately reached for his sword, his mind freezing at the sight of the shapeshifter outside of his cell. "What is he doing here?'

Novah quickly placed herself between them, and Bricru's chains rustled as Zale tugged him closer. "It's alright, he's still chained."

Bricru grunted at Zale's grip, a scowl etched across his face. "Novah—"

"It's *fine*, Kyler."

His gaze flickered to Vera. "Why is she here?"

"You were right. She found something." Novah stepped back, nodding to Zale.

The Sea Force commander shoved Bricru to his knees. The sound of him hitting the ground echoed through the study with a crack, and the shapeshifter cursed at the impact.

Novah straightened. "Vera believes the potion he drank was

counteracted by magic."

"Powerful magic," Zale interrupted, taking Bricru's chin in his hand to study his face like a physician. The shapeshifter flinched at his touch. "We needed to examine him out of the dark of the dungeon."

Kyler scoffed. "You couldn't have summoned for bit more light and left him behind iron?"

Novah grabbed a book off her desk, flipping lightly through it. "I wanted him here."

"He's dangerous."

"He's in chains."

"Why wasn't I consulted in this?"

Novah glanced up at him. "Do I need to ask your permission, Commander?"

"No," he said a bit too quickly. "No. I just don't trust him."

Bricru's voice rose. "I thought we were friends."

"We're not." Kyler released a frustrated sigh. "Vera, why do you think it was magic?"

"Look at his veins." She stepped toward him and took hold of his chains, tugging his wrists into the air. "They're white. He didn't heal from it naturally." Vera passed the gallot root to Kyler. "He had the same reaction the root did, except he recovered. That means that the root and Tophet are, in fact, connected and—"

"And someone in Tophet knows how to counteract it." Kyler handed the root back to Vera. He took a knee before Bricru, leveling himself with the shapeshifter. "Were you healed by magic, Bricru?"

"Ask your little alchemist."

Vera scowled.

"I'm asking *you*. Were you healed by magic?"

The ground rumbled beneath them, cutting Kyler's

interrogation short. He drew his sword as he stood, his heart jumping to his throat.

Bricru leaned back on his heels, tipping his head to the ceiling. "You're out of time, Caligari."

Footsteps pounded down the hall, and a panting Corbin came into view, his blade drawn.

"They're here." He hardly got the words out between gasps for air. "The gateway is open. Orisis is attacking."

Kyler's legs were heavy as he rushed down the hall, Corbin matching his pace. Shouts echoed across the castle as the roar of swordplay filled the air, and dust clung to Kyler's boots.

"Draven, get her *out*," Novah commanded. She shoved Vera into her brother's arms before racing after Kyler and Corbin. "Lieutenant!"

Corbin spared a glance over his shoulder to show he was listening as he moved.

"How many are there?'

Corbin didn't have to answer. The window to their left shattered into pieces as the tail of an amphiptere collided with it, sending shards of colored glass skittering across the floor.

Kyler shielded his head as glass grazed his hands and scraped his armor. Dust continued to spill from around the corner, where clashing swords and shouts echoed like a song of destruction from the great hall.

Novah pushed Kyler forward. "Keep your men close to the Temple. Keep the Pass open." She drew her blade and headed for the great hall. "I'll take Zale with me."

Kyler wanted to argue, to tell her that she needed him in there, but she was right. This was a land attack, and his men knew the land better than anyone. They were trained for this, and they needed their leader.

Kyler faced Corbin. "Split up. Find Adri and Salcon. I'll cut through the gardens and meet you at the Temple."

Corbin gave a sharp nod, his jaw locked, and broken glass crunched under his feet as he sprinted off. The shriek of an amphiptere echoed in the sky, and Kyler shoved down the fear that was beginning to chill his chest. He turned to the shattered window and leaped through the gaping hole. His legs scraped the jagged edges of the glass as he landed softly on the other side and raced toward the cries of battle coming from the direction of the Temple.

Shadows of black swooped like storm clouds in the sky, dodging the dragons of Adoni who attacked without mercy. Fire shot through the air like arrows, the smoke of the sky rivaling the dust of the ground.

Kyler's breath felt hot and jagged against the dry air. From the corner of his eye, he could see the wooden structure of the barracks, their walls consumed in flames.

The whistle of a blade swept past Kyler's ear, and he had barely lifted his own to block before the next swing came. Kyler shoved the afi away with a grunt, striking him in his side with a force that sent him tumbling to the fallen leaves. The tip of the commander's sword slipped through the enemy's armor, and the afi fell dead at his feet. Blood slicked Kyler's blade, mocking the red of the leaves around them.

He broke into a run, weaving between branches that snagged his clothes and scratched his armor. Smoke billowed ahead, and the sight only pushed him to move faster. A flash of green caught his eye as Corbin drew near. Adri trailed with soldiers at his heels, their sights on the sky and armor reflecting the flames.

"Commander!" Corbin called over the chaos, and Kyler adjusted his course to meet him. Corbin passed a bow into his hands. He accepted it gladly, taking aim for the sky.

Amphipteres shot past, fire falling from their fangs and catching on the dry grass. Kyler held steady as he reached the white brick of the Temple, his sights locked on the afi who rode atop the beasts. He loosed an arrow, not waiting to see if it'd made its mark before nocking another. They whizzed through the sky, piercing the smoke and darkness.

The rounded structure of the Temple was flooded by soldiers, both afi and Land Brigade, as the battle swept across the grounds.

"Corbin, take the back!" Kyler shouted.

Corbin's voice rose as he repeated the command to his men, guiding them to the other side of the Temple walls.

Kyler was ready to release another arrow when he was battered from behind. He tumbled to the dirt and gasped as the air fled from his lungs. His palms hit the ground, taking in the shock of his fall, and he scrambled to his feet to meet his attacker.

The prince of Potri stood before him, his golden-stitched robes covered in ash. He playfully spun his blade before swinging at Kyler, a grin splitting his face.

Kyler narrowly dodged his sword and drew his own, abandoning his bow on the ground. Smoke burned his lungs, coating his tongue and stealing his breath.

Above the mountains, more dragons burst from the Pass, filling the sky with color and flame.

The prince swung again, and Kyler countered, the hit jarring him.

An amphiptere dipped low to the ground, sending soldiers tumbling from its path, and rammed its side into the body of the Temple. Stone cracked at the impact, and fear leaped into Kyler's throat. Elizus swung with a strength Kyler couldn't best.

Another beast flung its body into the temple, and the flick of its tail sent both the prince and the commander rolling to the dust.

Kyler scrambled for his blade, but Elizus reached him first, pinning him down with gritted teeth. Kyler twisted and turned beneath him. Elizus held firm, his forearm digging into Kyler's throat.

"Watch, Caligari," he hissed.

The amphiptere hit the Temple again, sending stones tumbling. Shouts rose around him, disorienting and desperate, but those all sounded like whispers compared to the cry that filled the air with terror.

Kyler looked up. Atlas' white scales were slicked in blood as the dragon roared in pain. His wings struggled, pierced by arrow and flame, and then they stopped.

Atlas fell from the sky.

Orders and shouts turned into panic as soldiers turned their backs on the Temple, racing away from the dragon's shadow as Atlas' body crashed into the stone.

The Temple crumbled to rock and ruin.

Fragments of stone skittered across the ground. Kyler shielded his face as they flung toward him, scraping his skin, and pinged off his armor.

A snap echoed from the sky, louder than the shatter of glass, and the clouds above the mountains dissipated in a flash of white.

Kyler's body responded. A weight like steel fell onto his chest, hard enough to make him gasp. The blood that raced through his veins seemed to still for a moment as if suddenly unsure of itself.

And then it was gone. Every ounce of magic in Kyler's blood faded. He *felt* it leave.

The afi turned their gaze to the castle.

"I'll kill you!" Kyler seethed. He finally grabbed hold of Elizus and wrestled him off. His bones felt weaker. His mind was clouded.

"You can try." Elizus gripped Kyler's arms as the commander pressed him into the dust.

Arrows flew past Kyler's head, close enough to brush his hair, but all of his anger was channeled toward the prince. His knuckles crashed into Elizus' cheekbone, hard enough to make Kyler's fingers crack, and the prince shouted in pain.

Kyler used the opportunity to wrangle himself free, stumbling, and started for the castle. He took hold of his sword as he passed it, and he gripped the hilt as if it could save Sannir from ruin.

He cut down afi as he crossed the bridge. Dragons rose and fell like the tides of the battle, and soldiers with scales of all three colors fought with every ounce of strength they had.

But they weren't winning—not anymore. For they had no magic to wield.

CHAPTER FIFTY

FIRE WAS DEVOURING CARPETS AND TAPESTRIES AS KYLER reached the castle foyer, choking on the dense smoke that filled the air.

He pulled his cloak over his nose and squinted in the dark for signs of Novah or Zale. Flames licked at his ankles as he pushed his way through the smog. He kept a hand against the stone wall to orient himself in the low visibility. Heat crawled up his skin and he kicked at the rugs as he passed them, smothering what he could.

Distant shouts and the ringing of steel pulled his attention toward the west, and Kyler followed the sounds with his blade drawn.

Doors had been splintered and crushed. The roll of dust behind him made Kyler quicken his pace, hoping to remain unnoticed in the dark of the halls.

A grunt echoed through the smoke, and Kyler flexed his grip. His steps slowed as the glint of steel caught his eye.

Aeron shouted as he brought his blade down on an afi, the tip scraping the goat-like horns on the man's helmet. He dodged the hit, and Aeron struck again, severing the afi's arm.

Blood splattered, and the afi let out a cry of pain. He doubled over and clutched his arm as Aeron struck again.

Kyler moved to join him, but the sound of shifting armor rose behind him. He spun, and his blade caught an afi's sword just inches from him. The dark colors of the afi's clothes blended with the smoke, and Kyler dodged as the soldier of Orisis nearly sliced through his torso.

"Behind you!"

Kyler ducked as a second blade grazed over his head.

Novah was beside him in an instant, her warning now drowned out by the pounding of armored boots. At least three more soldiers were almost upon them.

Kyler sunk his blade into the man's stomach. The man screamed, collapsing to the marble floors. Kyler had little time to linger as another soldier reached him, attacking with no mercy and impressive strength.

Shouts and curses filled the halls. Beside Kyler, Novah gained the upper hand on her opponent. She battered him to the ground, turning quickly to assist Aeron as Kyler landed a finishing blow.

The afi cursed as Novah's blade caught his side, and his moment of weakness gave Aeron the opportunity to slice his throat.

"The queen?" Kyler asked, his breathing short, as he faced Novah.

"Safe." She flicked hair from her eyes, still panting from the heat of the battle. "Zale has Sannir surrounded and is catching amphipteres before they reach the island. The physicians are already working—"

"The Pass is closed."

Novah blinked at him. "What do you mean?"

"It's closed. The Temple is destroyed. The physicians can't do much."

She just stared at him, her breath still and lips parted. "It's not—"

"I felt it too." Aeron rolled his shoulders. "Commander, you were there, weren't you?"

Kyler nodded. "We have the dragons. We can still win this."

Novah set her jaw. Her back was to Aeron, and by the time Kyler spotted the afi behind him, it was too late.

"Lieutenant!"

He wasn't finished with his warning when Aeron released a guttural scream, the sound cut short as his body froze. An afi gripped his neck, fingers pressing into his skin as his eyes rolled.

Dust dripped from the afi's hand, swallowing Aeron until the lieutenant could no longer be seen beneath it.

And then the dust dissipated, and with it, so did Aeron.

Tophet had taken him.

"Aeron!" Novah's shout mixed with the clash of steel as Kyler thrust himself in front of her, catching the afi's blade before he took Novah as well.

He was large, making Kyler's arms shudder as he drove the commander back. The afi snarled under his helm, forcing Kyler to step with every swing of his blade. The sharp tip of his weapon whizzed past Kyler's ear, and the sting of blood rose to its surface.

With another hit, Kyler lost control, but a new figure stepped between them, tall and dark. He shoved the afi back with a grunt.

"We need him *alive.*"

Skin like fractured glass reflected off the flames, and it was only as he faded that Kyler recognized his savior as Ophir, shifting back into Bricru. Chains no longer dangled from his wrists, and his pale hair was coated in ash.

Novah swung at him immediately.

Bricru stumbled, his back slamming against the wall, and

ducked beneath her next swing. He held no weapons, yet there wasn't a glint of fear in his eyes.

"You should be thanking me, General!"

She ignored him, swinging again.

Kyler took the opportunity to rush at the large afi, letting the man's blood splatter across his armor as he ripped the life from his opponent.

Novah swore as Bricru dodged yet another attack, slipping behind her with as much skill as a snake.

"I'd rather I didn't die today," he said, panting.

Kyler caught him by the back of his collar and pulled him against his chest. "I'd rather you did." He brought his blade to the shapeshifter's neck, pressing hard enough to make him still.

Bricru sucked a slow breath, his voice steady. "You won't kill me, Caligari."

Kyler's blade scraped his throat. "You have too much faith in me."

Bricru swallowed, his nonchalance quickly fading. "You and I are alike," he said softly. "I know you see it too. You did not wish to kill me before, and I don't think you wish to now."

Kyler flexed his fingers around his hilt. The words rang truer than he wanted to admit.

Bricru's chest rose and fell in heavy gasps. For a moment, neither one moved, trapped in a silence of hatred and understanding.

Then Bricru's skin fractured, and Kyler struck.

The commander's blade bounced lightly off Bricru's neck. His tender skin hardened with scales of ebony. Wings rose into the air, as wide as the ceiling was tall, and Bricru's breathless pants became a flurry of smoke and embers as he transformed into an amphiptere.

Bricru dove for Kyler. The strength of his amphiptere form cracked the walls as he twisted in the tight hallway, snapping the wooden beams with his head and digging his wings into the marble as if it were made of sand. He curved like a snake, without legs or claws, each muscle rippling beneath his scales.

Kyler leaped from his path and shoved Novah back, flattening them both against the wall. Bricru's tail whipped past, brushing Kyler's chest plate as the smog grew denser. The scales at Kyler's ears tangled with the breath of the beast, and Bricru's gaze fell on him once more.

"No masks, Bricru!" Kyler shouted up at him. "Fight me as you are!"

He fractured again, falling to his knees as glass pieced his body back into a man.

"You wish to fight me as your equal?" He heaved, wincing in pain. "Then fight me, Caligari."

Kyler tossed his weapon to the ground. He ran at Bricru, striking him in the jaw hard enough to make him stumble. Bricru's foot caught on the corpse of a fallen afi, and he fell.

Kyler was on top of him in an instant, gasping as Bricru landed a knee to his stomach. Armor shifted as their limbs tangled, and Kyler grabbed for Bricru's wrists, attempting to keep them pinned. The shapeshifter writhed and kicked beneath him.

"Tired yet, Caligari?"

Kyler silenced him with an elbow to his brow, slicing the skin of his forehead open.

Bricru cursed.

"Pathetic snake," Elizus' cool tone filled the hall.

Kyler's head snapped up, and Novah pushed off the wall in time to catch Elizus' sword with her own as he appeared from the smoke.

He shoved her back, but she held her stance, swinging with a force that could only be fueled by anger.

Kyler turned back to Bricru, attempting to land another hit on his brow. But he moved, and Kyler hit the marble instead. A shock of pain raced up his arm like lightning, and another kick from Bricru sent him crashing into the blood and dust.

The destruction of Orisis coated the floor, rolling and twisting and clinging to every surface it could find.

Kyler scrambled to his feet and grabbed his sword, giving Bricru a kick to the ribs. The shapeshifter cried out, grasping his side. He curled onto the cool floor.

Novah had Elizus in a string of attacks, forcing him into defense. Kyler hesitated a moment. She could handle herself.

He looked at Bricru, who cowered beneath him. The two stared at each other, and Bricru made no move to flee as Kyler inched closer.

Kyler had killed him once. He didn't want to do it again.

He stepped over Bricru and hurried down the corridor. He followed the dust. It thickened as he neared the great hall, covering his steps, as if he walked the very ground of Tophet.

Kyler reached the doors of the great hall, rushing through without thought.

The moment he crossed the threshold, the world went silent.

Dust floated in the air around him, thicker than smoke, and masked him from the battle that took place beyond the room. He stilled, panting in the muted air, and blinked away the fuzz.

A figure stepped slowly from the smoke, his smile as cold as the air around him.

"Hello, Caligari."

CHAPTER FIFTY-ONE

THE GOD OF DESTRUCTION STEPPED THROUGH THE GATEWAY and entered Sannir, his hands clasped behind his back. His dark hair hung loose around his jaw, and his pale lips quirked into a smirk as he laid eyes on Kyler.

Dust spun violently around him, dressing him like the dark robes he donned and curling around his neck. It crept along Kyler's skin, grasping for him.

Orisis scanned the castle with a look of wonder. "Last time I stepped foot in this kingdom, your father was just a soldier."

This was a history Kyler did not recognize. He breathed in dust as Orisis went on.

"I suppose that's all he ever was—all *you* are. A soldier, facing a god." He stepped closer, close enough that Kyler could smell the stench of Tophet on his clothes. "I believe this is yours." He brought his hands from behind him, revealing a sword of leather and steel.

Kyler recognized it immediately. His jaw clenched. "Where did you get that?"

"You left it behind when the inn burned."

"I don't want it."

Orisis held it out, offering the weapon to him anyway. "A gift from your father, wasn't it?"

Kyler took the blade hesitantly, wrapping his hands around its hilt. It was familiar to hold, the divots in the grip fitting his fingers and resting balanced in his palm. He met Orisis' eye once more. "Call off your attack, and I'll let you live."

"That's a bold threat."

Kyler inched closer, his heart thundering within his chest. "You think that after all I've seen, I wouldn't be more than willing to drive this blade through your chest?"

He sighed. "I don't care how willing you are. There will always be something you want more." He sidestepped around Kyler, waving to the smoke. "General, why don't you join us?"

Kyler's heart jumped to his throat.

Uriah emerged from the dust.

Shackles still bound his wrists and feet as he strode into the room, his chin high and nostrils flared in anger. Blood as brown as dirt had dried along his head and neck, tangling into his beard, and his hair clung to his face, soaked in sweat.

Uriah looked worse than when Kyler had seen him last, and when their eyes met, Kyler feared his father would crack.

But Uriah had never cracked before, and he wouldn't now.

"What is he doing here?" Kyler motioned to Uriah with his blade, his voice stronger than he'd anticipated.

"He's come to make a deal." Orisis' smile seemed to flash with excitement, like he'd been waiting for this moment.

"I'm not making deals with you. Either of you."

Uriah's hard stare was fixed beyond Kyler.

"Go ahead, General. Tell him what you want."

Uriah's jaw ticked.

Orisis gave an exaggerated sigh, though he seemed to expect this. "I suppose I can be the middleman." He motioned to the dust, urging it to spin faster. "I will call off the attack. I will close the gateway to Sannir and leave you all in peace if you, Kyler Caligari, will do your father one favor. If you refuse, I will make true of the things you saw last time we met. Your Temple is already crumbled. What next? Your lieutenant? Your queen?"

Kyler ground his teeth. "I get the feeling this favor won't be small."

His eyes sparked as he glanced to Uriah. "The flick of a blade is all."

"Tell me, Orisis."

"Kill your father."

The words hit Kyler like a blow to his chest, and Orisis' smile grew wide.

"This is the fun part."

Kyler's knuckles were white around his weapon, his fingers growing stiff from the tension. "Why?"

He shrugged. "Because I don't think you'll do it. You're weak. You're too much like him."

Kyler swung his blade, pointing the tip at Uriah's throat. "Do I have your word, Orisis?"

"I swear it." There was a giddiness in his voice.

The sword felt heavier than it had a moment ago. Its weight shifted in Kyler's hold as he adjusted his grip. Every part of him begged to not look at Uriah.

"This is for Sannir," Kyler whispered. He focused on Uriah's throat, where the tip of the blade pressed a divot into his skin.

The former general didn't so much as flinch. He would be the hero one last time. His sacrifice would save them all.

A small trail of blood bubbled, blooming like roses, on Uriah's scarred skin. Kyler wasn't sure how long he stood there, staring at the bob of Uriah's throat against the tip of the blade, but it was enough to make the sword feel as though it were made of rocks.

"Any day now, Caligari." Orisis' voice broke the deadly silence of the room.

"That's not my name." Even as he said this, Kyler swallowed a sob that tried to surface. No tears for Uriah. Never again.

And yet, despite the hatred and hurt, Orisis was right.

Kyler couldn't do it.

The commander turned his weapon, swinging instead at Orisis' neck.

Dust leaped into the air, curling around Kyler's blade and deflecting it like a shield. He swore as he was shoved backward, his boots skidding on the marble, and the dust whipped through his hair and clothes.

"It seems I know you better than you thought," Orisis chided with wicked amusement.

Uriah pressed his eyes shut, releasing a breath, and tilted his head to the ceiling.

Kyler shielded his face, coughing as destruction swept through his mouth and tangled in his scales. He raised his blade against Orisis once more, only to be tossed aside. His back slammed against the wall, and Kyler fell to his knees.

"You don't know when to quit, do you, Commander?"

Kyler gasped, his legs threatening to give out as he stood once more. "You don't know when to die."

"I will never die." He towered over Kyler, and the amusement faded from his face. "You will. I will drain you of every drop of blood until your magic is all I can taste and your realm is my own. You will die, and I will live."

Dust strangled Kyler's throat, choking him. What did it matter? The Pass was gone. He had no magic to give.

And yet, Orisis' gaze darkened. "You will give me what I want."

A figure stumbled through the dust with a sword pressed to his back. Before Kyler could move, Elizus' hand snapped around the neck of the soldier, brushing the green of his scales as dust curled into his hair.

A scream ripped through the room, and Kyler joined in when he realized who it belonged to.

Corbin's face froze, his eyes wide, as Elizus dropped his grip and lowered his blade, a satisfied smile on his face. Slowly, the dust that surrounded them curled around Corbin, and his soul followed Aeron's to a world of torment and agony.

CHAPTER FIFTY-TWO

TEAR-SOAKED ASH BLURRED KYLER'S VISION AS CORBIN FADED, his soul sent to the one place that Kyler could not reach.

"Pity." Orisis frowned. "I liked him."

Kyler swung for the god. His blade was caught by dust once more, never touching Orisis. He forced his strength into every strike, swinging harder and harder, his rage all-consuming and directed at the god of destruction.

Orisis simply waved his fingers as he deflected each of Kyler's attacks.

"You look angry," he teased. "You look like your father."

Kyler choked a sob, swinging as hard as he could. This time, Orisis halted his blade with his dust, letting it hover just inches from him in a thin layer of destruction.

"Let's not get emotional, Kyler."

"You're vile," Kyler whispered.

"That, I am." He let Kyler's blade fall, watching it slip from his hand and clatter to the marble. "You know what I want. Uriah was willing to give himself up for his kingdom. Are you willing to do the same? Give me what I ask, and your friend will return from Tophet."

Kyler's fingers twisted in the dust as he clenched his fists. His voice shook. "If I fall, Orisis, you will fall with me."

The god grinned.

"Orisis!"

This voice was new, one that Kyler didn't recognize. It rose from the dust like a flame, and at its sound, the god of destruction seemed to forget about Kyler entirely.

Orisis straightened and turned from the commander, facing the dust where a soldier emerged.

He wore silver armor—the same armor that dressed Kyler. His chest plate was embossed with dragons, and his brown curls were braided at his temples. Rows of scales the color of bone, ivory, and snow trailed his elongated ears, and a cape just as pale swept down to his ankles. His wide jaw was set as he met Orisis' eye.

"How *dare* you show your face in Sannir." His voice was rough, its sound like the crackle of embers.

Orisis scowled, a hint of fear dancing across his face. "I knew you would come."

"Did you?" The soldier stalked closer, a sword hanging from his hand.

The dust seemed to flee from this newcomer, skittering away before even a speck could touch his battle-worn skin.

The god of destruction did not flinch. "Your Pass has fallen."

"I will rebuild it."

"Your soldiers are weak."

"I will shape them."

"You have *nothing!*" Orisis hissed the word like it was made of salt. "Where have you been hiding? Why wait until I have all but destroyed what you have built?"

The soldier's jaw shifted as brilliant anger flashed across his face. "I gave you the realm, Orisis. I allowed your hand to touch any life you wished to taint, but that wasn't enough for you."

"It will never be enough!" Orisis' voice rose to a shout. "Not until you yield to me, Adoni, and your magic is mine!"

"You will not create." Adoni inched closer. "I will not yield."

Orisis panted, his eyes wild with anger and jealousy. "Then you will lose everything."

Adoni swung, his blade slicing the dust as if it were cloth. Destruction split wherever he struck and tumbled away from his boots. Orisis blocked every strike, but unlike with Kyler, the dust exploded like fireworks on Eliab's Eve, scattering with every hit of Adoni's sword.

Across the room, movement caught Kyler's eye. He saw Bricru, whose scar stood out amidst the dirt and dust, limp toward the gateway, Elizus and Uriah close behind him.

Kyler rushed at them, his cloak slipping and tangling with his arms, and met Elizus' blade once more. The great hall filled with the clash of steel. The prince released his hold on Uriah, and the former general swung at Bricru, knocking the shapeshifter to the ground.

Elizus kicked Kyler's chest, stealing his breath, and shoved him back. Kyler had hardly regained his wits when he saw the dust take hold of Uriah. It lifted him as if he were a feather and shoved him back into the gateway from which he came.

Across the room, Orisis' attention was divided. Dust as fierce as a snowstorm encircled the gods, burning Kyler's skin as it whipped past his face. It grabbed hold of Elizus and Bricru and sent them through the gateway after Uriah. A moment later, Orisis followed.

The last thing Kyler saw was the scrape across the god's cheek as their eyes locked, and Orisis disappeared into the dust.

Kyler made for the gateway. His hands brushed the air as he tried to follow, but it would not open. Not for him.

Adoni was at Kyler's side in a moment, his weapon sheathed and palms outstretched. He took hold of the remaining dust like it were cotton, the whisps forming into something solid at his touch.

The gateway flickered before him and began to take shape in the center of the hall.

"They can no longer come through this way," he spoke as he worked, "but your soldiers can. This gateway will allow those who come from Sannir to return—Corbin and Aeron and anyone else Orisis has stolen—but it will not let the afi through."

Kyler's eyes burned with bitter tears, mixing with the tainted blood of the afi that was smeared across his face.

Adoni faced him, a sheen of sweat along his skin and a furrow in his brow. He stared at the commander for a long moment, his breath heavy and muscles tense. He looked as though he wished to wipe the blood from Kyler's face and promise him everything would be alright.

"End this, Kyler," he said finally. "Finish the war your father started. You are more powerful than gods; you can both destroy and create. I cannot dwell within destruction, but you can."

He gripped the back of Kyler's neck, pressing their foreheads together. His callouses were rough. He smelled like earth. "Trust me. And trust your general. I chose her for a reason."

Adoni dropped his hold on Kyler. Then, with another handful of dust, the god of creation formed a gateway that spun with sunlight and stepped through it.

CHAPTER FIFTY-THREE

ADONI WAS GONE.

Pain shot through Kyler's bones as his knees hit the ground. His chest shook. He attempted to regain control of his breath as tears burned his eyes, fiercer than flame. He pressed his forehead to the cold marble and let the salt of his tears fall across the dust on his mouth.

He could hear Corbin's screams, echoing through the hall like a ghost's. He could feel Uriah's touch, his father within reach, and yet the general was once again trapped in torment.

Kyler tried to stop. He tried to think and breathe and pull himself together, but every breath felt like a blade and every thought was consumed by what he had lost.

Footsteps quickened down the hall, slowing as they reached the room.

"Kyler." Novah knelt beside him and placed a firm hand on his shoulder. She tugged lightly, forcing him to look at her. "Are you hurt?"

"He took Corbin." His voice was raw.

He took Corbin. He took Uriah. He took the Pass.

She sat next to him without a word, and the scents of blood and pine surrounded him.

Kyler roughly wiped the soot and tears from his face and forced himself to breathe. He felt utterly useless—a soldier against a god. The threats Orisis promised seemed to fill the empty hall, lingering with the dust that covered the ground. Saints, he could hardly think.

But if Novah saw him as weak, she didn't show it. She stayed with him until his sobs turned dry and his breathing eased to a more reasonable pace.

"We'll get them back," she said softly. She reached for his face, using her thumb to clean the blood and dirt that splattered his skin.

He didn't respond. He pressed his eyes shut as her touch lingered, easing the tension in his jaw. He hadn't lost everyone. Not yet.

But he would if Orisis didn't get what he wanted.

She stood, pulling him up with her. "I'll take you to the castle guest rooms."

The barracks—they'd been destroyed.

Kyler's breath stuttered, and he ran an ash-covered sleeve across his face. "Adoni was here."

She nodded slowly. "I know. I heard his voice. What did he say to you?"

"He told me to trust him." Kyler blinked away the tears until he could see her clearly. "He told me to trust *you*."

She straightened, brushing ash from her chest plate. "Aiyanna and Cadmus will want to see us. Clean yourself up, and we'll assess the damage—"

Kyler pulled her into a hug. Their armor met with an echo that filled the barren hall, the sound so different than the clash of battle. Kyler dipped his chin to her shoulder, not caring that her scales caught his hair or that she smelled of ash. He simply held her there, feeling her chest rise and fall against his, and reminded himself that she was still alive.

After a moment, her arms came around him too.

"Sannir needed you," he whispered.

She didn't respond, and when Kyler finally released her, he found red brimming her eyes.

Novah sucked a breath. "Let's get you cleaned up."

The two of them walked in silence through the castle, the steady fall of their footsteps filling the halls. Destruction greeted them as they rounded the first ballroom. Frantic running and commanding shouts echoed from the surrounding hallways, and the glass from broken windows and oil lamps crunched under their feet. Several sections of the wall had been scorched or punctured, and the little light that did pierce through was pale and clouded.

The halls were full of people, many attempting to clear the floor of glass as they blocked off the shattered windows, and others were already beginning to repair the cracks in the marble.

Aiyanna stood at the center. Worry lines creased her brow where a crown usually sat, but she appeared otherwise unharmed. Her skirt, though wrinkled, was untouched, and though her hands tremored as she directed servants, there wasn't a drop of blood on them.

She scanned the room until her gaze fell on Kyler and Novah, and she immediately started for them. "Are either of you hurt?"

"We're alright," Novah answered.

Aiyanna took in the sight of the blood that splattered their armor. A worried look crossed her face. "The guest rooms are untouched."

"That's where we're headed." Novah motioned for Kyler to follow, and Aiyanna's attention returned to the castle.

They reached the guest quarters a moment later. Though a few nobles trailed up and down the wide staircases, the area was mostly empty and, like Aiyanna had said, untouched by destruction.

Novah led him to an empty room, the space filled with pale sunlight. "It's yours for as long as you need it."

She turned to leave but Kyler caught her hand, halting her. His thumb brushed across her raw knuckles, running along the cuts and callouses that marked her skin. He stared at her hand resting in his.

"Thank you," he said softly, the words catching in his throat.

Novah nodded before dropping his hand and left him on his own.

The room was large and decorated in pale blue. There was plenty of furniture and ornate décor, but Kyler didn't stop to admire any of it. He headed straight to the washroom, where a large mirror caught his attention.

The reflection that stared back at him no longer felt like his own. Despite Novah's attempts to clean his face, dust still clung to his nose and forehead, and splatters of blood still stained his skin. Reddish-brown blemishes smeared across his silver armor and soaked into his cotton shirt beneath, making him look even worse than he felt.

Almost.

Corbin's scream, as Orisis damned his soul to Tophet, echoed through the silent room, overpowering every clink of armor and rustle of scales as Kyler began to undress. His palms still felt heavy from the weight of his sword as he'd swung for Orisis. He could see Corbin fading, feel him slipping from his grasp.

The shock of the cool water hit his skin like needles as Kyler lowered himself into the tub. Trails of brown and scarlet traveled down him like raindrops falling from the wrong type of cloud, pooling and tainting the water. Every droplet seemed to sizzle against his warm face, and though chills spread across his arms, Kyler still felt as though he were on fire.

He took his time scrubbing the dirt and blood from his nails and hair before stepping out with a shiver.

The reflection that stared back at him now was much more presentable, but Kyler noticed the hollow look in his eyes and the warm flush of his cheeks.

Clean clothes had been left on the bed, fresh black cotton trousers and a white tunic. These were the base layers for the castle guards' uniform. Someone had gone out of their way to ensure their commander still looked like a soldier.

The clothes were loose and soft, allowing for room to move. Armor usually went on top of it, but whoever had brought the clothes must've taken Kyler's armor for cleaning, leaving him feeling bare without it.

He stepped to the mirror again and gently rolled the sleeves of the tunic to his elbow. Cuts covered his arms, nicks from blades and arrows, and he wondered how many of them would turn to scars. Blood still bubbled slowly on his left ear, where the afi's blade had caught his skin.

Everything ached. There was work to be done, and yet all Kyler wanted to do was lay atop his small bed back at the barracks and fall asleep to the scent of brewing potions and the sound of his men's laughter. He ran his rough palms down his face as he strode to the bed—much larger and softer than the one he was used to. It sunk beneath his weight as he lowered onto it, not bothering to pull the quilt over himself.

And Kyler slipped into a dreamless sleep.

CHAPTER FIFTY-FOUR

ALL THAT REMAINED OF THE TEMPLE WAS BROKEN STONE, jagged edges pointing to the place where the oldest dragon in Sannir had met his end. Ash still dusted the grass, catching in the wind, even though it'd been nearly a day since it landed onto what now felt like a graveyard.

Kyler flexed his fists against the cold air that blew across Sannir. Pink colored his nose and cheeks, and even with his heavy cloak, Kyler could feel the dry air clinging to his skin.

Aiyanna ran a gloved hand along the cracked stone, her fingers leaving trails in their wake, as she studied what remained of the Temple with a sunken brow. In the distance, the call of dragons echoed like birdsong. The beasts wandered the land, their path home having dissipated with the magic. Their shadows swooped as several landed near the Temple, the color of their scales more muted and their eyes duller. They watched from a distance as Aiyanna pulled her hand from the stone.

"We'll have to rebuild as quickly as possible."

"Where do we start?" Zale's boots pressed into the grass as he shifted, eyeing the Temple.

Most of Sannir had spent the previous day mourning the loss of their magic. The knowledge of what'd been taken from them hung heavier than the ash and soot, and the fear of failing to get it back was nearly suffocating.

Kyler thought of Vera—a young alchemist with a love for the magic she'd become skilled with—now stripped of her abilities. Without its magic, Sannir was nothing.

Where was Adoni when the Pass fell? Where was Adoni when their lifeline was torn from beneath them?

Where was Adoni when Corbin was taken?

He'd come too late.

The clink of armor announced Novah's arrival, trailed by Draven. His steps were mimicked by his dragon head cane, and a frown was etched onto his face. The red of his hooded cloak contrasted the gray of hers, and just like the rest of them, their cheeks were wind whipped.

"The Regiment is secure at the base of the mountains." Novah paused before Aiyanna, nodding her head in greeting. She notably ignored Cadmus, who'd sided up beside the queen. "For those of you who don't know, we lost Commander Idar to afi blade. This is acting Commander Draven Caelum, one of the soldiers who accompanied us in Potri. He'll hold the position until after this threat is neutralized, and then we can affirm his place as commander."

Aiyanna began to speak, but Cadmus cut her off. "Thank you, General."

Novah turned to him with raised brows and sounded her disapproval. "I was informing the queen."

He stiffened. "In case you've forgotten, I am the queen's advisor. You follow my orders."

"I follow *her* orders. I suggest you let the queen speak, Advisor."

Kyler stilled at her tone, and Zale looked like he might laugh.

Cadmus's gaze narrowed. "Watch how you speak to me."

"You forget your place."

"My place is at the side of the queen."

"As is mine." Novah faced Aiyanna, whose round lips tugged at the corners. "What have they done with the fallen dragons?"

Aiyanna's smile fell. "They've been brought to the mountains, as close to the closed Pass as they can be. They will be taken care of by their own kind."

Novah nodded, turning to Kyler. "I take it Bricru made it back with Orisis?"

"He did."

"Then we set our sights on Tophet." Novah made her way to the Temple, staring up at what little remained. "Zale and Draven, I want you working to reopen the Pass. The people are scared without it, and that fear is only going to turn to distrust if we can't open it again. Work with the architects to rebuild the Temple, and see if there's anything we can do to speed up the process.

"Kyler, we need a way into Tophet. See if any of Uriah's notes survived, and collect whatever potions remain. The soldiers we still have will need an alchemist, and the ones in Tophet need to get out."

Cadmus crossed his arms stiffly over his chest. "That's a large task, General. Are you certain Commander Kyler is the best person to be doing this?"

Anger flashed in Novah's eyes before she even opened her mouth, and Kyler decided then that he never wanted to be on the other side of it. "While your distrust is Commander Kyler is clear, it's not shared. I'm not in the mood to put up with your boyish grudges, Cadmus. Keep your mouth shut or walk yourself home."

Draven glanced at Kyler, his eyes wide, before he shifted back to Novah and Cadmus.

Aiyanna placed herself between them. Though shorter than both, she held her chin high as she faced her advisor. "Perhaps the general is right. We've had a long few days. Rest."

Cadmus ground his teeth, his nostrils flaring as he slipped around Aiyanna, leaving the soldiers and the queen to themselves.

"Well done," Novah muttered to Aiyanna before stepping toward the Temple ruins.

Kyler came to Novah's side, noting every scorch and chip that marked the Temple's surface. Draconic runes etched into the broken stone, words like *light* and *protect*, were now crumbled. Something in Kyler ached, knowing this was the creation of Eliab himself and, in one night, those trusted to guard it had failed.

He wondered if Novah thought the same as she tugged off her gloves and pressed her palm to the stone.

"I'm lost, Kyler," she whispered.

He kept his hands in his pockets. "One step at a time."

Her chest rose as she took a deep breath and dropped her hand from the ruins. "You said the gateway in the hall is no longer a threat?"

"Adoni built on it." Kyler turned, making sure the others could hear him as well. "It will let our soldiers back through if they can reach it, but it's locked to Orisis."

"It's also locked to us." Novah sighed, tilting her face to the sky. "That hasn't changed. We can't reach Tophet."

Kyler nudged her with his shoulder. "Not yet, but if Uriah could build gateways, so can we."

"Without magic?"

Kyler pulled his lips into a thin line. "I don't know. Bricru implied that Orisis sees something more in me. If Uriah built gateways in the depths of Tophet, perhaps I can build them in the absence of the Pass."

She huffed. "I think I need a nap and a large glass of Apola."

"Lucky for you, Sannir has plenty of that in stock." He tapped his potion belt, where the remainder of his potions sat securely in place. Without magic, his mixtures were equal to gold, but it would be a while before the Apola ran out.

Novah eyed his belt. "Work with Vera on making those last as long as you can. Check the barracks and see if any more of your bottles survived the fire."

Kyler didn't want to go to the barracks, not when those walls were filled with Corbin, but he nodded anyway. The wind stung his eyes as he turned from the Temple.

Cold ripped from the mountains, and he could make out the Sky Regiment camp with tents of red so dark they could've been black. Where the thick clouds of the Dragon Pass used to rise, there was now nothing but white-tipped mountains and blue sky. The pillar of Adoni still stood between the castle and barracks—strikingly white against the dying grass and trees—but utterly useless. It was nothing more than a reminder of what had been lost with the Temple.

It smelled like charcoal and bitterness as Kyler reached the front door of the barracks. The once-polished wood was now blackened with soot and charred by flames, leaving a trail of ash across his hand as he pushed it open.

The cleanup had already begun, and the hollow frames of hallways were filled with those working to make the building livable again. A few soldiers dug through the debris, looking for belongings that were sure to be nothing but dust by now.

The east side of the building suffered the least damage, and to Kyler's relief, the kitchens were mostly intact. Those working that evening had made it out with minor injuries, and Kyler clung to that thought as he reached his room.

The door itself was untouched, but as he stepped through the frame, he found that wasn't the case for the rest of his quarters. The right wall had collapsed, crushing the bed with cracked plaster and wood. The flames had eaten away at his quilt and traveled to his clothes chest, coating it in black. The chest seemed to have kept most of his belongings safe, though it was clear by the black stains that it wouldn't have lasted much longer.

The ceiling had begun to collapse as well, leaving Kyler's potion cabinet lopsided from the weight of the beams pressing down on it. The glass casing was warped and scorched, and several bottles of potions were shattered at the cabinet's base.

Kyler stepped to the case, picking through the broken glass and pocketing whatever vials were still intact.

The soft tap of boots approaching from down the hall made Kyler turn, and he found Vera in the doorway, taking in the damage. Her eyes traveled the scene before landing on the commander.

"I'm sorry."

"Some of your notes might still be salvageable." He nodded to the desk, where he'd stored a few of Vera's findings on gallot.

She came to his side and picked through the glass, passing him bottles that hadn't been cracked or spilled. The smells of sage and smoke drifted from her, like she'd scrubbed herself clean and yet couldn't quite shake the stench of fire from her skin. Kyler wondered how many others had close calls with the amphipteres.

She kept her gaze averted as she said, "I heard about Lieutenant Corbin."

"We're forming a plan to get him out, Vera. I know he was a friend to you too."

Her back straightened. "He can handle Tophet until you reach him."

Every minute he spent there, the more of himself he would lose.

Kyler picked up a vial of Ponos that was still half full. "I know the fall of the Pass changes things, but I can use your help. We need to make these potions last, and the gallot root still needs to be studied."

Vera's lips tugged into a smile that she tried—and failed—to hide. "I'd love to help, Commander."

Something in Kyler's chest eased. "Don't look so excited. It'll be terribly boring."

She chuckled and passed him the final vial with a sigh. "Thank you, Kyler." She turned to leave but halted, chewing on her tongue as if there was something more she wanted to say. "I don't think Corbin blames you, you know. I don't blame you either. Not for this, and not for Draven's leg."

Before he could come up with a response, she disappeared down the hallway, leaving her words hanging in the ash around him.

Muffled greetings passed through the wall, and a moment later, Salcon's head poked through the doorway. "Cleaning up?"

Kyler waved him in, and Salcon eyed the destruction with pursed lips.

"You'll be glad to know the fires didn't get anyone. They tore through quite a few walls, but the men who died did so in battle, not flame."

Kyler's bed creaked as he moved toward it, lowering himself onto the mattress and ignoring the plaster that poked at his skin. "We shouldn't have lost any."

"That's not the life we live." He pulled a letter from his pocket, passing it to Kyler. "This came for you."

Kyler frowned, instantly recognizing the neat handwriting that addressed the envelope. "Thank you. I'll find you later."

Salcon gave a tight smile and left the commander alone.

The simple seal popped as Kyler broke it open, unfolding a letter he wasn't sure he wanted to read.

Kyler,

I'm sorry to hear of the events which led you to write. I think we both know that Uriah is a stubborn man, and if I'm honest, I can't say I'm surprised at his betrayal of Sannir.

For my own safety, and to assist you in whatever you need, I think it would be best for me to return to Sannir, even if just for a short while, until things have settled and we are certain I am not in danger. I know we have not always seen eye to eye, but right now, we should stick together.

I might know something about that root of yours. We'll talk when I arrive. I'll see you soon.

Your brother,
Evander

CHAPTER FIFTY-FIVE

THE WORLD SMELLED OF ASH AND RUIN, THE SCENT FILLING
Bricru's lungs and burning his throat. He knew it well.

He was home.

And he was a dead man.

A foot collided with his side, and a grunt fell from his lips as
the shapeshifter rolled in the dust. His ribs still ached from the
beating he'd received from Kyler, and the metallic tang of blood
coated his tongue. His eyes focused on a barren sky, and then on
Elizus' face. When had he lost consciousness?

"Leave him be, Elizus," Orisis chided, his silky voice carrying
in the void.

Bricru managed a smirk that made his jaw pinch. "Yes, Elizus,
behave."

Elizus scowled deeper.

Sharp pain shot through Bricru's limbs as he tried to lift himself
from the ground. Blood oozed from his head, soaking his hair
and making his mind throb, and his vision blurred once more.

"Get up," Elizus hissed. When Bricru didn't, his voice raised.
"Get up!"

"Gods, can't you see I'm trying?"

"And failing."

Orisis moved closer, gently brushing Elizus to the side as he neared. The prince closed his mouth—something Bricru was grateful for—but his gaze was torn from the prince as Orisis knelt before him.

The god studied the shapeshifter, his pale face and dark eyes revealing nothing of his thoughts. "You look like you're in pain."

Bricru swallowed. "I'm fine."

He lifted his chin in cool hubris. "Is he lying, Elizus?"

"Yes."

Bricru said nothing.

Orisis lifted his hand to Bricru's throat, and the shapeshifter closed his eyes, waiting for what he knew would come next.

The feeling that overtook him was the most incredible torment he'd ever felt—worse than the gateway, worse than Kyler's potion. Bricru felt as though his every muscle was contorting and burning. He hardly recognized the scream that ripped from within him. It flooded the dust of Tophet and shook him to his very core.

When Orisis released him, the pain vanished as quickly as it'd come, along with the wounds Bricru had received. In their places, scars twisted his skin, bold and white and as crooked as his soul.

This magic was nothing new. Orisis had possessed it since the day Bricru had met him, but its origin evaded Bricru's knowledge.

The Healer. The Emperor. Orisis' Sixth.

Each time Orisis used this magic, Bricru became more curious of the one behind it, curious of the brother he knew nothing of.

Bricru brought a hand to his jaw and rubbed the bone, finding nothing but a dull ache where needle-like pain had been before. His legs shook as he stood, tremors rolling across his limbs.

Orisis eyed him. "Feeling better?"

Bricru forced his words through his sandpaper throat. "Yes."

"Good." The god turned, his dark cloak spiraling in the dust at his heels. "Come with me."

Bricru looked at Elizus, whose usual smug smile wavered. He watched as Bricru trailed after the god, never once intervening or speaking up for the shapeshifter's sake. He disappeared as Orisis closed himself and Bricru in a ring of dust, masking the sounds of Tophet.

Bricru dropped his head in a bow.

"I've been very patient with you," Orisis spoke slowly.

Fear crept along Bricru's skin. "I know. And I swear to you, if you just—"

"If I just *what*, Bricru?" Orisis inched closer, his lips curled into a snarl. "I gave you *everything*. The project of Uriah Caligari was yours, and what infuriates me the most is that it was good!" He dug his fingers into Bricru's hair, yanking hard enough to make the shapeshifter grunt as he forced his face toward him. "The moment Uriah locked that gateway, you lost your senses, Bricru. You've done nothing but fail over, and over, and *over again!*"

He thrust Bricru against the wall of dust, the spiraling particles snatching Bricru's clothes as he steadied himself. "I just need time," Bricru pleaded. His tone brought heat to his face. He sounded like he was begging. Maybe because he was.

"You're out of it."

"I can bring you Kyler Caligari."

"You had him!" His shout made the dust spin faster— violently, like a sandstorm. "Twice! Twice you've had him in your grasp and *twice* you've let him go!"

The dust lifted Bricru's hair, its spiral becoming dangerous. Orisis paced the small space, his anger toward Bricru forming the walls he'd made around them.

"Adoni closed the only gateway to Sannir that we had. He's hiding somewhere, but I can't reach my brother without Caligari blood. We can take the Islands and the mainland. We could even take Sannir if we tried again, but without Caligari blood, we cannot take *him!*"

Bricru flinched as the dust spun wildly, filled with rage. It struck his face with its grain. He remained pressed against the wall of dust, breathing in its destruction. What did Orisis see in Kyler's blood that Bricru did not?

"Please don't cast me away again." Bricru's voice came out broken and desperate.

Orisis stilled, and with him, so did the dust. The anger on his face melted into something kind, and instead of force, he placed a gentle hand on Bricru's cheek.

"I will not cast you away," he said softly.

Bricru met his eye, and the momentary relief he felt quickly vanished when he saw the darkness inside.

"I will curse you. I will leave nothing but the corpse of who you once were. You will live forever, child, in anguish and agony."

He dropped Bricru's face, his shoulders relaxing and head tilting slightly. "I hope that's promise enough for you. Now, bring me Kyler Caligari, or I will be your ruin."

ACKNOWLEDGEMENTS

THERE ARE SO MANY PEOPLE WHO HAVE SUPPORTED THE journey of this book that I could write an entire novel full of how grateful I am. For three years, this book has been crafted, and for three years, people in my life have encouraged me.

First, to the One who gave me, his creation, the ability to create. I can dream and think and imagine, but this book would be nothing more than a vapor of a thought without Adonai.

I cannot thank my husband enough. My wonderful, dyslexic husband who can't read a single word of this book, and yet listens to all my rants, handles my finances, takes pride in me and my work, and says this book is his favorite in the whole world. Chase Skyler, I love you to Pluto and ¾ of the way back.

My best friends in the entire world: Francine, Mara, Raina, and Alex. The four of you are my heart. I love you. (Check the map—there's a place named after each of you!)

This would not be possible without my *incredible* writing buddy, Kaylee Stepkoski! You read Guardian when it was full of plot holes and bad writing, and you believed in it from the very start. Kyler thanks you immensely (and Corbin says 'hi').

Samantha Mendell—someone who came into my life at the perfect time. You are a wonderful human being and the world's greatest editor. Thank you for loving this story as much as I do, and for enduring my horrendous typos.

Thank you to my family—my parents and in-laws—for bragging about me to your friends and supporting me no matter what!

And of course, I must mention some of my incredible creative friends: MK Ahearn, Allyn Hamrick, Kaia Bakken, Kimberly Byrd, and so many more. Thank you for believing in me and my books!

Finally, thank *you*, my reader, for picking up this book and giving it a chance.